BROKEN
GRACE

ALSO BY E.C. DISKIN

The Green Line

BROKEN GRACE

E.C. DISKIN

Published by Thomas & Mercer, Seattle

www.apub.com

Amazon, the Amazon logo, and Thomas & Mercer are trademarks of Amazon.com, Inc., or its affiliates.

ISBN-13: 9781503946187
ISBN-10: 1503946185

Cover design by Ben Gibson

Printed in the United States of America

For Jim

ONE

GRACE'S HANDS SHOOK AS SHE TRIED to put the key in the ignition. She looked back at the house, threw the gear in reverse, and backed out of the drive, the tires spitting up gravel. Shifting into drive, she slammed her foot on the accelerator and flew down the road.

The neighborhood was quiet, the sun still hidden, just an orange and pink glow rising through the barren trees. The car bounced over the railroad tracks, jolting her body into the air, smacking her head against the roof. She slowed as she reached Red Arrow Highway and made a right onto the empty road.

Breathe. She needed to get to the police. She glanced back, but there was no one following. She faced the road ahead. Which way was the station? Her fingers, gripping the wheel, tingled, turning white. She shook her hands, one at a time. *Breathe.*

She scanned the rearview mirror. There. The car was several hundred yards back—but it would catch up. As she floored it, watching the gauge climb, a deer darted out from the trees. She slammed on the brakes and wrenched the wheel hard left, but it was too late. The massive animal flew up; his body crushed the hood, his antlered head smashing into the windshield while she veered across the highway.

She felt the tires leave the pavement and power over the frozen ground. She went for the brake again but pressed the accelerator. Her body jerked as the car rushed forward over rocks and hollows. Her head whacked the driver's-side window so hard she heard it crack.

She tried to focus, but the windshield was a blur of shattered glass. And then she hit something—like a brick wall—launching the deer from the hood. Her body rocketed forward into the steering wheel. Suddenly, cold air enveloped her. Everything went dark. The only warmth came from something oozing down her forehead.

She understood, in the abrupt silence, the finality of this moment. She was not meant to survive. She closed her eyes and felt the pain dissipate, the trickle of cool, soft feathers on her skin that melted upon contact. She opened her eyes one last time. Snowflakes. Big, airy, lake-effect flakes. And then it was as if she just floated away.

TWO

Eight days later

GRACE SAT ON THE EDGE OF A CHAIR near the bed, dressed in clothes a stranger had brought her, and waited. The walls of her sterile room matched the blank canvas of her mind. She had stared at the white ceiling tiles for days—at the thousands of tiny holes in each square that must have allowed air and sound and matter to breathe—but they held no answers. And now it was time to leave. Outside the window, the world beyond this little box was white-washed, almost frozen in time, the only indication of life coming from puffs of smoke rising out of a nearby chimney stack.

Dr. Roberts entered, open laptop in hand, and smiled. "Big day, huh, Grace?"

She slowly stood to greet him. "I guess," she said in a barely audible voice. She cleared her throat and repeated the words. His light blue eyes and that dimpled chin had been a comfort all week, his tone and smile always able to calm her. But today she noticed rounded shoulders, dark spots on his forehead, pronounced bags under his eyes, and the mostly white stubble of a five-day-old beard. He was old and tired. He was ready to be rid of her.

"I know you're nervous," he said, closing the computer. "But what you really need right now is rest and time. You can do that at home."

Home. If only that meant something.

"Now, let me take a look here." He patted the bed for Grace to sit and put the laptop aside. She moved with caution, trying to minimize the strain to her ribs. Dr. Roberts gently guided her chin to her chest and checked the stitches in her scalp. "All is well here. How's the headache today?"

"It was pretty bad an hour ago, but it's a little better now."

When she'd woken and realized what was missing, the doctors explained that, among other things, she had a large gash in her head that had required a dozen stitches. Her response was an incoherent mumble, but inside, she'd screamed. She felt sure this gaping hole in her head had allowed everything she'd ever known to spill out.

Dr. Roberts lifted her chin and looked into her eyes with his tiny flashlight. "Good. Now take a deep breath," he instructed, listening with the stethoscope.

She winced from the strain.

"Yeah, the ribs are going to hurt for a bit longer, but your lungs sound good."

No one was paying attention to the real problem. The nurses and doctors had come in all week, checking machines and tubes and looking into her eyes and listening to her chest and examining her wounds, but no one focused on the massive black hole in her mind. She'd searched the contents of the small purse beside her bed, examining the driver's license and crumpled receipts for answers, but nothing helped. Even the cell phone failed to bring the world into focus. It held no photos, no notes, no texts. It was nearly as empty as she was. Only a few names in the contacts: Lisa, Dave, Michael. No last names.

Nurse Molly entered wearing her teddy bear–covered scrubs; those squeaking pink sneakers; and that big, fat, stupid perma-grin, with her curly bottle-red hair pulled into pigtails like a little girl. Leaving Nurse Molly was the only benefit to today's agenda. Finally, she could say good-bye to that relentless smile and incessant chatter about every reality show on TV. The nurse took Grace's temperature for the hundredth time.

"Ninety-eight point six," she said to Dr. Roberts. "You're getting out just in time for church, honey." Even the word *church* conjured confused images of the many churches Grace had seen, though she had no idea if these pictures were her own memories or remnants from books or television or movies. Did she even go to church? Was she a Christian? Maybe the answers were somewhere outside these white walls.

"You can't possibly want to stay here," the nurse said, wrapping Grace's arm to check her blood pressure. "After a week? You've got to be ready for some real food. Apple pie, mac and cheese, ice cream . . ."

Grace had the sudden desire to slap that stupid expression off Nurse Molly's freckled face. She imagined the shock it would cause the irritating woman and smiled.

The nurse obliviously smiled back, patted Grace's knee, and gave the "all good," before busying herself with more exit procedures.

"I still feel like I've been hit by a truck," Grace said to Dr. Roberts, who was typing notes into her chart.

Nurse Molly responded before the doctor could. "Well, it's probably not much different than a truck. If I were you, I'd be going to church today, thanking God for watching over me. You should thank him for protecting that beautiful face of yours. You're a lucky young lady."

Grace ignored her. The doctor took Grace's hand in his. "You've been through a major trauma, and it's going to take some time. But everything looks good in there," he said, pointing to her head, "and I feel confident that this is a temporary situation. Just take it easy this week. I want to see you in my office next Monday. We'll determine where things are and make a long-term plan. Okay?"

One week. It sounded like an eternity. She nodded.

"I know this must be scary, but you need to rest and let your sister take care of you. It's the best thing for you right now."

Grace looked at his eyes, her only comfort. "I don't even know her."

He squeezed her hand before letting go. "Yes, but she knows you. It'll help to be home."

As if on cue, a knock sounded at the open door, and Dr. Roberts and Nurse Molly turned and smiled. Grace slowly turned as well, trying to avoid straining her ribs. Lisa smiled, raising her coffee as a greeting, an extra coat draped over her other arm. She'd obviously overheard the conversation. "Besides that, your insurance won't cover any more days, so there's really no choice, sis."

Lisa had come to see Grace every day. She'd brought her clothes, a toothbrush, even an old blanket that she swore Grace had cuddled with for twenty years, but nothing about her felt familiar. She'd sat at her bedside speaking softly and slowly, like Grace was a fragile doll, and even held her hand when Grace was trying to sleep. She'd stared into her eyes, as if doing so might cause a spark, and didn't seem fazed by Grace's reluctance to connect. When Grace would pull back, shift focus, or give a clipped response, Lisa would smile, just as a preschool teacher dealing with a difficult child might, and say, "It's okay, Grace. This must be so weird."

Looking into Lisa's eyes felt a little like drowning in deep pools of water, so Grace focused instead on the mascara-covered lashes; the thick, dark liner; and how her dramatic features and porcelain, almost translucent skin reminded her of a Tim Burton movie character. (She could name at least five Tim Burton movie titles, she realized, though the titles existed in her mind as facts, unattached to any memories.) The idea of being released into Lisa's care put her on edge.

Lisa clomped into the room in her chunky heels and oversized, all-black ensemble, bringing with her the scent of cigarettes and a jarring, almost blinding energy, as if the day's agenda were worthy of celebration. Grace studied her face. It held no answers.

Dr. Roberts began rambling on about the medication schedule—the Norco for pain, Seroquel for agitation, Ambien for sleep issues. It was difficult to focus on his words. "People with TBIs often have trouble sleeping," he said, talking more to Lisa now, "and she might be forgetful and foggy. There are some side effects like dizziness and blurred vision . . ." Her head was starting to throb again.

Nurse Molly rolled a wheelchair into the room and helped Grace into it while Dr. Roberts continued. "The goal is for Grace to get a lot of rest this week. It's probably the best thing for her injuries." Finally he turned back to Grace. "No activity, okay? And absolutely no driving. These are pretty strong meds, and your reaction times are going to be slower for a while."

"Got it, Doc," Lisa said. "I need to work a lot this week, since I spent so much time here last week, but I'll be with her as much as possible."

Dr. Roberts nodded. "Hopefully she'll spend most of her time sleeping. But please check in with her every so often."

"Will do," Lisa said. "And there's no chance of driving." She looked at Grace. "Your car was totaled."

Grace felt no comfort at the thought of leaving with this woman, but no one else seemed to care.

"And what do you think about the memory loss?" Lisa asked.

"I'm hopeful that it's temporary and related to the brain injury." Dr. Roberts turned to Grace then. "Be patient. Your brain has been through a major trauma. You need to give it some time. And if you remember things, write them down. Take some notes. It's a process."

He put his hand on Lisa's shoulder. "You can help by keeping track of her meds—be sure she's taking them, make notes of any side effects, anything you notice about how she's doing. Call if you need me; otherwise, we'll adjust anything when I see you next week, okay?"

Grace didn't look up into the doctor's face; it hurt her neck and head to move. She lifted her arm toward the stitches on her head. "What about this? Can I take a shower?"

"Sure. But be careful. If you're dizzy, let's stick to baths."

"Got it," Lisa answered. "Now, it's freezing out there, sis," she said, offering the extra coat. With Nurse Molly's help, she put the coat on Grace, then wheeled her toward the elevator. The nurse came running out of the room behind them. "Don't forget this stuff, sweetie." She loaded Grace's lap with her purse and a bag filled with the clothes they'd removed when she came into the ER. "Good luck, hon," she added before squeaking away.

The sisters sat in silence as Lisa maneuvered out of the hospital parking lot and onto the city street. Grace examined the road signs and scanned the buildings.

"What are you thinking about?" Lisa asked.

"Nothing looks familiar."

"Well, that's not surprising. This is Kalamazoo. You've probably never been up here before. But it was the closest Level One Trauma Center."

"How far are we from home?"

"About an hour and a half. You might as well rest." Lisa wriggled out of her heavy coat, turned on the radio, and pulled onto the expressway.

The music was too loud, compounding the pain inside Grace's head, but she feared the questions and the energy of this woman, and the song seemed to distract her: Lisa was tapping the steering wheel to the beat, humming along with the heavy rock tune, completely absorbed. Grace couldn't help but stare as Lisa brushed her wild, shaggy black hair away from her eyes. Grace had spent a lot of time examining herself in the hospital mirror: the square of her jaw; the shape of her brows; the variations of brown, and a few streaks of something lighter, in her hair. This woman seemed so different—shorter, smaller, her face narrower, her nose thinner, her eyes darker, her skin lighter. She wondered if the hospital had asked for proof that they were sisters.

Lisa's fingernails, chewed and chipped, were painted black, multiple earrings hung from her ears, and the top of a tattoo was visible on the side of her neck. It was a tough facade, but her wrists were tiny, as if all of this were armor for something more fragile.

Grace examined her own hands. Her nails also looked chewed, but her wrists were a tad bigger, her skin a little freckled. And scarred. Dozens of small scars—straight lines, like hash marks—on her forearm. Lisa must have seen her looking, but when Grace glanced over, she turned her gaze back to the road without comment.

Grace stared out the window at the passing cars, noting the license plates: mostly Michigan, but sometimes Indiana, and even a couple Illinois. She rubbed her earlobes, massaging the tiny hard bits of cartilage that confirmed her own piercing. Lisa stopped singing. "What is it?"

Grace put down her hands. "I'm just trying to remember."

Lisa laid her hand on Grace's and interlocked their fingers. "Don't worry. It'll come. Everything will be okay."

Grace stared at their entwined hands, a gesture of intimacy that felt contrived. She pulled away, and Lisa continued singing along to the music. She actually had a nice voice.

"Joan Jett," Grace said abruptly.

Lisa turned down the music. "What?"

"You remind me of Joan Jett. She's a singer, right?"

Lisa smiled. "You remember Joan Jett? How random is that? Is it the hair?"

"I guess. I just heard you singing and her name popped into my brain."

"That's kinda crazy. Mom used to sing Joan Jett all over the house when we were young. She'd belt out that song 'I Love Rock 'n' Roll.' You remember?"

Before Grace could respond, Lisa began singing the lyrics, and suddenly Grace was sorry she'd mentioned it. She feigned recognition and turned to view the passing landscape, desperate for this to end. "So I'm in school?"

Lisa reached for a cigarette before responding. "Do you remember school?" The car lighter popped, and Lisa lit the cigarette, inhaling deeply.

"No, I just figured, because the doctor said I was twenty."

Lisa exhaled into the open slit of her window. "Wow, you really are a blank slate. Yes, you're a student and you wait tables. But don't worry, it's winter break, so you don't have classes for a few weeks, and I called the restaurant already. They've taken you off the schedule until you're ready to come back. Everyone wanted me to tell you that they hope you're feeling better soon."

"And what about you? Are you a student too? I don't even know how old you are."

Lisa chuckled. "No way. School was never my thing. I'm twenty-seven. I manage a bakery in Bridgman."

Grace nodded slightly and turned her attention back to the flat, desolate road surrounded by woods. Her neck ached from looking left. She tried to get comfortable and rest her head against the cold window.

"I'm sorry I have to work a lot this week, but I took off so much time to be with you last week."

"It's no problem," Grace said, grateful that there would be a break in the questions, the stares, the small talk.

"But I'll do what I can to make things easy for you, okay? And I can bring home some pastries and fresh bread. So that's not bad, right?"

Grace offered a fake smile and a nod, still gazing at the trees outside. Her focus dulled, the trees became a blur, and then it was impossible to keep her eyes open.

THREE

WHEN SHE WOKE, THE CAR WAS ON AN EXIT RAMP.

Grace sat up carefully; every muscle of her torso ached. "Are we here?"

"Not quite. But let me know if things start to look familiar."

They turned left, away from the highway, and passed a little brewery, a market, some antique shops, and restaurants. They continued past some small homes set back from the road.

"Is this our town?"

"This is Sawyer. It's not far from where we live, but we're a bit farther out."

They drove through a wooded area before the road opened up to expose acres and acres of farmland. Lisa took a left and drove along several more miles of cultivated land before the road wound around a series of bends. They turned again and passed an orchard of some kind and row after row of vineyards.

Lisa looked over with a hopeful expression. "Any of this look familiar?"

Grace was about to say no when Lisa turned left and the car rolled forward on a gravel road. It was unmarked, barely wide enough for two cars, sandwiched between a large field on one side and a forest on the other. The crushing sound of tires on gravel felt familiar. She didn't recognize anything, but she closed her eyes and let the noise fill her ears.

They traveled about a quarter mile before Lisa stopped the car and opened her window to gather some mail from a box. "I forgot to get this yesterday."

Grace sat up, gripping the seat, waiting for something to happen. "What is it?"

"Is this it?" She was leaning forward, trying to get a look through the trees.

Lisa smiled. "Yep. This is home." She turned onto an unpaved drive that cut through the dense trees for ten or fifteen feet before the view widened. She looked over at Grace for her reaction. "Do you remember?"

An old white farmhouse sat in the middle of a patch of open, snow-covered land, the center of the maze. Snow had slid off portions of the metal roof that hung over a covered porch; one of the gutters hung precariously from a corner. The white siding was chipped in several places. Two dormered windows extended out of the roof on the second floor. Two rocking chairs, turned upside down, flanked the front door. There were no other homes in sight.

"Is all this land ours?"

"Yep. It's, like, twenty-five acres."

An old red pickup truck was parked off to the side. A giant tree stood in the center of the front yard, a broken rope swing hanging from its massive branch. The woods in the distance seemed to wrap the home in a protective shell. "This is where I grew up," Grace said.

"That's right." Lisa stopped the car. "Are you remembering something?"

Grace couldn't take her eyes off the house. "I know this house. I knew that sound of tires on gravel, like I'd heard it thousands of times." She turned. "We still live here?"

Lisa nodded. "Our parents left it to us. In fact, that's Dad's old truck over there." She pointed to the pickup. "I've been meaning to get rid of it, but it's got sentimental value."

"They're dead?"

Lisa pulled closer to the house and put the car in park before answering. "It was a long time ago, Grace. It's a lot for you to take in, I know." She reached out and put a hand on Grace's knee. "It's just you and me now."

She got out before Grace could say more and came over to Grace's side of the car to help her.

"I'm fine," Grace insisted. It was a lie. She felt the cracked ribs with every step. Her head pounded with each movement, and she stopped several times, hoping to lessen the dizziness with a deep breath that only made her wince in pain.

Lisa ran ahead to unlock the door and hold it open. Grace followed, and as soon as she saw the bench next to the stairway in the hall, she sat. Lisa returned to the car for Grace's medications, letting the screen door slam shut behind her, and then threw it open again, scurrying past her in those obscenely loud shoes. A minute later, she was standing before Grace with a glass of water and some pills.

"Thanks." Grace didn't have the strength to say more. She threw back three tablets with a single swallow.

"Come on, you should lie on the couch," Lisa said, helping her stand. The living room, unlit but for the few sunrays spotlighting swirling dust, felt stale, as if everything in it—once fresh and loved—had spoiled. The floor was covered in a thick, brown shag rug that must have been older than Grace, and two antique chairs had long passed their expiration date. The wall in front of her was partially painted a shockingly vivid blue, while the other walls remained cream-colored, maybe a bit dirty.

"We were trying to update the place," Lisa said, "give it some new life, get some new stuff. But it's kind of a long process. Money's not exactly flowing these days. And it's in pretty bad shape. We sold most of Mom and Dad's stuff, but there are some things in the basement."

Grace propped up the pillows at the end of the leather couch, obviously a newer purchase, and lay down. Now facing the hall, she noticed swatches of red and orange paint marking two square-foot sections of the entry wall. Ripped magazine pages were taped up in various locations.

"Inspirational," Lisa said.

Grace smiled before covering her eyes with her forearm.

"Well, let me know if you need anything." Stair treads soon creaked under Lisa's feet as she headed upstairs.

When Grace opened her eyes again, the headache was gone, and as she sat up, she no longer felt the pain in her ribs. She rolled her head, stretching her neck, and carefully stood, taking a moment to adjust to the new perspective. "Hello?" she called out. No response.

She slowly climbed the stairs. It was that sound. The squeak of a tread when she put her weight on it. She stood on the spot and closed her eyes, waiting for something to come to her. Maybe if she stared into the darkness of her mind long enough, her eyes would adjust and see shapes. Nothing came, but then she looked at the spindles of the stairwell, grabbed the one beside her, and tugged at it. It was loose—completely detached from the stair beneath it. She knew it would be. At least that was something.

Lisa was in the room to the left, making up a double bed. Grace leaned against the dark-stained casing. "Hi."

"Oh, hey, how are you feeling?"

"Better."

"This is your room. I was just trying to straighten it up for you."

The room was fairly large, though mostly empty. The wood floors were bare, scuffed, and faded from the sun except for a large rectangular outline of darker wood in the center, as if it had been long covered by a rug. An old ceiling fan and light with four decorative glass shades hung in the center of the room. A white sheet, tied back with a yellow ribbon, hung above the single dormer window that flooded the room with light. The walls were bare, just like the hospital, except dirtier. The iron-framed double bed was covered in a white bedspread, its pillows fluffed, with an old milk crate propped beside it. A dresser, painted white but chipped, housed a small table lamp and a picture. Nothing felt familiar. Lisa took the picture from the dresser and brought it to her. "What about this? That's you, Grace. Do you remember this?"

Grace studied herself. Her hair was longer in the photo, nearly to her waist, and sun-streaked—or maybe highlighted. She was sunburned, smiling, squinting and holding up a hand to block the sun. She looked a little younger. She was sitting on a beach in shorts, leaning back into the arms of a shirtless man. An older man. He was cute—tan, with wild dark hair, blue eyes, dimples. "Who's that?"

"Michael."

Michael. One of the names in her contacts. "When was this?"

"I guess it was a few years back. It's such a nice picture. You looked so happy. But I guess that's over now."

"What do you mean?"

"You broke up last week." Lisa put back the picture.

"Why?"

"You wouldn't tell me." There were no other pictures in the room.

"He was my boyfriend all this time?"

"Oh yeah, you've been together for as long as I can remember."

"He looks a lot older than me."

"He is. Like, ten years older, I think. That was probably why it ended."

"What do you mean?"

"He . . ." Lisa hesitated. "It bothered you that he could be controlling sometimes."

She wondered if he'd controlled her phone, if that was why it was so empty. "Does he know about the accident?"

Lisa shook her head. "I wasn't sure you'd want to see him. You were so upset about the breakup." She smiled. "Come on. I'll show you around."

Grace followed her into the hallway but stopped to open the nearby door. She leaned in. "What's this?"

"We don't use that for anything," Lisa said, walking toward the other end of the hall.

Grace stood in the doorway, staring into the small bedroom, looking for memories. A shade pulled over the window prevented light from entering the space. The switch didn't work, but she could see several holes in the wallboard, like it had been punched. "What happened to the walls?"

Lisa came back and leaned into the room. "What do you mean?"

"Those holes."

She chuckled. "Jeez, I forgot all about those. Yeah, you had a little bit of a temper as a kid. Big fan of throwing tantrums—chairs too, if they were around. Come on." She walked across the hall, but Grace stepped inside to investigate further. How else would she remember? "How old was I when I did that?"

Lisa returned. "Oh, I don't know. Maybe twelve? Thirteen? That's probably right because that's about the time I moved out." She nudged her. "Guess you really didn't want me to go. Dad never even fixed the holes. He didn't care. Now, come on, the tour continues."

"Why'd you leave?"

"I was, like, twenty; it was time, that's all. But I came back to visit a lot." Lisa steered her to the other side of the hall, presenting her bedroom with a sweep of the arm. "And this is me," she said.

It was a large bedroom with a dormer window, like Grace's. A mound of blankets sat atop a sheet-less, queen-sized mattress in the center of the room. The wallpaper behind the bed was ripped off in sections.

"This was Mom and Dad's room. I'm redecorating in here as well. Gotta get that damn paper down and then I'll paint."

Grace studied the fragments of tiny blue and white flowers on the walls, looking for memories before glancing through the double doors to the left that opened into an adjacent smaller room. An easel stood in the center, a cup of brushes and a bucket of acrylic paint tubes on the small table beside it. Several canvases, some painted, some blank, lined the wall. The afternoon sunlight flooded the small space through the two windows facing the backyard. Grace walked into the room. "You're a painter?"

Lisa shrugged. "I try. I'm not as good as Mom was, but I like to think I'm an artist."

"Can I see some of your work?"

She shook her head quickly. "Oh no. Nothing in here is ready for anyone to see. And it's a mess. Let's go."

At the bottom of the stairs, large pocket doors closed off a room to their right.

"What's in here?"

"Too much." Lisa opened the doors a few inches. It was nearly impossible to enter with boxes piled high, a desk and built-in shelves barely visible behind them.

"There's a lot to do to fix up this place. Our parents were kind of pack rats. I tend to clean by moving piles, so the living and dining room are pretty decent now, but I haven't had the strength to tackle this room yet." She closed the doors, and Grace wandered ahead of her back to the living room, touching, holding, examining every-thing—furniture, books, figurines.

"Are there any more pictures?"

"Not really. Mom and Dad had pictures of us all over the place, but they're in storage. I guess we're not big on photos." Lisa called from the kitchen, "You hungry?"

"No. But I'll take some water." The nausea and cotton mouth had returned. She'd felt this way for days. Nurse Molly said it was the meds. She sat back on the couch, exhausted, and stared up at the water-stained ceiling.

The chime of a doorbell rang out slowly, eight notes climbing up and down a scale, the sound sparking something. It was connected to good things. It made her smile.

Lisa went to the door and Grace listened, unable to stand and look for herself. She heard voices without understanding their content until Lisa ushered two men into the room and subtly signaled Grace to sit up. Lisa's face gave no hint as to their purpose, but those raised eyebrows must have meant she was surprised by their arrival. "Grace, these officers are from the Chikaming Township Police Department. They're hoping to speak with you."

A big man in a black leather jacket held out his hand. He was maybe forty, more belly than legs. "How you doin'," he said rhetorically. His dark under-eye circles and scratchy tone mirrored her exhaustion. He looked serious, maybe angry. "Detective Bishop," he said, his arm still outstretched toward her. She didn't react quickly enough; he withdrew the hand, scanning the room.

A young man dressed in a police uniform followed behind. He was taller, fit, a little more fantasy cop than real cop. Dark hair, olive skin, a bright smile, perfect teeth. She slowly rose to greet him. But he seemed to be trying to control his demeanor, as if he wanted to emulate his partner's stoicism. He wiped the smile from his face as their eyes met, and he offered his hand. "Hello, Grace."

That voice. She stretched out her hand cautiously, watching his changing expression. He held her grip a little too long, staring into her eyes, studying her. "Do I know you?" she asked.

He looked over, and the big one, Bishop, answered for him. "This is Officer Hackett."

Hackett. It didn't mean anything.

Lisa gestured to the men to sit, then joined Grace on the couch. Hackett grabbed the nearest chair, pulled out his pen and notepad, and looked to his partner.

"So I guess this is about the accident?" Lisa said.

"Accident?" Bishop said.

"Grace was in a terrible car accident a week ago on Red Arrow Highway," Lisa said, perched on the sofa's edge, her back straight, her hand patting Grace's knee. "A deer hit her car and she ran into a tree somewhere near Warren Dunes State Park. We literally just got home from the hospital."

Bishop nodded. "Miss Abbott, can you tell us exactly when this accident occurred?"

Grace turned to Lisa for help. "It was a week ago yesterday," Lisa said. "What would that be? December seventh. Saturday morning."

"And where was she going?"

"I don't know," Lisa said.

Everyone looked at Grace. She just shrugged.

Lisa kept patting her knee. "She took a pretty big blow to the head. She cracked her ribs and punctured a lung, but she's okay. She's going to be fine." That last bit seemed to be for Grace's benefit. She vaguely remembered Dr. Roberts warning Lisa to look out for signs of depression.

Bishop focused on Grace. "I'm really sorry to hear about this, Miss Abbott. But do you remember anything about that morning?"

Mutely, Grace shook her head.

"Detective," Lisa said, "Grace doesn't remember anything."

Hackett leaned forward, eyes intense. "You mean you don't remember what led to the accident?"

Grace opened her mouth to speak, but Lisa beat her to it. "She was unconscious for quite a bit. She doesn't remember anything. She didn't even remember me. The doctors said she has a traumatic brain injury, a TBI, but they tell us to be hopeful." She turned to Grace. "We're just going to get some rest, right, Grace? And it's all going to come back." Lisa patted her knee again as if comforting a small child, and Grace stared at the hand, anxious to push it away and run. Her headache was returning.

Lisa looked back at the officers. "I don't understand. If you didn't know about her accident, what's going on?"

Grace could feel Bishop's eyes on her. "We've actually been trying to find you for the last few days, Miss Abbott."

"Please don't say that," she said, keeping her head down.

"What?" Hackett asked, his tone gentler, less accusatory.

She met his dark brown eyes. "*Miss Abbott.* Will you call me Grace, please? I'm not a librarian." Hackett looked at his partner, who now sat back, arms crossed, studying her.

Lisa frowned. "It's a side effect. The doctor said she might be a little off. Maybe irritable." Her black nails tapped Grace's knee. "It's okay. Grace, it's okay."

She wanted to jump out of her skin. Except it hurt to think about jumping. "Just tell me why you're here already."

Bishop's eyes narrowed. "This is about Michael Cahill," he said, watching her response.

"What about Michael?" Lisa asked. "Is he in trouble?"

Grace hugged herself, feeling chilled. "Who's Michael Cahill?"

"Michael is your ex-boyfriend, remember?" Lisa said.

"Ex?" Bishop sat forward, arms uncrossing.

Both Lisa and Grace answered, "Yes."

"But it appears that you and Mr. Cahill live together in Harbert."

"I thought I lived here?" Grace turned to Lisa.

"You do, Grace. Now, anyway. But the officers aren't wrong. You only asked to move in a week ago. It was last Friday night."

"Why?" she asked.

"I . . . don't really know. You were just really upset, you said it was over with Michael, and you asked to move in here. You ran up to your old room, so I let you be. I figured we could talk in the morning."

"What time was this?" Hackett asked.

"I don't know." Lisa shrugged. "Maybe ten o'clock. I don't really remember."

"Did Grace tell you in the morning what had happened with Michael?" Bishop asked.

"I never had the chance to ask. She was up and gone in the morning, and then she got in that terrible accident."

Grace sat forward as if she could take back some control of the situation, of a life that made no sense to her. "What is this all about? Is he in trouble?"

The two men glanced at each other again. "No," Bishop answered. "Mr. Cahill is not in trouble. I'm afraid he's dead."

Grace focused on that word: *dead*. She began picturing dead people. A casket. A funeral. A man being shot off a horse in an old western. Dozens of men in confederate uniforms lying dead in a field.

"My God!" Lisa said, her alarm puncturing Grace's mental tangent. "What happened?"

Bishop ignored her. "Miss Abbott? Grace?"

Grace finally returned her focus to Bishop, watching his mouth as he spoke.

"We're still trying to figure it out. He didn't show up for work on Monday, so one of his coworkers went to the house that evening. He found the body. After questioning the witness and a few others, we began looking for Grace."

"What happened to him?" she asked.

"He was killed," Bishop said.

"What do you mean?" Lisa asked. "Like murder?"

"Yes."

Lisa's hand covered her mouth. Grace watched her face, trying to read it like a new language.

"We believe he'd been dead a few days."

"How? Why? What do you think happened?"

Grace sat back, watching their discussion like they were actors in a play—like some sort of interactive theater in which she was supposed to participate. But they were strangers and she didn't know the story.

Bishop leaned forward more, as if proximity would make them friends. "We were hoping we might find out more from you, Grace. When we investigated the crime scene, it was pretty obvious from the bills and the clothes that you lived there. So when we couldn't locate you, we were concerned."

"I can't believe it," said Lisa, rubbing her face with her hands. She patted Grace's knee. "Oh my God, Grace, thank God you were here, what if you hadn't . . . ?" She didn't finish the thought, her eyes watering.

Hackett sat forward, his voice soft. "Grace, do you remember Vicki Flynn?"

She shook her head.

"She got a text from you last Friday evening around nine o'clock saying that you had big news and that you'd stop by in the morning after your run. She lives a block from Cahill's house."

Grace looked at Hackett, her mouth open, ready to speak, but she realized she had nothing to add.

"You don't have any idea what that might have been about?" Hackett asked.

She could barely keep up; this whole conversation was like a book she'd never read. "I don't know who Vicki is. I don't know anything."

"Did someone break in?" Lisa asked.

"We're still trying to figure that out," Bishop said. "There's no evidence of a break-in, but of course we're a bit hampered by the delayed discovery of the body and the snow that blanketed the area by midday Saturday."

"What can we do?" asked Lisa.

"Just help us if you can in piecing together Mr. Cahill's days before the crime. Our team is running down several leads from the crime scene. We'll be looking into everything about his life."

"Of course," Lisa said.

Grace turned to the younger cop but hesitated. "How was he killed?"

"Shotgun. He was in bed at the time."

Lisa covered her mouth and shook her head. Grace pictured a generic man in a pool of blood—like a character in a movie, about whom she knew nothing.

Bishop tilted his chin toward Lisa. "Since Grace is unable to remember, perhaps you can help us?"

"Of course," she said. "Whatever you need."

"Any idea where Grace might have been going when she got in the accident last Saturday morning?"

Lisa repositioned herself on the sofa, even closer, and looked at Grace before responding. "I wish I could tell you." She put her arm around Grace. "I slept in and then got the call from the hospital about the accident. But Grace is a runner. She always does her big runs on Saturday mornings. Maybe she wanted to go for a run in those trails by the dunes. Maybe she went out for coffee."

Hackett took notes. Bishop's attention shifted back to Grace who was staring at the shag carpeting.

"You can't think that Grace could have done this," Lisa said, her arm still wrapped around Grace, now pulling her closer. Grace leaned back and away from Lisa, mumbling about her headache.

She needed to catch her breath; Lisa's smothering felt like a bag over her head.

"We simply need to establish alibis for everyone who knew Mr. Cahill well." To Grace, Bishop said, "Given the fact that you lived there, when we couldn't locate you for several days . . ."

"You thought it was Grace?" Lisa's voice rose. "That's ridiculous."

Bishop held up a palm in Lisa's direction. "We're not accusing you, Grace," he said. "In fact, there was the possibility that whoever killed Michael had harmed you as well."

"We're relieved that you're okay," Hackett said, his voice soothing. "We're not accusing her of anything," he assured Lisa. "We simply need to gather information but, given Grace's condition, this might be a little more difficult."

"I'm sorry," Grace said to him. "I wish I could help. I wish I could remember." A bolt of pain shot through her temple, so sharp and sudden it was as if a nerve had been cut. She cried out, wincing and grabbing her head with both hands.

Lisa jumped up. "Lie down." She grabbed the pillows from the end of the couch. When Grace was settled, she turned back to the detectives. "I'm so sorry to hear about Michael, and please keep us posted on any developments. But you can see Grace is no help to you right now, and the doctor wants her to rest."

The men stood. "Grace, we hope you feel better soon," Bishop said. "We'll be in touch."

Grace couldn't respond.

Lisa ushered them to the door. She heard them talking but couldn't understand what was said. The door opened and closed. The house fell silent. A short while later, the door opened and shut again.

Lisa approached and laid a wet towel across Grace's forehead. She knelt beside her and leaned in. "Are you okay?"

Grace looked at this woman's face, her raccoon-like eyes, her squirrel-like movement, her total lack of respect for personal space. "I'm okay."

"Grace—did any of that ring a bell?"

"What do you think?" she responded sarcastically. Obviously she didn't remember anything or she would have said something. Lisa was starting to play the role of Nurse Molly, and Grace was starting to think about another face slap.

"Hey, the doctor warned us of this, remember? You may feel anger or irritation, even when it's not called for." She went to the kitchen and Grace heard the fridge open and close. "So I'm not going to take it personally, okay?"

This was a bizarre nightmare, that's what it was. And when she woke up, this blinding pain would be gone and—

Lisa popped the tab on a can of soda. "You went to Michael's house last Saturday morning. You were going to get some clothes because you said he'd be at work."

Grace grabbed the towel and sat up. "What?" Intense pain stabbed at her temple.

"Don't worry. Maybe it happened after you left. Or maybe you never got there."

Grace leaned back onto the couch. "Why didn't you say anything?"

"I'm not an idiot. I've seen shows about this. Cops look at the spouses, the girlfriends, the boyfriends. I'm not going to hand them information that could hurt you."

She didn't know what to say. And the pain in her head made it impossible to focus on anything else.

"But they did take your clothes from the accident," Lisa said, her voice fading for a minute. "That Bishop handed me a warrant at the door. The bag was still in the car, so I gave it to him."

She came over with a glass of water and a pill. "Here. And don't worry. Maybe that's good. Get you cleared from the radar so they can focus on who really did this. You want me to close these shades?" she said, walking to the bay window. "Maybe darkness is better."

"Good idea," Grace whispered. She had no reason to be fearful, no knowledge of wrongdoing, but suddenly she felt hunted.

FOUR

THE FROZEN SNOW CRUNCHED BENEATH their boots as the men walked back to the squad car. Hackett didn't know what to say or how to feel. Every day that he remained quiet potentially made things worse, but there she was. Alive. It hurt a little to face her blank stare, like they were strangers, but at least she was okay.

Be objective. Solve the case. That was the mantra he'd been silently repeating since he found Cahill's body and he saw the photo of Grace—smiling, arm in arm with the dead man—covered in shattered glass, the frame cracked.

They sat in the car, letting the engine warm up for a minute. "Well, that was interesting," Bishop said, rubbing his hands together in front of the heating vents. "I'd say that was a good enough reason to call me on my day off."

"Yeah, I figured as much. Why'd you pretend we didn't know about the accident?"

"I wanted to see if her story would match what we had learned."

Hackett was just glad to finally see her. After learning the make and model of Grace's car, they'd put a "Be On Lookout" on the network by midday Tuesday, but it was only yesterday that a cop from the Bridgman station had called, letting them know the car had been in a near-fatal crash the previous Saturday. After they determined where Grace had been taken, Hackett had wanted to jump in the car and drive all the way up to Kalamazoo, but Bishop had sent him to deal with getting the wreckage towed while he took care of securing warrants for her hospital records and clothing from the crash. Bishop had said they would head up to the hospital together on Monday, but Hackett couldn't wait. He'd driven up there this morning, only to learn from an overly cheery nurse that Grace had just been released to her sister.

"Well, what do you think?" Hackett asked.

"I think this girl is pretty lucky."

Nothing about this situation was lucky. "How do you figure?"

"Her boyfriend is dead. She may have been the last one to see him, and she can't remember a thing. I'd say that's pretty lucky."

"You think she's faking it?"

"I'm not saying that, but her accident happened within the window of our vic's time of death. Unless the medical examiner comes back with something in his final report that says Cahill definitely died after nine o'clock that morning, this may have simply been a case of the perp leaving the scene. Crashed. Done."

Bishop buckled in and filled his bottom lip with a wad of chew from a tin he kept in the driver's-side door.

"We should see if there was a motive though, right? We can't just jump to the conclusion that the girlfriend did it."

Bishop backed out of the driveway. "Motive is good, but if the evidence points her way, I don't care if we never understand why. People kill for a lot of reasons, and if you spend too much time trying to connect every dot, you might miss your chance to catch them. Crazy people do crazy shit for crazy reasons all the time."

"You sound like you're speaking from experience."

"Of course I am, kid. I'm old. That's why you're going to follow my lead, do as I say, and we'll solve this case inside of a week."

"A week? How can you be so sure? The lab work can take months."

"True. But nine times out of ten, the killer is right in front of you. It's young guys like you who want to overcomplicate things and miss the obvious. No offense," he added with a backhanded slap to Hackett's leg.

Hackett's throat tightened. Bishop was from the region's homicide task force, brought in to work the case with Hackett; he'd have to defer to him and all his experience, but he needed Bishop to value him and not discount his opinions.

"Pretty cool for you too," Bishop said as they drove the mostly plowed road that cut through the expanse of desolate, snow-covered farmland.

Hackett's face flushed. "How's that?"

"We're in the sticks. You can spend years doing nothing more than dealing with permits, speeders, drunks in the summer, and, if you're lucky, the occasional break-in. Not every day a young gun like you gets assigned to a murder investigation with a hotshot like me," he added with a grin. "And this one is starting out pretty interesting."

Hackett faked a smile and stared out his window. Bishop was right, of course, and it was great luck, given the situation. He couldn't let himself get removed from the case. "Have you investigated a lot of murders?"

Bishop smoothed the wisps of hair that remained on his bald spot and spit into a cup. "Sure. I spent most of my career in Detroit. No missing out on the rough crimes in that area. But about a year ago, the wife begged for a transfer. She grew up in Stevensville. Wanted the kids to live in a quieter town, experience life by the lakefront. Can't say as I blame her."

"I don't know Stevensville."

"North of Bridgman, south of St. Joe. What, you not from around here?"

"I'm down in New Buffalo, but I just transferred from Indiana last summer."

"And of course, this is your first murder investigation."

"Right."

"Well, lesson one, young squire. There's no perfect crime. People always make mistakes." He spit again.

Hackett couldn't get Grace's face out of his mind. Those chestnut eyes that had drawn him in the first time he saw her. Those lips. That smile. The thought of her connected to the blood and violence found at Cahill's was hard to process. If she had been there, if she'd seen that happen, he was relieved she'd blocked it out. Because how could she live with those images? "My cousin had a traumatic brain injury from a skiing accident up in the U.P. a couple of years ago."

"Oh yeah? Did he lose his memory?" Bishop asked.

"Well, he couldn't remember the accident or the whole morning before it happened, but he remembered everything else."

"Huh."

"He was pretty messed up, and his reactions were odd. He would start laughing when people were telling a serious story, or he'd lash out at people for no reason. The doctors told us that sometimes people with TBIs have no emotional connection to what you're saying."

"Well, that sounds about right. She certainly didn't react like someone who cared about the vic."

"She doesn't remember him." Bishop shot him a curious look. Had his tone been too defensive? *Be objective. Prove yourself.* Maybe then, even if Bishop found out the truth, it wouldn't matter.

"So what do you make of her?" Bishop asked.

"I don't know." It felt like a trick question. "What do you think?"

"I'm keeping an open mind, but we always gotta start with those closest to the vic."

Hackett gazed at a silo in the distance. "What's next on the list?"

"Food," Bishop said, slowing for the intersection. "I'm starving."

"I thought you were eating when I called you this morning."

"I was, but the wife's got me on some crazy diet. I'm starving all the time."

"Is it working?"

"I'm sure it would if I did what she told me. She usually packs lunches for the kids and me every day, but she's been too busy lately, so I'm getting a little reprieve."

Hackett reviewed his notes. "Well, after food, we gotta visit the victim's work again. We're waiting on the bank records and Cahill's cell records. We still don't know who was the last to see him, what he was into."

"That's right. And I need to get Miss Abbott's clothes sent up to the crime lab. If we're lucky, Cahill's blood may be on some of these items."

That was the last thing he wanted. "But even if his blood is present, that only puts her at the scene. It doesn't mean she did anything. Maybe she was running from the killer."

"We'll see."

Hackett put away his notes and pen. "I hope she wasn't involved."

Bishop spit into his cup. "Why's that?"

He shrugged, avoiding Bishop's eyes. He shouldn't have said that. "She's pretty cute."

Bishop gave his thigh another backhanded slap. "Don't do that, boy. First rule of murder investigation—stay objective. Don't want to cloud your judgment."

Hackett nodded. "I know. I'm just sayin', she's kind of cute. Don't you think?"

"Whatever, rookie. Just be smart." He glanced over. "She's a sweet-looking young chick, and you're what? Twenty-six, right?"

"Yeah."

"Single, right?"

"Yeah—"

"No kids, I assume?"

Hackett turned quickly to see why Bishop would mention kids, what he might know, but Bishop chuckled. "I know your generation is full of baby daddies," he said, like he was channeling the street lingo, "and people don't get married anymore."

He was closer than he knew.

"So I'm just saying, I know it's a small town and it's the off-season, so it feels even smaller, but you need to stay focused."

"I only said she was cute," he muttered. "Can we drop it?"

"Whoa. Little sensitive, there? Lighten up, Francis."

"What?" Could his new partner really not remember his first name was Justin?

"Name that movie. Come on. You must know that line," and then he said it again, with more gruff in his voice. "*Lighten up, Francis.*"

"No idea."

"The introductions in the barracks . . ." He started laughing. "*Stripes!*"

"Never saw it."

"Jeez, you are a baby. Okay, that's a required movie. I'll tell the chief you're not ready for the next level until you've seen it."

Hackett finally broke a smile. "Okay, okay. I'll add it to the list."

Bishop spit into his cup. "Good."

~ • ~

When Grace woke, a blanket covered her and her shoes had been removed. The living room was darker now, though light streamed in from the kitchen, where Lisa was cooking at the stove. Music played softly in the background. Grace pulled the towel from her forehead, sat up, and slowly made her way into the room.

"Hey, sleepyhead. Feeling any better?"

"Yeah. These headaches just wipe me out. I feel kind of woozy."

"Well, I guess that's better than the pain, right? Hell, that's why I drink this." Lisa raised her wineglass. "Nothin' wrong with a little woozy."

Grace sat on a barstool at the counter while Lisa stirred something in a saucepan, the fragrance of roasted tomatoes in the air. "Were you telling the truth before? To the police?"

Lisa froze. "What do you mean?"

"Did I tell you what happened when I came here Friday night?"

"No," she said, and lifted her glass for another sip. "I know this must be so strange. You probably don't know how to feel."

"I feel lost."

"Well, I can tell you that maybe this was a good thing." She set down the glass and continued stirring.

"How can you say that?"

"I don't mean good that he's dead. I just mean good that you broke up. At least we know he can't hurt you anymore."

"What do you mean?"

Lisa hesitated, looking at the grease-stained tiles behind the stove. "Michael had a temper. That's why you wanted to get your stuff when he wasn't home. You didn't want a confrontation. I asked you to leave him so many times, Grace. It wasn't healthy."

"Did he hurt me?"

"Well, that's a loaded question, isn't it," she said, her eyes avoiding Grace's like it was too hard to say what came next. "I never saw a black eye or anything, and you never said he hit you, but I don't know what went on behind closed doors. You just seemed afraid." She turned and must have sensed Grace's anxiety. "Don't worry. The doctor said you need rest. Your memory will come back. This will all get cleared up. They'll figure it out. He probably had lots of enemies. Now," she said, opening the oven door below her and retrieving two sandwiches, the cheese oozing from their sides, "I made tomato soup and grilled cheese. Sound good?"

It sounded perfect, actually. Much better than the stuff at the hospital, and despite everything, she was hungry. After dinner, she went back to the sofa and Lisa went up to work on her bedroom. Grace said she'd watch television, but she preferred silence. She scrutinized the walls: the scuffs, nail marks, the lightened rectangles of space indicating longtime locations of paintings or pictures. She studied the fireplace: the painted wood mantel, its ornately detailed design now grayed from soot; the iron grate; the remnants of wood, mounds of ash, and the cracked brick hearth. She'd been a child in this house, a little girl who probably sat in front of the fire, playing board games on that rug. But as she tried to conjure the image, to transform the space in time back to something recognizable, it felt forced, like she was simply drafting a story in her mind.

When she couldn't wait any longer to use the bathroom, she stood, bracing the arm of the sofa to regain her equilibrium. Specks of light clouded her vision, but she slowly made her way up the stairs and paused in Lisa's doorway to say good night. Lisa brought her an old T-shirt and some sweatpants from Grace's dresser, turned down her bed, and got her evening dose of medication.

When Grace opened her eyes again, the green digital display on the clock atop the milk crate next to her glowed in the darkened room: 1:36 a.m. She was wide awake. She sat up slowly, trying to protect the ribs that begged her to be still, and walked to the window, the cold wood floor creaking beneath her bare feet. The full moon cast a dim light onto the front lawn, and stars speckled the clear sky. It was peaceful. Beautiful. Or it could be; maybe it used to be. She put her hand to the window. In the frigid air, the icy-thin glass fogged around her fingers.

She found some socks in the dresser and wandered to the bathroom. She stood at the pedestal sink, bathed in the bright light bouncing off the white-tiled walls, staring at her mirrored image: the freckles, the mole near her chin, the teeth, the bite of her jaw. She had good teeth, very straight. Had she worn braces? She made several faces at herself—serious, goofy, tongue out, tongue in . . . could she flip her tongue? It was like playing with a new toy—this face, this body. She opened the medicine cabinet and examined the shaving cream, disposable razors, deodorant, toothpaste, floss—like a detective looking for clues. She pulled the cap off the Mennen deodorant and whiffed. Masculine, familiar. Did Lisa use this? Did she? Did Michael? A small makeshift table sat next to the sink, piled high with makeup, brushes, a hair dryer, and jewelry. She searched for a glass or cup—her cotton mouth had returned—but despite evidence of every possible item one might cram into a bathroom, found none.

She peeked into Lisa's room. Paint rollers and open paint cans sat atop newspapers lining the floor along the walls, now half-covered in a vivid turquoise that practically glowed in the dark. A pile of ripped wallpaper sat in a heap on the floor, and Lisa lay curled into a ball on the mattress like a baby.

Grace made her way down the creaking stairs to the kitchen for water. The house was quiet and dark. She stood in the center of the room and considered the space. It felt familiar. She shut her eyes and heard cabinets closing, a woman's voice calling her down to breakfast. Her muscles relaxed. She opened her eyes. There, in front of the sink—a tall woman, maybe forty, with wild, long, wavy dark hair, wearing a T-shirt, jeans, and a paint-covered apron, looking out the window toward the backyard, smiling. Mom. It was only a glimpse and then it was gone.

Perhaps everyone was right. Being here would bring it all back. She got some water and took another Ambien from the bottle by the sink. She sat at the table, enjoying the nanosecond of what must have been a memory before a loud clacking sound started up.

She walked into the hall, the noise growing louder. It was coming from below. Under the stairs, she saw a door, held shut by a hook-and-eye latch. She lifted the hook and the door opened, as if she'd given freedom to a force behind it. The air was cold and damp. The noise grew louder. It had to be the furnace. Lisa had said Mom and Dad's stuff was in the basement.

The switch on the wall failed to turn on a light. Still, she gripped the railing and descended the creaking wood treads, the total darkness of the basement engulfing her. She stepped onto the cold concrete floor and nearly shrieked when something touched her face. But it was just a string. Pulling it bathed the room in the dim light of a bare bulb above her head.

The furnace in the corner rumbled and then clacked to a halt. The room fell silent, but the space was calling out to her, almost begging for investigation—old pieces of furniture, boxes, piles of clothing still on hangers, framed artwork, laundry baskets and milk crates filled to the brim—all of it holding potential clues to her life. She walked over to a large roll of carpet, taped together, and, pulling back a corner, revealed a hint of white shag. She fingered the fibers and smiled. It was hers. She'd rolled around on that rug as a child in her bedroom.

Next to the rug was a white-painted table covered in butterflies. This was hers too. Her fingers traced the texture of the paint, the delicate brushstrokes on the wings. Her mom had painted this. Grace moved around the table, examining all four sides, the butter-flies, flowers, detailed trees and grass. On the back, in marker, were smiley faces, at least a dozen, drawn with a child's hand. Had she done that? Among the smiles were two circles, linked together, each containing one letter: *G* and *M*. Grace and Michael? But it was a child's work. Could that be *M* for Mom?

She sat on the floor and sifted through nearby boxes. A picture frame held a photo of a woman and a child, sitting on a blanket in the grass, staring intently at each other. The little girl—probably

Lisa—maybe four years old, with short, wispy hair, held the woman's face in her hands. The woman was a younger version of the mother she had remembered in the kitchen. She touched the glass, as if she could reach through it and touch the woman's hair. An ache welled up, an overwhelming sense of loss, of needing her mother, even if she couldn't remember her. What had happened to her? To both of their parents? She needed to ask Lisa more tomorrow.

Farther down in the box was another picture, this one of a little girl swinging under that giant tree in the front yard. The girl leaned back, her mouth open in joy, her long, wavy dark hair falling behind her, little bare feet high in the air. The hair was the same as Grace's. Closing her eyes, she tried to recall the breeze, the massive branch creaking against the pull of the ropes, the birds. It almost felt real, but was it wishful thinking? Was it her?

Something began to howl outside. She walked to the window above the washing machine. She couldn't see anything, but the howling continued. First one, then more. Coyotes.

As she stood there, a feeling of déjà vu rushed through her. She tried to understand the strange sensation gathering inside. There was nothing odd about what she was looking at: an old washing machine, a slightly newer-looking dryer beside it, a large cast-iron basin full of dirty laundry, and, above it, an old metal chute. A churning filled her belly, like nausea, but then rushed through her system like a locomotive. She tightened her grip on the machine, weakened by the sensation, terrified of a feeling she couldn't identify. And then it came like an alarm: a long, terrified scream.

Grace whipped her head around so quickly that she winced. There was no one else in the basement. But she heard it again, the sound of terror and panic. It was a child. She squeezed her eyes shut, trying to get that noise out of her head. It faded to a whimper and she took a breath and let her head fall back. She opened her eyes, staring at that chute. The voice was gone, but her stomach twisted in knots. She thought she might get sick. Was it panic? Memory? She rushed back upstairs and latched the door shut.

As she climbed the stairs to the second floor, she instinctively stopped at the midway point. Why had she known that spindle would be loose? She stood for a moment, eyes closed, gripping the railing tightly with both hands, slowly moving her foot toward the spindles, mimicking a kick, and she heard it: the heavy weight of thick-soled boots pounding up the stairs, stomping each tread, smashing the spindles like thunderclaps. The force buckled her strength. She fell back against the wall, sitting hard on the stair. It felt as if her mind were a damaged circuit board and she'd been messing with the wires, trying to connect pathways but causing only sparks and shocks and damage.

She returned to her bed and lay there with her eyes closed for what felt like years, wishing for sleep that wouldn't come, trying to think good thoughts—but what came instead were questions, one after the other. She played with them, sorting and reordering as though faced with a crossword puzzle, unsure which answers were needed most, which might give clues to answer other questions, what she might learn from this house. Finally, with exhaustion came sleep.

FIVE

IT WAS NINE FORTY-FIVE WHEN GRACE GOT UP. Lisa's door was shut, but she could hear the muffled sounds of music, of Lisa singing along inside. Grace opened the door and the full blast of the song filled the entire second floor. Lisa was bouncing around, flicking paint at the walls. Specks covered the floor and ceiling. When Lisa turned to work on the area toward the door, she jumped.

"Damn, you scared me," she said. "Good morning! What do you think of my masterpiece?" The four walls were all bright turquoise now, but Lisa's large brush was covered in black paint. Splatters of black covered random bits of the walls. Bright-eyed and covered with paint flecks herself, she smiled with pride at her creation.

Grace had no words for the chaos. It felt a little like a nightclub without the black lights.

"How'd you sleep?" Lisa asked before launching another splatter at one of the walls.

Grace envied her energy; Lisa seemed the embodiment of her polar opposite. "I don't know. I was up a lot. I wandered around a bit."

"Really? I didn't hear that. I've been up for ages. I'm good to go on, like, five hours."

Had she wandered, or was that a dream? "I'm a little foggy."

"Remember anything?" Lisa asked without stopping.

"I remember coming here yesterday."

Lisa turned to her and almost chuckled. "Do you remember the police coming here?"

"Police," Grace repeated, scanning her brain for the details.

Lisa stopped and came over, her tone softening. "Do you remember what they told us about Michael?"

Grace struggled to reach through the fog.

"Your ex-boyfriend?"

There were pieces there, she could see them, and yet . . .

"He's dead," Lisa said, like it was old news.

"Right." Grace nodded, relieved. "Right, yes, that's right. You made soup."

"That's right." Lisa smiled at her oddly, then turned back to her work.

"Please." Grace reached out and grabbed her arm, feeling a rush of panic. "Help me."

Lisa looked at her arm, turning red under Grace's grip. "Let go," she said, her voice clipped.

Grace withdrew immediately and watched Lisa's pinched expression shift back to the concerned look she'd worn at the hospital. "Of course I'll help you, Grace."

"I'm sorry. I need to know who I was. I need a history."

Lisa pulled her in for a hug, but it felt like a stage direction that made them both uncomfortable. She patted Grace's back softly. "It's okay. Go get some coffee and cereal. I bought your favorite. I need to clean up the brushes. I'll be right there." She guided Grace to the doorway and nudged her in the right direction.

Grace cautiously took the stairs down to the kitchen and let the aroma of roasting coffee beans guide her. After pouring herself a cup, she walked to the upper cabinet to the right of the stove for the cereal. She looked around the room then. "Right there," she murmured before walking directly to another cabinet for a bowl. She knew where everything would be, as if her body were on autopilot.

The coffee, hot and strong, felt good going down, and she sat at the table, looking out the window toward the woods. Every branch was covered in snow, creating a canopy of fluff atop the massive trunks. Lisa's footsteps creaked on the floor above her; furniture scratched along the wood planks. She covered her ears; it was too loud, like nails on a chalkboard.

Her gaze fell to the linoleum-tiled floor, the pattern pulling her in. She fixated on the lines within each square, but the pattern began to move. The shapes shifted. She sensed it wasn't real, but she lifted her feet to the safety of her chair's support rail just in case; pushed her fists against her eyes, like she could force out the hallucination; and shifted her gaze to the living room, to the beams of morning light streaming onto the carpet. She looked down. The floor had stopped moving, so she carefully returned her feet to the ground. She drank more coffee, poured milk on her cereal, and tried a few bites, but it was no use. The nausea had returned.

When Lisa joined her in the kitchen, she sat taller despite feeling weak. "Will you tell me about Michael? And our parents? Our childhood?"

Lisa sat across from her, tapping her fingers against the sides of her chair, as if she wasn't sure how to begin. "Okay. Michael. You'd been with him for a long time, but I can't say I ever understood why. But then again, I've never had the best taste in men either." She met Grace's eyes. "And you and I haven't always been close."

"Why not?"

"I don't know. I guess it's just because I'm older. I moved out when you were only thirteen, so after that it just wasn't that kind of typical sibling relationship. But you came to me and wanted to move in, and I was glad to have you."

"I don't understand. Why—?"

The phone rang before she could finish the thought. Lisa jumped like a startled cat. It was difficult to guess who was on the line. She was just saying, "Yes . . . okay . . . sure . . . and where are you? All right."

Grace sat with her head in her hands, pressing hard against her temples. The pounding had started again.

Lisa hung up, came over, and crouched down beside her. "What is it?"

"Another headache."

She went to the counter where she'd lined up the pill bottles from the hospital. "Here. It's time for your meds. This will help."

Grace swallowed the pills and returned to her former position, waiting for an effect.

"That was the police again," Lisa said. "They'd like us to come in."

"Why?"

"Well, there *was* a murder. They're going to have more questions. But don't worry. I'm sure it's no big deal. I need to get in the shower though. We're supposed to be there in an hour."

Grace needed a shower too, but she wasn't sure she could stand up that long. Perhaps she'd take a bath later. She carefully climbed the stairs, her gaze intentionally avoiding the shaky spindles. The closet was empty and there were just a few items in the dresser. She pulled out some jeans that had been folded neatly in a drawer.

The drive to the station took thirty minutes. When they arrived, Lisa helped her out of the car before ushering her into the building. Her ribs weren't too bad, but her equilibrium was gone and she couldn't walk without her sister's help. Hackett and Bishop greeted them in the lobby as they entered.

Hackett stepped to Grace's side to support her. "Are you feeling okay today?"

She rejected his arm and tried to force a smile. "Thanks, but I'll be okay. I just get a little dizzy when I stand up sometimes."

"This way," Bishop said, and led them to a private room. It was small and white, much like the hospital room, and entering brought with it the thought of crawling back into that hospital bed and closing her eyes, potentially forever.

Hackett pulled out her chair. "We really appreciate you coming in today. We'll try not to keep you for too long." She took the seat and Lisa took the one beside her.

Lisa removed her coat and offered to help Grace with hers, but she refused. Bishop and Hackett sat across the table, and Bishop took the lead again. "Any new memories, Grace?"

"I saw my mother," she uttered, barely above a whisper.

"What?" Lisa said.

Grace looked at her sister and waited a moment for her vision to clear before speaking again. "Last night in the kitchen, it must have been a memory. I saw her at the sink, wearing an apron."

Hackett leaned forward. "So you're starting to remember a few things?"

Grace looked at him; the movement caused more blur, so she closed one eye. But even then, she could see something in his expression and his posture. The way he was still, waiting for a response—he cared. "Maybe. It's almost like I'm remembering feelings as I walk around the house."

Bishop cleared his throat. "We'd like to share some information with you. Maybe it'll help all of us." He nudged his partner, like Hackett needed reminding of their purpose.

"Great," Lisa said cheerfully.

"There are some things we've learned about Mr. Cahill— Michael—at this point." Hackett arranged his pad and pen, ready to take notes. A white file box sat on the table next to him. Bishop crossed his arms and rocked back in his chair. "For one, Michael seemed to be a drug user. There was a pretty large bag of marijuana in the bedside table."

Grace wasn't sure if that was supposed to mean something, but it didn't.

"Do either of you know anything about that?"

"Don't look at me," Lisa said.

They all stared at Grace, waiting for her response. "No," she said.

Bishop nodded as if he didn't believe her, as if he'd interviewed tons of murderers and her responses were typical. She suddenly felt desperate to please this man, to say whatever he wanted to hear and help them solve the case, to get him to smile and stop examining her like a lab rat. But she didn't know what to say.

"We're also wondering if Michael may have been a gambler."

Grace looked toward Hackett, pleading for some relief. Lisa piped in. "Why do you say that?"

"His bank records indicate that he never used a credit card. His credit score is pretty low, so we're guessing he's had some money troubles in the past."

"What does that have to do with gambling?"

"Well, nothing directly. But he had pretty regular withdrawals of cash after he'd deposit a paycheck, and every few weeks he took out pretty large sums of money. Every once in a while there were large cash deposits."

"I don't see the connection," Grace chimed in without making eye contact with anyone. It was easier to keep her head still, so her eyes remained on the table in front of her.

Hackett spoke this time. "Honestly, Grace, we're just keeping the options and ideas flowing at this point. Someone with poor credit is bad with money, someone who gambles is bad with money, someone who takes out large sums of money might gamble."

Lisa snorted. "Is that all you've got? I mean, it's been a week since you found him. What about a murder weapon? Prints? What about DNA? Was anything taken?"

Bishop rocked forward, bringing all four legs of his chair back to the floor as he responded. "We're processing plenty of evidence, Miss Abbott. There's an entire investigative task force assigned to the case, and the state forensics lab is examining several items. Just because it's a small town doesn't mean we don't know what we're doing. But it's going to take a little time, particularly to get DNA evidence."

"Sorry," she said. "I didn't mean to offend you."

Bishop cracked a smile. "It's okay. Everyone seems to think that the lab can get back to us in an hour."

"Like on *CSI*," she said with a grin.

"Right, but you just have to be patient. There's one lab for the whole state."

"Then, by all means, please continue," Lisa said. "I just thought you'd have some real leads to share with us."

Bishop rolled his eyes at Hackett before continuing. "Well, I can tell you a few things we do know. For one, his car wasn't stolen. At first, that was a possibility because it wasn't at the scene, but it turns out he'd dropped it off for an oil change on Friday afternoon."

Everyone glanced over at Grace, trying to gauge any kind of response. She shrugged. "Okay."

"And," Bishop continued, "we hope that you or Grace might be able to shed light on some of this stuff." He nodded toward Hackett, who reached into the box beside him and pulled out some envelopes.

"This might be a little awkward," he said to Grace.

She waited for him to say more, irritated that with every sentence, she felt their stares, waiting for the reaction she didn't have.

Hackett pushed a clear evidence bag across the table. Inside was a large blown-up picture of Michael and an attractive blonde woman, smiling for the camera.

"Do you recognize this woman?" Hackett asked.

"No," said Grace. "Do you?" she asked Lisa.

"No." Lisa shook her head. "Where'd it come from?"

"The girl posted it on Facebook on the Friday before the murder. Michael was tagged in the picture and she'd written, 'Congratulations!'"

Grace glanced at him. The information was meaningless.

"Either of you know what she might have been congratulating him for?"

"No," she said, and Lisa echoed her.

"Okay, how about this?" Hackett pushed another evidence bag across the table. Grace picked it up and examined the prescription bottle of pills inside: Xanax, prescribed to Grace Abbott by Dr. Bethany Newell.

"These are mine?"

"It appears that way."

"What does that have to do with Michael?" she asked.

"Well, given the drugs found at the scene, we had the lab rush a toxicology screen. Those pills were in his system at the time of his death," Bishop said.

Lisa sat forward, her arm stretching in front of Grace like a shield. "What does that have to do with anything? It's not like this could be about drugs, right? I mean, you said he was shot."

"That's all true, Miss Abbott; we're not sure what it means yet," Hackett said. "There's something else though. We found these." He pulled several more evidence bags from the box. Each contained an eight-by-ten picture of two naked people in bed together.

"What's this?" asked Grace.

"These are not familiar to you either?" Bishop asked, incredulous.

She wanted to scream. It was like beating her head against the wall. Why didn't he get it? She massaged her temples before resting her forehead in her hands. "Nothing's familiar to me."

"Well, we can say for sure that the man is Michael," Bishop said.

Lisa examined the photos. "It's not Grace, obviously." The naked woman on top had her back to the camera; the only thing visible was her long, platinum-blonde hair.

"Yeah, the hair is definitely not Grace's," Hackett agreed. "And this doesn't look to be taken in Cahill's house, so we're assuming this is another woman. And see here, there's a date on the back. December first."

"What do you make of it?" Lisa asked.

"Don't know yet," Bishop said. Grace twisted some of her dark hair around her finger, inspecting its color, wondering if this was a good thing.

"Could this be the same woman from the Facebook picture?" Lisa asked.

"It's possible," Hackett said, taking the pictures back and laying them side by side.

"Dick," said Lisa. Grace looked at her. "I knew he was a dirtbag."

Bishop raised his brows. "Did you know Michael?"

"Of course."

"Why 'of course'?"

"We've known him forever. He lived next door when we were growing up. We played together for years. But I wouldn't say we were friends or anything."

"Why's that?"

"Like you said, he got into drugs. He wasn't a good guy, in my opinion. And he was too old for Grace. He was kind of controlling. So of course that put a strain on things. That's why Grace and I weren't all that close in the last few years."

Finally, Lisa was sharing a little more about their relationship. Grace sat forward, listening intently.

"Any knowledge of him dealing drugs?" Bishop asked.

"No," she said.

"Okay. Again, we're simply chasing possibilities. It was a pretty large stash of marijuana. Obviously if someone's involved in illegal activities, there are dangerous types one's going to run into."

"Well, that seems unlikely. I'd hope Grace would not have stood for that."

"Were you aware of Cahill cheating on Grace?"

Now it was Lisa who seemed taken aback by the cop's intense gaze. "I didn't say that."

Hackett followed up. "Is there anything else?"

Lisa glanced toward Grace again before responding. "I did wonder if maybe that's why Grace left him, that's all. I mean, isn't that the cause of a lot of breakups?"

Bishop nodded noncommittally. "Grace, we'd like to ask you for a couple of things."

She looked at him but couldn't maintain eye contact with that piercing gaze. She kept her eyes on the table. "Sure."

"First, we'd like to get your fingerprints. We have a lot of prints from the scene, but since both you and Michael lived there, we'd like to know which prints are yours and which belong to someone other than you or Cahill."

"Okay."

"We'd also like you to take a polygraph."

"What?" Lisa straightened like a rod.

"It's standard procedure."

"She has no memories; how the fuck could she be lying?"

Grace reached out to touch Lisa's arm, a surprise to both of them. Lisa was obviously trying to help, but it seemed like a mistake to make the police angry.

Bishop raised both hands, palms forward. "We're not suggesting that Grace is lying. But we'd like to confirm what she might and might not remember."

"I don't mind," Grace said, hoping her own calm would settle her sister. "I don't know how that will help, but if you say so, fine."

"That's great," Bishop said with a smile. "It will help a lot. We can get the prints from you today. We'll have to call you back to do the poly on another day."

"Fine," she said, satisfied at having extracted a smile. She rose from her chair but then stopped suddenly to brace the table, closing one eye for balance. Hackett came around quickly and offered his arm. He guided her out the door and down the hall to the fingerprinting computer.

"You doing okay?" he asked.

She withdrew her arm from his, regaining her equilibrium, and smiled up at him. "Sure, thanks. You're a lot nicer than the other one."

The compliment didn't get the reaction she expected. Instead, his smile faded.

But when he placed her fingers one by one onto the plastic board, holding them steady as the digital print was taken, he stood so close she could smell his cologne. She knew that scent. "What's your name?"

"Justin," he said without looking at her face.

"Justin," she repeated. "Nice name."

He looked at her, searching her expression, and she smiled.

"Do you remember something, Grace?"

"Should I?"

He smiled and shook his head. There was something about him, but she couldn't put her finger on it. She didn't feel hunted by him. She felt safe, even as he took her fingerprints.

When they returned to the room, Bishop watched her as if she were some sort of alien. "Is there anything else you remember about Saturday morning?" he said to Lisa. "Hearing Grace in the bathroom, perhaps, or shutting the door, or the sound of a car leaving? It would really help us establish her whereabouts."

"We've been through this. She was in a car crash."

"Yes, but the officers at the scene got there a little before nine in the morning. Their investigation concluded that the accident had occurred between thirty minutes and an hour earlier."

"And when did Michael die?" Lisa asked.

"We can't say for certain. Given the delay in discovery, the medical examiner has given us a window. It definitely happened in the early part of Saturday, but it could have occurred before or after the time of Grace's accident."

Grace sat up and confirmed what everyone was thinking. "So you think it's possible I did this."

Officer Hackett shook his head. "We can't rule anything or anyone out yet. That's all."

Lisa's cheeks flushed. "This is crazy. You don't know her. It wasn't Grace. It couldn't have been. Yes, she was upset, but . . ." She paused, maybe unsure of what might help.

"Can you think of where she might have been going at the time?" he asked.

"I already told you." Her voice rose again. "Maybe running. Maybe coffee. I don't know." She slammed her hand down near the pad of paper where Hackett was taking notes. "Hey, I know what you're suggesting." She stood. "I don't think we should continue this, Grace."

Grace didn't move right away. Lisa nudged her. "I don't want to sit here and help you build a case against my sister simply because she can't properly defend herself right now."

"Maybe I should go to Michael's house," Grace offered. "Maybe it would help me remember."

"That would be great," Bishop said.

"Absolutely not." Lisa pulled at her arm. "Come on, we're leaving."

Bishop stood as well. "Miss Abbott, we're only looking for help. No one is being accused of anything."

Grace carefully stood to join Lisa, who was now at the door, holding it open. "I understand you're doing your job and trying to solve a murder, but I'm trying to help my sister get better. Her doctor told her to take it easy, and now she's come home to a murder investigation. This must all be very confusing, and I don't think we should do anything to upset her, certainly not without speaking to her doctors first."

The officers followed them to the station lobby.

"As far as I can tell," Lisa said, "there are other possibilities here—gambling, drugs, who knows what else. Maybe Michael messed with the wrong guy at a bar. You don't know anything yet, and you'd better not just go after the easiest suspect."

Grace watched the confrontation and giggled. They all seemed very cartoonish—this scrappy, punk-rock chick, dragging a drugged-up basket case out of the room, and these two officers, like keystone cops, shuffling after them.

Bishop was trying to control her sister, who was obviously not going to be controlled. "Okay, Miss Abbott. Let's give her another couple of days. We've got some other things to track down. Do us a favor and stay in town."

"We're not going anywhere," Lisa said.

She yanked at the station's front door, causing it to bounce off its hinges and hit Grace as she trailed behind. It propelled her forward, causing a strain in her rib cage that made her yelp in pain, but Lisa was oblivious as she rushed to the car. Grace followed like an old woman in the ten-degree air.

Once inside the car, Lisa turned to her, deadly serious, her pointy little face scrunched with stress. "Grace, don't be stupid."

Grace forgot about her pain and laughed.

"You have no idea what went on Saturday morning. You can't blindly offer to go back to that house. They'll be watching your every move, your every reaction or lack of reaction. For all we know, they're trying to build a case against you. Don't help them do it."

"I thought you said I couldn't have done it."

"Just because I said that doesn't mean they'll believe me."

Grace's head began to ache again. She closed her eyes and let her head fall back against the seat.

"And quit laughing. This isn't funny. Come on." Lisa checked her watch. "Let's go home. You need to be resting and I need to get to work. And until you know what happened, don't volunteer to help the police, okay?"

Grace agreed.

SIX

HACKETT WATCHED THE WOMEN DRIVE out of the lot. "Why didn't you mention the casino?" he asked. They already knew the photo with the blonde had been taken at the Four Winds Casino, and the woman's profile listed it as her place of employment.

"We're walking a fine line here. Grace could be traumatized from that accident, she could be traumatized by something she saw at Cahill's house, or maybe she's our perp. I'm not ready to share all our cards yet."

"Shouldn't we get over there and find out more?"

"No need. We got what we needed this morning," Bishop said, walking back to his desk.

"What do you mean?"

"Kewanee, with the tribal police, checked it out. The Potawatomis own the casino, so their tribal police are deputized and help us out when it comes to tribal property. He already learned that the woman's a waitress, she arranged for another waiter to cover her shifts last week, and she's off this week. No one has seen her at home or work, and everyone assumes she's left town. She's not due back at work until this coming Friday."

"So this woman is connected to the victim the day before his death and now she's skipped town?"

"Well, yeah, but we don't know enough to assume anything too nefarious yet. She may just be on vacation." He sat behind his desk and reviewed some notes. "Anyway, how are you coming with Grace's cell records?"

Hackett went to his own desk that faced Bishop's and leafed through the paperwork. "I got the warrant processed last Thursday, but the phone company said it could be at least a week for the texts and phone records." He hoped it would take longer. It would all be over if Bishop saw the call logs before they figured out who killed Michael.

His boss sipped his coffee and continued working on the half-eaten muffin he'd abandoned when the women arrived. "We also got some new information just now."

Hackett took a seat. "What's that?"

"When you took Grace to get the prints, Lisa mentioned that Cahill had a temper. She said Grace was afraid of him." Bishop cracked a half smile, like he'd just gotten a great nugget. Like maybe Grace blew him away, a battered woman who'd had enough.

Hackett was surer than ever that he'd been right to keep quiet. Someone had to keep Bishop from going after the easiest target. "We don't have any record of abuse," he pointed out.

"True. But that doesn't necessarily mean anything. Call the crime-lab fingerprint unit, ask for Miles. Tell him we got Grace's prints and we need them checked against the prints found on the photos."

"Okay. Didn't he say there were more than one set of prints on them?"

"Yeah. But we know that Cahill's wasn't one of them. If Grace's prints are on those photos, that's motive."

Hackett made the call and said a silent prayer for Grace. And for himself. As he hung up, Bishop was grabbing his coat. "Come on. We're heading up to Berrien Springs."

~ • ~

The wind off the lake had picked up, swirling some of last week's snowfall into the road. The entire landscape was still covered in a thick blanket, and the temperature wasn't expected to let up anytime soon. Hackett rubbed his hands together, trying to get warm and focus on the facts—to play the part of investigator—but his thoughts kept falling into a ditch, where they went round and round, back to Grace's face and back to the phone call that might ruin him.

"Whatcha thinking about?" Bishop asked.

"Nothing," he answered, keeping his eyes on the white-covered fields.

"You watch *Stripes* yet?"

Hackett chuckled. "You just told me to watch it yesterday!"

"Well, what the hell else you gotta do? How does a young guy spend time around here anyway? You never seem to be hungover, so I'm guessing you're not that type."

"No," he said.

"Come on," Bishop prodded. "Give me something. I'm almost a half century. God, that sounds bad. My free time is spent at basketball games, ballet recitals, chores—did I say ballet recitals?"

Hackett laughed.

"It's my duty to live vicariously through my good-looking, young partner who's probably swinging from chandeliers. I mean, look at you!"

Hackett laughed. "Hardly. You'd be so disappointed."

"You got a girl?"

"No."

"And your family's in Indiana?"

"Yeah. Chesterton. I haven't seen them in a while."

"Well, I guess that'll change soon."

"What do you mean?"

"Christmas."

"Oh right, yeah, maybe." Maybe. His mom had left several messages, and he knew it might make things worse if he didn't go, but everyone else was much better at pretending the family hadn't been irreparably damaged. And he didn't want anyone looking at him like he was some wounded bird. He couldn't stand their pity.

"Well, we need to solve this case ASAP."

"What's the rush?"

"It's just shitty timing."

"Christmas?"

"That and I'm on double duty right now. Sandy's mom is in the hospital again. Doesn't look good."

"What is it?"

"Cancer. She's battled it for years, but looks like the fight is about over. Sandy won't leave her side, sure she's going to go any minute, so she's up in St. Joe night and day."

"That's tough."

"Yeah, and don't get me wrong, I love my mother-in-law and I know it would be shitty to lose a parent, but I've never been in charge at Christmas. She's leaving it up to me to make the magic happen."

"How old are your kids?"

"Fifteen, thirteen, eleven, and nine."

"Wow, that's a brood. At least they're older, right?"

Bishop shook his head. "You have no idea how hard it is to shop for these kids. The older ones understand that because of Grandma, it's not a great year, but Paige, my nine-year-old, is still talking about Santa. Last night she asked me to download this app on my phone that tracks his movements so we'll know exactly when he's getting close to Michigan on Christmas Eve."

"They have that?"

"Oh yeah. And the older ones just want electronics: PlayStations, Wiis, Xbox. Lucky for my boy, I enjoy a game or two. But those iPods, iPads, iPhones—I hate that frickin' *i* company. They need to stop marketing expensive shit to my kids."

Hackett smirked at his tirade.

"I say no to everything," Bishop added with a grin, "but nothing makes you feel like more of a failure than disappointed kids on Christmas morning."

Hackett's thoughts went to Donny, opening up his gifts on Christmas, probably the first one he'd understand. Beaming as he ripped through wrapping paper, content to play in an empty cardboard box—and Hackett wouldn't see any of it.

"Well, you're a chatty Cathy, aren't you?" Bishop said.

"Sorry." His thoughts were now stuck on Christmas, on how every future Christmas would bring nothing but dread.

They drove another twenty minutes in silence. As Bishop turned onto Shawnee Road toward the center of town, he smacked the steering wheel to break Hackett's spell. "Okay, I got another quote for ya."

"Hit me."

"Now, this is a classic. Everyone in the world has seen this movie."

"Okay."

In his most strained voice, as if he could barely get out the words, Bishop said, "I got no place else to go. I got no place else to go! I got nothin' else."

Hackett grinned, watching him mug for a few seconds before giving up. "I got no idea."

Bishop's tone was now deeper and gruff. "Oh, come on, May-o-nnaise."

"What?"

Bishop continued in his best imitation of the unnamed actor, throwing at him some insulting remarks about Oklahoma.

"This is all the same movie?"

"Yes! Kid, what have you been doing all your life? It's *An Officer and a Gentleman*. Richard Gere. Debra Winger." He clapped his hands and went into a high-pitched falsetto. "Go, Paula!"

Hackett cracked up, suddenly picturing his balding partner in a dress. "Same movie?"

Bishop chuckled and backhanded him on the knee. "Of course."

"Well, now I have to see it."

They pulled into the parking lot of The Rack, just a half mile down the road from Cahill's construction job. Cahill's foreman had said a stop at The Rack was like the second half of any shift. The building, enlivened only by neon beer signs in the window, was rundown, sandwiched between a thrift shop and a parking lot. Inside, the smell of cigarettes and stale beer greeted them as Led Zeppelin blasted from the jukebox. The bartender, mid-sixties, with long, graying hair pulled back in a ponytail, multiple earrings, tattoos covering both forearms, and a massive belly that spilled out from beneath his Harley T-shirt, leaned against the rail at the end of the bar, reading the newspaper.

Hackett and Bishop took seats at the bar and introduced themselves. The bartender offered them a drink, which they declined. "Had to ask." He smiled. "I'm Ed." He shook hands with both of them. "What can I do you for?"

"You recognize this man?" Hackett held up a photo of Cahill.

"This is about that murder, huh?"

He nodded. "We heard from Mr. Cahill's foreman that he and the boys often came here after work."

"Yeah, Mike was a regular."

"How often would you say he came in?" Bishop asked.

"Oh, I don't know, few times a week? There was usually a load of 'em who came in after their shifts over at the site to kick back for an hour or two before headin' home."

Bishop gave Hackett the nod to jump in. "We're trying to piece together his last days. Can you remember the last time you saw him?"

"Couple weeks, I guess."

"According to his boss, he'd worked four days on the week before his death." He checked his notes. "Sunday, Tuesday, Wednesday, and Thursday. Would you have any record of whether or not he was here any of those days—after his shift, perhaps?"

"Nah. No real bookkeeping. I mean, unless someone pays with a credit card, there's no telling who's been in and out."

Bishop spun his barstool away from the conversation, toward the pool tables.

"How well did you know Mr. Cahill?" Hackett asked.

"Not well. I mean, he's 'Mike' to me, for one. I ain't no Sam or nothin'."

"Sam?"

"You know, Sam—*Cheers*?"

Bishop turned back and smiled. "The reference is wasted on my partner, here. Turns out he doesn't know anything from before 1990."

"Come on, guys," Hackett protested. "I can't help it if I'm not old!" The men laughed.

"Shall we get back to it, please?" he asked. "When was the last time you saw Mr. Cahill? Mike?"

The bartender sipped his coffee. "I know he wasn't here after Sunday, week before last. I know because I was planning to give him some shit, bust his balls a little, but I never got a chance."

"So you know he was here that Sunday?"

"Yep."

"And why'd you wanna bust his balls?" Bishop asked.

"Oh yeah. Kinda funny, really. The boys are always hanging out. They're loud. Riding one another a bit. Placing stupid bets on the games. Sometimes I go in on them, but shit, I'd be broke if I did that with all the customers. Anyway, I remember that Mike was telling all the guys about how he couldn't place no more bets for a while, that his ring was setting him back a bit."

"Ring?" Hackett asked.

"Engagement ring. He was showing it off. Had it with him. He'd told the boys that he was finally gonna do it, and they all teased him a bit."

"So that's what you wanted to tease him about?" Bishop asked.

"Fuck no. I wanted to tease him because the very night that he's telling the boys how he's taking the big plunge, I seen him leave here with some other woman."

"How do you know it was another woman? Do you know his girlfriend?" Hackett asked.

"No, no. We don't get many chicks in this place. It's more of an escape. But this chick came in looking like, I don't know, like Sharon Stone or something. Fuckin' hot, that's my point. Mike's up at the bar, getting a few, and this girl, she starts chatting him up, flirting. She wasn't no girlfriend. I mean, I was at the other end of the bar, but you can tell when girls want some just by the way they hold a cigarette, you know?"

"So she smoked?"

"Well, not in here, of course. But she was holding an unlit one at the time. Anyway, next thing I know, he's leaving with the girl. Got his arm around her and everything."

"So this was Sunday . . . December first?" Hackett asked, looking at his notes.

"Yeah. Had to be."

"So he meets some girl and takes off with her? Can you remember what the girl looked like?"

"Skinny thing, high heels, long blonde hair. You know that white blonde, like a porn star. Yeah, I mighta left with her too, if she'd asked me."

"Did she come in with anyone else? Did you see her talking to anyone else?" Bishop asked.

"She might have come in with someone. I didn't see. But there weren't any other women in here. Grant you, it's not exactly normal for a looker like that to be hanging out in a shithole like this, but she obviously liked what she saw in Mike. I mean, I guess he's good-looking. *Was* good-looking. Fuck." Ed shook his head and crossed his arms.

"Just a second." Hackett pulled out his phone, searched "Michael Cahill" on Facebook, and found the picture posted a few days before the murder. "Is this the girl you saw with him?"

The bartender took the phone and squinted at the picture. "I don't know if I could say. The hair color is about right, but I didn't focus too much on her face, if you know what I mean."

Hackett took back the phone. "And you work on Tuesdays and Thursdays, and Cahill didn't come in?"

"That's right. I didn't see him, anyway."

Hackett turned to Bishop. "Cahill worked on Wednesday too."

"Who runs the bar on Wednesdays?" Bishop asked.

"Richie. He's got Wednesdays, Fridays, and Saturdays."

"So it's possible Mr. Cahill—Mike—was here on Wednesday."

"Hold on," Ed said. A customer waved him over. The bartender poured his shot and beer, then returned to Hackett. "No idea, man."

Bishop stood. "Well, this is helpful. Do me a favor. Write down Richie's number."

"Sure thing," Ed said, noting the number on a cocktail napkin.

"Does he live around here?" Hackett asked.

"He's about an hour away in Three Rivers. But like I said, he'll be in Wednesday, anytime after two."

Bishop held up the napkin. "Well, thanks. One other thing," he said. "In general, would you say that Mike was a heavy drinker?"

"No more than anyone else."

"Never belligerent, never had to cut him off?"

"No."

"You ever see him and wonder if he was on drugs?"

"Nope."

"And how would you describe him—nice guy, tough guy, difficult? Anything?"

"I don't know. Good guy. They're all good guys. Some rougher around the edges, but these guys keep me in business. So yeah, I'd say they're all nice guys."

"And on that Sunday you saw him, how many drinks would you say he had?"

"Maybe two beers."

Bishop nodded, then pulled out his card. "Thanks," he said. "And if you think of anything else, please don't hesitate to call."

"Sure thing."

Back in the squad car, Bishop turned to Hackett. "We need to talk to Wesley Flynn again."

"The guy who found Cahill?"

"Yeah. Flynn said he hadn't seen him since Sunday. Maybe they were here together. Maybe he saw this woman Cahill left with."

"Okay. What are you thinking?" Hackett asked.

"This girl he hooked up with, it sounds like the girl in the naked photos. Also sounds kinda like that girl in the Facebook post."

"True. And the 'Congratulations' comment on her post—you think that's about the engagement?"

"Maybe. But that's kinda weird, right? If that girl is the one in the photos, would she be saying 'congratulations' about marrying someone else?"

"I don't know."

"We don't know if they're the same woman. Cahill had a lot of Facebook friends, and many were women. He may have been quite the player."

Hackett's thoughts turned back to Grace. Why was she ever involved with this guy?

"You know what else," Bishop said. "Think about those naked photos. You know what's odd about them?"

"What?"

"Who took them? They only capture the girl from the back, like someone was at the foot of the bed."

"You think someone else is involved?"

Bishop shoved some tobacco inside his lower lip before answering. "Don't know. But the photos were taken somewhere other than Cahill's house. It wasn't his bed; it wasn't their bedroom."

"What about a webcam? Maybe it was part of some kinky sex-tape-type stuff."

Bishop spit out the window and continued. "But if I'm gonna cheat on my girlfriend, why would I have photos of another woman and me in the bedside table, where Grace would easily find them?"

Hackett wondered if Grace had found them or if she'd suspected Cahill was cheating. It would be a couple of days before the crime lab would know if her prints were on the photos.

"What if I wanted to blackmail someone?" Bishop said. "We now know Cahill took five thousand in cash out of the bank a week before he died."

"True. But we also know he had bought a ring by Sunday—a week before the murder. Maybe that's what the money was for."

"Also true."

"But you're thinking maybe this blonde girl was trying to break up Michael and Grace? Maybe she's the one we should be looking for?" He spoke disinterestedly, to avoid betraying his hope.

"I don't know," Bishop said before spitting into his cup. Then he laughed. "What if the blonde was Grace? Like some kinky game, like she's wearing a wig and they're spicing up the love life—playacting? Showing up at the bar in a wig, pretending to be a stranger."

Hackett faked indifference. "It's possible, I guess." It wasn't possible.

"Can't imagine my wife doing crazy shit like that, but maybe Cahill was a lucky bastard."

Until Saturday anyway.

SEVEN

WHEN GRACE OPENED HER EYES, she looked up at the water-stained ceiling, trying to figure out how long she'd been sleeping. After Lisa had dropped her at the house, she'd poured more coffee and made toast. The dry, crusty bread had crunched in her mouth, but the flavor of the jam and the cream cheese she'd smeared atop it was nonexistent, as if her taste buds had fallen out of her head with everything else. All she got was an amplified crunch in her ears and the useless chewing of flavorless, day-old gum. Nauseated and dizzy, she brought her coffee and meds to the living room, turned on the television, and sank into the couch, trying to focus on the screen. But her vision blurred. Her lids felt weighted. Eventually, she closed her eyes and the cushions swallowed her up as she fell deeper and deeper into a semiconscious state, able to hear things but unable to move.

Now a new program was on and the sun had fallen. She stood and leaned on the frame of a nearby chair to get her bearings. She felt drunk, definitely worse than before.

She sat back down, holding her head, reviewing what she knew. The days were blending into one another. Someone's dead, she remembered. Police station. Driving with Lisa. A wave of nausea returned. She had to get outside and breathe fresh air. She grabbed the coat hanging in the hall, slipped on a pair of boots, and walked out the front door.

The snow-covered landscape appeared like a painting, frozen in time; her breath, visible in the cold air, wafted into her sightline. But the picture was tilting—or was it she who was tilting? She wrapped her arms around the closest porch post, closed her eyes, and breathed slowly, trying not to upset her rib cage while inhaling the cold air—the life—into her body to get clear, to lift the fog.

After a few minutes, she opened her eyes. The spinning had stopped. She walked around toward the back of the house and spotted a small white shed off to the right, closer to the woods. She peeked into its windowed door at the fertilizer, garden tools, and a red, rusted wheelbarrow propped up against the wall.

Then, like a flash or a dream, she was sitting in the wheelbarrow. Riding in it. Laughing. But she was young. She looked back at the large, open yard behind her and saw a young girl, squealing with delight. The sun was shining on the little girl's long brown hair, and the green grass was covered with fallen autumn leaves. The girl was holding on tightly, looking back and giggling at the man pushing her around the yard. Dad? He was tall, thin, fair, with freckles and a red beard. She blinked and the sunshine, grass, and leaves disappeared. The world went back to white.

Something was unlocking inside her mind. She walked from the shed toward the tree line and looked into the woods at the underbrush, the bent twigs, coated in thorns. The lightness and joy left her. Tension crept up her spine. A single gunshot echoed loudly in the distance. She turned around to locate it, but there was no other sound. Was the shot real? She heard a scream—a little girl, crying. Grace spun toward the sound, but there was no one. She spun around again and again, until she lost her balance and fell to her knees in the snow. "What's happening?" she screamed to the sky. Her voice echoed through the woods.

~ • ~

Wesley Flynn strolled into the station with the faint smell of stale beer on him, a travel mug of coffee in hand. His unlaced Timberlands, unbuttoned flannel shirt, and beard stubble suggested a quick and recent dressing, despite the afternoon hour. Hackett thanked him for coming in on such short notice and brought him into the interrogation room where Bishop was waiting. Flynn pulled off his knit cap, brushing through his disheveled hair. Bishop told him to take a seat.

"What's going on, fellas? Am I in trouble or something?"

"No," Bishop said. "We were just hoping you could help us piece together Michael Cahill's last days. You said you saw him last Sunday, a week before the murder, right?"

"Yeah."

"Was that at The Rack, after work?"

"That's right."

Bishop shared what they'd learned from the bartender, but Flynn didn't recall the blonde. "Doesn't mean much though," he said. "I was playing pool most of the night."

"Do you recall Cahill talking about getting engaged?"

Flynn swallowed visibly. "I don't remember. Honestly, we were both there, but I was playing pool most of the time." He grinned at them, as if his easygoing smile could be a substitute for real information.

"Can you tell us the names of the other guys who were there?"

Flynn thought for a second and shared the names of a few other construction workers. Hackett took notes before pulling up the Facebook post. "Do you recognize this woman?"

Flynn scrutinized the picture. "No."

"It was apparently taken at the Four Winds Casino. It was posted on Friday before the murder."

Flynn shook his head, but frowned.

"What?" Bishop asked.

"We swore that place off. I mean, my wife absolutely forbids me from going anymore. We lost far too many paychecks after a few too many. I thought Mikey was done with it too." He stared at the photo. "What do you think it means?"

"We're not sure yet," Bishop said. "And you didn't see Cahill again until you found him the following Monday?"

Flynn sat back and began buttoning his shirt over the white tee. "That's right."

Hackett thought he saw something there. A hesitation or avoidance of eye contact. He couldn't be sure, but something made him asterisk Flynn's response on his notepad. "How long have you known Cahill?"

"Oh, forever, man. We've been friends since we started working together. That was, like, right outta high school."

"So does that mean you know Grace Abbott well?" Bishop asked.

"Of course. Grace is a sweetheart." Flynn leaned in. "Is there any news on Grace?"

Hackett nodded. "She's okay. She was in a car accident. She spent the last week in a hospital up in Kalamazoo."

"Shit, you're kidding." He smacked the table. "That's great news. My wife is going to be so relieved. She okay?"

"She's pretty banged up," Hackett said. "But she's alive."

"Speaking of Grace," Bishop asked, "do you know if she smokes?"

"Cigarettes? No way, she hates the smell. Where is she now?"

"At her sister's place in Buchanan," Hackett said.

Bishop's cell rang. He checked the number, stood to leave, and signaled Hackett to wrap up the interview. Hackett leaned forward as Bishop left and lowered his voice. "Do you know if Cahill ever cheated on Grace?"

Flynn sat back, stunned. "Why? You think a woman did this?"

"I'm just asking."

Flynn scanned Hackett's eyes and then the room before responding. "Michael loved Grace, I can tell you that for sure."

"That's not actually an answer to the question."

"My point is that Michael wasn't always the best boyfriend, but . . ."

"So he did cheat on her."

"I didn't say that."

"What are you saying?"

"I'm saying I don't know of any affair. I don't know of any cheating specifically, but Michael was a bit of a magnet. That doesn't mean anything, but if he ever slipped, I'm sure it wasn't recently. He was a good guy."

Hackett sat back, exasperated. "Wesley, do you think Grace could have done this?"

"Grace? Fuck no."

"Well, if you know something that could shed some light, out with it. It could help her."

Flynn looked around. "It's just that, now and then, someone would do something to Michael. His tires were slashed last year. It was just about a year ago. It seemed like he knew who did it but wouldn't say. That's all. And before that, someone threw a rock through his bedroom window. It kind of made me think of a woman, that's all."

"Why's that?"

"I don't know. We'd all been out for Grace's birthday that night. It just seemed like maybe a woman saw them and got mad. What can I say, he was a good-looking dude. Maybe I've just seen too many movies. But I never found out who did it."

Hackett thanked him, walked Flynn to the door, and went to his desk. He couldn't decide if what Flynn just shared could help or hurt Grace, so he wasn't ready to talk about it yet.

Bishop sat at the neighboring desk, finishing up the call. "That was Kewanee," he said, putting down the phone. "Turns out Cahill was a big winner at Four Winds last Friday."

"How big?"

"Ten thousand dollars." Bishop grabbed his coat and checked his watch. "Come on."

"Where are we going?"

"We're gonna get a warrant to get back into that house."

Two hours later, Bishop pulled into the gravel drive in front of Cahill's house. The snow had been packed down by all the squad cars, but the yellow tape remained at the front door. "Good," he said. "Looks like no one's been here."

"What do you mean?"

"That tape really has no meaning anymore. It's been a week. That's why we had to get a new warrant. I thought the landlord might have sent a cleaning crew to deal with this place by now."

"Wouldn't want that job."

"God, no."

There had been no chance to check for footprints or tire tracks or any evidence outside the house because the snow had fallen all day Saturday, days before the body's discovery. There was no point looking for anything outside now.

Bishop slipped on some latex gloves and tossed a pair at Hackett before they walked through the house again. Hackett went back to the bedroom and stood at the foot of the bed; the mattress was still covered in bloodstains. "So what are we looking for?"

"Look everywhere," Bishop said. "Think of places you might hide a lot of cash. If we find the money he won Friday, then I'm guessing this isn't about money. If we don't, well, who knows? There certainly weren't any deposits for that kind of money in his account."

Bishop checked the bathroom, the living room, and began opening cabinets in the kitchen. He emptied the contents of a small trash can on the counter. "Hey, Hackett, check it out."

"What? What's that?"

Bishop carefully lifted a large yellow envelope from the mass of discarded mail on the counter. "It's addressed to Grace. Date-stamped December fifth. A couple days before the murder."

"What are you thinking?"

"I'm thinking this envelope is the perfect size for photographs."

"It's only an envelope. Seems like a stretch."

"Really?" Bishop turned the envelope around so Hackett could see the front and the stamp PHOTOS DO NOT BEND. They both chuckled.

"Well, that was kind of easy," Hackett said.

"Maybe whoever took those photos of Cahill and the blonde wanted Grace to see them." Hackett took the envelope in his gloved hand and examined it. On the back side, in the bottom right corner in tiny print, were the letters *HBG*. "What do you make of that?" he asked.

"No idea."

Hackett went back into the bedroom and got down on the floor, searching under the bed for a box or anything one might put cash in. He didn't find any box, but he spotted an empty handwritten envelope, addressed to Michael Cahill, sent from Oaks Correctional, also date-stamped December fifth. He brought it back to the living room. "What do you make of this?" He held it up.

Bishop took the envelope. "Friends in prison? Anything in it?"

"Nope."

"Make a note to call the prison. See if Cahill ever went to visit someone there and, if so, who."

"Got it."

They spent an hour carefully reexamining the crime scene but found no sign of the cash.

"Well, I guess that leaves a lot of possibilities," Bishop said.

"You know what else?" Hackett said. "Cahill was allegedly gonna propose. You see a ring on Grace's finger?"

"Don't remember."

"Well, I do, because I was standing there when she gave her prints this morning. She wasn't wearing any jewelry. I wonder if he ever proposed."

"I'm still waiting for her medical records from the hospital in Kalamazoo. Maybe there will be a record of whether there was a ring on her finger when she came in."

They both stood at the kitchen counter, scanning the living room. The room, painted in soft yellow, gave no hint of the violence that had occurred in the bedroom, other than that broken picture of Grace and Cahill that had been found on the floor amid shattered glass.

Hackett thought about the moment he'd entered the house last Monday. He'd been the first responder at the scene. All he'd known at that point was that someone had been shot. Investigators were soon crawling all over the place, snapping photographs, bagging items. He'd hesitated to go into the bedroom, terrified he would find Grace there. Now he walked over to the spot on the floor where he'd found the broken picture of the onetime happy couple. He looked at the wall above it, at a small gash in the wallboard, and turned to Bishop. "Maybe you were on to something about those photos."

"What do you mean?" Bishop asked.

"Maybe they were about blackmail."

Bishop shook his head. "I don't think so."

"But remember that broken picture of Cahill and Grace?"

"Yeah."

"It was here, on the floor," Hackett said, pointing to the spot by his feet. "And here"—he pointed at the gash in the wall—"looks like the kind of mark that could happen if you threw the picture across the room."

"Doesn't mean much. Grace could have done that. Or Cahill."

"Or maybe it was a moment of jealousy of seeing the happy couple. We know he was with another woman. What if we don't see the money because he paid someone off?"

"The photos were in the bedside table," Bishop said. "Grace's side, from the look of things. And if they came in that envelope, they were addressed to Grace. If I wanted to blackmail Cahill, I'd send them to Cahill, not Grace."

EIGHT

GRACE WOKE ON TUESDAY WEARING only a robe. The wet towel had come loose from around her hair and dampened her pillow. She sat up slowly. It had been another restless night. She'd dreamed of the swing out front, maybe because of that photo she'd found. But she wasn't the girl on the swing. She was behind the girl, pushing her higher and higher as they laughed. Then the little girl fell, crying as she hit the ground, holding her ankle. Grace's own ankle throbbed in that moment, her tears and pain jolting her awake.

By three a.m., she'd gotten out of bed and considered wandering the house again, searching for clues to her former life. But the dull headache that seemed to have permanently installed itself behind her eyes and the weakness she felt when moving dissuaded her. Instead, she filled the tub with some bubbles and grabbed a washcloth. At least she'd finally feel clean. She shaved her legs and washed. But then it happened again—that feeling—the churning in her stomach, the uneasiness.

She lay back against the porcelain and closed her eyes, covered her face with the damp washcloth, and tried to focus only on her breath. But then a vision came like a rush. Splashing water, struggling for air, arms flailing. She screamed, "Stop! No!" And then she was sobbing. The cries were real. And loud. She sat up, wincing from the pain of her sudden movement and shocked by her own outburst.

Lisa barreled into the room. "What's happening?"

"I don't know," Grace cried. "I don't know what's happening to me."

Lisa came over to the tub. "Come on, let's get you back to bed."

"I feel like I'm losing my mind."

"It was probably a bad dream," Lisa said, gently positioning her hands under Grace's arms to help her stand.

"But I wasn't asleep."

Her sister helped wrap her in a towel and grabbed another for her hair. "When did you come in here?"

Grace put on the nearby robe and wrapped her head in the towel. "I don't know. Three?"

"It's five o'clock. You probably fell asleep in the tub. Maybe you had a nightmare."

It *was* a nightmare: every moment since she'd woken in the hospital.

Now the house was empty and Lisa was gone. A note on the kitchen counter reminded Grace that she was at work. Other notes on the counter reminded her to take her pills, which had already been separated into little piles marked *morning, midday, bedtime.* Lisa had made coffee and left chili in a Crock-Pot, and there were more notes reminding her to eat, along with a cell phone number if Grace needed anything.

She took the first pile of pills with her coffee and went to the bathroom. Another note was taped to the mirror: "Take your medicine!" Despite the shakiness in her step and the vague sensation that she might faint, she was relieved to be alone.

~ • ~

Hackett's alarm began buzzing at seven, but he smacked the snooze button and put a pillow over his head to block out the light pouring in from the uncovered windows. He really needed to get some shades. He'd tossed those purple curtains Olivia had picked out into the trash as soon as he moved in five months ago. He'd taken everything from their house, even the stuff he hated—which was most of it, since she'd decorated without his input and ignored his opinions. But taking the stuff was punishment. This bed was the only thing he'd really liked. It was king-sized, and the mattress had that memory-foam stuff that oozed around him when he fell into it. But even the mattress sometimes failed to comfort him when he began thinking of it as an actual bed of lies.

The alarm sounded again and he grudgingly got up and headed for the shower. Bishop wanted him in by eight thirty. The phone rang while he was in the bathroom, but he let it go to voice mail. It was his mom, of course, given that it was a Tuesday, her day to check in with all the kids. She probably didn't even expect him to answer at this point. He'd ignored her calls for months, though he had to make a decision soon. He'd never missed Christmas, but the thought of it still made him sick.

What did people do who didn't have a family? Go to the pub? He didn't know which option would depress him more. His whole life had centered around family—his parents, brothers, cousins, grandparents, in-laws, brothers of in-laws—for as long as he could remember: massive fifty-person gatherings for every holiday, birthday, engagement, baby, or even Little League game. But he couldn't imagine sharing a meal, asking *her* to pass the potatoes, having a beer with *him*, or, worst of all, watching Donny playing with his brothers or running over to wrap his arms around his dad.

He shaved, dressed, and was out the door in twenty minutes. After grabbing a muffin and coffee at his daily pit stop, he drove to the station where Bishop was at his desk, ending a phone call.

"Sorry I had to get out of here early yesterday," Bishop said. "Crisis at base camp."

"Kids okay?"

"For now. No one's burned down the house yet, if that's what you mean. You find anything good yesterday?"

"I called the prison and talked to the person in the visitor's center," he said. "Cahill isn't registered on their logs. No incoming mail from that name either." He didn't add that he'd then left the station and gone to Lisa Abbott's house. He'd wanted to see Grace, and the more he knew he shouldn't, the more tempted he was. He'd pulled up to the foot of her driveway and looked down the gravel path to that old house, silently praying that Grace would be okay. But when a curtain moved, revealing a figure backlit at the window, he'd driven off.

Bishop didn't respond, his eyes rooted on a family photo. "You okay?" Hackett asked.

"Huh? Oh, sure." He smiled. "Just tired. Sandy got home from the hospital at midnight, had a mini meltdown. It's not easy, kid, losing a parent. I don't care how old you are. And I hate seeing her so sad and there's nothing I can do."

Hackett withered inside; those words stung more than Bishop could know.

"Come on," Bishop said, grabbing his coat.

They drove in silence to Cahill's former work site while Hackett focused on the crumbling and abandoned barns along the way, neglected to the point of no return. The foreman they'd met with last week pointed them toward the management trailer. When they entered, a woman bent over some drawings at the table hollered at them to shut the door. The wind was whipping, making the twenty-degree air feel more like five. Hackett shut the door while Bishop asked for her boss, Joe McKenzie.

The woman, perhaps late thirties, looked up from her work, dropped her pen, and stood. She was disarmingly attractive and seemed to have mastered a sexy look for a construction site: tight jeans, "work" boots—like Timberland imitations with a little heel—and a long-sleeve thermal T-shirt that hugged her body, with a flannel shirt tied around her waist. She looked like she might model in carpentry catalogs as a side gig. She walked over to the officers and offered her hand. "That's me, fellas."

"Oh, excuse me," Bishop said, flustered. "We assumed you were a man."

The woman smiled, pointed toward the chairs facing her desk, and took a seat. "Yeah, I get that a lot. It's Jo, as in JoAnne."

Hackett grinned and watched Bishop fumble a bit as he sat.

"Sorry I couldn't get to you earlier, fellas," Jo said. "It's a busy time here. We had a crisis at the site and it was all hands on deck. And I had to get the new guy up to speed on what Mike had been working on. You have any suspects yet?"

Bishop did all the talking, as usual. "There are some strong possibilities, but we're trying to get the full picture of Mr. Cahill's life. We want to be sure we're not missing anything before we move forward."

"Sure. What can I do to help?"

"Tell us what you know about him. Was he a good employee?"

"Oh, hell yeah. He worked for me on my last build too—a strip mall up in St. Joe that we did about two years ago—and this project is pretty big, as you can see." She pointed at the posters lining the trailer wall—the current mass of steel beams and concrete pilings would one day become a twenty-story building. "So yeah, all in all, I'd say Mike's worked hard for me for several years. He was a good man."

"We found some drugs in his apartment."

"Drugs? I don't believe it. He'd have fallen off one of those risers and killed himself. What are we talking about?"

"Marijuana."

The woman laughed. "Oh, I thought you meant *drugs* drugs. I don't worry too much about a little pot smoking—no different than having a few drinks in my book, as long as you do it on your own time. No offense."

"Sure. We don't make the laws. Do you know if he had money trouble or was big into gambling? He didn't seem to have very good credit and didn't have any credit cards. Seemed to live exclusively on cash."

"Well, that isn't the norm, is it? I can't imagine life without my Visa. But then again, that bill is the death of me every month. Maybe he was onto something."

"So you don't know about any money trouble?"

She leaned back then, lit a cigarette, and blew the smoke off to the side. "Nah." On her desk sat an ashtray full of lipstick-covered butts. "He never asked for an advance or talked about payday loans, if that's what you're thinking."

Hackett asked the next question. "So, as far as you know, he was reliable, no money problems, nothing else?"

"Well, of course, he wasn't a friend. He was an employee. I wasn't his confidante, but yeah, he was reliable. He almost never missed a shift, and when he did, he even brought me a note from the doctor."

"Did that happen recently?"

"Yeah, actually. It was just a couple of weeks ago." She turned to a small cabinet and searched through her files. "It was a Monday. I know because we needed a big crew that day, and so I had to scramble a bit when Mike called in."

"So he called in sick last Monday? December second. The Monday before he died. And he brought you a note the next day?"

"Yeah. He said he was sick, and maybe he could tell that I didn't believe it. I mean, it's not that he'd faked it before, but I knew a bunch of guys had stopped at The Rack on Sunday night, and I think I even wondered out loud if he'd simply hit it a little too hard. But when he came in on Tuesday, he brought a receipt for services from the urgent care. Must have been a bug or something." She showed the officers the receipt.

"Could we take this with us?"

"Sure."

Bishop stood and shook the woman's hand. "Well, thanks again for your time, ma'am, and I apologize for the confusion. Thinking you were a man, I mean."

She stood too. "Happens all the time. Construction isn't exactly known as 'women's work.'"

"Right." Bishop turned away, blushing.

Hackett stood too. "Ms. McKenzie, do you ever go over to The Rack? Seems like the crew all goes there pretty regularly."

"Sure, I need a drink every now and then. But I tend not to hang out with my men. Conflict of interest, you know."

Hackett nodded. "Sure. Thanks."

Back in the squad car, Hackett turned to Bishop. "I take it you think she's hot."

"What are you talking about?"

"Are you kidding? You were like a twelve-year-old boy standing before the captain of the cheerleading squad."

Bishop chuckled. "Well, shit, she was a knockout, right? Not exactly what I expected. I felt like I was Tim 'the Tool Man' Taylor."

"Hey, I know that one—*Home Improvement.*"

"Thank God. You had to be alive for that show. I think it's still on in syndication," Bishop said as he grabbed some chew from the glove box.

"Yeah. Got a thing for blondes, eh?"

"Maybe just that one." He turned the key in the ignition.

"Remember what you told me," Hackett teased. "Don't go clouding your judgment."

"What are you saying, she'd be mixed up with Cahill? She'd be the woman in those naked photos?"

"It's possible, right? Or at least the woman at the bar. She's got the hair. And she's a smoker."

"Fuck," Bishop said before spitting into his cup. "You're ruining my buzz here, kid."

They went from the site straight to the urgent care facility in Bridgman. The receptionist took them to the break room, to the doctor, a gangly middle-aged man with thin wire-framed glasses, who'd been on duty when Cahill had come in. They exchanged pleasantries and offered an apology for interrupting his lunch. "We're here about a patient who was here a couple of weeks back. Hoping you could share the nature of his visit."

"Got a warrant?" the doctor asked, chewing a mouthful of sandwich.

Bishop smiled. "Not in hand, but we can get one if necessary. I thought you might help us out—since there's no expectation of privacy in this case."

"And why's that?"

"Because the patient is dead."

"Oh," the doctor said. "Do you think it's related to his visit here?"

"Not unless you all prescribed a shotgun to the chest." Bishop smirked.

"Oh Lord," the doctor said.

"We're piecing together his last days," Hackett said.

The doctor stopped at the laptop station in the hall, pulled up the record, and read through it briefly.

"Okay. I remember this one. He came in with his girlfriend at, like, six in the morning. She'd found him asleep in his car in front of their house. He'd been gone all night. He was slurring, not making sense, nauseous. She was worried about drug use. So we got him some fluids and tested his blood. He tested positive for alcohol and marijuana. He couldn't remember what he'd done the night before. Suffered a few hallucinations while he was here. Got a little crazy even—swatting the staff, telling the nurses to get off of him. We sedated him and then he was okay."

"Do you remember what the girlfriend looked like?" Bishop asked.

"Pretty girl. Maybe twenty or so. Long, wavy brown hair, slim. Here," the doctor said, pointing to the screen. "She signed the intake form. Grace Abbott."

"Okay, great. And what did his girlfriend think happened?"

"She knew he'd gone to a bar with friends after work. That was the last they knew. She said he had planned to come home early but he never did. Till she found him in the morning."

"But you didn't think too much of it?"

"Not really. I mean, his levels were low, not even legally drunk. It was odd not to remember anything, but everyone reacts to drugs differently. Perhaps he'd never smoked marijuana before. Or maybe it was laced with something we didn't detect. People get whatever they want these days. It's the age of the Internet."

They thanked the doctor and headed back to the car. "Well, that's interesting," Bishop said.

"What do you make of it?"

"He was a regular user and he'd only had a couple of drinks at the bar. Something went on with that blonde."

"You think she did something to him?"

"Maybe they did drugs together. I wanna find that girl."

"Maybe we should focus on that waitress from the casino. It could have been her. And she might have been the last person to see him. No one has talked of seeing him after the casino on Friday, and she's now skipped town."

Bishop shook his head. "Grace probably saw him on Friday night; she just isn't saying."

"You mean isn't remembering."

"Whatever."

"I don't think Grace has given us any reason to doubt her. She's trying to help. She's obviously been badly hurt. And yet you're acting like she's faking all this."

"Hey, I didn't say that. And why do you sound so protective? I'm just stating the facts."

Hackett opened his mouth to respond but thought better of it.

NINE

LISA CALLED TO CHECK ON GRACE around lunchtime and reminded her to take her medicine. Grace stared at the little pile on the counter. "Yes, got it."

"And don't forget to eat—I made chili, your favorite."

"Sure."

"Remember, the doctor said you need to rest. What have you been doing?"

"Nothing," she snapped.

"What's wrong?" Lisa asked.

"Nothing!" She didn't know what was wrong. But Lisa's voice and those little Post-it notes were smothering.

When they hung up the phone, Grace looked at the pills and the time on the clock. She pushed them aside. She was finally starting to feel clear. She was hungry too, but the thought of ground beef and beans and spices she couldn't even taste wasn't appetizing. She resented being told what she liked. She didn't know what she liked anymore, but she didn't want chili. She ate some Saltine crackers and a few slices of cheese while watching *The Chew*. The cohosts shared recipes and cooked and laughed. The banter felt familiar, and she relaxed into the chair.

Suddenly, she was watching a new program. She'd been in a trance. She hadn't been listening or watching anything for who knew how long. She turned off the TV and heard a faint buzz, a vibration. She followed the noise to where her purse rested on the counter. As she searched the bag, the noise got louder. When she finally found the cell phone, it had stopped, but she had messages. She knew which buttons to press. It seemed so odd that she remembered technology but not people.

The first message was from a man named Dave. He wanted to see how Grace was feeling. Everyone at the restaurant had heard about the accident, he said. They were all thinking of her, and her check was ready. "We'd love to see you," he said. She could pick up the check or he could mail it. She just needed to let him know.

Grace called the number and was startled by the loud reply on the first ring, "Brewster's, can you hold, please?" The woman put her on hold before she could respond. Grace waited, repeating the restaurant's name in her head, the sound of Italian music in her ear. When the woman returned to the line, Grace asked for their location.

"We're on Merchant in New Buffalo, right off Whittaker."

Grace hung up before the woman could recognize her voice.

"Brewster's," she repeated. She was leaning against the counter, thinking about it, when she spotted the key—a single key on a ribbon hanging on a hook by the door. She got closer. The key was branded FORD. Grace looked out the window at the old pickup truck off to the side. A Ford. She looked back down at her phone's apps and found the map function. *Don't drive*, her doctor's voice rang out in her head. But she let go of the counter and walked across the room as if to prove it to herself. She was finally feeling clearheaded. "I'm fine. I feel better," she said out loud.

This house felt like solitary confinement. Going to the restaurant might spark more memories. Excited by the thought of getting out, of driving down that gravel road to a place filled with people who might be her friends, she grabbed her coat and purse, put on the rubber boots by the door, and carefully walked to the old truck.

When she climbed into the cab, the smell of vinyl hinted at times past, like a perfume. She closed her eyes, picturing little bare feet on the dashboard, toes tapping to a Bruce Springsteen tune. What was it? "'Born to Run,'" she said, smiling. Her dad had loved Bruce. But as she sat in the seat, looking out at the house, the yard, the woods, her smile faded—that was all she knew. She turned the key in the ignition, but the engine only made a painfully weak noise before the silence returned. She tried again, pumping the gas pedal. It didn't sound good.

She looked back at her phone to check the mileage on the map. It was a fleeting thought: to walk. But it was twenty miles. The land was covered in a thick, white blanket, it was freezing, and every step jostled her sore ribs. She was trapped. Her excitement collapsed, as if someone had opened the gates to freedom and when she ran for them, he'd slammed them shut and laughed in her face. She closed the map app, defeated, when she noticed another message in her voice mail.

With the speaker function engaged, a woman's voice filled the cab. "This is Dr. Newell's office. The doctor wanted me to remind you that she hasn't seen you now in two weeks, and we wanted to be sure you're okay and that you'll still be coming on Friday. Please call if you need to reschedule." The woman left a number, and Grace immediately called back. Dr. Newell had been the name on that Xanax prescription.

When the receptionist answered, Grace gave her name and explained that she'd been in an accident, had been in the hospital, and was anxious to meet with the doctor. The woman offered to squeeze in a visit the following morning between appointments. Grace noted the address. Perhaps the doctor would be able to fill in some of her blanks.

She hung up and instinctively went to the calendar function and added a reminder. She punched the date and time into the phone and closed the day. She then scanned the days before the accident to see what she might have had planned. She saw doctor's appointments for Fridays at one, a repeating event. But there was no indication of why she'd skipped it the day before the accident. She only saw a note about working on Friday afternoon. She went further back in the week, but the only notes were work related. Nothing social, nothing that meant anything.

She tried the engine one more time. It started! The gas gauge slowly climbed to half a tank. The map guided her down several roads and then south on Red Arrow Highway. After a few more miles, she sat up straighter, predicting: "A river," she said, before passing one a moment later. "Hamburgers," she said before the Redamak's Tavern sign appeared. "Nails," as she passed a nail salon. She made a right turn in the center of town without checking the phone. She turned left a few blocks later without seeing a street sign, and there it was, on the left side of the street: Brewster's Italian Café.

Staring at the entrance, the cobblestone-walled exterior, and old-world lamppost by the door, Grace tried to envision the interior, the uniforms, the layout, but nothing came.

The woman at the podium by the front door wore a nametag: Sheri Preston, Hostess. Her face lit up when Grace stepped inside.

"Grace! How are you feeling?"

It was scarier than she thought it would be. This woman knew her, and Grace couldn't place her face. "Hi," she offered quietly. "I'm here to get a check. Dave called me."

"Of course. Take a seat," she said, gesturing to the benches by the front door. "I'll get him." She scurried away, pulling down her tiny miniskirt as she left, wobbling atop four-inch heels.

Grace sat, taking in the large bar, its tiled countertop, giant wood pillars, the wineglasses hanging by their feet from above, and the Tuscany-yellow walls, waiting for a spark of memory.

The girl returned a moment later, relaxing behind the podium, doodling and trying to make conversation. "Grace, we're so sorry about Michael."

"Michael," Grace repeated. It took a second. Michael, the dead boyfriend, she suddenly remembered.

"The police came here last week asking questions about you," she said.

"Oh."

"Don't worry, Grace. We know you didn't do anything."

Grace nodded silently and looked around the room.

"Anyway, I'm glad you're okay. We've all been worried."

Another girl came in then, wearing a hostess tag and equally high heels. "Hey, Grace," she said, waving. The two hostesses looked at each other with raised eyebrows. The gossip would begin the moment she left. Coming here had been a mistake. The world would think she'd lost her mind.

Finally, a man appeared, grinning as he approached. He towered above the petite hostesses, even with the rounded shoulders that pushed forward his already large belly. He stretched his arms toward her as he got closer. "Grace!" he said, waiting for her to return the excitement. She stood to greet him, trying to make a connection— the black hair, gelled back; the ruddy cheeks; the bloodshot brown eyes, with lids at half mast. Nothing clicked.

"Hi," she said.

He seemed to understand her discomfort and lowered his arms and voice. "We heard about the accident, Grace. Your sister called and said that you hit your head pretty good and were having some memory troubles."

"Yeah."

"Did you drive yourself here?"

She could see the concern on his face. "Yeah, I'm okay. I just wanted to get out." It suddenly felt awkward to speak to this man whom she didn't remember at all, pretending she did, pretending she knew this place and her coworkers and that she wasn't a total basket case. "I'd better go."

He handed her an envelope. "Okay, Grace, you take care. We're ready to have you back whenever you're ready."

"I'm outta here too, Dave," Sheri added, as the other hostess took center stance behind the podium.

Grace said a quick "Thanks" and left while Sheri held the door. Grace thanked her and hurried to her truck before Sheri could make any more small talk.

She sat in the cab, looking back at the building. How could she not remember those people? They all knew her. This was her life. She opened the envelope and found the paycheck, but when she pulled it out, another slip of paper fell out as well.

Grace,

Meet me at Cherry Beach if you can.
Two o'clock. We really need to talk.

Dave

Grace looked back at the restaurant. Dave the manager? She looked at her watch. It was 1:35 p.m. "Cherry Beach," she repeated. She started driving again. It felt familiar. She wasn't sure, but she wanted to try something—to just drive. Maybe she would remember where to go.

She instinctively got back onto Red Arrow Highway, heading north. She passed signs and businesses. Things were clicking. "Yes," she said aloud. "Antiques." She smiled as she passed a few shops. But a few miles later, she started to wonder if she were lost. She slowed, and cars zoomed past as she carefully read the street signs. And then she saw it: Cherry Lane. A little street on the west side of Red Arrow. She turned onto the tiny, winding road, flanked by homes and dense woods. It dead-ended into a big gravel parking lot overlooking a bluff. "Cherry Beach," she said with satisfaction.

The wind whipped over the lakefront, but the water glistened in the sunshine, drawing her in. It felt familiar. The steep, long wooden stairway down the hundred-foot bluff toward the beach was covered in snow, but boot prints had packed each stair, and she slowly descended, taking in the vastness of Lake Michigan.

Snow covered the beach near the bluff, but gently lapping waves exposed the fine sand along the shore. As the wind fought to blow her hood from her head, she held it with one hand and trekked a few feet, following the tracks of previous visitors, hunting for memories. The sound of the water seeping up the shoreline was calming. A pile of old, rotted driftwood sat, abandoned, covered in snow. It sparked a vision: a bonfire on the beach.

"Grace!" a man called from the distance. She looked up. He stood on the deck overlooking the lake at the top of the bluff, waving at her. She slowly climbed the stairs, each step a little harder than the last, each one reminding her that going up was so much worse than down, that perhaps taking on a hundred steps in the freezing weather was a bad idea for her ribs and lungs.

"I'm so glad you came," Dave said. "I didn't mean for you to go down to the beach, but I thought this would be the right place to talk alone."

"It felt familiar. I wanted to see if I remembered."

"So this is for real? You don't remember anything?"

"No."

"Like, you don't remember the accident? Or you don't remember that day, or what?"

"I don't remember much. I didn't remember the restaurant. I didn't recognize you." It was as if she'd kicked a puppy. "Sorry. I don't remember my life. It's—"

"That's awful."

"I've had some flashes; at least I think they were memories. Honestly, they've got me on so many meds right now, it's hard to know what's real and what's not."

"But you remember this place?"

"Yeah, something about this place feels good."

Dave's smile returned. "We came here together."

"You and me?"

"I wanted to call you so badly, but your sister said that you had to rest and that you weren't to be disturbed."

"I don't understand."

"So much has happened. I just wanted you to know that I didn't do anything."

"What do you mean?"

"To Michael. I mean, of course I wanted to," he added—lightly, like there was something funny about the comment—"but I would never hurt him."

"Why would I think that? Were we together? I thought I was with Michael."

"You were. It was . . ." He paused and smiled before adding, "Complicated."

She studied him: this old guy—well, maybe not old, but midthirties—with a big belly and clumps of greasy hair that kept blowing into his eyes. She didn't know what her type was, but she couldn't imagine he was it.

"You're not a bad person," Dave continued. "I didn't mean to call you here and add to the confusion. I just wanted us to be able to talk alone. I thought you might be scared. I want you to know that I'm here for you. Anything you need." He tried to take her hands in his, but she pulled away.

"Was I not happy with Michael?"

He stared into her eyes before answering. "I don't know. I wish I could help, but of course you've never been the easiest person to read."

"What do you mean?"

"I mean you looked happy on Friday, the last time we worked together." He stopped, as if there was some significance she was supposed to understand. She didn't. "He was killed that weekend, right? What do the police say? Who do they think would have done it?"

"I don't know. I don't seem to have an alibi for the time of death, and I can't remember anything, so I guess they don't know what to make of that."

"Shit. Well, it's probably better if you don't mention our relationship to the police if you're a suspect. If they think you were cheating on Michael, I'm guessing that wouldn't look good for either of us."

Cheating, and with this guy? She couldn't believe it. Grace looked back out at the lake. "You and I were here together?"

"Right here. This is where I first kissed you." He reached out to her hands then, as if they could savor this memory together.

The thought turned her stomach. She didn't know anything about herself, but she instinctively wanted nothing from this man. His proximity was unnerving, his clear attraction almost scary. She shoved her hands into her pockets.

"Do the doctors think this memory issue is temporary?" he asked.

"They're optimistic. They said that usually memory loss from head trauma is less global, but it's like someone's taken an eraser to my mind. They say it will improve in time. I've been getting flashes. I knew where to turn for the restaurant and how to find this place, so maybe it's starting to come back."

"Jesus, Grace. Are you able to get home okay? I could lead you if you like."

"No, no. I've got it. And my phone has a map, so I should be fine."

"Well, if you need anything," he said, lifting her hands from her pockets in an awkward move for both of them, "call me."

He seemed to know too much about her history. It felt creepy. His body was too close to hers. She pulled her hands from his grasp.

"I'd better go." She started toward the truck.

"Okay. You have my number. Call anytime. And don't worry, they'll figure it out."

She stopped and pulled out the phone to check the contacts—Dave. She stepped back and showed him the screen. "Is this you?"

Dave looked at the number and nodded. "That's me. I mean it. I'm here for you, okay?"

She stepped back from the man, suddenly unable to get away fast enough. "Okay, thanks. I should go." She walked to the truck and got in. He raised his hand in a weak good-bye.

TEN

GRACE WOKE IN A DARKENED LIVING ROOM. Clouds had rolled in and the sun was gone. She sat up, turned on the table light, and checked the clock on the kitchen wall. She'd been out for a couple of hours. Her headache had only dulled, though her body no longer ached. She'd found her way back to the house by memory after leaving Dave at the beach, which felt like a great improvement, though her head had pounded from the effort, and maybe from skipping her meds. She had put the truck back where it had been parked so Lisa wouldn't know—she didn't want to hear the scolding—but struggled to get out of the cab. Every move had felt like swimming in molasses. She knew that staying in the truck was a sure way to freeze or, worse, upset Lisa, so she'd held her head in her hands and tried to breathe, disregarding the pain brought on by each inhale. She'd made it to the kitchen, grabbed the pile of pills from the counter, and found her way to those couch cushions.

Now she almost felt like a new woman. She raised her arms all the way over her head: incredible. She stood, breathed again, surprised that her ribs expanded with ease. She felt a wave of energy. There was so much to think about.

She opened the giant pocket doors to the onetime library, now filled with boxes. The chaos mirrored her mind. Everything was here; it had to be: her history, memories, family—but they were packed away, trapped beneath masses of tape. She pushed her way into the room and found an old desk practically buried under boxes. Using a knife, she cut open the nearest box. It held hanging files labeled *Credit cards, Utilities, Mortgage, Insurance*. Nothing that would mean much, but she studied the bills, reading charges, expecting a spark that didn't come. Buried among insurance documents were several bills for psychiatrists, psychologists, and counselors. Years and years of bills. Did she really want to remember? Maybe there was a reason she'd forgotten. One of the files was marked *New Haven Fertility* and inside the file were statements for treatments dating back to the early eighties. Perhaps that explained the age gap between Lisa and her.

The next box was more promising. A file labeled *Grace* contained her history—at least her school history. Report cards, school projects, even a few photos from elementary school. She scanned one picture, a kindergarten class posing in front of a playground swing set. The sun was shining into their eyes; the grass behind them was green. It took a minute, but she found herself in the group. It was that dress, a yellow sundress with gigantic daisies. Her favorite. All the children beamed at the camera except her. She looked distracted, maybe sad.

Grace skimmed through the report cards and teacher comments from year to year. *"Grace is a lovely girl," "I hope that she will get more comfortable with the group and begin to join in the discussions," "She's so quiet, sometimes so distracted, but when I see that smile come out, I know she's in there," "Keep working on her math."* She reread one several times. It was written by her kindergarten teacher: *"In light of all she's been through, I think she's doing fine."* What had she been through? Sitting among the open boxes and files, she felt overwhelmed by the history of a life she didn't recognize.

She went back to the basement and opened the boxes of clothes marked *Girls' Dresses*. She wanted to find that daisy dress, to tap in to her younger self. She sorted through a dozen neatly folded dresses of assorted sizes and colors without feeling a real connection, but then she saw it: a simple, bright-yellow cotton sundress with big daisies. She pulled it out of the box and held it to her nose, inhaling deeply, as if smelling it would take her back. But it didn't.

She looked down into the box and saw another one. The exact same dress, but instead of yellow, the primary color was orange. She pulled it out and checked the labels. Both were size 4T. The two dresses seemed a hint of something, maybe her own pleading, her love of that dress. She envisioned a little girl in a store, begging her mother for both. But it was wishful thinking. She was crafting a history, trying to fill the void with meaning. Her momentary nostalgia for something she assumed was a symbol of happiness began to dim. She laid the dresses side by side. Was it just the emptiness of staring at her past without remembering it, or was it something else?

~ • ~

"I think we found our murder weapon," Bishop said, hanging up the phone. "That was the crime lab. Turns out some officers in the New Buffalo station submitted evidence last week after getting a call from the recycling company that sorts trash bins behind Bellaire Apartments. They found a shotgun and a bloody shirt."

Hackett dropped his half-eaten sandwich on the desk and wiped his mouth. "When was this?"

"Monday, before we'd found the body. They turned over the items to the crime lab. A faded yellow T-shirt with a smiley face on the front, a 'Be Happy' logo on the back, covered in blood that's a match for our vic. The gun was registered to Michael Cahill. They're sending us scans of the evidence photos."

"Anything else?"

"The gun was wiped clean. No prints. But maybe we can link that shirt to Grace."

Hackett stopped himself from responding, but he shook his head and looked away.

Bishop threw down his pen. "What is it?"

"Cahill won a lot of money that we can't find. He was a gambler and drug user. We've got pictures of him having sex with another woman. But I'm getting the sense that you just want to pin this on Grace."

"I learned a long time ago not to overlook the obvious. You do and it'll bite you in the ass."

Hackett blew out a breath. "What are you talking about?"

Bishop rocked back on the hind legs of his chair, like a professor ready to school his charge. "We had a suspect for a murder years ago. Had motive, opportunity. No one else. But we kept trying to find the smoking gun. Just to be sure. In the meantime, this person killed again. Sometimes, rookie, you don't get to be a hundred percent. You just have to go with your gut. Grace lived with him, had every reason to want him dead from what I can see, and she has no alibi. That car accident may very well have happened after she ran from the scene."

"Well, my gut says she didn't do it."

"We'll see."

Heat rose to his face. Hackett took a sip of soda and let his focus shift back to his desk. He let a minute pass until the tension faded from the air. "Maybe we should see who lives at those apartments, right? I mean, what if the perp lived there and was just dumb enough to dump the murder weapon? And we're still looking for some blonde who was with Cahill at The Rack. Those naked photos are dated the same day he was seen leaving with the mystery woman."

"You're right. But as soon as we get those scans of that shirt, I want you to go through Cahill's Facebook page. Grace didn't have an account, but he had tons of pictures in his profile. I remember that she was in some. If we see that shirt on Grace . . ."

Hackett dropped his pen. "Wait, even if the shirt is Grace's, what does that prove? She lived there. The perp could have mopped up some blood with a T-shirt he or she found at the scene and disposed of it."

Bishop nodded halfheartedly.

Thank God. "Of course, if we can prove the shirt is definitely not Grace's, well, then it could be our perp's, right?"

"Maybe so," Bishop said.

An hour later, they pulled into the Bellaire Apartments parking lot. "The New Buffalo police question anyone here?" Hackett asked.

"They didn't have a known crime in the system at the time. But now we need to find out if anyone saw anything odd on Friday night or Saturday morning."

An older woman, maybe sixty, with strikingly silver hair and flanked by two Labradors, answered the door at the management office. She turned off the television, closed her *People* magazine, and moved a pile of older issues from the sofa, offering them seats. She seemed glad for the company, and when they told her their purpose, she pulled a list of tenants from a desk drawer.

Hackett scanned the list while Bishop asked a few questions. "Do you have any security cameras in your parking lot?"

"'Fraid not. A couple of officers came by after those things were reported being found here, but I wasn't much help. As far as I knew, no one had seen anything. I certainly didn't. My unit is in the front of the building. The bins are out back. You can go see. They're a bit removed from the main parking area. And when it's dark, they aren't lit."

"Okay, thanks," Bishop said.

Hackett looked up from his list. "Ma'am, by chance do you know if any of these female tenants are blonde?"

"Well, sure," she said as she stood up and went over to the list. "There." She pointed at unit 306. "She's my only blonde."

The men thanked her and headed outside. "So let's start with 306," Bishop said.

When they knocked on the door, a petite woman with long platinum-blonde hair answered. Hackett's radar perked up. She was definitely a looker, just like the bartender at The Rack had described.

Bishop handled the introductions. "Hello, ma'am, I'm Detective Bishop and this is Officer Hackett. May we come in for a moment?"

"What's this about?" She wore a little black miniskirt and scoop-neck top pinned with a name tag. Her bare feet shuffled back and forth as the cold air seeped into the apartment.

Bishop pointed at the name tag. "Miss Preston, may I call you Sheri?"

"Okay."

"Did you know Michael Cahill?"

"Yeah, he was that guy who was killed, right?"

"That's right."

"He was Grace's boyfriend. You came into the restaurant last week. I was there."

Hackett's heartbeat thumped. "So you work with Grace?"

"Yeah." She relaxed a bit against the open door.

"May we?" Bishop asked. "It's pretty cold."

"Sure." She let them in and closed the door. Hackett scanned the room while Bishop continued asking the questions.

"Are you a friend of Grace's?"

Preston went to the couch and sat. "Sure, kinda. We know each other."

Hackett sat on the arm of a chair, but Bishop continued standing. "Did you socialize with Grace outside of work?"

"Yeah—when we were working the same shifts. We usually all go out for drinks after our shift. We're pretty wired after running around for hours. She's nice enough. I mean, we didn't confide in each other or go to the movies, but we hung out. She's pretty quiet, that's all."

Unlike this one, Hackett thought. It was the way she walked—she was an attention grabber, just like Olivia. "And were you friendly with her boyfriend as well?"

"I knew who he was—I knew the name, but I didn't know him."

Hackett slid out his pad and noted Preston's connection to Grace, her physical match to the woman at The Rack, and her denial about knowing Cahill.

Bishop walked around the room, casually scanning pictures and knickknacks. "So, Sheri, it seems that some items were found in the trash bins behind your apartment recently that can be traced back to Cahill's death."

Preston crossed her legs. "Like what?"

"Like the murder weapon and a shirt covered in his blood."

"Oh shit." Neither Hackett nor Bishop spoke right away. Preston looked at them, then around the room. She didn't seem to know what to do with her hands, so she slid a cigarette from a pack on the coffee table and tapped it against her knee. "So what does this have to do with me?"

Bishop cleared his throat. "Well, we've been trying to figure out what Cahill was up to in the days before his death, and it seems he was seen leaving a bar with a blonde—a blonde who sounds a lot like you."

"What? Well, you're wrong. I didn't even know the guy."

"You ever been to The Rack in Berrien Springs?"

"The Rack?" She scowled. "What kind of name is that? Sounds like a strip club or something. No. I never heard of it."

Bishop made another circuit around the room. "So if we show your picture to the men who were in the bar that night, no one will recognize you?"

She sat back, blowing smoke toward the ceiling, and shook her head. Not even a hint of fluster. "I've never been to Berrien Springs. I don't even know where that is."

"Really?" Bishop said, incredulous.

She smiled. "Really. I'm from Chicago. I just moved to New Buffalo last summer. Thought it would be a summer job, hang at the beach. But I decided to stay. College sucks. So yeah, I don't know every town around here."

Hackett didn't buy it. "Can you tell us where you were on Sunday, December first?"

"Jeez, I don't know." She stood and walked into the kitchen to look at the calendar posted on the fridge. "Well, I wasn't working. But that was more than two weeks ago. I don't remember. I'll have to think about it."

Bishop said what Hackett was thinking: "It seems a bit of a coincidence to find evidence from a crime scene right here, just steps from your place, and to hear about Cahill leaving a bar with a woman matching your description a few days before his death. And I must say, the clothes look to be about your size."

Of course that was a stretch, but Bishop was obviously looking for a reaction, and he got one. "You're crazy. This is a huge apartment building. I'm not the only person who lives here. And who says you even have to live here to use the dumpsters?"

"Can you tell us where you were on Saturday, December seventh?" Hackett asked.

"You can't be serious." She plopped down on the couch again. "I take it that's the day he died?"

"Yeah," Hackett said.

"I was sleeping. I got up about eleven in the morning, then I went to work. I had a three o'clock shift."

"And is there anyone who could verify where you were in the morning?"

She leaned back and crossed her arms. "In fact, there is. I was with Dave Jacks. My manager."

The men looked at each other.

"We'd hooked up, okay? No big deal. A bunch of us were partying on Friday night."

"And he was with you all night?"

"Yes."

"At your place or his?"

"His."

"I don't suppose you know where we could find Dave now?"

"I'm guessing at his apartment. We both got off a little while ago, but he's going back in this afternoon. He lives downstairs in 104."

ELEVEN

WHEN HACKETT AND BISHOP KNOCKED on Dave Jacks's door, they found a man half-dressed and visibly stoned. He stood in the doorway in boxers, a white tee, and an unbuttoned blue dress shirt. They smiled, held out their badges, and introduced themselves.

"Hello, Officers, what can I do for you?" His voice cracked mid-sentence, betraying any attempt to be casual, while his face remained sandwiched between the door and the frame, preventing them from seeing inside his apartment.

"Can we come in?" Bishop asked.

Jacks didn't move. "I'm not really ready for company, guys. How can I help you?"

Bishop stepped closer. "Mr. Jacks, do you remember us? We came to the restaurant last Thursday in regard to the Michael Cahill murder?"

"Sure, sure, I do. Yeah, what's up?"

Bishop put away the badge and rubbed his hands together. "It's freezing out here, Mr. Jacks. Could we please come in and speak with you?"

"Oh, sorry guys, it's just—" Jacks glanced back into his living room. "Maybe I could come down to the station to meet you? I'm not dressed and I really need to get in the shower for work."

Bishop put his foot in the doorway and stepped closer. "I don't smell marijuana, do I?"

Jacks shook his head, but his shit-eating grin carried far more influence than his denial.

Bishop's hand was on the door, pressing against it. "I think you'd better let us in, Mr. Jacks."

Jacks let go of the door in defeat and walked into his bathroom as they entered the apartment. A two-foot-tall bong sat on the coffee table. Jacks returned from the bathroom wearing a robe. "It's recreational, guys. You're not gonna make a big deal of it, are you? Hell, I'm sitting in my own apartment, not hurting anyone."

"Where do you get your stuff?" Hackett asked. Bishop lifted the lid of a cigar box on the coffee table and pulled out a sandwich bag of weed, a small pipe, and a little bag of pink-and-white capsules.

Jacks said nothing about Bishop's discovery. He took a seat on the arm of the couch. "Come on, guys, what's this about?"

"We're here to talk to you about Michael Cahill," Bishop said. "But maybe you'd better tell us where you get your drugs, Dave."

"I don't know. Weed's not exactly hard to get. It's not even that much."

Bishop held up the bag of pills. "What's this?"

"Vitamins," Jacks said, looking anywhere but at the officers.

"Really?" Bishop said. "In a sandwich bag in a box on the coffee table?"

Jacks crossed his arms. "Yep."

Hackett stepped forward to look at the bag. "What kind?"

"Multivitamins."

"Great," Bishop said. "You won't mind, then, if we take these with us? I could use a multivitamin."

Hackett grinned. "Me too."

Jacks rubbed his face, like a dry wash would awaken him to this new reality of police in his smoke-filled living room, planning to take his stash. "I thought this was about Cahill."

"It is," Bishop said, as he sat on one of the matching leather couches in the living room, getting comfortable. "Did you know him?"

"Not really."

"He wasn't your dealer?" Hackett asked.

"What? No! Why would you ask that?"

Bishop continued. "We found a lot of pot at Michael's place. We're trying to piece together his life and contacts. Can you tell us where you were on Saturday, December seventh?"

"Are you accusing me of something?"

"We're simply asking questions."

"I was here."

"Were you alone?"

"Is this about Grace? She didn't kill Michael."

"No one said anything about Grace," Hackett said as he perused the room, picking up several framed photos. He walked into the kitchen, examining the photos posted on the fridge. Most were printouts of partying twenty-somethings—close-ups, toasting with beers, card games, smoke-filled rooms. A few were taken of the staff at the restaurant. He recognized Sheri Preston and Grace Abbott in several shots.

When he moved toward the bedroom, Jacks got up and followed. "Can I help you find something?"

Hackett peered into his bedroom. A picture of Grace sat perched by the bed.

Jacks followed his gaze. "Hey, guys, I don't mean to be rude, but I don't recall inviting you in. I'm starting to feel a little uncomfortable here. And I've got to get ready for work."

Hackett looked back at Jacks and rejoined Bishop in the living room. "Can you answer the question, Dave?"

"What question?"

"Were you alone here, last Saturday?"

"No, I wasn't alone. I was with Sheri Preston until about eleven in the morning. I threw a little party here on Friday night after our shift. It went pretty late—"

"How late?" Bishop interrupted.

"Like six or seven in the morning. Sheri spent the night. After she left, I watched TV until about two o'clock, and then I went to work."

"Did Grace and Michael come to your party?"

"Of course not."

"Why 'of course not'?" Hackett asked. "I thought Grace often went out with the work crew."

"That's true, but her boyfriend never did."

He could hear the disdain in Jacks's voice. This guy seemed more and more suspect. "Well, then, did *Grace* come to your party that night?"

"No."

"But she worked that night."

"Yeah, but she didn't go out with us afterward."

"Was that normal?" Bishop asked.

"I'd say it was normal for that day. I mean, she'd just gotten engaged."

"Engaged?" The word caught in Hackett's throat and he repeated it.

"Yeah. She told us on Friday at work. I guess he proposed on Thursday night."

"So she looked happy to you?" Bishop asked.

"People are usually pretty happy about getting married," Jacks said.

"You didn't know about any breakup?" Hackett asked.

Jacks backpedaled. "Well, if she said they did, I guess they did."

"You sound like you know something you're not telling us."

He retied his robe. "I don't know anything, man."

Hackett looked at Bishop. "You see that? I think there was some sort of spark when I said Grace and Michael might have broken up." Bishop smirked.

"I have no opinion about that," Jacks said. "Why? Did she say something about me?"

"Why would she do that?" Hackett asked.

"No reason. Listen, if that's all, I really need to get in the shower."

Bishop stood and they both followed Jacks to the door. "Just a few more questions," Hackett said. "How long has Grace worked at your restaurant?"

"Two years."

"And you've been manager all that time?"

"Yeah."

"And you've regularly gone out together after work—you've socialized?"

"So?"

"So you know her pretty well."

"I know her really well. I care about her a lot."

"Maybe too much?"

"What does that mean?"

"I see a lot of pictures of Grace in here. You take all these pictures?"

Jacks looked around. "It's not a big deal. I just take them with my phone."

"And then print them out and frame them."

"What's your point?"

Hackett raised his eyebrows at Bishop. "There's a picture of Grace by your bed," he said to Jacks. "That doesn't seem like a normal boss/employee relationship, don't you agree?"

Bishop smiled. "You're right about that."

"It's no big deal, guys. It was actually of several people, but their eyes were closed so I just cropped it. It's a good picture of her. We're friends, that's all."

"Sure," Hackett said. "I'd say you seem to have some strong feelings for Grace."

"I'd do anything for Grace, and yeah, I'm worried about her. Her boyfriend's been murdered, she doesn't seem to remember anything or anyone, and she must be scared. But I can't help you, fellas. I don't know anything. And I need to get to work."

They wouldn't get anything more from the guy right now. "No problem, Jacks," Bishop said. "We'll be in touch."

~ • ~

Grace made her way back to the kitchen for some pills and a little coffee before it would be too difficult to stand. Her headaches were becoming predictable, as if every attempt at prolonged concentration set off the ice pick behind her eyes. But after twenty minutes, she had a new wind.

Now an almost frantic energy was aching to break through the closed doors of her mind. She paced the room, mumbling, reviewing the day. There was a gap. She remembered the restaurant, Dave, Cherry Beach, but what about before that? She couldn't remember driving there. What was before that? "What the hell?" she shouted. Her mind began to speed up, as if she couldn't process thoughts fast enough. Was this what it was like to be crazy?

What was wrong with her? She'd remembered something today, she knew it, but now she couldn't remember what it was. She paced the house, looking around, pointing at items on the wall, listing what she knew and what she didn't. The walls were closing in; the ceiling was coming down. After ten or so laps, she collapsed on the kitchen floor, barely conscious, focusing only on the light fixture above her.

When Lisa walked in the back door an hour later, Grace felt her presence, but it took considerable effort to open her eyes. Lisa dropped her bag and keys and fell to the floor beside her. "Grace," she shouted, slapping her in the face, "are you okay?"

Grace looked up at Lisa. "What's going on?"

"What happened?"

She sat up with Lisa's help. "I feel crazy."

"Did you remember something?"

"I don't know. I thought I did. But now I'm not so sure. Just the roads."

"The roads?"

She instantly regretted saying it. "I mean this place. I remember you bringing me here. The roads to get here."

Lisa looked at the counter where she'd laid out the pills. "Did you take all your medication today?"

"I skipped the dose at lunch. They make me feel awful. But then I felt worse later, so I took them."

"Don't you remember what the doctor said? You can't skip them."

"But I can't sleep! How am I going to get rest if I can't rest? I feel like I could crawl out of my skin." She squirmed to get up.

Lisa stood too. "The doctor warned us that your brain injury can mess with your sleep patterns. And maybe you've always had insomnia—maybe that's why you had the Xanax. He gave you Ambien. Here," she said. "Come on, let's get you to bed."

Grace sat at the table and rested her head in her hands. "Something in this house scares me."

"What do you mean?"

"I keep hearing things. Yesterday I heard a little girl crying. I saw a girl, maybe it was me, in the yard."

Lisa joined her at the table. "In the yard?"

"I was walking around outside. I needed some fresh air. I saw the wheelbarrow in the shed, and then I saw this girl being pushed around the yard in it. She was little. It was fall. There was a man pushing her. They looked happy."

"That was probably you and Dad."

Grace smiled. "So that was a real memory."

"Probably."

"But then I felt scared. I heard a scream and I swear I heard a gunshot."

"Well, I don't know about the scream, but you might have heard a gunshot. It's always hunting season for something around here. I think it's pheasant season and maybe still deer season too. Till around Christmas."

She sat up, staring at Lisa. "Tell me about our parents. Why don't I remember them?"

Lisa went to the fridge and stood at the counter, opening a beer before she responded. "I don't know if we should do this right now."

"Why? I'm a black hole over here. Please. I need to piece my life together. Someone's dead. Someone who I was apparently living with. And it looks like . . ." She didn't want to say it.

"You're supposed to rest. I don't want to upset you."

"What do you mean?"

Lisa took a swig before answering. "Our parents weren't exactly good people."

"What does that mean?"

Lisa took another sip and opened the fridge, staring at the half-empty shelves. "Have you eaten yet?" she said.

Grace stood. "I'm not hungry." Suddenly, she felt very tired. She collapsed back into the chair. "Could I have killed Michael? I don't know who I was. I don't know if I could have done something like that."

Lisa put down the drink and came over. "I don't know. Come on."

With her help, Grace stood. She took another pill for sleep and let Lisa support her up the stairs. She crawled into bed without changing clothes, as weak as if she had the flu, unable to raise her head, suddenly so drowsy she felt as though she were melting into the sheets.

Lisa pulled the covers up and stood to leave.

"Wait," Grace said, in not much more than a whisper. "Tell me what you know about me. About Michael and me. Did we seem happy?"

Lisa sat next to her on the bed and brushed hair from her forehead. "I told you, we weren't always close. So I didn't see the day-to-day. I just saw when things happened. Like when you came here upset on Friday."

Grace nodded.

"And when you slashed his tires."

"What?"

Lisa chuckled. "I thought it was kind of funny, actually. I mean, I figured he deserved it, but you never said why you did it."

"When did I do that?"

"About a year ago. You told him that you'd come out of work and found them slashed, but you told me the truth."

The drugs had a strong hold on her now. She couldn't sit up and could barely register a reaction, but something about this story felt familiar. "It was my birthday," she slurred.

"Yeah, it was. Do you remember that?"

Grace couldn't keep her eyes open. She didn't answer, but she pressed for more. "Our parents . . . you said they were bad."

Lisa pulled the covers higher over Grace's chest. "The only thing a kid needs from a parent is love. Let's just say they didn't do their jobs."

"Did they hurt us?"

Lisa didn't answer and Grace forced her eyes open. Lisa was looking around the room, maybe searching for the words.

"Why do I have these?" Grace said, weakly offering her forearm to Lisa, showing her the methodical scars.

"I don't know."

"You're lying," she slurred. "You saw me notice them in the car. You know."

"I told you. Our parents were not exactly the best."

"They did this?"

"Dad wasn't big on spankings. Liked to do little things that carried a big punch."

Grace looked at her forearm in disbelief, unable to focus.

Lisa smiled. "That's nothing. Look at this." She pulled back her sleeve to reveal the inside of her forearm. Five small round scars, each the size of a pencil eraser.

"What's that?"

"Cigarette burns."

"He did that to you?"

"Guess he thought he could keep us in line this way."

It felt like pure fiction—some wild fantasy that didn't fit any instinct in her confused and darkened mind. But here was the evidence, a history that couldn't be erased. Two unhappy kids. Abuse. Maybe it was good that their parents were gone, like Lisa said.

"What happened to them?"

"Someone broke in."

Grace tried to sit up but couldn't. "Relax," Lisa said, her voice softening. She took Grace's hand in hers and held it gently. "It's an awful thing to think about. I didn't want to tell you. You don't remember anything. You don't know how lucky you are."

"When? How?"

"About three years ago. We weren't home."

"It happened here?"

"Yeah."

"Where were we?"

"You were over at a friend's house. I'd moved out a while before."

"How? Who did it?"

"Some drug addict trying to rob them. He's in prison now."

"Oh my God."

Lisa didn't say a word. She continued to pet Grace's hand as if Grace were a little girl.

"Why are we living here after such a terrible thing happened? And if they were bad? Why—?" She tried to sit up again. "Was it in here?" She looked around the room in a panic.

113

"No, not in here. They were asleep. It wasn't easy to stay, Grace, but this is the only thing they left us. Our parents gave us nothing." Suddenly her voice was laced with anger. "And life is hard enough. I really don't want to get into it right now."

Grace relaxed back into the pillow. It was too difficult to sit up. In fact, she was having trouble keeping her eyes open. "I went to the basement the other night. I had the strangest feeling when I was by the washer. I heard this little girl crying."

Lisa pulled the covers up higher, continuing to prep Grace for sleep like a small child. "Maybe your brain is protecting you. Some things are better left behind. Some memories are too painful. I've been trying my whole life to forget. You just got the slate wiped clean."

She had so many questions, but she could feel that the words weren't coming out right. She was losing consciousness. She heard Lisa walk out of the room, her footsteps crossing the hall, the squeak of her door shutting, and then a click. Had she just locked her door? Was she afraid? And then every thought in her head faded to black.

TWELVE

GRACE WAS TRAPPED UNDER SOMETHING HEAVY. It was dark. She broke free and began crawling out of the darkness. When she stood, tiny blue and white flowers covered the walls in front of her. Her vision telescoped in on the pattern, then expanded to a circle of fuzzy images surrounded by blackness, as if they were miles away. She walked closer. Closer. The images became clearer. The wrought-iron-frame bed. Mom. Dad. The bed covered in blood. Grace stood at the side of her parents' bed, screaming. Her own nightgown drenched with red. *"No no no no no no."*

The shaking finally woke her. When she opened her eyes and saw Lisa, she grabbed her and held her tight, ignoring the pain it brought.

"You were having a nightmare. What happened? Did you remember something?" Lisa maneuvered to sit by her side, still bracing Grace's shoulders. "What is it?"

"I saw them."

"Who?"

"Mom and Dad. They were dead. There was blood everywhere. I was standing there. Mom's face was frozen. Her mouth open like she was shouting. Did I see it happen?"

"No. No. It was just a dream."

"But I was there. I was there!"

Lisa relaxed her grip and pulled the covers up over Grace. "I just told you about the murder. You were probably imagining it. See, this is why I didn't want to tell you. I thought it might be too upsetting."

"But it was real." Sweat trickled down her forehead. "Please, get these covers off me."

Lisa left the room and returned a moment later with a wet rag, gently laying it on Grace's forehead. "It's okay. You weren't there. It was just a dream." Lisa sat on the edge of the bed and stroked her hair.

"I'll never sleep."

Lisa checked the clock, then left the room. The stairs creaked beneath her as she went down, and a minute later she returned with a glass of water and a pill.

"Here." She sat. "It's been more than four hours. You can have another."

Grace swallowed the pill and relaxed back into the pillow.

Lisa put aside the empty glass and stroked Grace's hair. "It's going to be fine," she said again and again.

The pill took effect. Like a wave, Grace floated out to sea.

She woke several times in the night, but she didn't dare get up, terrified of the visions and sounds that exploration brought. She stared at the water spots on the ceiling, the room dimly lit by the moon. She thought about Michael—and the photograph of the two of them—trying to make his face come to life, to see his smile, to hear his voice. But she couldn't conjure him. Instead, those officers' faces filled her mind, the younger one's especially. *Justin.*

~ • ~

Hackett sat on the couch, beer in hand, staring at the console that used to house his TV. Olivia had convinced him that she had to have it. Joe didn't have a flat screen, she'd pleaded, and Donny watched *Yo*

Gabba Gabba! every afternoon. *Please don't make this worse*, she'd said. Bullshit. All of it. But it had all happened so fast, and his goal had been to get the hell out of there as soon as possible, to leave and never look back, so he'd caved.

It was late, but he put on his coat and walked the two blocks to The Pub, hoping it would still be open. He needed some ESPN on a big screen to turn off his racing mind.

Alice was pouring drinks for a few men at the far end of the bar, but otherwise the place was empty.

"Hey, Officer!" Alice waved. She knew his name at this point, but he was pretty sure she'd be calling him "Officer" forever. She'd carded him his first time in. He'd smiled and pulled out his ID and newly acquired badge. "Sorry, honey, but you do have a baby face," she'd said. They'd both had a good laugh, and she'd welcomed him to the neighborhood.

She brought him a draft Bud, his usual—it was good enough and he was on a budget—and told him to holler if he needed anything.

Hackett turned his attention to the television in the corner and tried to focus on the scores, but his mind was on the case. There was something about that Jacks guy. He had a thing for Grace, Hackett could feel it. He didn't trust Sheri Preston either, though it may have just been that her air was too reminiscent of Olivia. But after they'd left New Buffalo, Bishop wasn't as impressed. He was more excited by the engagement news, which bolstered his working theory: Grace got engaged on Thursday, found pictures of her fiancé cheating on Friday, ran out, then returned Saturday morning to blow his brains out.

Other than getting those pills from Jacks's apartment analyzed, Bishop was ready to move on. But Hackett knew that couldn't be it. There was something wrong with that guy.

Twenty minutes later, the men at the other end of the bar left, and Alice offered Hackett a refill. He agreed, not ready to go home yet, even though *SportsCenter* was ending.

"So, Officer, why don't I ever see you in here with friends or girls? You gotta be beatin' them off with a stick."

It made him smile, which set her off again. "Look at those dimples. Come on, don't tell me you don't have a girl."

He shook his head and laughed.

Alice had already offered up her life story during a previous evening: divorced, two kids, deadbeat ex-husband, but a new boyfriend who was her true love, her destiny. She was nice and friendly, but he couldn't help but wonder why he had such bad luck when this woman—forty pounds overweight; an unruly mound of frizzy, gray-streaked hair; and arms covered in decades-old tattoos that were stretched and faded into unidentifiable blobs of black ink—was so in love. Maybe it was her edge. Maybe nice guys did finish last. His brothers had pounded that mantra into his brain for years, trying to get him to be more aloof, cooler, somehow more appealing to the girls.

"Come on," she continued. "What about that pretty young thing I saw you with a few weeks back?"

Shit. "Who?"

"I don't know, but I remember you were talking in the corner there. Seemed to be getting along. I think you walked her out—you remember?"

"No, I guess not." *Fuck.* "Well, couldn't have been anything, or I'd remember, right?"

Alice smiled flirtatiously and took a sip of her beer. "If you say so."

~ • ~

When Grace woke on Wednesday, Lisa was already gone. She'd left another note in the bathroom about her work schedule and more reminders about taking the prescriptions.

Grace was heading downstairs when a squad car pulled into the driveway. She froze on the step. Were they coming for her? Or perhaps there was good news.

The young officer—*Justin*—got out of the car and came to the door. She opened it before he had a chance to knock.

"Hi," she said, suddenly hopeful.

"Hi, Grace."

"What's happening? Do you have news?"

He shook his head and flushed slightly. "I just wanted to check on you. I'm on my way to the station, but I was wondering if you're feeling any better. I hope that's okay."

"Sure," she said, stifling her disappointment. "Come in."

She led him to the living room, and they both sat. When the silence between them grew awkward, Grace finally broke the ice. "This is kind of weird, but I kept seeing your face last night."

He smiled, a shallow dimple appearing on one cheek. "What do you mean? Did you remember something?"

"Not exactly." It didn't seem right to talk about her parents and the blood. "I was having these disturbing thoughts and, for some reason, when your face came to mind, it kind of calmed me down. Weird, huh?"

Hackett leaned forward in his chair, lips parting slightly, as if he wanted to say something, as if maybe he knew something he wasn't telling her, but he didn't speak.

"What is it?"

He shifted uncomfortably. "I probably shouldn't be here right now. I'm guessing my partner wouldn't be happy about it, but I . . . I want you to know that I don't think you did this."

Relief nearly made her laugh. "You don't? Because I'm sure it doesn't look good."

He sat back and said gravely, "We have to follow the evidence, and some of it doesn't help you, but I also have to follow my gut. I don't think you killed Michael."

She hadn't even realized how much that meant until he said it. She'd been focusing simply on piecing together her history, unable to deal with her present reality, but somewhere in the back of her mind, the idea of having committed a crime, of killing another person, of being sent away for life for something she didn't even understand, felt like a rockslide that had buried her alive. The moment he said he believed in her, it was as if a boulder had rolled aside, light streamed in, hope emerged.

"You know, I almost feel like you and I are doing the same things," she said lightly. "I feel a little like an investigator. I've got almost nothing to go on but the contents of this house and the fragments of memories that seem to pop up, but I spend most of my time around here searching for answers."

"And have you figured anything out yet?"

"Only that I didn't have a great childhood. It seems there might have been some abuse, and something about this place scares me. Last night I found out my parents were murdered here."

He nodded, brows furrowed. "I know. I'm really sorry, Grace."

"You know?" she asked, but she answered before he could. "You've investigated me."

He nodded. "That crime was solved, and we'll solve this one too."

She looked down, picking at a seam in the leather. "I just can't believe that nothing really clicks. I obviously lived here. I have fragments of memories, but everything I learn is like this crazy fiction."

"You can talk to me. If you remember anything. I'm on your side."

But those words, *I'm on your side*, took on a menacing tone as they repeated in her head. A little voice inside suddenly wondered if this was a trap, if she could trust him. Maybe this was a good cop/bad cop routine. But how could they trap her into some sort of confession when she didn't know anything? She sat back, distancing herself, suddenly anxious.

Officer Hackett looked around the room, combing his fingers through his thick, dark hair. "I wish I could snap my fingers and give you your memories. But I want you to know that I'm working on leads that are pointing away from you."

"Like what?"

He hesitated. "Michael won a lot of money the day before he was killed. Ten thousand dollars. I'm thinking maybe his death was about the money, that someone knew about the winnings, or maybe he owed someone a lot of money."

"I wish that meant something to me. It doesn't."

"There's also reason to believe someone may have had a long-standing beef with Michael. Someone threw a rock through his window, and about a year ago his tires were slashed . . ."

"On my birthday," she said. *Shit.* She couldn't say what Lisa had shared, that she'd done it.

"Do you remember that?" Hackett asked.

"I don't know, exactly." She smiled, nervousness pinballing through her. "This must seem nuts to you."

"Not at all." He stood and walked to the mantel before turning back to face her. "Grace, do you remember your boss, Dave Jacks?"

She swallowed hard, remembering the unpleasant feeling when he'd touched her on the beach. If she'd cheated on Michael, that wouldn't look good. "I . . . met him. I went to the restaurant for my check." That was true. "Why?"

"I think he has feelings for you."

She said nothing. She felt trapped again. Maybe he was just supposed to come here with his good looks and his kind smile and trick her into some sort of confession. "I'm sorry, I don't feel very good. I think I'd better lie down now."

Hackett nodded, obviously surprised, but he walked to the door, then turned back. "I'm on your side. I just wanted you to know that."

She watched him walk to his car. Was she getting paranoid? His face, his expression, his voice soothed her, but he was a cop. There'd been a murder and she was a suspect. Lisa had warned her not to say too much. And suddenly she was equally sure she shouldn't tell Officer Hackett's gruff partner that he'd been to see her.

She went to the kitchen and poured a cup of coffee, but before she could even take a sip, she heard her phone vibrating in her purse. When she pulled out the phone, a reminder filled the screen: She was supposed to see that doctor today.

She put down the coffee and got dressed, her heart pounding. The appointment was in an hour. This doctor knew her. If she was a therapist, she was bound to have some answers. Grace swung into the kitchen to grab her purse and looked down at the pill piles. Her head was feeling okay and her ribs were less sore than the day before. She was getting stronger. She needed to stay clear to drive. She put the pills in her pocket and mapped out the address.

THIRTEEN

WHEN HACKETT ARRIVED AT THE STATION, he went straight for the coffee machine for a strong dose of caffeine. Seeing Grace this morning, making her smile, had brought a jolt of energy he'd needed, though there was something distant in her reactions. She obviously didn't remember him at all. He wondered if she ever would.

His initial silence about knowing her was starting to feel like it might back up, roll him over, and crush him. Maybe if he'd come forward, Bishop could have dealt with it, let him off the hook. But it was too late now. He needed to be sure the real perp was found. For all he knew, whoever killed Michael could have intended to harm Grace too. She could be in danger.

But Alice's comments at the bar last night hadn't made him feel any better about his secrets. He'd lain awake much of the night, wondering if she knew who Grace was. He'd been to The Pub too often to count since moving in last summer, and he'd only seen Grace there twice, so maybe he had nothing to worry about. But saying that to himself didn't help him sleep any better. He'd even pulled up *An Officer and a Gentleman* on the tablet, watching until about four a.m., thankful to be absorbed in the story and chuckling when he heard the dialogue Bishop had mimicked. Though if he'd realized it would be a love story, he'd have watched *Stripes* instead.

Bishop was on the phone when Hackett got to his desk. They'd asked forensics to rush the tests of Grace's clothes from the accident, so Hackett called the crime lab to see if they'd made any progress. Miles said it would be another day or two before he had an answer, but then came the zinger: "Hey, I did get that drug identified though," Miles said.

The pills they'd found at Dave Jacks's place. "Yeah, what is it?"

"Scopolamine. It's prescribed for motion sickness."

"Jacks said they were vitamins, but that doesn't sound too bad."

"Actually, it is. What you sent us wasn't a prescription. Those were cold capsules that had been emptied and refilled with scopolamine powder."

Hackett frowned. "Do people take that to get high?"

"Not that I know of. And the dose in those capsules was many times greater than what's medically acceptable. Those are some dangerous pills."

"What do they do?"

"On the street, it's used in connection with criminal activity. Robberies, rape, things like that. Makes people totally submissive." He went on to describe some of its side effects, including hallucinations and violence.

Hackett took notes during the call, circling the drug name as they spoke. "Do you know how long it stays in the system?"

"Depends what you mean. Its effects can be felt for nearly twelve hours. But it's not easy to detect. Doesn't come up in blood or urine tests. We could test his hair sample for it though. Drug tests on hair can go back, like, ninety days."

"What if it was given to him around five days before his death?"

"I don't think we'd be able to tell. It generally takes between five and ten days for drugs to show up in the hair. Sounds like he died before it would have gotten into the shaft."

"Can you do it anyway? Just to be sure."

When Hackett hung up, he shared the drug findings with Bishop. "What about Grace's clothes?"

"Nothing yet. But I think we should focus on Jacks and this drug for a minute. All that stuff of Grace's from the hospital—it was all running gear. We know from Vicki Flynn's text that Grace had planned to run on Saturday morning. Lisa seemed to think she could have been out running too. Or getting coffee after her run."

Bishop's cell rang then, and after looking at the number, he walked into the break room to take it. A few minutes later, he returned and grabbed his coat from the chair. "That was my wife," Bishop said. "I gotta go."

"Everything okay?"

He shook his head. "Not really. She thinks it's going to happen today. She wants me to pull the kids out of school and bring them up to the hospital to say good-bye to her mom."

"Oh God, I'm so sorry."

"I don't think this is it. That old bird has faced death so many times. I wouldn't be at all surprised if I get up there with the kids and she's sitting up, smiling. But," he continued, putting on his coat, "I do what I'm told. No one would forgive me if she's right and they didn't get to say good-bye." He checked his watch. "Do me a favor. Put some pressure on the phone company about those cell records. I want the names of every person Grace called in the two days before the murder. If we're lucky, maybe she even made a call in the car just before the crash. And call that other bartender from The Rack and see if he saw Cahill on that Wednesday. I'm sorry to leave you hanging, kid. I'll try and get back here by late afternoon."

Hackett nodded, idly tapping his pen against the notes in front of him.

Bishop gave him a shove. "What are you thinking, rookie? You look a million miles away. You solve this case?"

It was Miles's comment about the effects of the drug in Jacks's apartment. Memory issues, robberies, and that doctor at the urgent care said Michael had no memory of the day before. He'd had hallucinations and was violent with the staff until they'd sedated him. He looked up at Bishop. "Not yet," he said, closing the notepad. "Sorry. I know you gotta go."

"I got a second. Out with it."

"I was just thinking. We didn't find the ring or the casino winnings at the house. The ring wasn't on Grace when she got to the hospital—I checked. Couldn't this be a robbery?"

Bishop bobbed his head from side to side. "Maybe, but nothing about this seems random. An iPad was sitting on the coffee table, and Cahill's wallet too. If someone took that money, he or she was looking for it."

Hackett nodded, but a robbery felt like a viable angle. "If that Facebook comment was about the money, we know that every 'friend' he has saw that. And he has a ton of 'friends.'"

"But the only responses to the post were question marks and guesses. No one knew what it was about. There was nothing indicating that comment was about money or how much."

"What about the waitress's friends?"

"What do you mean?"

"She posted the picture and tagged Cahill. Everyone in his network got that picture, but everyone in her network got it too. Her friends would know she works at the casino. Maybe they'd guess it was about a big win. Maybe someone did a little digging and saw him as a target." Before Bishop could respond, Hackett rushed on. "Or maybe she posts pictures like that as a signal. She watches for big winners, takes a picture, and posts it. Next thing you know, these guys are robbed. Maybe this one went wrong and she's skipped town. We need to find that waitress."

Bishop zipped up his jacket and put on his gloves and a hat. "Well, that's not gonna happen before Friday," he said. "We hardly have a basis for some national search for the woman. And I certainly hope you're not right about this Facebook stuff."

"Why?"

"Because I want the possibilities to narrow, not expand. We don't solve this inside a few weeks, we're looking at a case that's going to get as cold as that snow." He nodded toward the open field of frozen white outside the station window. "And Christmas is right around the corner. I'd love to be able to stamp this baby closed by then."

As soon as Bishop left, Hackett jumped online and began reading up on the black market uses of scopolamine, known on the street as Devil's Breath, a pretty common street drug in South America, particularly Colombia. Even the US State Department website posted warnings for travelers to be wary of leaving drinks or food unattended in that region, where criminals use the drug to rob and rape. It was an odorless, tasteless powder, put in cigarettes, food, drinks, even blown into the faces of intended victims, who became little more than zombies, conscious and coherent but deprived of any reasoning skills. According to reports, once the drug wore off, victims had no memory of what had happened to them. One man learned that his bank account had been completely drained, and the investigation uncovered video footage of the same man walking into his bank with two strangers, calmly asking the teller for his money. He had no memory of it. Another victim, a mother desperate to find her son, reported waking up naked in the street with no under-standing of what had happened to her. Her last memory had been of being on a bus with her child heading to the market. Colombian prostitutes reported giving it to victims before taking all their money.

Hackett's thoughts turned to Grace: Her memory loss wasn't unlike victims of this drug. He looked down at his notebook, reviewing everything they knew. Her name was on those initial notes from the crime scene, her full name, as found on a cable bill by the door. Grace Abbott. Circled several times. *Missing? Suspect?* he'd written. He looked down, remembering the feel of her small hand in his and the moment he'd felt her fingers press against his, like it wasn't just him. She'd felt something too. The guilt in her eyes had faded as he'd pulled her closer, and that kiss—hesitant, tender, but then so passionate—had filled his thoughts for days. She was It.

The trail of blood had to lead to someone other than Grace. She wasn't a murderer. She was the girl whose smile, whose eyes, had haunted him since they'd first met. The girl who'd made him see that he was going to be okay.

~ • ~

The doctor's office was a block from Brewster's, right off the main strip in New Buffalo, on the second floor, above a coffee shop. Grace walked up the narrow staircase and knocked on the heavy wood door. "Come in," she heard. It was a small reception area. An older woman, maybe fifty or sixty, smiled and said, "Hello, Grace. Take a seat. The doctor will be right with you." Nothing about the woman, who had already turned back toward her computer screen, was familiar.

Grace sat across from a large framed photograph of a lighthouse surrounded by thick ice, with pointed shards like spikes expanding toward the water. It was like a sculpture or an artifact from the ice age. She'd seen it before. Here? She stepped toward the photograph and read the description in tiny print at the bottom: ST. JOSEPH, MICHIGAN. How many times had she sat in this office?

Grace flipped through a fashion magazine, unable to focus on anything other than the hope that Dr. Newell held answers. A heavyset man suddenly emerged from the inner office, avoiding eye contact, and behind him, a tall woman in black-rimmed glasses stood and smiled. "Come on in, Grace."

Grace followed the woman into her office and scanned the shelves, pictures, and furniture. Nothing sparked. The woman wore wool pants and a sweater, her perfectly cut platinum-blonde hair neatly pulled back. She looked like some sort of cross between sexy and smart, maybe forty, and she exuded control and confidence, everything Grace lacked. She sat in her chair and suggested Grace take a seat beside her on the sofa.

Grace quickly explained the situation—the accident, the memory loss, Michael's death. The doctor's slightly raised brows were the only visible signs of surprise as she took notes. Grace stopped talking and watched the doctor continue to write for another minute.

When Dr. Newell finished, she dropped her pen and sat back. "Well, I'm glad you're okay, Grace, and I'm glad you're here. I was concerned when you'd missed these last two weeks, but obviously this explains it."

"But you, of all people, can help me, right? I'm so foggy. I didn't even remember making this appointment yesterday until I got a reminder on my phone. It's like everything's a dream. Not only my life before the accident but since then—like bits of each day disappear when I go to sleep. I only knew who you were when your assistant left me that voice-mail message because the police told me about some Xanax in the house you'd prescribed to me."

"Are you still taking them? Are you sleeping?"

"The police have the pills. They're evidence. There was Xanax in Michael's system."

The doctor nodded, making another note.

"But the hospital gave me a bunch of stuff for the pain and some stuff to help me sleep."

"Okay, I'd like to get the names of those medications."

"Why?"

"There are a lot of potential side effects with medication, and it's helpful for me to know what to look out for. Grace, you don't remember why you were on the Xanax?"

"No. I think the police are looking at me for this guy's murder, and I'm starting to wonder if I could have done it. Apparently things were not good."

"Why do you say that?"

"Well, you should know, right? I mean, if you were my therapist, what did I talk about?"

"A lot of things. What you wanted to do with your life, stresses you were having. And you were starting to talk about your parents a bit."

"How long have I been coming to you?"

"About a month or so."

"When was the last time I came?"

"You were supposed to come on Friday, the sixth, but you canceled."

"Did I say why?"

"No."

The silence rose up between them. Eventually, Grace said, "I've learned that Michael had a temper. He was also apparently a gambler, a pot smoker, and a cheater."

Dr. Newell nodded and took more notes. "I had not heard any of that before."

"But then again, apparently, so was I."

Dr. Newell stopped writing and looked at her. "What do you mean?"

"My boss at work seems to know me intimately. He wanted me to know that he didn't kill Michael and he wants me to lean on him. The thought made me sick."

"And your boss"—she paused, reviewing pages in her notebook—"is that Dave?"

"I mentioned him?"

"Yes."

"I'm starting to wonder if this memory loss is a way to avoid dealing with who I am and what I've done."

Dr. Newell closed the notebook, removed her glasses, and smiled at Grace. "I know that we didn't have a lot of time together, but I'm pretty good at getting a sense of my patients, of knowing who's unstable. I think you were—you are—a young woman trying to figure out what to do with her life. I never got the sense you would be capable of violence."

She wondered if she'd ever shared her history of punching walls and slashing tires. "Do you know about my childhood?"

The doctor replaced her glasses and opened her notebook. "How do you mean?"

Grace pulled up her shirtsleeve and offered her forearm as evidence. "I guess my dad did this to me."

Dr. Newell glanced at the scars for a moment without expression. "You had not shared that before," she said while taking more notes.

Grace shifted in her chair. This wasn't getting her anywhere. "I thought you'd have some answers. I can't sleep. I seem to wake up because of disturbing images or sounds. Last night I dreamed I was standing over my dead parents."

The doctor looked up. "So you remember them?"

"I've had a couple of visions. But last night I learned they were murdered. I dreamed I was in the room, standing over their bed. My mother's eyes opened suddenly with this horrified expression. There was blood everywhere. There was blood on me." She felt physically sick, recalling the image, and wiped the tears falling down her cheeks. "What does that mean? Lisa said I wasn't there. Some drug addict went away for the crime, but I don't know . . ."

"You've had that dream before. You often had trouble sleeping because you knew how they died and often pictured it. That's pretty normal. When horrible things happen to those we love, it's common to vividly work through how it might have happened, what it was like for those loved ones. It might not mean anything. As far as your parents, you never said anything negative about them."

Grace rubbed her eyes, desperate to open the doors of her mind.

"Grace, stopping the antianxiety meds cold turkey causes insomnia—so it's no wonder you're having trouble. You were an insomniac when you came to me. That's why I gave you the prescription. And apparently it was helping. The last couple of visits, you had said you were sleeping soundly."

"So I never talked about my parents being abusive?"

Dr. Newell shook her head. "Therapy is a slow process. We were getting to know each other. It seemed that your feelings about your parents were complicated."

"Why don't I remember anything? Is this all because of that damn accident?"

Dr. Newell sat back, dropping her pen onto her pad. "I don't know. This kind of amnesia rarely happens from car accidents or head injuries. Memory loss can happen, but usually that involves what's called retrograde amnesia or transient global amnesia. In those cases, you remember who you are and you recognize people you know well, but you forget the events leading up to and surrounding the time of the injury. You seem to be blocking a lot more than that. This type of amnesia—psychogenic or dissociative amnesia—is more often caused by emotional shock or trauma."

"Well, Michael's death apparently occurred around the time of the car accident. Do you think that means I was there?"

"It could mean a lot of things."

"It could mean I killed him."

"It could also mean you saw who killed him."

"And how long will it be before I remember?"

Dr. Newell's mouth opened, then closed, before she finally said, "There are a lot of unknowns. This kind of memory loss can last hours or years. We haven't been together that long, so I can't fill in your gaps too much. But I have two suggestions." She checked her watch. "Unfortunately, my next appointment is starting momentarily, but I want to see you again as soon as possible. I've got Friday afternoon entirely open."

"Okay." Two more days. She just needed to get through two more days.

"And I want to give you this." She walked to the desk and pulled a cassette tape from her drawer. "I always record my therapy sessions with this old tape recorder so I can take notes later if necessary. Perhaps in this situation it would be helpful if you heard the tape."

"Yes, please!" Grace rose from the couch for the tape, wincing from the sudden pain in her ribs.

"Okay. Just be careful with this. I've never offered tapes to a patient before."

"Why?"

"Well, just remember that I'm bound by doctor/patient confidentiality. But that's for your benefit. It's your privilege and, legally speaking, you can lose that privilege if you share the contents of these tapes. It would be like allowing a third party to be in the room, in which case the privilege is gone."

"Okay." Grace put the tape in her purse and sat back down.

"I'm sorry my technology is so outdated. Do you have an old tape machine you can listen to?"

"There's a tape deck in my truck."

"Good. Bring this back on Friday and we'll talk. Maybe hearing yourself will help unlock some memories. Also, I think we should try some relaxation techniques. How do you feel about that?"

"Like hypnosis?"

The doctor smiled. "I don't like to use that word because it suggests I'm somehow in control of the process, but I think in the proper relaxed state, you might be able to tap in to more memories."

"I want to remember. I keep having these feelings at the house. When we first pulled up, it was familiar. I felt fine and I've had moments of recalling random things—laughter, playing—but I get near the woods and it's like I'm a little kid, scared of monsters. When I went to the basement, I heard a little girl's scream. It was so real that I turned around. It was like I was having a panic attack. And then it happened again—at least I thought it happened again, but Lisa made me wonder if it was just a nightmare. I was drowning in the tub, like someone was holding me under. I feel like I'm losing my mind."

"Well, I'm glad you're back, Grace." Dr. Newell stood and walked her to the door. "We're going to work through this together and figure it out, okay?"

Grace nodded, feeling a tiny thread of hope.

"How about Friday at one o'clock?"

"I've got nothing else to do."

"Great. So come back Friday with a list of your medications. Until then, get plenty of rest. If you're having memory fragments, you may even unlock this on your own."

Grace stopped before Dr. Newell could open the door. "What if I did something?"

"Let's not get ahead of ourselves." Dr. Newell put an arm around her. "Remember, everything that happens in here is protected by doctor/patient privilege. In fact, I could lose my license if I shared what you tell me."

After leaving the doctor's office, Grace climbed into the truck, turned on the engine, and examined the cassette tape. Three hours of history right here. She said a little prayer for answers before inserting the tape into the deck.

FOURTEEN

AT FIRST, THERE WAS NOTHING BUT SILENCE. She feared the old tape deck was eating the tape, but then Dr. Newell's voice said: "November fifth, Grace Abbott," before she heard the doctor walk to the door and welcome Grace into the office. Dr. Newell advised Grace of the recording, then asked what had prompted her to make the appointment. Hearing her own voice on the tape, Grace leaned in, closed her eyes, and tried to wrap her head around the fact that this was her life.

She was telling the doctor she'd been suffering from insomnia for the last six months. She explained that she had worked on changing her diet and limiting caffeine, but it had no effect. She thought maybe the doctor could prescribe something.

"Is there something that's happened in the last six months?"

"Well, I'm stressed a lot."

Dr. Newell pressed for more, and Grace listened as she shared concerns about her current situation, Michael, and her future. She'd started college classes at Southwestern Michigan College, the Niles campus. But it was a struggle. She had difficulty balancing classes and restaurant shifts, and she and Michael were never on the same schedule. "He's annoyed by it all," she'd said. She was starting to wonder if maybe her interest in college was the beginning of the end for them. "And I'm annoyed by him a lot these days." He always wanted her to be available when he was in the mood to hang out, but he was always getting high or playing poker, sometimes late into the night, and he would wake her even when she had a big test coming up. She'd even applied to live in the on-campus housing next semester, though she hadn't yet heard if she'd gotten it, and she wasn't sure she could go through with it or how Michael would take the news.

Dr. Newell asked her how long they'd been living together. Three years, she said. The doctor remarked that it was a long time, particularly since Grace was so young. "I've known him my whole life. He's like my only family."

"So thinking about leaving him must be difficult."

"Yeah."

Grace rested her head on the steering wheel near the speaker, not wanting to miss a word, a sound, an inflection. But her cell phone rang. She hit the stop button on the tape deck and answered.

"Is this Grace Abbott?" a man asked.

"Yes."

"This is Donald over at Harbor Country Jewelers. Your ring is ready."

"My ring?"

"Your engagement ring, ma'am. I know it took me a little longer than I said it would, but it's done and looks beautiful."

What? "Would you remind me where you're located and I'll get right over there."

"Of course. We're on Whittaker, just west of Merchant."

"I'll be right there." Grace looked up the jeweler's address on her phone. It was only a block down the road.

The storefront window display glowed, the light bouncing off jewels, a large SALE sign attempting to entice passersby. Grace opened the door, triggering an elegant chime. Pink satin damask drapes covered the walls, and antique glass cases exhibited row after row of jewelry. An older gentleman in suit and tie, a perfect match for the tired elegance of the space, entered from the velvet-curtained back room. Wisps of gray hair rested atop his smooth but spotted head, reading glasses perched low on his nose. "Well, that was fast," he said with a smile.

"You remember me?" Grace asked.

"Sure. It was just about twelve days ago, right? I don't get much traffic this time of year."

She walked over to the counter. "I'm sorry, this is a pretty strange situation. I was in a bad accident and I'm having trouble with my memory. I don't remember being here."

"My dear, how terrible. Well, I'm glad to see you're okay. Maybe this will help." The man bent down and brought out an engagement ring from the case, offering it to her.

Grace stared at the ring while the man described it. "One-point-five carats, two baguettes, fourteen-karat-gold setting."

"Nice," she said. She'd never seen it before.

"Here." He gently took her hand and slipped the ring on her finger. A perfect fit.

"When did I bring this to you?" she asked.

"Let's see," he said, retrieving the receipt from his drawer. "Friday, December sixth. It was in the afternoon. When were you in the accident?"

"Saturday. The next day."

"Oh, how terrible. A car accident?"

"Yeah." Grace was still focused on the receipt. "And I filled this out?"

"You did, ma'am."

She looked at her name, her phone number, her address. An address she didn't know.

"Was the ring bought here?"

"Of course. The gentleman had been in a week earlier."

"Michael?"

"Well, I don't actually recall his name, but you would know," he joked. "He'd been a little nervous, said it had to be perfect. He didn't seem certain that you'd say yes. But obviously, you did." The man grinned.

"Could I see that receipt—for his purchase?"

His forehead creased. "I'm sorry, miss, that's a bit unorthodox. I'm not accustomed to sharing receipts. I'm sure most men don't want their brides to know exactly what they spent on the ring. Could be too much, too little . . . wouldn't want to get him in trouble. You understand."

"Right. I know this is weird. But . . . he's dead."

"Oh my Lord." He put his hand on her now-ringed hand and squeezed. "I'm so sorry."

She pulled away. People needed to stop touching her. "Thanks. But, like I said, I'm just trying to piece it all together."

"Of course. Wait here." He went into the back room and returned a couple of minutes later. "Here. The ring was bought by Michael Cahill, Saturday, November thirtieth. One-point-five carats, thirty-eight hundred dollars."

Grace stared at Michael's receipt, then at her own. The address was the same. So on the Friday before his murder, she was having her engagement ring resized. She'd said yes.

~ • ~

Hackett was grabbing more coffee when Bishop walked in. "Oh shit," he said under his breath. "Hi. I didn't expect you back so soon."

"Don't look so surprised. It wasn't exactly a party." Bishop poured a mug of coffee and Hackett followed him back to their desks. "We got up there before eleven. We were out by noon. I took the kids to lunch before sending them back to school."

"How'd it go?" He immediately regretted the question. How could it go?

"I don't know. But Sandy might be right. She's really weak, and none of us were even sure what to do. But Sandy swears she can hear us all. The kids were scared, especially Paige, but it was good. I mean, they were glad to have been included. She was a good woman," he added, his voice trailing off, like his mother-in-law was already gone.

Hackett kept glancing at the door, wondering if this was a good time to change topics, but Bishop did it for him. "Enough of that. What'd I miss?"

He wasn't sure where to begin. Certainly not with the fact that he'd forgotten to call the bartender from The Rack, or that he'd intentionally put off calling the cell company about those records.

The station door opened and Dave Jacks stood there, holding it for Sheri Preston, who breezed past him, barked at the clerk, then marched toward them in her tiny miniskirt and four-inch heels, while Jacks followed meekly behind.

"What's this?" Bishop said, setting his mug on his desk.

Hackett cringed, then straightened his back. "I called them."

"What?"

"I did some research on that drug in Jacks's apartment. This might be something. There's no legitimate reason to have those pills, and their effects feel eerily connected to this case. I figured that because Jacks and Preston are each other's alibis, and she met the description of the woman who met Cahill at The Rack, I should talk to them again." Before Bishop could respond, he added, "I was just following my gut, like you said."

Bishop smirked at him like a young pledge. "All right. Well, let's do this."

Preston dropped her purse on Hackett's desk. "Really, Officers, I don't have time for this. I had nothing to do with Michael Cahill. I barely knew the guy. Met him maybe one time. Do I need a lawyer or something? Because I'm about ready to scream harassment."

Jacks didn't speak.

Bishop smiled. "Thanks for coming, Miss Preston, Mr. Jacks. Let's go back here."

He turned to Hackett. "Put 'em in one and two."

Hackett led the suspects into separate interrogation rooms, told them to take a seat, and came back out to Bishop.

"Let's do Jacks first," Bishop said. When they entered, Jacks's coat was off, and he sat back, smiling, looking as stoned as he had during their first meeting. Before they'd even sat, Jacks began his defense. "Guys, I'm happy to help you, but I have no idea what happened to Mike. I didn't know the guy. Ask anyone."

Bishop took a seat across the table. "We're not so sure, Dave. Your alibi for Saturday morning is Sheri Preston. And her alibi is you."

"So?"

"So, we're not so sure we should trust the two of you."

"Why?"

"Well, we had those pills from your place checked. Looks like you had a good supply of scopolamine. A drug Cahill was given in the days before his death."

Hackett looked at Bishop. Could they really just make stuff up? Bishop didn't meet his eyes. He obviously had a strategy.

"What? Not from me. They're relaxation pills. They help me sleep. Maybe he took them—"

Bishop turned to Hackett. He was up.

"There're a few problems with that theory," Hackett said. "One, that drug isn't taken for sleep. Two, what you had was not a brand-name version of the drug but a homemade concoction. And three, if you had a lawful reason for having those drugs, we don't think you would have called them vitamins. Also, Cahill was seen leaving a bar with a blonde a week before the murder, and the next morning he had no memory of the previous evening and suffered hallucinations—known effects of scopolamine."

"Sounds to me like he drank too much. What does this have to do with me?"

Bishop leaned in toward Jacks's face. "We've got Miss Preston, who meets the description of the blonde he left with, and you, who had the drugs, and you're connected—on the morning of the murder, in fact. You want to help us understand why you'd drug Cahill?"

Jacks shook his head. "You're crazy. I didn't drug anyone. And I don't know for sure, but I don't think Sheri knew the guy either. He never even came to the restaurant. Grace was with the guy for years, and he never came in. Completely uninterested in her friends at work, far as I could see."

"Sounds like you've thought about this a good bit. Maybe you wanted to break them up," Bishop said.

"Why would I want to do that?"

"You're into Grace," Hackett interjected.

Jacks looked down. "I care about Grace, but not like that."

Hackett looked at Bishop, who nodded toward the door and smacked his hands against the table. "Well, stick with that story, Dave, and this could take a long time."

Jacks stood. "Hey, are you arresting me for something?"

"Nope. This is just a friendly conversation. You can leave anytime you want. But I'd advise against it. The more you cooperate, the quicker we can figure this all out."

The two stood and Jacks sat back in his chair.

Out in the hall, Hackett asked, "What do you think?"

"Let's talk to Preston for a second. See where this goes."

When they entered the room, she was pacing. "What the fuck is this about? Do I need a lawyer? I told you, I didn't even know the guy. I am not involved in whatever you think is going on here."

Bishop stepped forward. "Here's the thing, Sheri. A woman of your description was seen with Cahill the Sunday before he died. We think he was drugged that night."

"You think? What does that even mean? And what does that have to do with me? Or his murder?"

"Well, your alibi for the murder is Jacks, and he seems to have a good supply of a drug that may have been used on Cahill. That connects Jacks to the vic, and maybe you too."

"I'm telling you, I barely knew the guy. I'm not the one you're looking for. You don't even know if he was drugged. This sounds like a lot of fishing."

"Perhaps you and Dave were trying to break them up?" Bishop said. "Maybe something went wrong?"

Before she could respond, Hackett added, "If Dave has gotten you involved in something, the best thing you can do is share everything you know."

"This is ridiculous," she said, taking a seat at the table. "Listen, I'll tell you everything I can, and I'm happy to help. I have nothing to hide, but I really don't know what you're talking about."

The men joined her at the table.

"What kind of drugs are we talking about?" Preston asked.

"Scopolamine," Hackett said. "You heard of it?"

"No. What does it do?"

"It makes people completely submissive. It's known mostly for use in robberies and in sexual assault—like a roofie. Victims have no memory of what happened."

Her eyes widened as she processed the information. "And Dave had this drug in his apartment?"

Hackett nodded.

Tears filled her eyes. "Oh my God. That asshole."

"What?"

"Hooking up with my dirtbag of a boss, Dave, that's what. I was mortified when I woke up in his apartment on Saturday. He acted like we'd had this passionate night, but I didn't remember anything." Her face flushed red. She slammed her hand against the table. "That fucker must have drugged me."

"So you're telling us that Dave drugged you on Friday night?" Hackett said, trying to hide his excitement about a potential new development.

"Well, I can't prove it, now can I? I mean, this was almost two weeks ago. But I can't remember shit from that night. Dave hosted a party after work on Friday at his place. Lots of people from the restaurant, a few of his other friends, the usual. I didn't do shots. I didn't smoke any of his weed. Nothing crazy. I even remembered thinking I'd head home at one point. But I woke up in Dave's bed, naked. I was horrified."

"Did you ever leave your drink unattended?"

She was fighting back the tears that began to fall. "Well, sure. I mean, of course I did."

Hackett took notes while Bishop kept going.

"Do you remember anything specific about Dave? How he was acting that night? Anything unusual?"

She sat back and wiped her eyes, mascara now trailing down her face. "He seemed kinda depressed at work—quiet, preoccupied. I pressed him to go out with us. Then he offered to host at his place."

"Do you know what he was upset about?" Hackett asked.

"He didn't say, but it was Grace. We all knew he had a big crush on her. You could tell by the way he talked to her, the way he watched her. She always got the best stations during her shifts. And she'd just gotten engaged. I thought he could use a drink. Fucking dirtbag."

Bishop and Hackett left Preston and went back into the hall. Bishop turned to him. "What do you think?"

"I believe her."

"And if she's telling the truth, then it sounds like Jacks is obsessed with Grace," Bishop said. "She gets engaged. He kills boyfriend?"

"Maybe he drugged Preston so she'd be his alibi," Hackett said.

"Don't jump there yet. Maybe Jacks would do anything for Grace, like disposing of the murder weapon for her."

"Disposing of it behind his own apartment is stupid."

"Well, he's not the brightest bulb." Bishop smiled. They walked back toward the room where Jacks was being held. "Let Preston go," Bishop said. "We'll give her boss a ride later."

When Hackett joined Bishop in the other interrogation room, Jacks was pacing, his voice raised. "You have it all wrong. I didn't do anything, I swear."

"Sit down, Dave," Bishop said.

Jacks postured for a moment as though he might walk out, but then he sat. Hackett sat across from him, while Bishop remained standing. "Here's the thing. We know you're in love with Grace. We know you were upset on Friday about her engagement. So from our point of view, either you killed Cahill or you're helping Grace because she killed him. Unless you want to go down for this all alone, you should probably start talking."

Hackett winced. He wished he'd been able to do this interview alone—had he done nothing but give Bishop further ammunition against Grace?

Jacks finally sat up straight. "You're crazy. Yes, I care about Grace. That's no secret. But I was not so nuts that I'd kill a guy. I'm not a psycho."

Hackett piped up. "And yet you drug women to get them into bed."

Jacks ignored him. "I was upset because I didn't think it would happen. Last I knew, he'd gambled away the ring. Fucking asshole. What kind of guy gambles away an engagement ring? He didn't deserve her."

Hackett's pulse picked up. "What are you talking about? I thought you didn't know Cahill?"

"I didn't. But he joined a poker game I was in a few days before he died."

"So you did know him."

"No. I'd never seen him there before. I realized it was him as the night went on."

Bishop pulled out a chair. "Tell us about the poker game."

"It's a high-stakes game. Up in Bridgman. Sometimes the pot gets into the thousands."

"Where is this?"

"Back room of a car repair shop."

"And when was this?"

"It's a Tuesday night game, so I guess that would have been the Tuesday before he died."

Bishop waved a hand. "Go on."

"I know the guy who runs the game, Tom, but usually the players are strangers. I don't go all the time. Can't afford it. But I was there and Cahill and this other guy came together. I'd seen the other one before."

"And how did you know it was Cahill?"

"Because when he offered up the ring, his buddy said something about gambling away 'Grace.' He'd been calling him 'Mikey' all night, so I put it together."

"So exactly what happened?" Bishop said.

"He was up most of the night, like, three grand at one point, and then the cards started turning on him. But he didn't want to quit. Then in the middle of a hand, the stakes got really high. He didn't have enough money to stay in. He threw the ring on the table."

"What happened then?"

"His buddy told him he was an idiot. They argued for a bit, but Tom examined the ring and said he'd accept it if Mike lost the hand. So he stayed in the hand and used the ring, all the while saying it was worth far more. I guess he was super confident. Maybe he thought it would intimidate. Hell, it worked for me. I folded."

"And?"

"And they finished out the hand, and Mike turned over a straight flush with this shit-eating grin and leaned in to sweep up the pile. But then this guy George had a royal flush. And that was it. Fucker lost the ring."

"How did Cahill react?"

"Like a douchebag. He stood up and threw some chips at George. Accused him of cheating. Mike was drunk, and the boys by the door were on him in a flash. Pinned him to the ground. You don't mess with these guys. His friend got him outta there."

Bishop pushed a pad of paper at Jacks with a pen. "I think you'd better write down exactly where this auto shop is."

FIFTEEN

BACK IN THE TRUCK, GRACE STARED at her newly ringed finger before turning the ignition. She hit the tape deck play button and pulled out of the lot. Dr. Newell was asking how frequently she suffered from insomnia and whether she could discern any pattern. Grace explained that it was pretty much all the time now. She'd fall asleep, but most nights she was awake by two or three, struggling to get back to sleep. Her mind raced with school stuff, Michael issues, or even childhood memories. When she went out with the restaurant crowd after a shift for a few drinks, she might make it till four before waking.

Grace was leaning over the steering wheel, focusing on the taped voices as traffic zoomed past her in the left lane. Dr. Newell wanted to hear more about Michael. To her, and now to Grace too, it sounded as if trouble with her boyfriend could be a source of the insomnia. Grace answered the questions, explaining that they'd been a couple since she was fifteen.

"So it's safe to say Michael was your first love?"

"For sure." Grace laughed. "I never paid attention to anyone else."

She missed the turn, engrossed in her history. Finally, she pulled over.

"So you've never been with anyone else?"

Grace's tone changed. "Once. I did something really stupid." She'd cheated on Michael. A one-time thing. She'd gone out with a group after work and had too much to drink. She said she'd never been attracted to Dave, her boss, and she didn't even remember doing it, but at work, he had reminded her of their night together. "He grinned and told me how happy he'd been that I finally gave in to it." She was terrified Michael would find out.

Dr. Newell pressed her, wondering if on some level Grace might have wanted to end the relationship, if there was a part of her that hoped Michael would find out—perhaps it would be her ticket out. But Grace had been emphatic. "No way. First of all, Michael's like family. He's an idiot sometimes, but I love him. I wouldn't want to hurt him like that. I don't want to hurt him. I think that's the problem."

"What do you mean?"

Grace could hear the strain in her voice, the sniffling, as she responded. "I think I know we shouldn't be together anymore. But I don't know if I could ever leave him. He's . . ."

"What?"

"He's all I've got."

When Grace finally arrived back at the house, her head was pounding. She wanted to ignore all those pills on the counter, but the throbbing tentacles reached down the back of her neck, like they would eventually take over her entire body.

She got inside and took one pill, not sure if it was for pain or insomnia, but she didn't want to take them all, fearing the powerful side effects. She got a wet cloth for her forehead and collapsed onto the couch, sinking into the fog, the pain.

It must have been an hour later when she woke. The sun, now higher in the sky, was her only indication that the world continued to turn. Her headache was gone and she could walk across the room without getting dizzy.

She turned on the television and found an old *Seinfeld* episode. As she watched, she laughed, anticipating the punch line of a joke. "I know this one," she announced to the empty room, amazed by her own recall.

She closed her eyes, determined to remember more. "Michael," she said. Why was she thinking about him? She went to the bedroom, to that picture of the two of them together, and studied his face, touching the glass. "Michael loved *Seinfeld*!" she said suddenly, smiling. It was only a flash, but she pictured him on a couch, laughing, watching TV—*Seinfeld*. "Leather couch, yellow walls, glass coffee table," she said. "Our place."

She had to know. She grabbed the keys to the old truck and went to her purse, digging out the jeweler's receipt for the address. The tape was still in the truck's deck, and she hit play as she backed out of the drive, turning up the volume.

Dr. Newell was asking her what she meant about Michael being her only family. Grace explained that her parents had been killed, and he'd helped her get through all that. Grace let the phone map guide her while she listened intently. On the tape, she explained that it had been a break-in and they'd been killed in their bed. Dr. Newell asked how Grace had survived and if she'd been the one to find them.

"I was at a friend's when it happened."

"And how did you feel when they were killed?"

Her response sounded annoyed. "Well, obviously, I was upset."

"And how old were you when it happened?"

"Seventeen."

"Now, is it just you, or do you have siblings?"

She hesitated, and then it was almost a chuckle as she said, "It's kind of both. I mean, it's not just me, but it might as well be."

"What do you mean by that?"

She sounded reluctant. "You know, I get how this works," she said. "I came to you and I'm supposed to tell you all about my life, but I really don't like talking about all of this. It took me a long time to put all that behind me. I just need help with this insomnia."

"Isn't it possible it's all related?" Dr. Newell asked.

"Can't you just give me some meds? I mean, maybe I just need a little Ambien or something."

"I can, but if we don't get to what might be causing it, nothing's going to give you long-term results."

"I'd take a Band-Aid for now."

The doctor pressed on. "What happened to you after your parents died? It must have been very frightening."

"I had Michael," she said. "We moved in together after that."

Finally, as the session had ended, the doctor prescribed Grace the Xanax and warned her against mixing it with alcohol. She agreed to return the following week.

Grace pulled up to the address on the jeweler's receipt. She turned off the tape and studied the house in front of her: a tiny, one-story, aluminum-framed ranch with a single door and two windows flanking its sides. Under each window was a red flower box, now topped with snow. Grace studied those boxes and thought of spring, of planting flowers, and of Michael, working in the yard. But the front door spoke of the tragedy inside: yellow police tape wrapped around the handle, blowing in the wind.

She crunched through the hardened snow to the front windows and peered through the glass at the brown leather couch, yellow walls, glass coffee table. It was real. She trekked through the frozen snow to the back, spotting a couple of broken patio chairs; a rusty grill; and, deeper into the yard, an old stone well surrounded by flowerpots filled with dead plants, frozen in their plastic tombs. She peered into the windows where she could. One was covered in a shade. "The bathroom," she said. And then she saw the bedroom window. Her breath fogged against the glass, but she could see a bare mattress on an iron frame, a large black stain in the middle of the bed. Blood. Acid churned through her stomach; a sharp pain stabbed at her temple. She closed her eyes and held on to the siding, unsure whether her brain was trying hard to remember or forget.

"Grace?"

She turned to the breathless voice behind her.

~ • ~

"We gotta keep our eyes on Jacks," Hackett said after they'd dropped him back at his apartment. "If he drugged Preston, who knows what he's capable of."

"Agreed, but let's not assume too much yet." Bishop drove north on Red Arrow. "Jacks is a creep, but we've still got the fact that Grace was engaged to Cahill on Friday but may have broken up with him the night before the murder. That makes her a suspect as well."

Hackett stared down at his notes and resisted the temptation to defend Grace. *Be objective.* "So where are we going?"

"Well, since you never called that bartender, let's get over to The Rack. He's on now, as I recall."

Hackett remained silent, not wanting to make excuses for ignoring orders.

"What did you learn from the phone company, by the way?"

"I told the guy that we had to have those records, but he said it would be a little bit longer. Sorry." Bishop nodded, his trust widening the guilty trench winding through Hackett's stomach. "I saw *An Officer and a Gentleman* last night," he said, desperate for a topic change.

Bishop spit some chew into his empty soda can. "And? Great movie, right? What do ya think of my impression?"

"Terrible," he said with a laugh. "And you didn't tell me how sad it would be."

"What do you mean? It's got a happy ending. He gets his wings. He gets the girl. It's all good."

"But the blonde, Debra Winger's friend, is so cruel, and the best friend kills himself."

Bishop nodded with a smirk. "Well . . . blondes are bitches." Hackett chuckled. He had to agree with that one—Olivia was a blonde.

Bishop began another anti-Christmas-gift rant and gave his best impression of Billy Bob Thornton in *Bad Santa*. Hackett feigned interest, glad to have lightened the mood but now stuck on the cruelty of some women.

Another aging biker, thinner and taller but similarly tatted, stood behind the bar when Bishop and Hackett entered The Rack. There were few customers. They introduced themselves, pulled out the photo of Cahill, and the man confirmed he'd known him.

"So we spoke to your buddy, Ed, on Monday," Bishop said. "He said that you worked on the Wednesday before Mr. Cahill's death. We know Mr. Cahill worked on Wednesday, so we're wondering if you saw him in here after his shift."

The man nodded. "Sure, he was here. Sitting over there." He pointed to a booth in the corner.

"And this was Wednesday?"

"Had to be Wednesday. We were pretty dead. It's always busy on Fridays and Saturdays."

"And around what time was this?"

"Oh, I'd say sometime after six o'clock. That's when a big load of 'em come in."

"Was he with anyone?"

"For a bit, yeah. His buddy Wesley came and joined him a little while later."

Hackett immediately flipped back through his notes.

Bishop beat him to the punch. "Wesley Flynn?"

"I don't know last names. Just 'Wesley'—one of his buddies from work. They been coming in for a couple a years, so I know a good many of 'em by name—first names, at least."

"So they're sitting there, having a drink. Nothing out of the ordinary?" Bishop asked.

"Well, they fought. Wesley slammed down his drink and took off."

"Could you tell what they fought about?" Hackett asked.

"Hey, I ain't no eavesdropper. I just know it was a fight because there were a few choice words thrown around and then, like I said, the guy stormed out. That's all. I'm not saying he's a murderer or anything though. These guys get a little hot now and then. Don't mean nothin'."

The sun was setting when they came out of the bar. Hackett was ready to burst. "Flynn lied. He said he hadn't seen him since Sunday."

Bishop smiled. "Yep, maybe we're finally getting somewhere."

Bridgman, and that auto shop Jacks had fingered as the location of the illegal poker game, was only another ten-minute drive from Berrien Springs. When they arrived, they asked for Tom and were shown to a back room, where the owner sat behind a cluttered desk with a stack of receipts and a laptop in front of him. His gray shirt was covered in oil stains, his red-and-white name patch barely legible, his face marked with grease. He stood, offering his hand to Bishop first, his fingernails embedded with oil.

"Hey, fellas, what can I do you for?" He sat back down, wiping his hands with a rag.

"We heard you got a weekly high-stakes card game going on here," Bishop said.

The man stopped momentarily before continuing to work on his nails, his eyes never meeting theirs. "I don't know where you'd hear that. Must have me confused with someone else."

"Cut the shit," Bishop said. "We're not interested in your back-room gambling. We're interested in a couple players who were here week before last."

Tom stopped wiping his hands. "What do you mean?"

"Tuesday, December third. You hosted a game. Michael Cahill came here with another man. We're investigating his death. Apparently he lost an engagement ring in the game."

"So?"

"What'd you do with it?"

"I sold it."

"Where did you sell it?"

"Here. His buddy came in to see me the next day. Apologized for his friend. He wanted to get the ring back for him."

"So you gave it to him?"

"I sold it to him. That ring was worth about four grand. I have a buddy who knows these things."

"So the friend bought it back from you for four grand?"

The man smiled. "I'm a generous guy. I cut a deal and gave it to him for three."

"How nice of you. And what was the name of the friend you sold it to?"

"Wesley Flynn."

SIXTEEN

Grace turned to the voice behind her.

"I knew that was you!" A young woman, probably the same age as her, clomped through the snow, trying to catch her breath. Her cheeks were flushed, her nose red. "I saw you pass the house in that truck a minute ago. Oh my God, Wesley said you were in an accident." She pulled Grace into a tight embrace. "I ran over as soon as you passed."

The braided yarn on the woman's brightly colored knit cap flew into Grace's face. But Grace remained still, trying to place the woman and quiet the nerves that spiked through her chest with the sudden embrace. She pulled back to study her: same height, wavy dirty-blonde hair pulled back into two messy pigtails, a big white down coat that fell to her knees, red sweatpants, snow boots.

"Grace, are you okay?"

Grace took a step back.

The woman took a step forward. "I was so worried. Mike was killed and you disappeared. We didn't know what to think. And then Wesley told me that you'd been at the hospital all this time!"

"I'm sorry. Who are you?"

"What? Grace—what's going on?" She removed her cap. "It's Vicki! What happened to you?"

"I don't remember."

"Oh my God, Grace . . ." Then Vicki noticed the view inside the bedroom window. "What are you doing out here?"

"I wanted to see if I could remember . . ."

"Oh, Grace, you shouldn't go in there."

"It's okay," she said. "The police told me what happened. You know me well?"

Tears pooled in Vicki's eyes, and her voice softened. "We've been friends for, like, ten years." She was pleading for recognition.

Grace held her gaze, something she'd been unable to do with Dave Jacks or that hostess or even Lisa. The woman seemed heartbroken. Finally, someone who might be able to fill in more gaps. "Can you help me?" she asked.

Vicki pulled her in for another embrace. "Of course. Come on, let's go. It's freezing out here."

Grace pulled back slowly, not wanting to let on that the hug had hurt her cracked ribs. "Where do you want to go?" she asked.

"My house. I left Sammy. I've gotta get back. Come on. I'll get us some coffee. We can talk."

She drove Vicki back to her house, a block down the road. It was a similarly small house, barely bigger than a matchbox, but at least there were signs of life, maybe of laughter and fun silenced by the harsh winter: a swing set in the side yard; plastic Adirondack chairs, covered in snow and positioned in a circle around what must have been a fire pit. Hanging above the front door, covered with a dusting of snow, was a hand-painted placard: HOME SWEET HOME. And sitting on the nearby windowsill, a small ashtray filled with butts.

She sat at the kitchen table, finding nothing about the space—the toddler toys strewn about, the dried wildflower bunches hanging from hooks by the door, or the family pictures—familiar. But this woman, with her big green eyes, her worn-out Stray Dog sweatshirt, her skinny legs, felt familiar. Maybe it was her smile. One tooth wasn't quite in line with the rest. It felt right, like she knew that smile. She could trust it.

Vicki grabbed some mugs and turned on the coffee before joining her at the table. "I wish I had known sooner. I tried to find Lisa last week and see if she'd heard anything, but no one answered at the house, and when I called the bakery, she was never working."

"Yeah, she was by my side at the hospital all week."

"God, there's so much to talk about. We were so worried. I showed the police your text from Friday, but of course once we'd been interviewed, I never saw them again. I called your cell a few times, but you never answered. I planned to come over and see you at Lisa's, but Sammy's been sick. I tried to call again, but no one ever answers."

Grace looked at her phone. "I didn't have any messages."

"I didn't leave any. Grace, you can't believe all the crazy stuff I worried about. Mike was murdered and you were gone. I thought"—the tears returned and she quickly swiped them away—"I thought, what if you were kidnapped?" She shook her head. "I thought of a lot of terrible possibilities. I figured if you were alive you'd call me. His funeral was last Saturday."

"Funeral—for Michael?"

"Yeah. His mother had it up in Grand Haven. Guess she saw no reason to have it here, but still, it seemed wrong. He never lived there. All his friends were here. But maybe she wanted to be able to visit his grave or something. Anyway, we did the two-hour drive. Everyone said a prayer that you'd be found safe. Grace, we were all so worried."

"People didn't think I killed him?"

"No! Why would we think that?"

"I don't have an alibi. I can't remember . . ."

"Oh, Grace." Vicki took her hand. "I've known you for ten years. Michael's mother has known you forever. We knew this had nothing to do with you. The police will figure it out soon." She stood and fetched the coffee. "So, is everything okay? You're staying with Lisa?"

"Yeah, she seems nice. But we're strangers."

"Well, she did move out when we were thirteen, and you never really talked about her. But then again, maybe in a crisis . . . well, you *are* family."

Vicki poured the coffee, and Grace put both hands around the hot mug, heat spreading up through her fingers. "When's the last time you and I spoke?"

"About a month ago. I'm busy these days with Sammy, and you're busy with school and work. But you texted me the night before it happened. You were gonna stop by after your morning run. You said you had some news."

"Did you know I was engaged?"

Vicki smiled and shook her head. "But I knew he was going to ask." She took Grace's hand and smiled at the ring. "I'm so sorry . . ."

"It's okay. I mean, I don't remember him. It's hard to process what to feel. I guess you knew Michael pretty well, then?"

Vicki took a sip and nodded. "God, this is so weird. Yes, I knew him well. I called him Mike, actually. You called him Michael only when you were mad. Mostly, you called him 'babe,'" she said with a smile. "Anyway, Mike and Wesley were best friends."

"Wesley?"

"My husband. Grace, this is fucked up. You can't remember anything?"

Grace looked around the space, suddenly self-conscious about freaking this woman out. "I'm getting flashes but I don't know much. Can you tell me what you know about my relationship with Michael? Were we happy together?"

"Well, that's a loaded question, isn't it? Are any of us happy?"

Grace waited for a real answer.

Vicki took a sip and looked out at the yard. "I just mean I know there were ups and downs. They're men." She shrugged.

Grace took another sip. "So, we're close friends, right?"

Vicki nodded and smiled.

"Did you know if I ever cheated on him?"

"You mean with Dave?" Vicki asked.

It was still a horrifying, baffling reality. "You knew about that?"

"Yeah. But it doesn't mean you didn't love Mike. I know you did."

"But was I thinking about leaving him? Did I ever say anything?"

"No."

So obviously she didn't confide in Vicki about everything. "If the police find out I had an affair, it's not going to look good."

"Affair? Hardly. It was a one-time thing. Did Dave tell you that you were having an affair?"

"It wasn't what he said. It was the way he looked at me. It seemed like we were . . ."

"Dave is obsessed with you. I told you to quit that job. He's a freak."

"Why did I do it?"

"You went out with a bunch of coworkers, got shit-faced, and it happened. You didn't know why. You didn't want Mike to find out. You loved him."

"Do you think he found out?"

"Not that I know of. I mean, I think he'd have told Wesley. And you are engaged," she said, gesturing toward Grace's hand.

"Did he have enemies?"

"Not that I knew of." Vicki got some milk from the fridge and added a little to both cups. "Sorry, it was a little strong, right?"

Grace thanked her before sipping again. "Better." She put down the mug and continued. "What did you think of him—of Michael? The cops say he smoked a lot of pot and may have been a gambler."

Vicki chuckled and pulled the rubber bands from her hair, redoing the mess of waves into a bun. "That doesn't mean much. You could be describing Wesley like that too. But it's not like people were out to get them."

Grace watched her play with her long blonde hair and reached forward. "I remember that."

"What?" Vicki froze.

Grace smiled. "You, playing with your hair."

"You always said I should be a makeup artist or hair stylist. Do you remember anything about your life?" Vicki asked carefully. "Your childhood?"

"I've had a few flashes. But mostly I'm learning from everyone else. I learned that my parents were murdered." Grace studied her mug, the crayon declaration WORLD'S BEST MOM, wondering what it all meant.

Vicki nodded. "I don't think I'll ever forget that morning the cops knocked on my door."

"Why did they come to you?"

"You were with me. We were having a sleepover."

"That was you?"

Vicki nodded. "I remember that night like it was yesterday." A noise came from the baby monitor on the counter. She smiled. "That's why I remember every detail of that night."

"What do you mean?"

"It was the night I got pregnant."

"But I thought we were together?"

"We were together, but not the *whole* time, of course. We snuck out. We always used to sneak out. You were dating Mike; I was dating Wesley."

"And no one knew?"

"Well, your parents knew about Mike. They were against it, of course."

"Why?"

"Because you were seventeen and he was twenty-seven. But we were smitten kittens."

Grace sat back, drinking the coffee, not even sure what to ask.

"We snuck out a lot back then. You and Mike were so in love. We were all so stupid in love. You were even talking about running away together. But then your parents died. You didn't need to run after that."

"You said you got pregnant that night—where did we go?"

"Cherry Beach. It was late September. We made a bonfire in the sand, smoked some weed, went our own ways for a bit." She raised her eyebrows. "And about an hour later, we got back together and went home. Ten months later, I had a new baby."

"Do I smoke pot? The cops found a lot of pot at the house."

Vicki shook her head. "No. If it's one thing I know for sure, you and I have come a long way, baby. We may have been idiots when we were teenagers, but there wasn't much to do. We grew up. At least you and I grew up. We may be only twenty, but I think it's safe to say that you and I are the more mature ones in our relationships."

"What do you mean?"

"I mean, men are stupid," she said with a smirk. She stopped and looked at Grace. "I'm sorry. I don't mean to disrespect the dead."

Grace smiled. "It's okay."

"At least you can get a fresh start," Vicki said.

"What?"

"I mean, oh, nothing, I'm sorry. I just had a fight with Wesley, so he's kind of on my shit list right now. I shouldn't act like death is a better alternative. It's just not always a good thing when your life decisions are made by seventeen, you know?"

She didn't know how to respond, so she sipped the coffee. It was much better than Lisa's.

Vicki perked up. "But hey, I got Sammy out of it, so I'm not complaining."

"Did anyone ever know that we snuck out with Michael and Wesley that night?"

"Hell no. I would have gotten in so much trouble. It's not like it mattered. Not after what happened."

"I've been trying to piece it all together—walking around my house, searching through basement boxes, but I—" She didn't know how to describe it—would she sound crazy if she told her about hearing the crying girl?

"You've been to the basement? The whole time I've known you, that basement was off-limits."

"Why?"

"You refused to go down there. You said it was creepy."

"What did you know about my parents? Did I talk to you about them?"

"Not really. I mean, they were parents; we were kids. Our goal was always to get away. And from the time I met you, even back when we were twelve, you didn't like being at home much."

She listened while her thumb traced the lettering on her mug, wondering if her aversion to that house was based on fear.

Vicki continued. "They seemed okay. I mean, we were teenagers. We all thought our parents were idiots. And it didn't help that you started dating Mike. They forbade you from seeing him—they even threatened to report him to the police. So, of course, you fell in love and snuck out constantly."

"Did I ever talk to you about my parents being abusive?"

Vicki looked a little stunned, like the idea was entirely new. "No," she said. Neither said a word, the allegation hanging in the air. "You always wanted to sleep over though. We almost never went to your house. You once said your mom popped a lot of pills, but that's it."

"Did you ever know me to have a temper?"

Her blue eyes widened. "Not with me. No. No, Grace."

"Did I ever tell you that I'd slashed Michael's tires?"

Vicki laughed. She stood and put her mug in the sink. "That was you? You told me it happened, but you never said you did it."

"Do you think I could kill someone?"

"Absolutely not. Well—I take that back. We could all kill someone, couldn't we? I mean, if someone hurt Sammy, I think I'd kill him."

Grace wondered if her old self would have agreed, if everyone was capable of crossing that line if pushed to a certain limit. "Did Michael have a temper?"

Vicki was looking back outside, messing with her bun, letting the hair fall again before braiding it. "I never saw it. Though when he drank too much, he could get a little . . ."

"What?"

"He had some demons, a rough childhood, that's all." She returned to the table and sat. "You're freaking me out, Grace. Did Michael hurt you?"

"I don't know."

Vicki looked wary, like she'd made an important connection. "Someone keyed your car once. You said you didn't know who would have done it, but I didn't believe you."

"You think it was Michael?"

"I had no idea, but it seemed like you did." She hesitated. "Have the cops mentioned Wesley to you?"

"Wesley, your husband?"

Vicki's eyes drifted to the window. "Yeah, he's freaking out."

"Why?"

"He's the one who found Mike. He was so upset. But he's a little worried they might be looking at him."

"Why?"

"They got in an argument at that bar they go to after work. He's afraid someone might have overheard and misunderstood. He's just a hothead."

"What was it about?"

Vicki waved a hand. "It was something stupid. Mike owed him some money, that's all."

"How much?"

"Nothing big. Like, a hundred bucks. Not so much that you'd kill someone, if that's what you're thinking, but enough to piss you off. He was just being a guy. But now with what happened, obviously, we're both a little freaked out." She began cracking her knuckles.

Grace smiled broadly as she reached out toward Vicki's hand. "I remember that."

"What?" Vicki asked.

"Cracking your knuckles. Whenever we had a test," she said, her grin growing as she envisioned young girls in a classroom.

Vicki put her hands on Grace's. "Like I said, we've been friends forever."

"That's right." Grace laughed, feeling a momentary calm and joy in the pleasure of reliving a sliver of a memory with an old friend.

The sound of a little girl suddenly poured out of the baby monitor, filling the space: *"Mama, up, up."*

"Oh shit, Sammy's up from her nap."

Grace stood. "I'll go. Thanks for talking to me."

Vicki pulled her in for another hug. "I'm so sorry about everything. I'm sorry about Mike; I'm sorry you don't remember anything. It'll come back. And call me. I'm here for you, anything you need."

It was that phrase again, ringing around in her brain. Menacing. *I'm here for you.*

Grace shook her head, trying to banish the threat from her mind. She pulled out her phone. "How can I reach you?"

Vicki took it from her and went through the contacts. "Why aren't I in here?" Before Grace could respond, she said, "Jesus, no one's in here. What the hell?" She created a new contact for herself and gave it back to Grace. "Here, call me anytime."

Grace sat in the truck contemplating the conversation. Michael was ten years older. It sounded wrong, almost criminal. No wonder her parents hadn't approved. But maybe it was about trying to get away from them. Maybe she was desperate to be loved. Maybe her parents were bad. But it sounded so odd, like a line in a story that didn't fit. The two visions she'd had of them were harmless, peaceful, even joyful. Then again, maybe those were the only memories she could handle.

SEVENTEEN

GRACE SAT IN THE TRUCK OUTSIDE of Vicki's house, looking at the street, the houses. This had been her neighborhood. She'd sent a text to Vicki about popping over after a run, the police had said. And Lisa said she was a runner. She rested her hands and chin on the steering wheel and closed her eyes. She felt the cold air in her lungs, the steady rhythm of her feet hitting the pavement, the peacefulness of those early mornings, of the quacking ducks in the distance, the occasional deer in the woods. It was real. It wasn't wishful thinking. She remembered running.

Her cell rang, pulling her from the trance. It was Officer Bishop asking her to come in again.

Lisa's outburst after their last trip to the station echoed in her ears: *Don't volunteer to help them.* But maybe they had a new lead, or maybe going would show that she was cooperating. And Officer Hackett was on her side. She told Bishop she'd be there shortly. Lisa would want to go with her, but she was so paranoid and hostile toward the police, and Grace felt about ten years old when she was by her side. She would handle this herself.

She pulled out of Vicki's drive and, once on Red Arrow Highway, remembered the route Lisa had taken to get to the station. It felt like an improvement.

She listened to the tape on the way over. It was Grace's next session, and Dr. Newell began by asking if the Xanax was working—if she was sleeping better. Grace said that it was helping. She said she felt like a new woman. She could hear the lightness in her own voice.

Dr. Newell asked if she'd noticed any negative side effects. "You could say that. My boyfriend seems to like them too." The doctor was not amused and threatened to discontinue the prescription if Grace was sharing them. Grace quickly apologized—she hadn't given him any or suggested he take them; that was the problem, she said. Michael seemed too interested in getting high all the time. It was part of why she wondered if she could stay with him. She had told him about seeing the doctor and about her relief at getting the pills, and then noticed several missing by the end of the week. The doctor made Grace promise to hide them if necessary—or she'd end the prescription.

"Well, beyond that, anything else troubling? Any changes in appetite, anything that you're concerned about?"

"Only that I might get fat," Grace said.

The doctor questioned her meaning, and Grace said that a few days earlier, she woke and found the fridge wide open, chips and dip on the counter and the remnants of what looked like melted ice cream in a bowl. Michael had been at an all-night card game and wasn't even home yet, so she knew it had to have been her, but she didn't remember eating any of it. "Can that happen?" she'd asked. "Sleepwalking and eating?" The doctor confirmed it was possible and suggested reducing the dose.

Grace turned off the tape as she pulled into the station.

Officer Hackett came to the lobby to get her. As soon as they made eye contact, he smiled, and a portion of her anxiety dissipated. It would be fine.

"You remember anything new, Grace?" Detective Bishop asked as they escorted her to the interrogation room.

Dr. Newell had said not to let anyone listen to the tapes. Could she share what she'd learned? Would she lose all privilege? What if something bad came out? "Nothing of significance. I drove over to the house today." She sat at the table with Hackett, and Bishop shut the door behind them.

"Really?" Bishop leaned against the door. "Did you go inside?"

She couldn't tell whether he was annoyed. "No. I didn't have a key or anything, but I remembered something and wanted to see if it was real."

"What did you remember?" Hackett asked.

"The inside, the living room. I remembered that Michael loved *Seinfeld*. When I walked around, I felt like I knew the house. I remembered planting flowers in those flower boxes. But like I said, nothing of significance."

"So things are coming back. That's encouraging."

Bishop clapped his hands together, and joined them at the table, like the real discussion was beginning. "Grace, we questioned your boss, Dave Jacks, earlier today."

"Why?" Her thoughts raced back to their conversation at the beach, to his advice that she not mention him to the police. He'd said it would be better for both of them.

She looked at Hackett. Had she made a mistake this morning, admitting to seeing him? Had he intended to trap her into some sort of admission?

"Did you have a relationship with Dave outside of work?" Bishop asked.

Her heart felt like it was going to leap out of her chest. "I'm told that people from work would go out together after shifts. That's all I've learned."

"What about Sheri Preston, the hostess?"

"I met her when I went in for my check."

"She says you were friends."

"Okay—if she says so."

"We found a lot of pictures of you in Dave's apartment," Bishop said.

Oh God, they knew. They knew she'd slept with him. "Of me?" she said meekly, the words barely getting out. "What—?"

"Michael's shotgun and a T-shirt covered in his blood were found in the dumpster behind Dave's apartment," Hackett said. "And he had a highly dangerous drug in his apartment that's used among criminals. It affects memory."

Bishop cleared his throat, glaring at Hackett. He'd obviously said too much.

Grace sat upright and Hackett leaned in, ignoring his partner. "Do you remember taking Michael to the urgent care in Bridgman early Monday morning?"

"I don't remember anything before the accident. I've had flashes here and there, but they seem to be older memories."

"So you don't recall if Michael thought he had been drugged a week before the murder?"

"No." Michael's abuse of her Xanax came immediately to mind. Was that it? Maybe he'd taken her pills again. She opened her mouth to speak but stopped herself. This was from the therapist's tape. Could she share? Would it mean that anything she said to her therapist could be used against her? The questions raced through her mind, and she wondered if her face would give away the panic that was building.

"Do you remember Dave? Do you remember that he has feelings for you?" Hackett asked. Did he want her to remember? Would it help? She didn't know what to say.

Bishop didn't wait for a response. "Have you spoken with Dave since the murder?"

What if they knew she'd cheated on Michael with Dave? What if they knew she'd met him at Cherry Beach? How would it look? She fidgeted with her hands, feeling the heat rise to her face. "I—"

"Nice ring," Bishop interrupted.

Grace looked down at her hand, now the focus of everyone's attention. "Oh yeah, thanks."

"I don't think you were wearing that when you gave us the fingerprints." He said it nonchalantly, but his words were somehow loaded. "When did you get engaged?"

"I got a call from the jeweler yesterday. He told me I took the ring in for resizing on Friday." She nervously rolled the ring around her finger.

Bishop turned that intense stare up to full wattage. "You and Michael became engaged two days before the murder. I wish you had shared that with us," he said, pointing to the ring. "We'd like to think you're cooperating with our investigation."

"I am," she said in a voice that sounded unconvincing even to her.

"When you learn something about the days before the murder and you don't share it, well, it doesn't look good."

Suddenly, she felt like a trapped animal, unsure whom to trust, what to say. Her heartbeat was racing. Heat was rising to her neck; her entire face suddenly felt hot. She stared at the table, unwilling to meet their eyes. What if Dave had drugged her? Vicki had said she'd been mortified about being with Dave and that she hadn't remembered anything about it. But she couldn't prove she was drugged. And she'd be admitting to a relationship with their new suspect. "Is there anything else you wanted to ask me?" she said, her voice small. "My head hurts. I think I'd better get home."

"Sure," Officer Hackett said. "Do you want me to drive you?"

He didn't sound angry like Bishop, but was this the good-cop routine? "No, thanks, I'll be okay."

~ • ~

"She's hiding something," Bishop said as Grace walked out the door.

"She looks like a deer in headlights to me," Hackett said. "Don't you think it would be crazy not to remember your life?"

"I think my head would hurt if I felt the police getting close. Any luck finding that T-shirt in any of Cahill's Facebook pictures?"

"No."

Bishop rubbed his eyes before looking down at his case notes. "So Flynn bought the ring back. And soon after, Flynn and Cahill are seen arguing. We need to talk to him again." Bishop's phone chimed and he checked a text before grabbing his coat. "I've got to go. Do me a favor—call Flynn's work and find out where he'll be in the morning."

Hackett's desk phone rang as Bishop walked out the front door. It was Miles at the forensics lab. One set of prints on the naked photos was a match for Grace. She'd seen those pictures. Maybe that was why she went to Lisa's Friday night. And if she was upset enough to break off the engagement, a jury might think she was upset enough to kill him.

~ • ~

It was dark when Grace left the station. She drove home in silence, almost in a daze. A few cars honked as they passed her on the right, and suddenly she noticed lights coming straight at her. She quickly corrected back into her lane and pulled over onto the shoulder. She shouldn't be driving. She took a careful, deep breath. A twinge of pain in her rib cage remained. Another headache was coming on. She closed her eyes, willing the ache to recoil, but it was no use.

She carefully pulled back onto the road and continued home. The approaching lights began to stretch out into bright streams like laser beams. She blinked hard to correct her vision, but it was no use. She drove slowly, painfully, and finally turned onto the familiar gravel road. When she pulled into the driveway, Lisa's car was there. She opened the door slowly, careful not to upset the delicate balance in her head, as though her brain was a fragile boat, floating on the water, and if the water didn't remain still, the waves would start, pounding the boat against the walls of her skull.

She climbed out of the truck, grabbed the tape, and put it in her pocket.

Every step caused pain. As she opened the front door, a pan slammed down onto the kitchen counter, and Lisa flew at her with an intensity that almost brought Grace to her knees.

"Where have you been?" She didn't wait for a response before continuing. "Who have you been talking to? Where did you go?"

Grace held up her hand and closed her eyes. "Stop. Please. Calm down." She made her way to the living room couch and sat. Four empty beer bottles were lined up in front of her.

"You're not supposed to drive. I'm responsible! I'm responsible, okay? I told the doctors I'd see that you took your meds and you rested and you didn't drive. And look!" She pointed to the pile of pills on the counter. "You didn't take the fucking meds! You drove a car. What am I supposed to think?"

Grace kept her voice low and lay back. "Jesus, Lisa. Take it down a notch. I was feeling better, okay? The pills make me so groggy. I don't think I can handle the side effects."

"But look at you. You're obviously in pain." Lisa sat on the arm of the sofa and took a quick, deep breath. "The doctor was very specific. You're to take the medicine. We'll see him on Monday, and then you can tell him you want to get off. But I don't want to be responsible for anything happening to you. Please, take the medicine."

Grace sat up and looked at Lisa, who was wiping tears from her cheeks. "What's going on with you?"

"Just take the goddamn pills. You have to take them."

"I'm okay, Lisa. I get it. You don't want anything to happen to me."

Lisa stood. "That's right." She wiped at her jeans, the conversation a mess she'd finished cleaning up. She grabbed the empty bottles, headed for the kitchen, and returned a moment later with a glass of water and several pills. She held them out.

Grace took them without a word. This was a fight she couldn't win, and she felt guilty. It couldn't be easy dealing with her right now, taking care of a loved one who treated you like a stranger. She lay back on the couch and closed her eyes, draping her arm across her face.

"So, where were you, anyway?" Lisa's tone had calmed considerably, and she was back in the kitchen.

"Police station. They called me back in. They questioned my boss, Dave Jacks. They wanted to know if I remembered anything else."

"What? Why? What's happened?"

Grace jumped at the sound of her voice, suddenly so close. She looked up at Lisa standing over her.

"Why him?"

"I guess Michael had been drugged the week before he was killed, and Dave had the drugs at his place."

"What do they think?"

"I don't know. I don't think they know. But Michael's shotgun was found in some dumpster at Dave's place."

"What? Oh my God."

Grace sat up then to look at her sister. "But I found out something today."

"What do you mean?"

"We were engaged." She held her hand out for Lisa to see the ring. "Why didn't you tell me? You said Michael and I broke up."

Lisa sat on the arm of the chair. "Where did that come from?"

"I dropped off the ring for resizing on the Friday before he died. The jeweler called me."

Lisa sat, silent for a moment, staring down at the shag rug. "I didn't know."

"Tell me the truth. What happened Friday night? What did I say?"

"You were really upset. You said Michael was a bastard. But you didn't want to talk about it. You weren't wearing that ring. You didn't mention the engagement. You asked to be alone, and the next morning you left to get your stuff."

Grace lay back down and stared up at the ceiling. "I think I need a lawyer." She felt like she was just starting to find out about who she was. She couldn't really kill a man, could she?

Lisa took her hand. "Grace, they're just fishing. Stop volunteering to help them, okay? I told you, it's not going to help things."

"You should have seen the way that Bishop guy looked at me. It's like he knows something I don't. I need help." She looked at Lisa. "I need professional help."

"Okay. I'm just worried that if you get an attorney now, it might make you look more suspicious. I mean, don't people with something to hide get lawyers? I just feel like we need to ignore the police until they start accusing you."

"I can't. I . . ." She looked at Lisa's eyes and couldn't hold back the tears. "I'm scared."

Lisa reached out and hugged her. Finally, it didn't feel awkward when Lisa held her tightly and rubbed her back. "Okay," she said. "I'll see if I can find you a lawyer nearby. I don't have to be at work until noon tomorrow. I'll take you."

The tension in Grace's body eased. She relaxed into her sister's embrace and closed her eyes, finally feeling grateful for Lisa's care.

The meds helped her headache and she fell asleep easily, but the fall woke her. Her body jolted in the bed, and she opened her eyes to a sudden realization that it was a dream. She'd been scared and crying, maybe five years old. The yellow sundress with daisies. Her arms tied behind her back, her eyes covered by fabric, when the ground disappeared beneath her and she tumbled forward and fell at least four or five feet into a pit. She'd shrieked. Wet leaves, grass clippings, garbage. That stench. What was it? Another nightmare or a memory?

She closed her eyes. Terrified of returning to that vision but wanting more. Had it been a game? The details were already fading from her mind. "Someone get me out of here," she begged into the still air.

She was not going to wander the house again. She wanted Dr. Newell; Friday couldn't come soon enough. She'd been in this house only four days, but she wanted out. She wondered if being back in Michael's house would be better. If the owner would have it cleaned, maybe she could stay there. Maybe it would help. How could her childhood home be more unsettling than the house where the man she'd once loved was murdered? And yet, it was.

She lay in her bed, eyes shut, and thought of Michael. She'd said yes. Why? According to her therapy sessions, she'd been having serious doubts about their future. She felt like an outsider looking in, and from her view, she and Michael didn't look like a good match. What held them together?

And then there was Dave. Why in the world would she have slept with him? There was nothing about Dave she was drawn to. That greasy hair, those bloodshot eyes . . . the thought of touching him—of being naked with him—felt wrong. She tossed and turned all night wondering if it were possible for a head injury to cause someone's personality to change.

EIGHTEEN

HACKETT SAT AT THE BAR WAITING for a refill. He stared at the scores on the television but couldn't focus on the information. Those damn print results would not help Grace. It did sound coincidental for Cahill to be murdered right after she found those pictures. Bishop would be thrilled. But he kept circling back to Dave Jacks and that drug, and to Cahill's urgent care visit, and the money. There had to be something else going on.

Miles had confirmed two different prints on those photographs. Neither was Cahill's. He'd asked Miles to compare the other prints on the photos with any other prints found at the scene. Maybe the other prints belonged to the person who'd sent them. And if he could place whoever sent them at the crime scene, well, that might be something.

Alice brought him another beer. The stragglers were leaving and she warned him that she needed to lock up soon. "Oh shit," he said, looking at the time. "Sorry. I didn't mean to stay so late."

"That's okay, hon. You look like you got the weight of the world on your shoulders tonight."

"Not quite," he murmured.

"This about a case or a woman?"

He shook his head but couldn't help smiling at her accuracy.

"Woman," she said with a grin, like his smile was the only answer she needed. "Come on. Tell Alice. I am a woman, after all. I'm sure I can help."

Of course she couldn't. And he couldn't get into it.

"Someone broke your heart?" she said, as if his silence were an offer to go fishing. "Christmas is coming?"

She was two for two.

"Feeling the pain of losing her again?"

Jeez, this woman wouldn't quit. "Let's just say I'm not looking forward to the holidays."

"Family trouble. Honey, everyone got family trouble. If my own holidays didn't involve one good throw-down, we'd all think something had gone horribly wrong."

He grinned. Hell, she'd probably get a kick out of his drama. Maybe make him think it wasn't so bad. So he told her about his big family: his massive Italian family that was so close and connected that every gathering involved fifty people.

She opened another beer for each of them and egged him on. So far, nothing sounded bad to her. In fact, she said, it sounded like one of those TV families you dream of.

So he moved on. "There was a girl, Olivia." He told her of their high school romance, the on-again, off-again, then moving in together.

"I take it she's finally out of your life."

He shook his head. That wasn't it. And then he changed his mind. He couldn't talk about it. It was hard enough without rehashing all the details. He thanked Alice, left some money on the bar, and went home.

The next morning, Hackett was pouring his first coffee at the station when his cell rang. It was Bishop, running late. Hackett told him that Flynn was off until noon and they could call him in or head over to his house. Bishop suggested they meet at Flynn's house in twenty minutes.

Hackett did as told. When Bishop arrived moments later, Mrs. Flynn greeted them at the door and left them while she woke her husband. They sat at the kitchen table drinking coffee and waited. Bishop looked awful. Not that he didn't always look a little haggard—but the bags looked deeper, his eyes were puffy, and he had foregone a shave, adding black and gray stubble to the already rough terrain. Hackett conveniently forgot to mention Miles's phone call. At least until Miles got back to him regarding the other prints first. "You okay?" he asked.

Bishop shook his head. "Not now." Neither said another word while they waited.

Flynn emerged from the bedroom in a robe. His wife followed.

"Hey, Wesley, sorry to disturb you, but we need to talk."

He went straight to the coffeemaker and poured a cup. His hand seemed to be shaking a little. His wife leaned against the doorway.

"Mrs. Flynn, would you mind giving us a minute alone with your husband?" Bishop said.

"It's okay. I don't have any secrets from my wife. Have you learned something about Mike's death?"

"We've learned a good bit. But Wesley, you told us you hadn't seen Cahill since the Sunday before his death, and we've learned that's not true."

Flynn looked over at his wife, who didn't seem surprised. She offered the explanation. "Wesley panicked. He didn't do anything. They were best friends."

"Vicki, stop," Flynn said. "We had an argument. It was no big deal. We've been friends forever. I loved him like a brother. I didn't hurt him."

"What were you fighting about?"

His wife answered. "Mike owed Wes a little money. It was no big deal, really. We knew you'd blow this out of proportion. It was only a hundred dollars." She sat at the table with the officers.

Bishop looked at Flynn. "That's not what we hear. Take a seat, Wesley. Tell us about the ring."

"What ring?" his wife said.

"Grace's engagement ring," Hackett answered.

"What are you talking about?" She turned to her husband. "What's going on?"

Flynn ignored her. "Like I said, we were best friends. Mike made a stupid mistake. I wanted to help him get out of it."

"Someone please explain to me what you're talking about!" she said.

Flynn said nothing, so Bishop responded. "Wesley and Cahill were in a high-stakes card game on Tuesday night, and Cahill gambled away his engagement ring. Wesley bought it back for him the next day."

"What? Wes! You swore you were done with that game!"

"I was. I am. Mike begged me to take him. Said the ring was settin' him back and he needed to get the cash."

His wife said what everyone was thinking. "So he wanted to gamble?"

"He wouldn't let it alone. He came to me Tuesday and begged me to get him into that game. But he fucked up."

"Why did you buy the ring back?" Bishop asked.

"Because I knew he was afraid Grace was going to leave him. I knew she was good for him, and I wanted to help."

"So what happened next?" Hackett asked.

"We met on Wednesday at The Rack. I told him I got the ring back and, at first, he was relieved and thankful, but when I told him I had to pay three grand for it, he got pissed."

Vicki Flynn slammed her mug onto the counter beside her. "What? We don't have that kind of money!"

"This is why I didn't tell you. It was a loan. He was my best friend!"

"It does seem like a lot to do for a friend," Hackett said.

"I did it for Grace too." Flynn looked at his wife. "You told me she didn't seem happy." He turned back to Bishop. "That girl's been through a lot."

"Like what?"

"Like losing her parents. We've all been friends for years. I thought if Michael got his shit together, he might make her happy."

"You should have told me," his wife said.

Bishop put out his hand to stop the couple's fight. "Wes, what happened next?"

"He said there was no way he was spending another three grand on that thing. I got pissed. I mean, I don't have that kind of money to spare. Look around."

"You're telling me," she added.

"So what happened next?" Hackett asked.

"I told him he needed to give me some money and I'd give him the ring back. I didn't even need it all upfront. I only wanted him to promise to pay me back. I told him it was safe in my dresser, waiting for him."

"You should have told me," his wife said again.

"Well, we know he gave Grace the ring," Bishop said. "She took the ring to be resized on Friday before work."

Flynn jumped up from the table. "I didn't give it to him," he said as he ran to the bedroom.

His wife looked at the officers. "He should have told me."

Flynn came back in. "It's gone."

"Of course it's gone, you asshole!" she yelled. "You didn't tell me! Mike came here on Thursday after his shift and said you were holding the ring for him so Grace wouldn't find it at their place. He said he needed it so he could propose!"

"Shit," Flynn said. "Why didn't you tell me?"

"Because we don't talk anymore, obviously!"

Bishop looked at Hackett before turning back to Flynn. "You're saying you didn't know he took the ring back?"

"No."

Bishop stood and Hackett did the same. "I don't know, Wesley."

"I didn't kill him."

Bishop rubbed his stubbled cheeks, unconvinced. "You lied about the last time you saw him. He owed you money. He stole from you."

"And he won ten thousand at the casino on Friday," Hackett said.

"What?"

"You saying you didn't know about that?"

"No!"

"Because if someone owed me several thousand, and then stole from my house, and then I found out he had the money and didn't pay me back, I'd be pretty pissed," Hackett said.

Bishop added the final blow. "You *were* the one who found him."

"I didn't do it."

"Did Michael pay you back on Friday?" Hackett asked.

"No. But I didn't see him. I swear. I didn't know anything about him winning money." Flynn's voice cracked. "He was my friend."

"My husband did not do this," Vicki said, putting her hand on his. "I may not be okay with loaning a friend that much money, but that's no reason to kill anyone. I don't know who would do this, but it wasn't Wes."

Bishop said they'd be in touch and told Flynn not to leave town.

As soon as the front door closed, Hackett turned to Bishop, grinning. "What do you think?"

"It's interesting. Get in my car for a minute so we can talk." He followed Bishop to his car and got in. Bishop rubbed his eyes hard before speaking.

"What's going on? You look like you haven't slept."

"Sandy's mom died last night."

"Oh shit. I'm sorry."

Bishop held up his hand. "It's okay. Kids are home from school today and Sandy's home. But frankly, I'd rather be working. So let's just focus on that, okay?"

"Got it. I think we just got a new lead, right?"

Bishop brushed through the thin strands atop his head. "None of this is helping to clear Grace. What if she knew that he gambled away the ring? This guy was an idiot. We've got gambling, drugs, sex with another woman. Do we need more motive?"

"Well, she's not the only one with motive, obviously. Cahill screwed over his best friend."

"True, but there's no evidence that Flynn knew about the casino win, and it seemed like he didn't even realize Cahill had stolen the ring. Grace has no alibi and she has motive. Flynn just said she was thinking about leaving him. So I'm thinking Cahill proposes, she says yes—maybe against her better judgment—and then she finds those pictures. Maybe even finds out about the ring and the gambling and pow, she loses it. Runs off to her sister's, drives over there Saturday morning, kills him while he's still asleep, takes off, and hits a tree. Case closed."

Hackett looked out the window at the frozen white landscape. It couldn't be. There were other possibilities. Was it all just wishful thinking? "Maybe Wes knew about the win. Maybe he saw that post." He pulled out his phone and went to Cahill's Facebook page, searching his friends. "Here," he said excitedly. "Wesley Flynn. He's in Cahill's network. He could have seen that post from the casino."

Bishop didn't respond. He just stared out the window at the house.

"And what about Jacks? Maybe this was all his doing?"

"Maybe. But I'm not sure I see him doing this if she wasn't somehow involved."

"She doesn't seem like she could do this."

Bishop turned to his partner. "We've interviewed her two times. How can you even have an opinion on what she could do? Besides, she might not even resemble the person she was. She's got a brain injury. She may seem like a shy, sweet girl now, but maybe she was a raving bitch."

Hackett didn't respond. It was all starting to back up on him, the secrets, lies, withholding evidence. How had it gone this far?

"What was Flynn talking about in there about Grace's parents?" Bishop asked.

Now Hackett focused on the landscape in front of them, unable or unwilling to look at his partner. "They died three years ago. I thought I told you."

"No, you didn't."

"There was nothing to tell. You told me to check her out. She's never been arrested. Never in trouble. Student, waitress. Paid bills on time. I don't know, I didn't think of it."

"How'd they die?" Bishop asked, grabbing for some chew.

"A robbery at the house. They were shot in their bed."

"You never thought to mention that?"

Hackett turned to him, defensive. "It was an open-and-shut case. The guy who killed them is in prison. It happened several years ago and we're dealing with this right now."

Bishop tucked the tobacco under his lower lip before responding. "You know how often we get murders in this area?" He didn't wait for an answer. "Almost never. And now you're telling me that we've got a double murder three years ago and another murder, and they're all connected to Grace."

"Yeah, but the girls weren't even in the house. They both had alibis. And some guy was sent away for it."

They both sat in the car in silence, and Hackett wondered if he'd said enough to get Bishop off Grace. Bishop shook his head and turned to Hackett. "You can go. Meet me back at the station."

He drove behind Bishop, feeling like a scolded child. When they got back to their desks, Bishop said, "Pull it up."

"Huh?"

"Pull up the parents' murder case."

Hackett went to his desk, navigated through the network, and found his way to the official case report filed by the Buchanan station regarding the Abbott murders. "Okay, here it is."

"So who did it?" Bishop asked.

Hackett quickly reviewed the case notes. "Stanford Jones is serving time at West Shoreland Correctional." He continued to read. "He was caught on tape pawning some of their valuables in St. Joe."

"And what was the murder weapon?"

"Shotgun. It was found hanging up in the basement. Assumed it was the parents' gun—it had been wiped down, but the evidence showed that it had been used within hours."

Bishop looked at him. "So the perp kills the parents with their own gun, wipes it down, hangs it back up, and leaves?"

"I guess."

"Fucking strange MO for a robbery. And was there a connection between this Jones and the Abbotts?"

"None mentioned."

"I want to know more."

"I just don't see—"

Bishop interrupted him. "Here's the thing. I don't know shit about who went down for the parents' murder, but both of these crimes are connected to Grace. The victims all died in their beds, killed by shotguns. Just feels a little coincidental."

"What are you thinking?"

Bishop finally took off his coat and put it on the back of his chair. "I just want to be sure we don't have a sweet little twenty-year-old on our hands who solves her problems by killing them."

NINETEEN

GRACE FINALLY WOKE AROUND NINE O'CLOCK and came downstairs. Lisa was dressed and pacing the kitchen floor. "Oh good, you're up. Have some coffee and take your meds," she said, handing her a mug and the pills. "I found you an attorney. We need to be there in an hour."

"Okay," Grace said. "I'll get dressed." She took the coffee and pills with her upstairs. She poured the coffee down the drain of the bathroom sink and tucked the pills into her front jeans pocket. There was no fighting Nurse Lisa, but none of this made her feel better. She could live with the lingering headache, but she couldn't live with those side effects. And Lisa's coffee sucked.

They drove for about thirty minutes to Saint Joseph, passing the small downtown area until they found a half-vacant strip mall. Lisa pulled the car into the lot and parked in front of the office. The door was covered with advertisements: DUI? DON'T WORRY!, UNDER INVESTIGATION? CALL ME!, SEX CRIMES, VIOLENT CRIMES, MEDICAL MARIJUANA, WHITE-COLLAR CRIME—I'VE DONE IT ALL!

"You sure about this guy?" Grace asked. "Doesn't look all that professional."

"Hey, he had the best ad in the yellow pages. It'll be fine."

They went into a plywood-paneled office where an older woman in a large beehive hairdo sat behind a desk, talking on the phone. Lisa told her who they were and the woman smiled, passed her a clipboard seeking basic information and a contractual agreement for payment, and pointed to the chairs against the wall. When the attorney came out to greet them, Grace felt no better. His toupee was askew and his shirt was desperately fighting to stay tucked in to his size-forty pants. Nothing about him suggested legal prowess. The women stood and the man asked that Grace alone come into his office. Lisa seemed reluctant, but he insisted. "I know that family is always concerned and wants to help, but we need to maintain our attorney/client privilege, so it's gotta just be her and me, okay?" Lisa smiled and sat back down. Grace followed him into his office.

The odor of a McDonald's Egg McMuffin wafted through the air, a surprisingly familiar scent. He crumpled the wrapper, still on his desk, and tossed it in the trash. "Breakfast of champions," he joked while gesturing for her to take a seat, as he took his behind the massive and equally disheveled desk. She stared at the placard facing her. OZZY MARSHALL, ESQ.

"So, tell me what you're up against. What's going on?"

Grace told him about her car accident, her memory loss, Michael's death, what she'd learned from Dave, what the police had found, and how she feared the evidence might be pointing her way. "In fact," she added, "they want to give me a polygraph, which I don't mind because I honestly can't remember anything, so I can't imagine it will hurt, but they're asking about my relationship with Dave, and I don't know how to handle this."

"Understandable."

"I thought maybe I should get some advice. I don't know what happened or what to believe, so I don't know how cooperative I should be."

"You did the right thing coming to me."

She looked around the room again, unsure he was right. "Have you ever dealt with a . . ." The word caught in her throat. "A murder?"

"Sure," he said, leaning back and stroking that fake hair on top of his head.

It wasn't a convincing reply.

Marshall sat forward. "Don't be fooled by all that marketing for petty shit. I need to do whatever comes to me to bring in the bacon, but I'm a litigator. I do it all. I may not have been the top of my class, but I get my clients off. Doesn't matter the charge; I'm the shit," he said, tossing his pen onto the desk, as if that speech would win her over. "Don't worry."

She did.

"I want to be by your side whenever you meet with the cops. And I want to talk to your doctors at the hospital and see the police records from the car accident before you do a poly. I'll contact the police and tell them that we'll have to delay until I can get up to speed."

Grace took a breath and continued. "I've learned that I lived with Michael, and we got engaged on Thursday before the murder. He was killed sometime on Saturday, I think. Apparently, we got in a big fight Friday night and I went to my sister's, asking to stay with her. I was in a car crash the next morning. I guess that's about when he died. I have no alibi."

"Your sister won't say you were with her in the morning?"

"Well, I don't expect her to lie. She woke and I was gone. She told me that I'd said I was going to get my things from our house. But we haven't told the police that part yet. I don't know if I actually got there. Maybe I got in a crash on the way. She's trying to protect me, but I wonder if we should share everything. If they find out, it might look like I was trying to hide something."

"What were the medications in your name?"

"Xanax. I guess I was an insomniac. I'd started seeing a therapist, who I met with yesterday. I'm hoping she can help me remember. The cops found pictures of Michael with another woman in the house—so I'm guessing they think I might have killed him out of jealousy or anger."

"And you've seen the photos?"

"Yeah. The police showed me."

"Did you recognize the woman?"

"No. But you can't see her face. Only her backside."

"What else?"

"There were drugs in the house, large money withdrawals. Lisa says that he was a bad guy—and gambled and smoked pot."

Marshall took lots of notes and threw the pen down again. "Okay. We've got a lot to work with here. There are plenty of potentials, and my job, if you end up being charged, is not to prove that you didn't do it. It's to prove that there are plenty of other potential scenarios. We just need reasonable doubt. Worst case, even if all arrows point to you, we've got the drug defense."

"What do you mean?"

"There are some pretty serious and documented side effects from antianxiety meds—sleepwalking, sleep driving, sleep eating, there have been cases even of sleep murder. The perps weren't conscious when they committed the acts, so they couldn't be found to have 'intended' harm—there was no intent." Grace's mind returned to the taped session, to her unconscious eating while on Xanax.

"In fact, I'll see if we can find out what drugs were in your system when you got to the hospital. If you took Xanax the night before the murder, we might be on to something."

"That happens?"

"Sure. It's rare, of course, but it's happened."

"Are you saying that I could have driven over there, killed him, and left—all while sleeping?"

"It's possible. Obviously we wouldn't say that unless the evidence is clearly pointing at you. Right now it sounds like they're still fishing. But my point is, even if it looks bad for you, it's a great thing that you were on meds. It's a great thing that you got in a car crash. It all works. And this sleepwalking stuff—it's a real defense. Hell, it could even explain your car accident. You hit a tree, right?"

"Yeah, no other cars involved, no witnesses. The cops said it was a deer."

"This is a pretty interesting possibility." He leaned back in his chair. "Give me the names of the officers you've been speaking with. I'll call and let them know they need to deal with me. And if they call you to the station again, we go together. If someone shows up with a warrant for your arrest, I'm the first call. Got it?"

"Okay," she said, feeling slightly better. He wasn't a total moron.

"If you remember anything, call me. Let's stay in front of this. And I'll advise you not to discuss this meeting with your sister or anyone else—lest you open the door for the prosecution to challenge our privilege if we need it."

"Okay."

He stood and came around his desk, signaling the end of the meeting. "Be sure Betty out there at reception has your credit card imprint before you leave. It's a hundred for today. We'll go hourly until you get charged, then we can move to a fee schedule for the defense. Sound good?"

"Yeah." She couldn't believe this was her life.

After dealing with reception, they left, and Lisa finally turned to her for information. "So, what did he say?"

"He said he'll represent me if I need him and to contact him if anything else happens."

"Does he think it looks bad for you?"

"He told me not to talk about it. I guess it puts the whole attorney/client privilege in jeopardy."

"Oh. Okay." She put her arm around Grace. "See, it's going to be okay, Gracie. Now, how are you feeling? I know those meds can wipe you out."

"Oh yeah, I'm exhausted," she lied.

Lisa dropped her at the house, told her to rest, and went to work. Grace relished the time alone. She had to finish listening to the doctor's tape. She went to the kitchen where she'd left the key to the truck, but it wasn't on the counter. It wasn't on the hook. She opened one drawer, then another, then another. Then each of the cabinets. It was gone.

She searched the main floor and moved upstairs. Lisa's closet was jammed with clothes, most of which were on the floor. Paintings lined the walls in the small connected room, and she suddenly pictured her mother again—that paint-stained apron, the disheveled hair, a brush in her hand. Grace sat on the floor in front of a brightly colored abstract that bore the name *Elsi* in the bottom right corner—her mom. She studied the flowers, birds, globs of paint that created texture she wanted to reach out and touch, like layers of thoughts and ideas had come together. It was joyous, almost celebratory. She felt along the patterns, examining the tiny details, and noticed some little phrases, affirmations, hidden treasures lightly embedded into the piece: *Family is forever, Love, Peace.* And then, written in the top left corner, she saw her name: *Grace.* A few inches below, written on the petal of a flower with a slightly darker green color and a fine-tipped brush: *Lisa.* She searched for more, like her mother was talking to her through the painting. And then on the petal of a sunflower, written in a delicate orange tint: *Mary.*

Her breath caught in her chest, and the light faded from the room as her mind hurled down a dark tunnel. She heard her mother's bloodcurdling scream, the depth of a despair from long ago. She fell back, the weight of revelation pushing her toward the floor. *Mary*. Tears fell from her closed eyes as she felt the loss. It all made sense now—those initials on the back of the butterfly table, linked together forever, *G* and *M*; the daisy dresses. Mary. Her sister. Her twin.

It had been Mary on that swing. Mary was the one who fell, she suddenly remembered. They'd always felt each other's pain. They'd slept in the same bed, shared clothes and toys and dolls. They'd been inseparable. "We were only five," she said aloud as the pain of losing her twin came back like a violent storm. Mary's death had become a dark cloud that covered this house. It had covered everything.

The painting beside the colorful abstract mirrored that darkness. It was smeared in black, purple, blues, greens, hints of yellow, the brushstrokes weaker. The lightness, optimism, gone. There were no names or words in the piece. She compared the works side by side and sensed her mother's presence. This was Mom: sometimes exquisitely cheerful and loving, other times dark and sad. And Mary's death had brought with it the darkest period. It wasn't a memory or a guess. She just knew.

Grace stood and looked out the window at the backyard, the woods, the shed off to the side. It was the same view her mother must have had when she painted. How did her mother fit in to these traumatic sensations? The screaming, the fear? And where was her dad? She looked down at her arm, at the little scars. It was a horrifying thought, that her father could have done that. How could she forget something like that? Then again, it was almost too disturbing to envision. She wondered what else he might have done.

She went back to Lisa's closet. She didn't know what she was looking for, but she began digging through the pile. It was probably a figurative inclination, but she felt compelled to dig.

A garbage bag full of clothes sat in the back of the closet, under mounds of Lisa's clothes. Grace began riffling through it. Men's clothes. She pulled out several items and thought of the dad she remembered. That vision with the wheelbarrow. He was tall. He was a big man. These clothes wouldn't fit him. And they didn't seem old. A Green Day T-shirt, skinny jeans, too small for someone his size. So whose clothes were they? Why were they hidden in the back of Lisa's closet?

She sat on Lisa's bed, surveying the rest of the space. She'd asked her so many times for information about their past, but what had she really learned? That Michael had a temper? That their father hurt them? It wasn't enough. She'd said Grace was lucky not to remember, that she'd spent years trying to forget. Bullshit. There was nothing lucky about this. Grace was sick of being protected from whatever the truth was. Nothing could be worse than not knowing. And Lisa was obviously hiding more than the key to the truck. She felt sure of it.

She scoured the bedside tables, then moved on to the dresser. The drawers were overstuffed with clothes, 90 percent of which were black, but in the bottom drawer, she saw a small box. She sat in the midst of the mayhem she'd created, opened it, and found pill bottles. At least ten bottles—Ativan, Valium, Lithium, Clozapine—prescriptions for Lisa, for their mom, for Grace. The dates were old, some four years old, some ten. Some bottles were empty, some had a few pills, and one had a funny clink when she shook it. Grace opened the bottle—the key! She got up, put on her coat and boots, and headed for the truck.

With the engine on and the tape playing, she sat back to listen to the last of her sessions with Dr. Newell. The doctor was asking her to share a little about her childhood. Grace leaned forward, her chest practically on the steering wheel as she listened. The silence felt endless. Was she thinking of a response? Had something happened to the tape? But then she heard her voice. It was almost a mumble.

"It was okay."

"Were you a happy child? Did you have friends?"

"It was difficult."

"Why was that?"

"I really don't like to talk about all this. Can't we stick to the present?"

"Grace," the doctor said, "this is the whole point of therapy."

"But the meds are working. I'm sleeping better; isn't that the point?"

"You don't want to be on medication forever. It won't even continue to work forever. Your body will get used to it. I want to know what may be bothering you. What were your parents like?"

"They were sad a lot."

"Depressed?"

"It was a stressful house."

"Go on."

She heard herself take a deep breath before continuing. "My sister died when I was five. After she died, I was alone a lot. I was scared a lot."

"What were you scared of?"

"I never wanted to sleep alone."

"So you were afraid of nightmares?"

"No."

"What were you afraid of?"

Grace didn't respond and the doctor pressed for more.

She finally spoke again. "They said I was a nervous kid. I couldn't go to the woods behind my house or down to the basement."

"And what made you scared of the woods and the basement?"

"I don't remember."

"Come on, Grace."

"Seriously, I've been afraid for as long as I can remember. I don't know why. But I have panic attacks if I get even halfway down the stairs or even a few steps into the woods. It's been like that for as long as I can remember. At some point, I stopped trying to go."

"What did your parents say about it?"

"My mom understood. She knew not to ask me to do laundry because I refused to go down there. Mary and I played together in the woods and in the basement. Mom figured that was why I couldn't be in those places."

"Was she right? Was that it?"

Grace paused before answering. "Honestly, I don't even remember anymore."

"How did Mary die, Grace?"

Grace couldn't hear her response. Then she heard the doctor's voice move farther away from the tape. She was comforting Grace. They agreed to end the session.

Grace sat in the cold cabin of the truck, her chin on the steering wheel, her eyes staring out the windshield at the house. It all felt so close, as if a word or a name was on the tip of her tongue. This was her life. She looked to the house, the shed, the tree swing, the woods. The answers were all here.

TWENTY

BISHOP TOLD HACKETT TO GRAB ALL the evidence and photos from the Cahill file while he began reviewing the information online on the old Abbott murder.

"Who worked that case?" Hackett asked.

Bishop read from the file. "Detective McDougal out of the Buchanan station led the investigation. He retired the next year."

They both quietly read through the notes in the files. It didn't take long.

"Okay. We've got the parents dead in their bed. This went down as a robbery because some of the vics' things were discovered at a pawn shop up in St. Joe a few days later, and the front door glass was broken from the outside. But these people were found in their bed." Bishop paused, like he'd give that tidbit a second to marinate before continuing. "So, if someone breaks in and ransacks a house the way this place was—drawers overturned, furniture knocked over—don't you think you would wake up? But they're both in the bed. They were shot with their own gun."

"What are you thinking?"

"I'm thinking someone snuck into the house, grabbed the gun, shot the parents, and then turned the place upside down. That doesn't sound like the actions of a stranger to me."

Hackett knew this was what he'd do, immediately start looking at the girls, even though someone had already been convicted of the crime.

"In fact, what if it wasn't even really a robbery but staged to look like one?" Bishop continued to scroll through the documents online. "This file is for shit."

"But they got the guy."

"They got *a* guy. A guy who was pawning their stuff in a town thirty minutes away. He said he'd found it under a viaduct. What else did they have on him?"

Hackett abandoned his own case notes and stood behind Bishop, reading the screen over his shoulder. "His fingerprints on a water glass," he said, pointing toward the screen with some satisfaction. "Guy proclaimed innocence but his alibi was another junkie. No credibility."

"A water glass? What, killing people makes you parched?"

"How else do you explain them being there?"

Bishop shook his head and continued to scroll. "No confession. No witness. Dammit. The wife of the guy even said he didn't have a car. She said he sometimes disappeared for days, but she'd always find him under the viaduct with the other drug addicts. He never left town as far as she knew. They didn't even have a logical explanation for how he'd get to Buchanan to commit the murders and get back up to St. Joe with the stuff. Seems to me he may have simply been an easy scapegoat. I don't know. Maybe it was a faulty fingerprinting."

Hackett returned to his desk. "Grace was seventeen years old, and she and Lisa both had solid alibis. And they certainly didn't have a connection to the guy who was convicted. He was some forty-year-old drug addict."

"If I'm right though, and this murder has actually not been solved, the murderer knew exactly where to find the gun and entered quietly. That means the kids should have been prime suspects. You'll see this more in your career, Hackett, but there's pressure to solve a case. Community pressure, sometimes political pressure. Now, I don't know squat about the guys over in the Buchanan Police Department, and I know I'm not from around here, but I'm guessing they have the same pressure facing every department I've ever known. No one likes to have these kinds of crimes go unsolved. Makes them feel unsafe, makes them stop trusting that law enforcement will protect them."

"Are we getting any pressure about this case?" Hackett asked, unable to hide the accusation in his tone.

"You trying to say something?"

His emotions were taking over. "I just feel like we keep circling back here. We've had some interesting leads, but you seem hell-bent on going after Grace. Now you're unearthing an old case, a *solved* case, and pointing fingers at Grace."

Bishop sat back and stared at him. "You'd better watch that tone, kid. Let's remember who has experience between us, shall we? I'm not ignoring anything."

"Maybe you are. Maybe you're determined to pin this on Grace because . . ." He stopped himself.

"What? You got something to say, say it."

"Nothing."

Bishop looked around the small station. No one else was in view. He leaned forward anyway and lowered his tone. "You think this is 'cause of what happened back in Detroit?"

Hackett didn't know what he was talking about. He just thought that maybe Bishop's personal life, his own distractions, made him want to solve the case quickly, too quickly.

"Well, it's not. I've just learned from my mistakes, rookie. Don't ignore the obvious. And if we're gonna point some fingers, I'd say you're the one who seems hell-bent on proving it wasn't Grace Abbott. I think you'd better check yourself." He tossed his pen and went to the break room.

Was he right? Was it his judgment that was too clouded, too emotional, too attached to Grace's innocence, or was it Bishop, too determined to find her guilty? He tried to think methodically, to take out his feelings and focus on the facts. She wasn't happy but she hadn't left Cahill. She'd gotten engaged. She'd hit a tree. He pictured her then, sitting in the wreckage, the shards of glass, her head smashed, when just a few days earlier he'd looked into those beautiful eyes, felt her soft hand in his . . . His thoughts were falling back into a ditch of emotion. "Fuck!" he said. He wasn't objective. He wasn't sure he could be. But there was evidence that made others look bad. Flynn, Jacks, whoever was in those photos, that casino girl. How could they just hone in on one suspect so quickly? But fighting with Bishop wasn't going to help anyone.

When Bishop returned with his coffee, Hackett stood. "I'm sorry. I didn't mean to suggest anything."

Bishop gave him a light punch on the arm before returning to his seat. "No worries, rookie. We're on the same side here. Let's just remember that."

He faked a smile. "Have you heard from Cahill's mother? I was just thinking about what you said about pressure. You'd think she'd be worrying about whether we'd solved this case."

"I haven't, surprisingly. She was certainly anxious to get his body from the ME so she could have a proper funeral. But let's just be glad for that. I don't need any more pressure right now." Bishop returned to reading the case notes on the computer.

Hackett flipped through the papers in front of him, no longer sure what to do. But it was just a moment later when Bishop snapped his fingers. "Hand me that picture from Cahill's crime scene. The one of him on the bed." Hackett complied and Bishop smiled as he turned the screen toward him and held up Cahill's picture beside it.

"What do you see?"

"A lotta blood."

"Come on—look!"

"What?"

"It's the same bed—the wrought-iron frame. Look at that."

"Yeah, so?"

"You don't think that's a bit morbid? Your parents are killed in their bed and you take the bed frame?"

"I don't know. It's only furniture. I took whatever hand-me-downs I could grab when I moved out."

"What was Grace's alibi for her parents' murder?" Bishop said, taking a moment to scroll back through the file and answer his own question. "At a friend's house for a sleepover. Parents of the girl and the friend vouched for her."

"And what was Lisa's?" Hackett asked.

"Also cleared. Lived an hour away at the time. Now, what was the friend's name where Grace stayed that night?" Bishop asked himself.

Hackett waited while Bishop found his own answer on the screen. "Vicki Beckerman," he said with a grin. Bishop looked up from the screen at his partner. "And what do you want to bet that Vicki Beckerman's married name is Vicki Flynn?"

Hackett didn't respond, though he wasn't sure it was necessary. Maybe Vicki Flynn was Grace's alibi three years ago, but so what? Bishop's phone rang and Hackett stood to get some coffee and clear his head.

When he returned to his desk, Bishop was hanging up the phone. "Well, that was interesting."

"What's that?"

"Grace has secured an attorney. He just called to tell me that if we have any further questions for Grace, we should contact him. I told you she was holding something back yesterday. She knows she's in trouble. She left our station and got a lawyer."

Hackett didn't say a word. He needed to figure out a way to deal with these other leads, and quickly. Bishop continued. "I just called my buddy up in Muskegon too."

"What for?"

"West Shoreline Correctional is there. That's a couple hours away, but my buddy owes me a favor." Bishop smirked. "He's gonna pop over there today and talk to Stanford Jones."

Great.

"Kids kill their parents, Hackett. Happens all the time."

TWENTY-ONE

VICKI FLYNN WAS HOLDING HER TODDLER in her arms when she answered the doorbell. Her facial expression dropped when she saw Hackett and Bishop at her door again.

"Officers, did you forget something? Please don't tell me you're here for Wes. He couldn't have done this. I swear."

"May we come in? We need to talk about something else."

She took them back to the kitchen. "Wes just left for work."

They all sat around the kitchen table, and Mrs. Flynn put her daughter on the floor. The toddler quickly scampered away. "Have you found out something new about Mike's death?"

"We want to talk to you about Grace's parents, actually."

"Oh," she said, visibly relieved.

"We noticed from the files that Grace was with you on the night of her parents' murder," Bishop said.

"That's right. I was telling Grace about that yesterday. It's so crazy that she doesn't remember anything."

"You saw Grace yesterday?"

"Sure. I've been so worried about her."

"Well, we realize it's been several years now, but would you mind walking us through what you and Grace did that evening?"

"Why? You don't think that the cases are related, do you?" Before either officer could answer, she continued. "That would be so crazy. But they caught the guy. What—"

Bishop cut her off. "Let's not get ahead of ourselves. Just tell us whatever you can remember about the night Grace slept over."

"Like I said to Grace, I remember that night like it was yesterday. Thanks to my two-year-old, constant reminder."

"What do you mean?"

"Sammy. We conceived her that night." She smiled.

Hackett looked up from his notes. "But Grace was sleeping over at your house, right?"

"That's right, but we hooked up with our boyfriends."

"I don't recall noticing that from the file," Bishop said.

"No. We were only seventeen. They were older. We both, well, I—I would have been in so much trouble with my parents. I figured no one needed to know—it didn't matter. It only mattered that we were together."

"Can you tell us exactly what you all did that night?"

She told them the specifics.

"And when you and Wesley reunited with Grace and Cahill after splitting up for a bit on the beach, how much later was it? Did you go back to the bonfire?" Bishop asked.

"I really don't remember, but I don't think we went to the bonfire. No, the fire was out. Grace and Mike weren't around, so we walked up the stairs and found them in the car already."

"Was either of them acting strange? Anything out of the ordinary?"

Hackett knew what Bishop was doing and held his breath while she responded.

"No," she said, like it was the strangest thing to ask.

"And when the police came to your house, do you recall what time that was?"

"It was in the morning. I remember the doorbell rang. It kind of woke us up and my parents got the door. Then they called us both down."

"And when they told you what had happened to Grace's parents, how did Grace react?"

"Well, obviously, she was in shock."

"Did she cry? Did she faint? How did she react?" Bishop asked.

"She was frozen. Like I said, she was in shock. I don't think she knew how to react."

"And did the officers ask you if she had been at your house all night?"

"Yeah, I mean, not immediately. We all went to the couch to sit. My mom and I were both holding on to Grace; we kind of walked her over to the couch. It was awful."

"But they also wanted to confirm her whereabouts?"

"Well, it was obvious. I mean, they probably said something like, 'And Grace was here all night?' and I'm sure we all said, 'Yeah.'"

Hackett knew what Bishop would think of that—the investigators hadn't focused on Grace at all.

As they drove along the gravel road, the sound of rocks popping under their tires filled the car. They turned onto a paved street and made their way back toward Red Arrow Highway and the station. The air felt like it was getting thicker by the minute, as if the silence building between them was becoming a wall.

"Cherry Beach is about twenty or thirty minutes from the Abbotts' place," Bishop finally said.

"You think she and Cahill killed her parents."

"I don't know. But she was thinking about running off with him. The parents didn't approve and her alibi wasn't actually with her all night. I tell you what, if they did kill her parents, then Cahill'd have something to hang over her if she ever wanted to leave him. I want to know more about this family and—"

"I'm on it," Hackett said. *Be objective; solve the case.* Fuck his gut. He needed to stop thinking about her and just follow the facts. If he did, it would all be okay.

Bishop's cell rang while they were driving back to the station. The caller was obviously one of his kids. One of the younger ones, from the sound of it. It was strange to hear this side of Bishop. The gruff tone was gone. He was trying to soothe the sadness of his child. "Love you, baby," he said before hanging up. Hackett looked away, unsure of the protocol of being privy to this private conversation, but Bishop didn't seem to mind. "I'm gonna head home for lunch today."

"Sure," Hackett said.

"I just think . . ." His voice trailed off then, and his thoughts appeared to be miles away.

Back at the station, Bishop dropped Hackett in the lot and told him to read through the parents' murder file more closely, focusing on the girls. "And get me everything you can on the Abbott family. Any news, police reports, trouble in school, anything."

Hackett grabbed a soda and pulled up the scanned notes from the Abbott file, as well as the interview videos. He clicked on Grace's first. She looked a bit younger than she did now as she sat quietly in her T-shirt and sweatpants, answering the officers' questions. When they were through, she'd asked for tissues, and then, without even looking up from the table, she quietly asked where her sister had been. The officer's first response had been to comfort her, to assure her that her sister was okay, that she hadn't been there either. But Grace shook her head. "No. There was an argument." She explained that Lisa had fought with her parents because they had cut her off financially.

Hackett closed the file and clicked on Lisa's interview. She'd admitted to the argument with their parents, but her parents had been right, she'd said, and she'd said as much in an e-mail she sent to them two days before the murder. Their relationship was fine, she assured the officer. She was living up in Benton Harbor with some guy named Bichon, who confirmed that she had been home with him all night.

Next, he scoured the public records. He looked for arrest records, business licenses, property records, county clerk records, media coverage, anything that search engines or internal records could find.

When Bishop came back to the office an hour later, he went to his desk without acknowledging Hackett and sat there, staring at a family photo on his desk. It looked like it was from a Christmas card, one of those staged shots of the whole clan, all dressed in coordinating colors and posing in front of the fireplace. Bishop's wife sat by his side, the older kids knelt beside the parents like bookends, and the younger two were down front. Their smiles looked natural, a moment of genuine happiness captured for posterity, that rare perfect family photo. Hackett had noticed it before mostly because it brought to mind his own dysfunctional family and their dozens of failed attempts at doing something similar.

"You okay?" he asked.

Bishop snapped out of the trance and gave him a weak grin. "Oh sure, sure. Just not an easy day for the Bishops." He leaned back in his chair then. "I tell ya, kid, it's pretty brutal to see your wife fall apart. And I've been watching that for a few weeks now. But she's strong. I know she'll pull herself together. And she can rationalize the situation, her mom's age, the pain of sickness. She knows she's in a better place. But my kids are so heartbroken. They're just genuinely devastated. And I can't fix it for them. And there's just nothing worse than that helplessness." He wiped his eyes. "It sucks." Hackett nodded, not because he'd known the same loss, but he knew nonetheless. And the image would probably always haunt him: Olivia peeling Donny's arms off of Hackett's neck as the baby wailed, not wanting to let go. "So what'd you find out for me?" Bishop asked, getting them both back to business.

Hackett briefed him on the girls' interviews and alibis and moved on to his more interesting finds. "The parents don't look like they were in trouble with the law. The mother was some sort of painter, had a few pictures hanging at a local coffee shop. But otherwise, she stayed at home with the kids. Found a LinkedIn profile on the father—some sort of tech guy. But this was interesting. Back in 1998, the Abbotts lost a child."

"What do you mean 'lost'? Like a missing person's report? A social services situation?"

"No, I mean dead. A kid, five years old, Mary."

"And were the parents suspected? Any charges filed against them?"

"Initially the mother was questioned pretty seriously. I guess she didn't call for help right away. She couldn't say how long the girl had been missing. She'd said the kids had been playing, and she'd been painting for hours. The mother admitted to bouts of depression. She was on some pretty serious meds at times. But the kid, Mary, was found within a couple of hours in the neighbor's field. Her neck was broken. The neighbor was charged with murder. He was a known violent drunk, and cops had been to his house dozens of times over the years for domestic-abuse stuff."

"And how'd it turn out?"

"Sentenced to twenty-five years. Sent to Oaks Correctional. And guess what else?" He didn't wait for a response. "The neighbor was Michael Cahill."

"As in, Michael Cahill, our vic?"

"As in our vic's father, Michael Cahill Sr. He killed Grace's sister."

"Shit."

"There's more."

"Well—don't leave me hanging. What do you got?"

"He'd been on a bender. Officers found him passed out on the kitchen floor after finding the little girl in his field. The wife had been at the store. Our vic, young Michael Cahill, had been at the Abbotts' house all day."

"And why were they sure it was Cahill Sr.?"

"He'd worked at the Abbotts' house a few times doing handyman-type stuff, and his son played with the Abbott girls all the time. Appears the Abbotts stopped asking him to do work when they noticed bruises on his son. I guess they were all afraid of him. They said he'd had a history of yelling at the Abbott kids, threatening them whenever they came on his property. His wife and child both testified at the trial. He'd been violent with both of them."

"Did he have any kind of defense?"

"Not really. And there was a hair fiber found on the little girl's shirt that didn't match her own."

"And I'm guessing it was a match for Cahill."

"Yep. A mitochondrial DNA test was done. Had to be Michael Cahill's or his son's. And of course the son had an alibi. Cahill Sr. had no alibi, no character witnesses. He couldn't remember anything about the day after breakfast, when he'd started drinking."

"How old were the kids when all this happened?"

"Michael Jr. was fifteen. Lisa was twelve. Grace and her sister were five—twins. The kids, Michael and Lisa, said they'd been playing hide-and-seek, and Lisa saw Mary run to the Cahills' property. The kids said they'd tried to find her for, like, an hour or so before telling anyone."

Bishop didn't respond, so he continued. "This family has had some serious tragedy. I'd say they're about as cursed as the Kennedys."

"I'll give you that. But none of this helps clear Grace Abbott." Bishop rubbed his stubble. "Maybe we're getting sidetracked here. I mean, what do we do with that information? And we're only two people. We can't chase every possibility at one time. We have to stay focused on what's right in front of us."

"But I feel like there might be a connection. Remember when we went through the trash at Cahill's place? There had been an envelope addressed to Cahill. The return address was Oaks Correctional. Remember? There was no letter inside. Don't you think that's interesting?"

"What, do you want to talk to Cahill Sr. in prison and ask what he said?"

"That's the other thing. We can't talk to him. He committed suicide three days before Cahill's murder."

"What?" Bishop pondered that a moment before shaking his head. "I think we're getting lost in tangents. His father may have written him letters for years. Doesn't necessarily have anything to do with anything. We know Cahill never visited him in prison. We still have a girlfriend with no alibi and a solid motive, thanks to those pictures."

"Well, we've also still got ten thousand in cash missing," Hackett said. "Could have been motive, and we've found no connection between that cash and Grace. And what about Jacks and the scopolamine? You wouldn't believe the shit I've read about that drug. You can grow it almost anywhere. Scariest stuff I've ever heard of. And what about the blonde in those pictures?"

"Well, give me another theory."

"Lemme talk to Dave Jacks again. I can't get that drug out of my mind. If nothing comes of it, I'll let it go."

TWENTY-TWO

GRACE WALKED AROUND THE PROPERTY AGAIN, traipsing through the hard, crusted snow that would probably remain on the ground until spring. The temperature was dropping, the wind picking up, and the forecast predicted more snow. She looked down at the ground, at the footprints from her first walk, and followed them back to the shed. That wheelbarrow. Maybe if she'd touch it, she could get that vision back. But the door was locked. She wandered down toward the woods again. She refused to be scared. She needed to face whatever these memories were. She began wandering around the back side of the property. Lisa had said they had more than twenty acres. Perhaps she'd recognize the property line.

She buried her hands into her coat pockets and attempted to shield her face from the cold air with her collar. Up ahead, something, a structure, had been built in one of the trees. A treehouse? She approached the old oak, its trunk at least two feet wide, and looked up at the wood platform in the branches, perhaps twenty feet off the ground. No walls, no roof, only a makeshift railing on two sides. Didn't seem like a treehouse. On the back side of the tree, she saw an old ladder pieced together with various woods. She reached out and touched it. Yes, this was something. She'd been here. She'd climbed this ladder before. She pulled on the rungs to test their strength. Still strong. She began to climb.

Once at the top, she brushed off the snow with her boot and sat cross-legged, taking in the view. She must have done this so many times as a child. The house looked so small and isolated in the center of all this land. There was that big old tree in the front yard, the swing that must have provided at least some moments of joy (or so it seemed from that picture she'd found), Dad's old truck, the shed, and acres and acres of woods.

And then it happened again. She started to feel sick, the taste of saliva filling her mouth, the instinctive need to swallow down whatever was coming up. She closed her eyes for a moment and opened them. The view blurred. She felt dizzy. She took deep breaths. What was it? "Why am I afraid?" she shouted into the void. And then, as if the voice in her head answered, she heard herself, a younger self, a little girl's voice scream, "Stop, no, get me down. I wanna go down!" The sound of laughter followed. Not the girl's. Someone older, someone who found her pain and fear funny. She wrapped her arms around herself, closed her eyes, and concentrated on breathing. Her heart rate slowed. "I'm not scared; you're not scared. We're to-ge-ther, best friends for-ev-er." The words flowed out of her mouth like a singsong chant, something she'd said a thousand times. They'd said it together. She and Mary, their voices blending, their arms holding each other. Her stomach calmed and she felt better. She opened her eyes. "We have each other," she muttered. It's what they'd always said.

Grace carefully climbed down the tree and continued walking along the wood line, looking into the underbrush, her arm outstretched, feeling the branches as they swatted her hand, bending, springing back, their limbs sharp and brittle. As she headed toward the house, she noticed footprints. Not hers, she realized. She traced her former path with her finger: walking to that shed, the woods, collapsing into the snow. She remembered seeing the area where her knees had hit the ground. She scanned the path back up to the house.

No, this was an entirely different path, toward the woods over there. What was over there? And then she saw her mother again, carrying something—a bucket. What was in there? Trash? Food scraps, she remembered. She was going to the big compost pit. The vision faded into the ether. Grace walked in that direction, following the footprints that ended at the edge of the woods. She looked into the brush at a clearing up ahead, about ten feet inside the wood line. But she didn't see a pit. Just dirt and snow.

She made her way back to the house and into the basement. Daylight flooded the space through the windows above the washer, and she stood in front of the mound of stuff in the center of the room, determined to face whatever was down here.

She sat on the cold concrete floor, emptying the contents of an old steamer trunk filled with photographs: school pictures; landscapes; close-up shots of flowers, birds, Grace's young face. Her mom took these shots, she thought. The artist, always observing, studying her surroundings. She stopped at one of the pictures—the backside of a young girl, maybe seven years old, brown wavy hair flowing over her shoulders, sitting with an older boy under a tree. He was smiling. It looked like he was reading her a book. Grace stood and walked to the window, looking out into the backyard. There was the tree.

She found more photographs, birthday cards, art projects. Her parents were in several pictures. Both smiling for the camera. Both looking happy and loving.

She found some photos of Lisa when she was younger too. Nothing too remarkable. Except that she was never with Grace in the pictures. They were each pictured in various moods and moments, but never together.

Grace continued emptying the trunk. She pulled out a painting with her name scrawled along the bottom with the word *Kindergarten*. She studied the picture. A man with a beard, a woman in a skirt, and a child with pigtails, all stick figures, all standing beside a white house, holding hands. The man held a big umbrella that extended over their heads, shielding them from rain. Lots of rain. But the rain didn't come from clouds. Along the top of the picture were drawings that looked like giant insects crawling across the page, with long legs extending out from their oval bodies. A few of the legs were drawn jagged, almost like lightning. Grace rotated the drawing and realized she was not looking at giant insects but at eyes with long lashes, some of which became stormy. The eyes were crying. The family and the house were covered in tears.

She piled the contents onto the floor and studied the empty trunk's interior. Its scent, like mothballs or mildew, was familiar. Yellow satin, torn in several places, lined the inside of the top. She traced her fingers through the ripped material. Her heart began to race. She heard pounding, like feet or hands, kicking a box, a young girl shrieking. She felt queasy and tried to calm her breathing—it was all happening too quickly. Her rib cage ached; she felt possessed by this little girl's cry. She slammed the trunk shut and scooted away, shaking, hands over her eyes, desperate to stop the screaming that filled her head.

But she couldn't escape it. She was inside, blinded in darkness, scratching frantically, tearing fabric, shouting, *Get me out! I want to get out!*

She opened her eyes, shocked, and sucked in air. Rocking back and forth on the cold concrete, she wept. She wanted out of this house, out of this mind.

~ • ~

Bishop made it clear before Jacks arrived that he was simply humoring his partner. Hackett didn't care. He hoped it meant Bishop would let him take the lead this time, and he said as much as Jacks walked into the station. Bishop patted him on the back. "Sure, rookie. Have at it." They led Jacks to an interrogation room and suggested he take a seat, but he refused.

"Guys, if I need an attorney, you have to tell me. It's the law."

Hackett smiled and sat at the table. "You can call an attorney anytime you want. You don't have to talk to us. But I was just hoping you might be able to help us. Please," he added, motioning for Jacks to join him.

Jacks pulled out a chair, and Bishop took the seat directly across from him and leaned forward. "I think you'd better tell us how you were involved with Grace and Cahill." He patted Hackett's arm and sat back in his chair, nodding, as if Hackett could now begin.

So much for giving him the lead. "I wasn't involved," Jacks said, removing his hat and coat. "Grace works at my restaurant. That's it." His expression remained steady but his voice cracked. Hackett opened his mouth to speak, but Bishop said, "Come on, Dave. You're in love with Grace. You want to protect her. We get it." Hackett almost threw his pencil in frustration.

"Who said that?" Jacks asked.

Hackett jumped in. He had to take charge. "There are pictures of her all over your house. She gets engaged, and the next morning her boyfriend is dead."

"I told you, I was with Sheri that morning."

"You drugged Sheri," Hackett said. "That alibi isn't gonna work for you."

"That's bullshit, man. Fuckin' women. They're all over you and then it's like they wake up and you're not good enough anymore."

"Cut the shit," Hackett said. "You had a nice little supply of scopolamine at your place. All we have to do is run a hair test on Sheri and it's gonna confirm what we already know."

"Hey, man, I may have had some pot at my place, but nothing else in that house is illegal."

Bishop leaned in again, but Hackett put his hand on his arm. This was his tangent. "You didn't have a prescription. And a medical dose is less than one milligram. Those little capsules had about eight times that amount. It may not be a controlled substance, but you're obviously aware of its powerful side effects. That was a homemade supply, and the woman you were with the morning of the murder says she was drugged. No memory of sleeping with you. Someone drugged Cahill with something too. All roads are leading to you, Dave."

"Sheri Preston is a fucking liar. And those pills are recreational. I take them to relax. We both did."

"Come on, Dave, it's a little late to play dumb."

"I'm not a murderer!"

Bishop jumped back in. "If you're protecting Grace, you might want to rethink this. She put you up to it?"

"What?"

Hackett opened his mouth, but Bishop beat him to the punch. "Whoever killed Cahill didn't act alone. Right now it's looking like a good circumstantial case against you—you want to take the fall?"

"Oh my God, this is crazy," Jacks said.

Bishop turned up his intensity. "Everyone says you were obsessed with Grace. Maybe she took advantage of your feelings. Convinced you to do something you didn't want to do. You don't seem like a violent guy, Dave. No record. Don't let that girl get away with something and spend your life in prison. Maybe she said if you got rid of Cahill, you could be together?"

"What? No!"

Hackett didn't like where this was going. Jacks might throw Grace under the bus just to get off the hook. He needed them to stay focused on that drug. "What are you doing drugging people without their knowledge?"

"I didn't!"

"I've been reading up on that stuff you had in your apartment, Dave. 'Devil's Breath,' some call it. Big in Colombia. Used to rob, rape. Doesn't take all that much, and the victims don't even know what's going on. They become so docile you can make them do anything."

Jacks opened his mouth but stopped himself. He wiped his brow. Hackett let him have a moment. Bishop leaned forward, but Hackett threw his arm out to stop him again. He wanted to see where Jacks would go with this.

"I didn't know it was that bad. I swear."

Hackett nodded. "You heard of roofies, right, Dave? When a person is given a roofie, he can be hypnotized later and will usually recall what happened. With scopolamine, it isn't possible to remember because the memory is never recorded. The drug interferes with the part of the brain that records events. Do you have any idea how serious it is to even have that stuff?"

Jacks's face and neck flushed red; his eyes watered. "I didn't do anything to Michael Cahill. I swear to God. Yes, I've always had a crush on Grace. Yes, I was sad that she got engaged, but that's it."

The truth was finally emerging. Hackett pushed a piece of paper and pen across the table. "Write down the names of every person who was at your party on Friday."

Jacks took the paper and began writing. "I don't even know everyone's last name. I know the staff's, of course, but other friends are really first name only."

"Just do the best you can."

Bishop obviously had less patience. "So you're going to go down for this alone, huh?"

"I slipped Sheri a pill. But that doesn't mean anything. I never did anything to Michael."

"Why'd you slip her the pill, Dave?"

"So she'd consider me."

"What do you mean?" Hackett asked.

"I was told that they'd loosen someone up. Make 'em give someone another look. I don't have the best luck with women, okay?"

"Dave, who else have you given the pills to?"

He didn't respond immediately; Hackett could sense he was trying to calculate how much to say.

"You're in a heap of trouble here," he said. "Slipping someone a drug and sexually assaulting her? We're talking criminal sexual conduct in the first degree. Of course, we haven't decided whether or not to charge you. But if you can help us in this Cahill case, things might go a little better for you."

His head dropped, his focus now on the table. "I've only used them twice."

"Who else?"

Jacks hesitated and Hackett slammed his hand on the table.

"Grace," he finally admitted. "One night we were all out drinking. She always looked at me. I got the sense that maybe she could like me, but she had a boyfriend."

"So you thought you'd drug her."

"It wasn't like that. I only wanted her to give me a chance. Drop her defenses."

"When did this happen?"

"Like, a month ago."

"Did you bring Grace back to your place?"

"No. I took her to Cherry Beach. We kissed. She didn't resist. I looked in her eyes and knew there was a chance. We got in my car and I knew she'd go anywhere with me. I started driving to my place, but then I played it out. Michael was a pretty big dude. I panicked. I drove her home and got her inside before I left."

"Was he home at the time?"

"His car was there. It was, like, four in the morning though. He was asleep. I laid her on the couch and left."

"Did Grace remember being with you?"

"If she did, she never said so. I told her at work that I enjoyed our night together."

"And what did she say?"

"Not much."

Hackett nodded.

"But I never drugged Michael. I barely knew the guy. No one ever asked me to kill him, certainly not Grace."

"Where'd you get the drugs?"

"This guy I know, Tucker. He's into all sorts of homegrown shit. We were hanging out one night at the restaurant, and I shared my girl troubles and he offered them to me. Said they'd be fun. Said they make girls take a second look, that's all. Open up to the idea. I never knew they were considered a 'date rape' drug."

Bishop snorted. "You had to know that drugging a woman in order to get her into bed is a crime."

Jacks rubbed his eyes hard before answering. "I wasn't thinking. It was dumb." Hackett and Bishop glanced at each other. "I swear," he said, "I didn't kill anyone!"

"And when did you buy the drugs from this Tucker?"

"I didn't even buy them. He gave them to me!"

"And if we met with Tucker, you think he'd tell us the same story?"

"I don't know. But it's the truth. Go find him. He works at that auto shop where they have the card games."

Hackett's brows rose. "Was Tucker there last Tuesday night when you went to the card game?"

"Yeah, he was the one who took down Mike when he started going crazy."

"So Tucker's like a bouncer at the card games?"

"Kind of, yeah. He's actually always trying to get in on the games, saying how broke he is, how he needs a chance to win one of those big pots. But his boss never lets him. Makes a good bouncer though. He's not a big guy, kinda scrawny actually, but no one messes with him 'cause he's crazy. I heard he bit a dude's nose once."

Hackett continued. "Did Tucker know Michael Cahill?"

"No idea."

"Did you hear any words exchanged between Cahill and Tucker when he was kicked out?"

"Nah. I mean, Tucker's not a bad guy, really. He may look like a badass with all those tattoos, but he's always nice to me. He's a good time. He's just not afraid of anything. Fancies himself a psychonaut."

Bishop piped up. "Psycho-not?"

"That's what he called himself," Jacks said. "Like an astronaut. I guess there are a lot of these people. He said it was about 'exploring the frontiers of the mind.' He thought that all these different drugs unlock different portions of our brains. Very new-agey, really. They all are."

"Who?"

"These psychonauts. I guess there's a whole subculture that is completely into experimenting with psychotropic drugs—allegedly for religious or spiritual purposes. I asked him where he got the stuff, where he learned about all this, and he told me everything he ever needed to know was on the Internet. Anyway, he's a cool guy."

"Sure he is. He gives out free drugs to rape women," Hackett said.

Jacks closed his eyes and rubbed his face.

Hackett stood and Bishop followed, and they left Jacks to stew for a bit. Jacks didn't even ask whether he'd been arrested or if he needed a lawyer. He seemed willing to stay, as if somehow confessing to loving Grace and slipping her the drugs would show that he was cooperating and had nothing to hide.

Bishop leaned against the wall in the hall, arms crossed. "So what are you thinking here?" His cell rang and he held up his hand while he took it. Hackett watched Bishop walk to his desk and jot down some notes during the call. His own line rang then and he went to his desk to answer. It was the phone company. They'd finished gathering Grace's phone records and had e-mailed the logs to the station. Both he and Bishop were to look out for copies in their in-boxes. He was out of time.

A moment later, Bishop hung up the phone.

"So?" Hackett asked.

Bishop threw down his pen. "That was my buddy who went over to see Stanford Jones in prison. Stanford Jones, now recovering addict, three years sober thanks to the state of Michigan, seems to have found God. Still says he didn't kill the Abbotts. Maintains that he found the stuff under the viaduct where he and several other junkies spent most of their days. Said he'd never even gone to Buchanan. He didn't know the Abbotts and didn't have a car."

"What about his prints found on that glass at the house?"

"Said he'd spent a lot of time wondering about it. Apparently, he got pretty philosophical with my buddy. Said he wasn't sorry to be in prison, that prison saved his life, that maybe someone or something wanted to save him."

"Oh boy."

"Yeah. He said prison was a blessing, and he hated to think of where he might be if this hadn't happened. Said no one deserved the shit he'd put them through."

"What shit? Who?"

"His wife, the kids. A bunch of fosters. I guess they had foster kids for the state money. Sorry excuse for a man, that's for sure." Bishop stood up. "Come on, let's wrap this up with Jacks."

Hackett remained in his chair. "Wait. I think we've still got something here."

"What?"

"Jacks has drugged two women with this scopolamine, and his supplier, someone who's a known crazy guy and desperate for money, is also now connected to Michael Cahill. We know the drug is used to rob people, and Cahill had ten thousand dollars when he was murdered that we can't find. I'm telling you, this scopolamine turns people into zombies."

Bishop chuckled and took a seat on the side of his desk. "Rookie, I think you're getting a little carried away here. Let's stick to the facts."

"I'm serious," Hackett said, pulling out his notepad and quickly flipping the pages. "I spent a lot of time reading all about it. The drug was used in the 1900s during childbirth because it helped women get through labor. They couldn't remember anything even though they'd been awake and coherent and able to have a conversation and participate in the birth process. Then the CIA started using it to interrogate criminals because they realized people had no free will while on it. They'd do or say whatever."

"Where'd you get all this information?"

"Internet. Listen." He checked his notes again. "CIA stopped using it because of the undesirable side effects—hallucinations, disturbed perception, blurred vision, headaches, et cetera. But at least in South America, where so much of the"—he turned back to his notes then and struggled with the pronunciation—"the *Borr-a-chero* tree it comes from is plentiful, it's a commonly used criminal weapon. Only takes a few minutes to kick in, and if the dose is strong enough, the effects can last anywhere from eight to eighteen hours."

Bishop put his hands up in defeat. "Okay, pull back a little. Jacks is right; it's not even a controlled substance. I'm thinking some of what you've heard might be a little overblown. And we still don't know if that's what was given to Cahill, or even if that had anything to do with his murder. It might be that this is some new recreational drug that's going around right now, totally unrelated to our murder investigation."

Hackett interrupted again. "This is serious shit. People are growing it in the States, buying seeds online, and raising plants hydroponically or in gardens."

"Okay, okay. I believe you. But we don't know what, if anything, that has to do with our murder. What I do know is that we've got a girl with no alibi and a motive to kill, and so far, no other leads are floating to the surface. I think it's time to share our progress with the prosecutor."

Hackett's face flushed; his heart pounded in his chest. His personal feelings were in the way, but someone had to protect Grace. He was almost shouting now. "We've stumbled onto this memory-blocking drug, and your prime suspect currently has no memory."

"What are you saying, that Grace has been slipped this drug? That Grace committed this crime while under its influence?"

"I don't know what I'm saying yet. I mean, I guess it's possible," he had to admit. He flopped back against his chair in frustration. Had the drug made her do something she would never normally do? "We need to find this Tucker guy. Maybe we just got a lead. This whole 'psychonaut' business is too weird—Tucker's obviously on drugs much of the time. Jacks said he was a loose cannon and people think he's crazy. If he knew Cahill won that money, I mean . . ."

He was losing Bishop. "I'd rather see if Grace's prints were on those naked pictures. We should have found out by now, so—" Bishop's cell buzzed and he looked down to read a text, then began typing a response. Hackett waited for him to finish. He had to tell Bishop about the print results, but if he could just follow up on these leads first . . .

Bishop put down the phone and looked at Hackett. His expression had changed. Bishop eyed him cautiously. "Come with me," he said. Hackett silently followed him to the hall. Bishop opened the door to the empty interrogation room opposite Jacks's. "Get in here." Before he could speak, Bishop shut the door behind them. "I think you'd better start telling me what the fuck is going on here."

Oh shit. Hackett didn't speak immediately. He felt like a child, as his automatic expression of incredulousness tried to mask his guilt.

"I wanna know why you're concealing evidence."

It was an instinctive reaction: "I'm not."

"That was a text from Miles, saying he found another match for the second set of prints on the photos."

"That's great," Hackett said carefully.

"Why didn't you tell me that Grace's prints are on those pictures?"

It was the prints. Just the prints. Relief weakened his knees, but before Hackett could respond, Bishop growled, "You know, you accused me earlier of tunnel vision, but all I see is someone determined to find a way to punch holes in our leads and prevent me from seeing evidence that implicates my prime suspect."

That was when he knew it was over. He had to confess now—the phone logs would only make things worse. But how would he make Bishop see what he knew in his heart?

He took a seat at the table, allowing several chairs and space between them. He exhaled slowly. "I have to tell you something about Grace."

TWENTY-THREE

HACKETT LEANED FORWARD. There was no turning back now. "I kind of know Grace."

"What?" Bishop's face grew brighter, his eyes wide.

Hackett held up his arm, as if Bishop might jump up and tackle him at any moment. "Hold on. Here's the thing. I didn't even know her name before this case happened. I swear. I had dinner at her restaurant a few times. I saw her a couple of times out at bars in New Buffalo, and I tried to make conversation. She was always nice but with other people, and I never got her name."

It must not have sounded too bad yet. Bishop's face softened and he sat back and crossed his arms. "Why wouldn't you tell me this?"

"A couple of weeks before the murder, I saw her at this bar, The Pub. She was with some friends who were playing pool, but she was staring off into space, sitting alone in the corner, looking distracted and sad. I tried to make conversation, but she was polite, brushed me off, and said that she had a boyfriend. Then about a week later—this was just about a week before Cahill's murder—I saw her again and she was in much better spirits. I asked why I never saw her with her boyfriend—I was flirting a bit—and she shared that their relationship wasn't exactly good. I've been through some shit myself, and I could see that she wasn't happy. I said she was too young to waste time with someone who wasn't good enough for her. I suggested she break up with whomever it was and meet me for dinner."

"When exactly was this?"

"Sunday before the murder. We know now that Michael Cahill was at The Rack that night. The dinner date I proposed was for the following Thursday."

"What did she say?"

"I knew she was considering it. She actually said that she'd been thinking about leaving him for a long time, and she had just gotten word that she'd been accepted for on-campus housing. But she obviously didn't feel like it was right to talk to me about it. I was just some guy in a bar. She asked about me and I told her about my last relationship. I figured she'd see that I knew it wasn't easy to end something even when it was wrong. We sat in that corner talking for a long time. Granted, it was mostly about me, but we made a connection. She asked a lot of questions. When she was getting ready to leave, she almost told me her name, but I stopped her. I said she could tell me her name at dinner. It would mean that she had broken up and was free to be with me."

Bishop leaned forward, elbows on the table, and put his head in his hands without a word. Hackett knew he had to go on. "There's more."

Bishop didn't even look up but waved his hand to continue.

"After she walked out with her friends, I ran after her. They'd all turned the corner, and I asked her to hold up for a moment. She stopped and I took her hands in mine. I said something like, 'I really hope I see you Thursday.' She smiled at me without saying a word. And then I kissed her."

Bishop's head shot up, the anger in his eyes highlighted by his clenched jaw. "What?"

"It was just a kiss. It was only for a moment, but she wasn't upset; it wasn't offensive. Nothing too demanding, it was just . . . I wanted her to remember me. We smiled at each other and she thanked me. She said it was the best birthday present she'd had in years. Then she ran off to join her friends. And I went home pretty sure that we had a date for the following Thursday."

"And did she show up at dinner?"

"No. Now we know that she got engaged on Thursday instead."

Bishop stood from his chair and slammed his fist against the table. "Why the fuck didn't you come clean as soon as you saw her picture?"

"Please. Sit." Hackett lowered his voice. "I'll tell you everything."

"I can't believe the shit I'm hearing right now. I'm given a rookie officer for this case, a guy who's never worked a homicide, and this is the shit you pull."

"I couldn't say anything. When she didn't show, I was upset. I even went to the restaurant again on Friday, hoping I could see her and talk to her . . ."

Bishop sat heavily. "Oh my God, it gets worse."

"She called me. I'd given her my number. She left a message and said she was sorry for not showing. That it was simply bad timing. And she hung up."

"When was this?"

"I heard the message late Friday, but I think it was from earlier in the day. I'm guessing you'll find my number on those call logs we just got."

"Don't you see what an absolute idiot you are? This is all relevant to the case. For fuck's sake!"

Hackett dropped his head. "I was afraid. I . . . I saw her on Friday. Leaving the restaurant where she worked. And I chickened out. She looked fine. I mean, I don't know what I thought she'd look like. I guess I feared I'd see a black eye or something. But she drove off in her car and I followed her home."

"Goddamn. You're . . ."

"I know. I don't know what I thought I'd do, but I watched her walk inside. And then I drove away."

Bishop was shaking his head.

"I know it's crazy. I'm not some crazy stalker. I just . . . You know when you meet someone and there's this spark. It's so real, it's like you've known this person your whole life, or you're going to know her your whole life. I couldn't believe that she didn't show, and I got worried. I thought, what if this guy is abusive?

"Then on Monday, when I got the call about something going on at that address, I was terrified of what I'd see. I thought I was going to find her dead. I couldn't even speak. I couldn't say anything. I just needed to get inside. And then we found him. There was a part of me that was terrified for her but also terrified for myself. What if someone saw me follow her home or saw me with her at The Pub, saw me kiss her? And I walked through the crime scene stunned, my mind reeling, realizing I could be a suspect. I got back to the station and met you and heard I'd been assigned to the case. I had to take it."

Bishop had no words. His head was in his hands, his fingers circling his temples while veins bulged in his head. He took some deep breaths.

"I know it doesn't make sense to you, but I really felt something for this girl. We'd barely met, but I knew . . . this girl would change my life."

Bishop began to speak but Hackett cut him off. "If I'd told you I had asked her out, you'd remove me from the case, saying there was a conflict of interest. I couldn't do that."

"Of course there's a goddamn conflict of interest."

"I had to find out what happened to her. And then when we found out she was alive and went to the Abbotts' house, when I saw her, I knew in my gut she didn't do anything. I know her. I needed to be on this case."

"You didn't even know her name."

"But I know her."

"You're an idiot. And now you've jeopardized our entire investigation."

"I—"

"Say we charge Grace, which I still see signs pointing toward. Say her attorney finds out that you asked her out. That she stood you up. Don't you think a defense attorney is going to scream 'FOUL!'? That this is a vendetta, that she's being railroaded?"

"We can't charge Grace. There are too many unanswered questions. Too many potential suspects here. There's still a lot to figure out."

"Well, you're not figuring shit. You're off the case. If I have my way, you're suspended too, and goddammit!" He stood up.

"But . . ."

Bishop pointed toward the door. "Get the fuck out of here."

TWENTY-FOUR

LISA CAME IN THE BACK DOOR around dinnertime, carrying a bag of fresh bread from the bakery. Grace was lying on the couch in the darkened living room, watching her. "Hey," she said, without moving from her spot.

"Holy shit, Grace, you scared me." Lisa walked into the room and began turning on the lights. "What're you doing in the dark? Headache?" She didn't respond immediately and Lisa stopped at the sight of the beers on the table. "What are you doing? I didn't think you were supposed to have alcohol."

She sat up slowly. "No big deal. I was just thirsty." She didn't tell Lisa that she'd stopped taking the medications or that she'd had both beers in a quest to calm her nerves after another day of what were starting to feel like panic attacks. She didn't feel like explaining herself anyway. She wasn't the one who needed to talk. She was jealous of Lisa's memories, angry that she hadn't shared more, irritated by her coddling. She was sick of it, and she wanted some answers.

"What happened to Mary?" Grace asked.

Lisa's pale face seemed to turn blue. "What are you talking about?"

"Our sister. My twin. How'd she die?"

"Did you remember something?"

Grace stood. "Answer the fucking question! Why won't you tell me about my life? Why are there all those bottles of pills in your dresser? Why are there men's clothes hidden in the back of your closet?"

Lisa threw her purse across the room, stalked over, and shoved her. "Who do you think you are, going through my stuff? Who told you to go in my room? You're lucky I'm even letting you stay here." Lisa's rage was palpable.

"I'm sorry," Grace said, startled by the anger. Was Lisa resentful of her too? Maybe she resented her caretaker role, Grace's constant questions, her distance. Grace softened her voice to a near whisper, hoping a meek tone would soothe Lisa. "I sit here all day trying to sort through my life. This is our house! I feel like all the memories, everything I need to know, is right here, right under my nose. I need to remember."

Lisa collapsed onto the sofa with Grace and took her hand. Grace instinctively winced and tried to pull away, but Lisa held firm. Grace looked at her and Lisa smiled. "It's okay. I'm sorry I freaked out on you. I guess I'm just used to being by myself. Don't get me wrong. I'm happy to have you here. I guess that just felt a little too much like what it was like when we were kids—you were always getting in my stuff. It drove me crazy," she said, her tone and mood softening. "This house has always been a bit of a pharmacy. Those pill bottles are old though. I know it's weird, but it's part of how I remember them, how I remember all of us together. Mom was a mess. She suffered from depression, and after Mary died, it only got worse. I had some stupid diagnosis of anger issues as a kid. It was bullshit. We were all a little fucked up. How could we not be?"

Grace opened her mouth to ask more, but Lisa cut her off. "The clothes you found, those were my ex's. He left a couple of weeks ago."

She watched Lisa's face when she spoke, aching to catch every movement, hint, feeling, or subtext. "Why haven't you talked about him?"

Lisa's eyes welled with tears. She let go of Grace's hand and covered her face. "And when would I have done that?" she said sarcastically.

Grace didn't respond.

"I'm sorry. I don't . . . I didn't want . . . It's just been hard, that's all. You don't even remember me, you don't remember anything, you have your own problems. It just didn't seem worth mentioning."

It felt like a breakthrough. Lisa was finally sharing, at least a little. "Did he live here?"

"Off and on."

"Was it serious?"

"I thought so." She swiped at her tears. "Typical girl, right? I think it's a big deal, and he thinks I'm nothing special."

Grace took her hand. They both looked at their entwined hands and then at each other and smiled. It felt momentous. "And this happened right around the time of the accident?"

"Yeah. I haven't seen him in, what"—she paused—"almost two weeks. I should be done crying by now. Fucker." They both chuckled.

"So why keep his stuff? I say get rid of it. Right?"

"I just hoped he'd come back."

Grace patted her hand then. "Well, sis, I know you're older, but seems like we both could use some lessons in self-esteem. I mean, don't we both deserve guys who will treat us right?"

Lisa nodded. "Yeah, but it still hurts. Even if he wasn't the right one, he was mine. And maybe it's just inevitable."

"What?"

"History repeats itself, right? We had a volatile childhood and we both ended up with volatile men." Lisa stood up and went to the fridge for a beer. "You want another?"

Grace relaxed back against the sofa. "Sure. I know you think it's better that I don't remember what happened to us, but it's not. I need to know what happened in this house."

Lisa opened her bottle and chugged half its contents before answering. She didn't turn, just stared at the fridge. "Let it go, okay? Our parents sucked. Our family sucked. You were . . ." She stopped herself.

"What?"

"Nothing."

That tone. She felt an unspoken accusation. "Are you mad at me?"

"That's stupid."

Grace wondered if she'd done something to Lisa. She stood and went to her. "We weren't close. And now you're taking care of me. Maybe you'd rather I go . . ."

Lisa turned to her with a smile so fake it was like a clown's painted face. It was difficult to look at. "You're my sister. I love you and I want to take care of you." It was like a script. Like she was being recorded. "Now go into the living room and relax while I make us some dinner."

Grace had hit a brick wall. She'd only succeeded in creating more distance between them. "Well, hopefully you won't have to take care of me too much longer. I feel like things are starting to come back. So far, just little snippets from childhood, but it's just a matter of time, right?"

Lisa didn't answer.

"Oh, and I have some good news," Grace said.

"Yeah, what's that?" Lisa said, like she was barely paying attention.

"Officer Hackett came to visit me yesterday. He said he doesn't think I killed Michael, and he's looking into a different angle. He thinks it may have been about a robbery."

"A robbery?" Lisa said. She opened a cabinet and shuffled through some of the canned goods. "That's weird. I mean, what did you guys have at that house that was worth anything?"

Grace wandered back toward the living room, feeling her headache start to return. "Well," she called out, "they discovered that

Michael won ten thousand dollars at the casino on Friday. Hackett seems to think that might be what this is all about."

"That's great news," Lisa said. "Why would you steal from your own fiancé?"

"Exactly." She lay down on the couch, watching Lisa grab the can opener.

"How's your head today?" Lisa called from the kitchen.

"Not too bad."

"You take all your meds?"

Lisa was standing over the empty counter, where the little piles of pills had been sorted for Grace's ease. "Yes," she replied, instinctively feeling her jeans pocket, now full of pills.

"Good," Lisa said. "I'm making soup, okay?"

"Sounds nice."

Grace turned on the television while Lisa focused on getting a meal together. Grace felt the beers kicking in, and she was now too tired to say much more. They ate in silence and twenty minutes later, Grace could barely get up from the couch. Lisa came over to help. "Here, sis. Let's get you off to bed. It's getting late anyway."

"What time is it?" she asked, though she heard her words slur as they came out of her mouth.

"Late," Lisa said.

She tucked Grace into bed like a child, and Grace felt herself sinking deeper and deeper into the mattress as if she weighed a thousand pounds. She couldn't keep her eyes open. Lisa sat, stroking Grace's hair, saying, "Don't worry. It'll all be over soon."

Within minutes, Grace was out.

~ • ~

Hackett sat at the nearly empty bar at The Pub, amazed by the speed at which he'd fucked up this investigation, his job, maybe his whole career path. Alice had allowed him a steady flow of drinks since he came in, but now the bar was beginning to quiet down, and his refill requests seemed to be conveniently forgotten. Just a few other patrons remained, shooting pool.

A cold air blew into the room as the front door opened. A moment later he felt the presence of someone standing behind him. "Hey, bro."

The voice was as familiar as his own. He didn't turn around. "I got nothing to say to you."

"I know, but we gotta deal with this." The man took a seat next to him.

Hackett looked straight ahead and sipped his beer. "How'd you find me?"

"Mom gave me your address. I saw you walk in here an hour ago. Just took me a little while to get up the guts to come inside. Figured maybe it would be better if you'd had a few drinks first."

"I don't want to talk to you."

"I never meant to hurt you, J."

He'd been called nothing but kid, rookie, and Officer Hackett for months. No one had gotten close enough. Except Grace. He'd told her his name was Justin, and she'd repeated it, smiling. *Nice name,* she'd said. His heart had melted. But his family called him J, Little J, Baby J, J.Z., J.J., and countless other nicknames. Hearing it now, the pain of missing everyone came rushing back.

"Please, come home for Christmas. Donny misses you."

Hackett tried not to flinch at the sound of that name. He refused to look at Joe. "Get out of here."

"Come on, I drove all this way. Have a beer with me. Let's forget everything that's happened for thirty minutes. Pretend I'm not the asshole. I'm still your brother."

Hackett turned and punched him, square in the jaw. Joe fell back, stumbling into the chairs behind him, until he was on the floor.

The few patrons immediately took notice and scampered back in case a full fight was beginning.

"No, no!" Alice yelled. "Not in here, Hackett, you know I can't have this in here."

Joe put up his arm, waving toward Alice. "It's okay." He wiped his lip, licked the blood, and slowly got back to his feet. "Nothing happening here."

Hackett ignored him and turned back to his beer.

Alice stepped over to Hackett. "You okay?"

"Sorry about that. It was a long time coming."

She turned to Joe, who was making his way back toward the bar. "Sorry, fella, but I think you'd better get outta here. I don't want any trouble, and it's pretty clear that Officer Hackett doesn't want to talk to you."

"Okay, okay," he said to Alice. But then he put his hand on Hackett's shoulder. "I love you, bro. I'm sorry."

After he left, Alice asked, "What was that all about?"

Hackett didn't answer.

"That why you don't want to go home for Christmas?"

"Yep."

"Your brother."

"Yep."

"Wanna talk about it?"

"Nope."

She refilled the nut bowl in front of him and poured him another Bud. "On the house," she said.

He sat at the bar for another thirty minutes, staring into his beer, examining his hand—he hadn't punched a guy in years—and wondering how he'd been able to throw away his career in one week.

Alice came back over to him. "You know, sometimes it helps to talk."

Her persistence made him smile. Hell, it was nice to have someone to talk to these days. He rested his elbows on the bar, massaging his temples, scanning the room. "I never wanted to be here."

"Where? Michigan? This town? This bar?"

"You know, my dad's a cop. My brothers are all cops." Alice's eyebrows rose and he knew what she was thinking. "So yeah, I just punched a cop." They both chuckled. "Everyone's in Indiana. Same town, some even down the street from each other."

"Well, I guess that could be fun. Depends on the family, of course."

"It was awesome. And when I was gonna get married, I got a house just down the street."

"Kid, don't take this the wrong way, but what was your hurry? You're only, what, twenty-five?"

He smiled. "Twenty-six. My girl got pregnant."

"Ah. That'll do it."

"I wasn't even upset. I wanted what my parents had, what my brothers had. I had been dating Olivia on and off since eighth grade. I'd had a crush on her first. She was 'that girl,' you know? The one who commanded attention, who knew she was hot shit. She walked into a room and all eyes went her way. I worshipped her."

Alice propped herself up to sit on the back counter. She was in no hurry for this to end.

"So a couple of years ago, we move in together, down the street from my family. I wanted to get married, but she said she wasn't ready. I figured we were young, it would happen. But then she got pregnant. So, obviously, I begged her to marry me. I loved her. I love kids. Hell, I have, like, nine nieces and nephews already. I thought it sounded great. Our kid would have lots of cousins and grandparents around. The families would all be together. She said she wasn't sure she wanted the baby, but then everyone got involved and she agreed.

"She wanted to wait until after the baby was born—she didn't want to be a pregnant bride. I could understand it. My folks are pretty old-school Catholic, so are hers, but I knew it didn't really matter."

Alice poured herself a fresh beer and leaned onto the bar for more. "I feel like I know where this is going," she said, nodding.

"When the baby was born—best day of my life. We named him Donald after her father and called him Donny." He pulled out his phone and shared a photo.

"Nice," Alice said.

"Olivia kept putting off the wedding planning. I mean, after a few months, I thought, what are we waiting for? But I came home early one day and heard her yelling. She was standing in the kitchen, her back to me, banging pots around, and didn't see me come in. She yelled into the phone, 'So what am I waiting for?' I thought maybe she was on the phone with the cable company—they were supposed to come out and maybe they hadn't shown up. Donny was in his bouncing chair—he was five months old by then, and that kid's smile when I entered the room was all I needed for a greeting. He was reaching out to me, and I went to pick him up when I heard her say, 'But he's your son.'"

Alice shook her head and took a sip.

"Yeah. Somewhere deep inside, I think I knew she'd cheated. There was always a part of her that was a mystery. I'd always thought there were layers to her that might take years to uncover. I kind of liked the idea of growing closer over time. She turned and saw me holding Donny. She dropped the phone, and it was like there was nothing else to say. There was no misunderstanding. Donny wasn't mine."

"I'm so sorry, kid. And your brother? I take it he's involved in this."

"'Fraid so. Everything exploded pretty quickly after that. She said she knew I would be a good dad, but she was in love with someone else. She was sorry. And my brother, that asshole you met earlier, he tells me to take off, that I'm young and the town's too small. He said I should get a fresh start. 'Marriage is a bitch,' he said. In fact, his wife was leaving him too. Taking the kids. Just across town, but still. 'Don't look back,' he said."

Alice was shaking her head. She knew exactly where this was going.

"It was all a lie. Donny was his. He just didn't have the balls to tell me."

"So now Christmas is coming and you're supposed to go back and be with them."

"Yep. My mother calls every Tuesday like clockwork. I mean, after that bomb went off, the family just swept it aside and returned to life as normal. Joe and Olivia moved in together. His ex has even moved in with another guy already. He's getting divorced and acting like nothing ever happened. It's the new normal. But Donny was mine. I was at the hospital when he was born. I fed him. I changed his diapers. I held him all those nights. And now I'm supposed to move on."

Alice put down her drink and moved closer. "Well, I know you seemed a little cagey before when I brought this up, but I did see you flirting with a young girl a few weeks back. Looked to me like you were really hitting it off."

"Yeah," he said almost wistfully.

"So, yes, it sucks what happened. But that little boy, at least he'll always be in your life, right? I mean, he is your nephew. And that girl Olivia wasn't the one for you. Her heart wasn't there."

She was right, of course.

"That could have been a lifetime of misery. It's never all about the kids. You gotta have something real, something solid with the partner."

Hackett nodded. "That's what I liked about that girl you saw me with. She was beautiful, right?"

"Absolutely."

"She's the opposite of O. She doesn't walk into a room like she owns the place. She's quiet. But I saw her at work dealing with customers. And the way she talks to the kids . . ."

"So why are we drowning sorrows over that Olivia bitch? Let's focus on this new girl." She raised her glass then, waiting for Hackett to agree.

Hackett reluctantly lifted his glass and clinked with hers before finishing and wiping his mouth. His thoughts returned to Bishop, to the case. "You're right." Bishop would probably focus on Grace even more now, simply to prove a point. He had to do something. He had to find that Tucker guy. But as he stepped off the barstool and stumbled, he knew that he couldn't do anything tonight. He thanked Alice for the beer and for letting him unload on her. She took his hands in hers. "Anytime, Officer."

TWENTY-FIVE

HACKETT HAD SET THE ALARM BEFORE passing out. When the annoying beeping began, he ignored the headache that had settled in between his temples for the night, focused on a painfully hot shower, three Advil, and a quick stop for coffee down the street before driving up to Bridgman, determined to make things right.

He pulled up to the auto body shop and found legs and a torso popping out from under a car. "Excuse me?" he said.

The mechanic rolled out from beneath the car, his hands completely covered in grease. It was the owner, Tom, who rolled his eyes at the sight of him.

"I've got a few more questions," Hackett said.

"Look, I told you about the ring. I got nothing more to share. I got a business to run here." He rolled back under the car. "I gotta finish this one before nine."

Without Bishop by his side, he was getting a whole lot less respect and attention. "Hey, we can do this here or at the station, but I need to speak to you."

Tom rolled back out and slowly got up from his knees to an upright position. Couldn't be an easy job for a man that age, with that much belly. "What is it this time?"

"I need to see one of your employees—Tucker—but I also wanted to ask you some questions about him."

Tom wiped his hands on a rag hanging from his belt. "Well, I can't help you there. Don't work here anymore. Who said he did, anyway?"

"Dave Jacks. He said Tucker was here at that card game, Tuesday, December third."

"I'd take whatever Jacks said with a grain of salt. That fucker's not welcome here anymore."

"What do you mean?"

"I have only two requirements of players—come with enough money to play, and don't be a compulsive liar. I don't need the hassle."

"And Dave Jacks is a compulsive liar?"

"Well, you tell me," Tom said with a smile. "We're all playing cards that night and Cahill starts ribbing Dave. Someone said something about him being the manager of Brewster's down in New Buffalo, and Cahill said something like, 'Oh, I heard all about you.' Dave looked uncomfortable and Cahill seemed to enjoy it. Told us all about Grace and a few other girls going into Dave's office at work one day, finding his computer on, his profile from this dating site up on the screen. Guess the whole thing was a bunch of lies. Called himself a widower; an entrepreneur; used a different name; said he loved kids, travel, boating." Tom laughed. "I mean, what a piece of work."

"And how did Dave Jacks react to Cahill saying all this?"

"He said it was bullshit. He tried to get the conversation back to the cards, but the guys had a bit of a field day with it. Pretty funny night, actually, until Cahill freaked out over losing the ring."

"Okay, so Tucker. He was here that night as well?"

"Yeah. But he hasn't shown up for work in more than a week, so I'd say his employment here is over."

"So you didn't fire him and he didn't quit; he simply stopped coming?"

"That's right."

"And when was the last time you saw him?"

"He was here the rest of that week. He worked that Friday. But that was it."

Hackett's pulse picked up. "And when was he supposed to work next?"

"The next day. He didn't show."

The day Michael Cahill was killed. "What can you tell me about Tucker?"

Tom rolled his eyes. "Well, Tucker's a bit of an odd guy, but he's a genius under the hood, so I put up with him."

"What do you mean 'odd'?"

"Listen, I don't want to get anyone in trouble. That kid's seen enough trouble, I'm guessing."

"Meaning what?"

"He was a loner, a foster kid at one point, he'd said. I think he got messed with pretty badly; that's what my other guys said, anyway."

"Your other guys—other employees?"

"Right. I mean, I wasn't surprised. He was kind of an angry kid when he first got here. Threw tools a lot when he was frustrated, but he'd mellowed out in the last year. Anyway, he had dozens of tattoos on his arms and even his neck. Some of the images were kinda violent, but he was always coming in, sharing his latest marking, excited about it. Seemed like he was a little addicted, frankly. I mean, I heard of getting a tattoo here or there, but he was kinda covered. Then again, it did make people think he was sorta crazy, and that helped me keep people in line at card games."

Hackett nodded, adding up the details in his mind. "And I heard that he wanted to play in the games, but you never let him?"

Tom nodded. "He couldn't afford it. I knew that. He was always desperate for cash, asking for advances on his paycheck, but it's not like anyone's going to fix his money problems at a card table. I'm not a total asshole."

"How long did he work here?"

"About two years."

"Two years and he suddenly stops showing. Did you get concerned? Did you call anyone?"

"Yeah, I called someone. I called his house and heard he'd left town. That was that."

"Do you have any pictures of Tucker around here?"

Tom chuckled. "This ain't no modeling agency."

"Can you describe him—his age, height, hair color, weight, eyes?"

"He's about twenty-six, I'm thinking. Not too tall or big; kinda scrawny, actually. Maybe five nine, one sixty."

"And his hair?"

"White blond. Though that was a dye job for sure. His roots are pretty dark. He wears it all spiked."

"Anything else?"

"Not really. Not like I looked into his eyes enough to tell you their color. But like I said, lots of tats, some earrings. That's about it."

"And do you know if he did drugs?"

"Certainly possible. Look around this place. It's not IBM. I'm not drug testing. These guys come to work, do the job, and punch out. Don't need no education or references. They show me what they can do and do it. He did the job. He was great with cars."

"He have a locker here or anything? Someplace where he might have kept his things?"

"Sure, everyone's got a locker in the break room." Grudgingly, the owner took him into the cramped space at the back of the building. Fast-food wrappers sat crumpled on the table. "Animals," Tom grunted as he threw the trash into the nearby bin. He pointed out the locker. "This one was his." The lock was still on it.

"Well, he's not working here anymore, right? Let's open it up."

"Sure." Tom walked out and returned with a bolt cutter.

They opened it. An old sweatshirt, a baseball cap, and some loose change and receipts were piled on the bottom shelf, like a junk drawer. Hackett carefully reviewed the contents. "I'd like to take this. Okay with you?"

"What do I care?"

Hackett went out to his car to get some latex gloves and bags. He didn't know where any of this would go, but maybe fingerprints on the papers, maybe DNA, maybe they'd find a connection. "You said he was last here on Friday, the sixth, right?"

"Yeah."

"What time did he come in?"

"Oh, like, one o'clock. I think he was on till eight."

Hackett read one of the receipts. A parking stub from Four Winds Casino. Clocked at noon, Friday, the sixth.

"Is that it? I gotta get back to work," Tom said.

"Sure. Just a couple more things. I need to know what kind of car he drives and his home address, and then I'll get out of your hair."

"No car, drives a motorcycle. Honda. Follow me to my office and I'll get you the address."

When Hackett pulled up to Tucker's house, he looked to his GPS for confirmation that he was at the right place. He'd driven down a narrow gravel road, the width of a driveway, several miles from the center of Buchanan. The nearest neighbor was at least a quarter mile away. The house, set fifty feet back from the road, was a simple farmhouse, worn down by decades of neglect and harsh Michigan winters. There was an old station wagon in the driveway, no motorcycle. A huge barn, twice the size of the house, sat back even farther, off to the right. A little one-sided shack sat perched near the road, and remnants of old farm equipment, a giant metal wheel, some tires, and a few plastic crates were piled up along the fence.

Hackett knew that this was stupid. He wasn't on the case; he was probably suspended and maybe even fired. But he had nothing to lose. He got out of the car and zipped up his jacket. The temperature had dropped again and was now about twenty degrees. He felt his waistband for his gun. Luckily, Bishop had been so incensed, he hadn't thought enough to even ask for his gun or drag him in to see the chief.

He walked the well-worn path to the house and rang the bell. No one came. He rang it again and pulled back the old aluminum storm door, but its springs were broken and a gust of wind pulled it from his grasp, pounding it against the house.

He walked around the perimeter. Sheets hung over several of the windows, but as he reached the side of the house, one window was bare. Cupping his hands and pressing his face up against the glass, he could see the living room, complete with a large flat-screen television and thrift-store furniture. On the coffee table, a plastic bag of capsules. Just beyond that room, the kitchen, a metal press of some kind on the table.

He walked around the rest of the house, but the shades were pulled. Tracks extended from the back door to the barn doors off to the right. Light from inside poured out of the cracks between the doors and the frame.

The massive barn door creaked when he pushed it open. A blast of warm air hit him, thanks to a series of heaters buzzing from the rafters. In front of him was a massive grow operation. At least ten long tables covered with plants, lights hanging above them. He reached for his gun. If this were a drug operation, he knew to expect weapons. But the place wasn't even locked. He stepped closer to the tables, each labeled with different names, each one ending in the name Datura. Not pot, but whatever they were was unfamiliar to him.

A pair of plastic lounge chairs sat at the far end of the barn, a little crate between them. He stepped closer. Someone was there, lying on one of the chairs, his arms behind his head, earplugs in his ears. Hackett stepped closer, gun drawn.

"Police," he said.

The man didn't move.

Hackett stepped closer and nudged the man's arm with the tip of his weapon.

The man slowly turned and opened his eyes.

Hackett took a couple of steps back. "Police. Hands up where I can see them."

"Whoa, dude. Calm down," the guy said, his arms lazily extending halfway into the air. He smiled. "Dude, this is private property."

"Yes, and this," Hackett said, waving his gun toward the plants, "is probable cause."

The man sat up straighter and removed his earplugs. "Look, I don't know what you think you've found, but nothing in here is illegal. Certainly no marijuana, if that's what you're concerned about." He stood then. "How can I help you, Officer?"

"What is this?" Hackett said, waving around the room.

"These are my plants, man. What can I say, I love horticulture."

"Are you Tucker?"

"No, man. Tucker don't live here anymore."

Hackett looked around, not sure what his next move should be.

The man sat back down and patted the lounger next to him. "Come on, dude. Take a seat. Tell me what you need."

Hackett stepped closer and relaxed his weapon. "I need to find Tucker. How about you tell me when you last saw him. I assume you live here too?"

"That's right. But Tucker was always in and out. It's been a while," he said as he lay back and put his hands behind his head. "He really only used the place for mail and growin'."

"And when's the last time you heard from him?"

"Oh, couple weeks, I guess," the guy said before yawning and closing his eyes.

Hackett shoved his arm. "Wake up. Come on. I need specifics. When exactly?"

The guy opened his eyes and looked up at the rafters. "It musta been Friday." He pulled his cell out then and punched some buttons. "Yeah, here we go. He texted me. Friday, December sixth, two o'clock." He showed the screen to Hackett. "Said he'd hit the mother lode. We were gonna meet up on Saturday."

"But you didn't meet?"

"Nah. Bastard never showed."

"And what do you think he meant by 'hit the mother lode'?"

"Cash, I guess. We're not exactly good savers," he said sheepishly. "You seen that house? Kinda shitty, right? And we needed cash for our business."

"What kind of business?"

The guy sat up then, excited by the chance to share. Suddenly, he was full of energy. "Well, you know the marijuana biz is coming to Michigan. Legal. Medical, whatever. We're kind of entrepreneurs."

"I can tell. So you thought you'd get into medical marijuana? But this isn't marijuana."

He smiled. "Got that right. No, man. We're into something way better. And legal. Mind-altering legal, man. This is the future."

"Lemme guess, you're one of those psychonauts."

His chest came out, proud. "Hell yeah, man. Why limit your experiences to walking this earth, man, when you can literally take a walk through your mind."

"Sure."

"Telling you, don't knock it till you've tried it."

He needed this guy to focus. "Do you know Michael Cahill?"

"Who?"

"Did you sell drugs to Michael Cahill?"

"I don't sell drugs, man."

"Really—what do you do?"

"I'm like a scientist, dude."

"Sure—and how do you make money?"

"In the summer, I do some farming. Sell some fruits and veggies, you know, whatever it takes. Sometimes I get lucky at the casino."

"So what happened Saturday? Tucker didn't show. Did you call him?"

"Yeah, but then I heard he left town. Fucker. Probably thought twice about sharing anything with me." He lay back down as if that was all there was to it.

"Who told you he left town?"

"His old lady."

Hackett pulled out his notepad. "What's your name?"

"Henry."

"Henry what?"

"Henry David."

"Your last name is David?"

The guy smiled. "No, man."

"What's your full name, including last?"

"Henry David Thoreau." He nodded repeatedly, grinning. "That's right."

Hackett rolled his eyes. "Your legal name is Henry David Thoreau?"

"Check it out," the guy said as he reached back and pulled out his wallet. He handed over his driver's license. "Had it legally changed a few years ago."

"And why's that?"

"Because, man, a road diverged in a wood. I chose the one less traveled by. And that has made all the difference." His glassy eyes beamed with pride.

"Well, I hate to break it to you, but that's Robert Frost."

The guy sat up, momentarily panic-stricken, but seconds later he relaxed back into his lounger and smiled. "Bullshit. Quit messing with me, man."

It was rare for Hackett to feel like a scholar, but he had been forced to memorize that particular poem in English class. "Not messing with you. Regardless, what was your name before you changed it?"

"Marty Kesler."

"Okay then, Marty." He jotted down the name so he could pull this guy's records. Or maybe Bishop would. "I need you to give me Tucker's cell number, his full name, and where I can find his girlfriend."

Kesler sat up. "You're really not fucking with me about Thoreau?"

"Sorry."

"Thoreau was a poet though, right?"

"Yeah. I think he's more famous for that quote about how most men lead lives of quiet desperation."

Kesler smiled. "Well, all right then. I can live with that. Something to avoid, don't you think, Officer?"

Hackett shook his head, unable to keep up with this guy's wacked mind.

Kesler seemed able to focus again and pulled up his contacts. He handed the phone, filled with the requested information, to Hackett. "Here you go."

"Shit," Hackett swore. He recognized Tucker's last name immediately. "Thanks," he called out as he ran for the barn door.

TWENTY-SIX

IT WAS THE FIRST TIME GRACE hadn't woken several times during the night, but she still felt awful. Just lifting her body out of the bed seemed to take twice the normal effort. Sun streamed through the windows, and when she glanced at the clock, she was surprised to see that it was already noon. She'd slept for more than sixteen hours.

Downstairs, the kitchen was void of Lisa's usual coffee and morning notes—a nice change. Something was supposed to happen today. But Grace couldn't remember what. She pulled out her phone and sat, weighed down by exhaustion from simply coming down the stairs. She checked the calendar and nodded. Today was the day. Maybe she'd finally get her answers.

The temperature had dropped but the sun was blazing from a cloudless sky onto the white fields as she drove toward New Buffalo. She had trouble staying within the speed limit. It had been only two days since she'd seen Dr. Newell, but it felt like much longer, and she wanted to be in that office more than anywhere else in the world. So much had happened, but so many questions remained. The visions, tidbits of information, meeting Vicki, Mom's paintings, her panic attacks, her increasing fear of staying in that house—everything she'd learned or felt brought on more questions.

Dr. Newell welcomed her into the office, and Grace handed the cassette tape to her. "This was helpful," she said before taking a seat on the couch.

The doctor sat in the chair across from her. "Did it bring back memories?"

"I wouldn't say it brought them back. I don't remember saying those things to you. I don't remember Michael any more than before, but it was informative, and some things are coming back." She hesitated. "I'm so sick of not knowing who I am or what I've done. We're gonna get to the bottom of it, right?"

Dr. Newell smiled reassuringly. "I can't make any promises, but I'll do what I can. First, I want to know what medications you're on and how you're feeling."

"Here, I brought them all with me." She'd remembered at the last minute, just before she left the house. She pulled the pill bottles from her purse and placed them on the doctor's desk. "Lisa freaks out on me when I skip a dose, but they're not making things better. I've been skipping doses whenever possible. The headaches have dwindled and I feel too foggy when I take them. I can't sleep; I can't remember shit."

The doctor put on her glasses and read the labels, taking notes. "You're following up with the doctor on Monday, correct?"

"Yeah."

"Then I think it's fine for you to hold off on taking any more. These are some strong medications."

"Okay." Grace turned on the couch to lay back and said, "Let's go."

Dr. Newell smiled. "You're awfully anxious. Now remember, Grace, this isn't a guarantee. Hypnosis is kind of like meditation. We're simply going to try and create a highly relaxed state of inner concentration and focused attention. Your willingness to focus and relax is key. You can't be hypnotized against your will, and you'll be conscious the entire time. I'm not inducing you into any kind of sleep state, so if you decide you want to stop at any time, you just say so. My hope is simply that if you relax and open up, you might be able to remember a little bit more."

"I'm ready."

"Also, I want you to know that some people believe hypnosis can lead to false memories. That our mind can simply create ways to fill in the gaps, and so it can be very confusing. But I've had good results with my patients, and the key is for you to lead this journey. I will not plant suggestions or ideas. I will simply walk with you, metaphorically speaking, and see what we can find."

"Okay." Grace adjusted her head against the pillow.

"What I'm going to do is simply try and get you to relax to a point that you're still conscious but you're able to tap into memories that you might be blocking. First, I want you to close your eyes. Focus on your breathing."

Grace followed the instructions. Dr. Newell led her through several exercises, and before long, Grace felt relaxed enough to proceed.

"Now, Grace, it was two weeks ago that you ended up in the hospital. Can you tell me anything about that day?"

"I got in a car accident."

"Can you tell me anything about that crash?"

"No. I don't remember anything."

"And what about before the crash? Do you remember where you were going or what you were doing that morning?"

"No."

"Okay. Let's go back a little bit. Your parents died a few years ago. How did you feel when that happened?"

"I was sad. That's not right. More than sad. I felt guilty."

"Why did you feel guilty about your parents' deaths?"

"I wanted to be with Michael. I was fighting with them a lot."

"How did you feel when you found out they were dead?"

"I was sad. But there was this part of me . . ." She stopped.

"What?"

"I loved Michael. I wanted out of that house. We wanted to be together and they forbade it. We were even talking about running off together."

"When were you going to do that?"

"As soon as I finished the school year."

Dr. Newell waited then.

"But when they died, I didn't have to run away."

"Is that why you felt guilty? Because there was a benefit for you when they died?"

Her voice cracked. "It was just a little part of me. There was this little voice in my head that realized we didn't have to run away."

"Is there any other reason you felt guilty?"

"Yeah."

"Can you tell me about that?"

"I wasn't there."

"Where were you?"

"I slept over at Vicki's. We snuck out with Michael and Wesley. We went to Cherry Beach."

"What did you do there?"

"We made a bonfire, smoked some pot, and then . . . then . . ." It was like her mind was walking down a road and suddenly fell off into a ditch. She felt stuck for a moment, like she was at a fork and unsure which way to go.

"What is it?"

"Vicki and Wesley went off into the dunes for a while to fool around."

"And what about you and Michael?"

"I loved him."

"What did you two do when Vicki and Wesley left?"

"The fire started to go out. We went up to sit in the car. We kissed. We talked."

"Did you talk about anything special?"

"We talked about confronting my parents, to force them to allow us to be together."

"And did you do it?"

Grace shook her head.

"Is there something else? What is it, Grace?"

"It was my fault. They died because of me."

"Why do you feel responsible for your parents' death?"

"My mom and I got in a big fight."

"When, that night?"

"No. A few days before. She said I was too young to be with Michael, to want to move in with him. She said, 'Why do my girls make such bad decisions?' It made me so mad."

"Why?"

"Because she compared me to Lisa. I was nothing like Lisa. My mom didn't know anything."

"What do you mean when you say your mom didn't know anything?"

"My mom was . . . she was oblivious," Grace said, her voice now laced with anger.

"Go on."

"She spent all her time taking pictures, painting, observing, and yet she never saw me. She never knew what was happening in that house."

"What happened in that house, Grace?"

Tears began falling from her closed lids. She didn't attempt to wipe them away. She shook her head, but nothing came out. Her lips felt like they were fighting against the words.

Dr. Newell moved her chair closer to the couch. She reached out and held Grace's hand. "You're safe here. Nothing can happen to you anymore. It's okay. Tell me what happened."

"That house was a nightmare. Even after she was gone, it never ended."

"Even after who was gone?"

"Lisa."

"Go on."

"We played in the woods. We had lots of woods. Everyone said we needed to know them inside and out so we'd never get lost."

"Who's everyone?"

"My parents."

"Okay."

"So she blindfolded us."

"Your mother?"

"No."

"Who?"

"Lisa."

"And when you say 'us,' who are you referring to?"

"Mary and me."

"Your sister. Okay, and how old were you at the time?"

"She did it a lot. I don't remember them all. But the last time it was just me. I was, like, six."

"And what happened?"

She felt like she was right back there, just six years old, standing in the middle of those woods in her daisy dress. "She spun me around five times and said I needed to feel my way home. She said she'd stay right next to me. I would trip on a branch and tumble forward. She'd laugh, help me up, and say, 'Oh, watch out for that branch.' She said, 'Follow my voice.' So I did. I got smacked by tree branches and scratched all up and down my legs. 'Come on, you're doing great,' she said. 'Just a few more steps.' And then I took a step and nothing was there. I fell into this hole, landing in something wet. The smell was rancid. I started screaming. Lisa just laughed. 'You should have seen the look on your face,' she said as I pulled off the blindfold. I was in the compost pit, surrounded by rotting leaves, banana peels, eggshells, coffee grinds."

"Did you tell your mother?"

Grace shook her head. "Lisa ran ahead and told her I'd fallen in the pit. My mom assumed it was an innocent mistake. I didn't say anything."

"Did you think she wouldn't believe you?"

She shook her head again, trying to walk through the woods in her mind. Mary was by her side.

"Is that why you get nervous or you hear that crying girl's voice when you're near the woods?"

"No."

"Do you remember something else?"

They were climbing together, giggling. "Mom and Dad said we weren't allowed up on the hunting platform."

"Okay. Did you go up anyway?"

She nodded. "It was supposed to be our special place—our secret."

"Whose secret place?"

"Mary's and mine."

"And how old were you?"

"I don't know. Four? Five?"

"Did something happen up there?"

"Lisa came up. She scared us. Pushed us each back so far that we were sure we would fall. We both cried and climbed down. I never went back up."

"It sounds like Lisa was not the easiest older sister. Was she always mean to you?"

"She was always making up games we had to play."

"Were they fun games?"

"No."

"Can you tell me of any other games?"

"Hide-and-seek."

"Was that scary?"

Grace couldn't answer.

"What are you thinking about now, Grace?"

She was trying to remember . . . or not to remember.

"Grace, where are you?"

"I'm in the basement." Standing there with Lisa.

"Go on."

"She said it was a good place to hide. But it was so small. I couldn't breathe. The latches closed." She started to feel agitated. Her voice rose. "She wouldn't let me out. I was ripping the fabric from inside the lid. It won't open! I can't breathe." Her breath started to come in gasps.

"What are you in?"

"The trunk. Stop it! Open! Open!" she screamed.

Dr. Newell squeezed her hand. "It's okay. You're not in there anymore. Take a deep breath. You're with me now."

Grace inhaled deeply and blew out the air.

"How long were you in there, Grace?"

She felt tears wetting her cheeks.

"You're okay, Grace. You got out."

"She let me out."

"Who?"

"Lisa. She said it was a game. That I needed to stop being such a baby."

Nausea rolled through her. She was in a tunnel. She could feel that sensation coming. "Ouch!" she cried.

"What is it?"

She started whimpering, a little girl's voice. "I'm stuck."

"Where are you?"

She reached down and grabbed her shin. "I'm bleeding!" she cried out.

"Where are you bleeding?"

"My leg, I cut my leg!"

"Where are you, Grace?"

"I'm in the chute."

"The laundry chute? Did someone put you in the chute?"

Her own voice sounded like a child's. "She said it would be fun. 'Look at Susie!'"

"Who's Susie?"

"My doll. She threw her down the chute and put pillows in the laundry tub. She said it would be like a ride."

"And you got stuck in there. What happened?"

"There was a turn. My leg caught. I scraped it against something sharp."

"Where's your mommy, Grace?"

"I don't know."

"Where's your daddy?"

"Don't know."

"How'd you get out?"

Grace screamed. Her body bounced. She threw her hands up to shield her head from the downpour and closed her eyes even tighter, straining her whole face.

"What happened?"

"It's wet and cold—"

"What is it?"

"It's heavy. Thick. Slippery. *'Move!'* She kept yelling to move my leg." She curled up into a ball on the couch, wiping the tears as they came.

"What happened? Are you out of the chute?"

Grace nodded, wiping her tears. "She poured oil down the chute."

"Did Lisa ever do anything else to you?"

She nodded.

"It's okay, Grace. You're okay. Breathe."

She felt her breathing begin to calm. But when she began to speak, her tears exploded into sobs. "She tried to drown Mary in the tub. I came in and she was holding her head under the water. Mary's arms were flailing. I screamed for Lisa to let her up. Lisa turned to me like I was an idiot. 'It was only for a second, Gracie. You guys need to learn to hold your breath.'"

"What did Mary do?"

Her stomach turned at the thought of it. "We were four!"

"Did your parents ever know about any of this, Grace?"

She shook her head.

"And why didn't you tell them?"

"We knew what she'd do."

"Come on, Grace," Dr. Newell said. "You're doing great. Tell me what you mean when you say, 'We knew what she'd do.'"

"I hate her so much." Her voice grew stronger. "Mom never sees. She sees what she wants to see. She pops her pills and paints her pictures and cries for Mary. I couldn't tell her."

"So you were afraid of upsetting your mom, or you were afraid of Lisa?"

"She would have killed me. I watched her do it once."

"What do you mean?"

She was silent for a moment—what did she mean? She waited for the memory to come. "She took me into the woods. She brought me to a dead tree that had fallen. Its thicker limbs were still intact, but the smaller limbs had snapped off. She wanted me to see something. We walked around the trunk and I saw a cat. It must have been a stray. It wasn't moving. It was just hanging there, its head caught on the branches. Its eyes were open and its belly was moving. It was choking." She stopped, gasping to catch her breath. "I moved the branches to help it get free. But Lisa grabbed my arm. 'No, don't touch it!' I looked at her eyes. She was like a stranger. 'I wanted you to see it happen.' 'Why? Why are you doing this?' 'It's a cat, a stray, no big deal," like how could I be so stupid. And then she said, 'But how often do you get to watch something die?'

"I screamed and hit her. She put her arms around me like a bear. 'Gracie. You don't want to be next, do you? You'd better not say anything.' I broke free and ran toward the house. Mom was in the yard painting. I was hysterical. She asked me what happened but I couldn't catch my breath. Then Lisa ran up and said that I'd seen a dead cat in the woods and got freaked out.

"Mom hugged me and said that a coyote probably got to it. Lisa was staring at me. Watching me, watching to see what would come out of my mouth. I didn't tell. If I told I might be next. And then I was really trapped. I should have told. I should have dragged my mom into the woods and saved the cat. But I believed she could do that to me."

"Grace, did your parents ever hurt you? On Wednesday, you showed me scars on your arm that Lisa said your father inflicted."

"He didn't do that."

"Who did?"

She took a deep breath, like she was swimming for the surface of a deep pool and needed air. "I did."

"Why?"

"Lisa would smoke cigarettes in the woods and burn herself. She said it made her feel better when she felt out of control. I wanted her to go. I just needed to survive until then. Every time she did something, I began cutting myself. It became like a survival badge. I'd look down when I was sad and see what I'd survived. I'd remember that I could handle it."

"And did you ever tell?"

She nodded. "When Mom compared me to Lisa, I snapped. I told her everything."

"What happened?"

"A week later they were dead."

"Grace, are you saying your sister killed them?"

She was looking down on herself as she sat in the police station that morning, a social worker by her side, the woman's hand on hers, squeezing as the officer, another woman, tried to explain what had happened. "Police said someone else did it."

All the fights, the tension between her and Lisa came into full view. It had never stopped. Even after she'd moved out, even after their parents were gone. "I want to stop."

"Okay, Grace. But keep your eyes closed for another minute. I want you to take a few breaths. You did really well. Just listen to my voice as I count from five to one. When I get to one, you can open your eyes." Dr. Newell began counting.

Grace opened her eyes and sat up slowly. She wiped the tears that continued to fall. "She tortured me," she said. "But I should have told. I should have told them what was happening so many times. That cat died because I didn't tell . . . She made me as bad as she was."

"It's not the same, Grace. There is something to be said for self-preservation, don't you think? At our core, aren't we all just trying to survive? You were afraid."

She sat back on the couch, both hands pressing against her face, plugging the leak. "But if you know someone is bad, maybe even evil, and you don't do anything about it, what does that make you? At school they would say that if you ever saw a kid bullied and you did nothing, you were as bad as the bully."

"I don't think this is the same, Grace. Lisa was much older, and you had good reason to fear her. You can't blame yourself for how you responded at such a young age."

Grace let her head fall against the cushion. "My head hurts."

Dr. Newell stood, walked to the side table, and poured a glass of water. "Let's relax here for a bit. You've obviously been blocking some childhood trauma." She brought Grace the water. "Perhaps your brain has gotten pretty good at protecting you from difficult memories."

Grace looked at the ceiling, following the molding around the room. "I remember them now."

"Who?"

"My parents. They weren't bad people. They didn't hurt me." She sat forward and put down the glass. "I need to go. Thanks, Doctor. This has helped so much."

"Grace, what is it?"

"It's okay. I just need to get home. I'll call you later."

Dr. Newell checked the calendar on her phone. "I want you back here next Friday again, okay? I think we should continue to talk about all of this."

"Absolutely. I'll call you Monday." She was out the door before the doctor could say any more.

Grace pushed the speed limit all the way home, her mind reeling from the light shining through the dark tunnels of her mind. Her childhood. Her family. Lisa was at the center of it all, the trauma, the tears, everything. Her memories, shattered and broken into hundreds of pieces, were coming back together. But a few holes remained.

The answers were in that house, she was sure of it.

TWENTY-SEVEN

HACKETT FLEW UP THE DIRT ROAD as fast as he could. He pulled open the station doors and silently waved at the clerk, hoping he could enter without anyone else, Bishop particularly, noticing. Bishop was at his desk, talking on the phone.

Hackett ducked behind the partition and looked around the corner. He needed to get to a computer. Bishop was walking now, heading for the break room. Hackett rushed into an empty office and shut the door. He typed Tucker's name into a search field to pull up his records: DUI, assaulting an officer (and yelling nonsense), public indecency (running around naked in someone's field, intoxicated). According to the report, he'd gotten violent with the arresting officer—had to be tased. Hackett pulled up the records from the Abbotts' murder, searching for the case notes on Stanford Jones, the man serving time for the crime.

He found what he needed. Bishop was back at his desk, drinking coffee, when he approached. "I thought I told you to get out of here." He set down the mug and started scribbling on a Post-it.

"You did. I know I'm off the case and I might get fired, but I have to tell you something. It's important."

Bishop didn't look up. "What?"

"I went to find Tucker this morning. First at the auto shop and then at his house."

Bishop dropped his pen. "You did what?"

"Wait. He wasn't there. He hasn't shown up for work since the day of Cahill's murder. And I found a receipt in his locker for Four Winds Casino from the Friday before. I also picked up his sweatshirt and baseball cap. Thought maybe you'd need them for DNA. Anyway, I met his roommate, another one of these psychonauts. They've got a grow room in their barn that we need to investigate, by the way. But he hasn't seen Tucker either. Tucker texted him on the Friday before the murder, telling him they needed to meet, that he'd hit the 'mother lode.' But then he didn't show. The roommate tried to track him down, but Tucker's girlfriend said he'd left town."

Bishop finally looked interested.

"That's not the best part. Tucker's last name is Bichon. You remember that name?"

"Should I?"

"That's the name of Lisa Abbott's boyfriend, the one she was living with in Benton Harbor who provided her alibi for her parents' murder. And guess what else?" He didn't wait for Bishop to respond. "Tucker was a foster kid. I just checked his records. Tucker Bichon was one of Jones's foster kids."

Bishop leaned back in his chair, methodically digesting the information. "So, Lisa Abbott's parents are murdered, and the guy who went away was someone who had abused her boyfriend. That sounds awfully coincidental."

Hackett nodded, his excitement building. "And the MO for that murder was a shotgun, owned by the victims. They were shot in the bed and robbed. Michael Cahill was shot with his own gun, in his bed, and maybe he was robbed too. We haven't found the ten K, and it sounds like maybe Tucker knew about that win. He was at the casino. He told his roommate he'd hit the mother lode. And then he disappears."

"You think Lisa was in on this?"

"Don't know. But she is the one who told his roommate he'd left town. Maybe she's in the dark—or maybe she's covering for him." His mind was reeling. Lisa might have killed her parents. Or Tucker killed them. Either way, the thought of Grace in her care, oblivious to any danger, made his stomach turn.

Bishop rubbed his head, looking more and more disturbed. "Well, I've got some news too. I heard back from the crime lab last night. Grace's clothes from the car accident—there's no evidence of Cahill's blood on them. And there were traces of scopolamine in Cahill's hair. Sounds like you might have been right about him being drugged on that Sunday."

A massive wave of relief poured over Hackett. He could barely contain his smile. He wasn't sure if now was the time, but . . . "I fucked up. I'm sorry. And I don't want to mess up your investigation, but I wanted you to know everything."

Bishop sat forward in his chair. "Well, as long as we're sharing, I got one more interesting tidbit too. I was working through Grace's hospital records last night. She came in on Saturday morning unconscious and spent several hours in surgery. The hospital didn't track down Lisa until Sunday."

"So?"

"When I first asked Lisa what time Grace left her house on Saturday morning, she said she didn't know because she'd slept in and woken only when the hospital called to tell her about Grace's accident."

"Another lie. You know what else?" Hackett added. "The only reason we think that Grace and Michael Cahill even broke up is because Lisa said so. Everyone else reported them as happy and engaged. The only reason we think Grace went to Lisa's Friday night is because Lisa said so. Maybe despite the protective sister act, Lisa wants us to think that Grace did this. Maybe despite what we know about Michael Cahill, Grace loved him." He swallowed hard and moved past it. "She'd agreed to marry him and that was it. She went for a run on Saturday morning, and she came home and either saw him dead and ran or saw the killer and ran. Maybe she saw Tucker. Maybe Lisa is more interested in protecting Tucker than her sister."

"Get me Tucker's vehicle registration, and get me Lisa's while you're at it."

Hackett moved over to his own desk to pull up the records. The top paper on his case files was Jacks's list of party attendees from their meeting yesterday. Hackett quickly scanned the sheet of more than twenty first names: Tracey, Sheri, Bill, Bobby, Nina . . . and near the bottom: Tucker, Lisa. So he could place them at the scene where evidence was found. And how had she been home for Grace if she was at Jacks's party?

Bishop picked up the phone, called his contact with the tribal police, and asked him to pull up the casino's security tapes from Friday, December sixth, from the time of Michael Cahill's win and any tapes from the parking lot for the window of time when he must have left. He began describing Tucker, looking to Hackett for more.

"Lots of tattoos, skinny, around five nine, spiky bleached-blond hair," Hackett provided.

Bishop gave him a thumbs-up and finished the call. When he hung up, Hackett brought over a note with Tucker's and Lisa's registration records. "I know I'm off the case. No matter what happens, I don't want to fuck it up anymore. Good luck with everything." He headed toward the door. At least Bishop was now on the right track.

"Oh shit," Bishop said. Hackett turned back and Bishop waved him over. "Look at this." He jogged over to his desk as Bishop placed the photographs of Michael Cahill with the naked woman next to an image of Grace's dead parents on his computer screen. "You see what I see?"

"What?" Hackett said.

"Look closer," Bishop said, his finger on the wall behind the bed. "Oh shit."

TWENTY-EIGHT

GRACE BARRELED INTO THE HOUSE. Lisa's car wasn't there. "Lisa?" she shouted. Silence. She went back into the office where she'd already found the insurance files and school documents. Maybe there would be more about Lisa—about whether she'd ever been diagnosed with anything, or more about Mary's death. Her parents never wanted to discuss the details. All she'd ever been told was that a bad man took Mary from them.

She found the box with the hanging files and scanned the tabs. There was the file marked *Grace*—nothing but old report cards, school projects from elementary school, other memorabilia that her parents had obviously thought worth keeping. She found Mary's file. Projects from preschool and several photographs filled the thin folder; all of them featured the two little girls: in the yard, in bed—the double bed that Grace had spent the last week in—in the kitchen, at school. They were always together, arm in arm, leaning in, heads together, matching smiles for every photograph. Grace ran her fingers across her sister's face. She could feel her spirit—as if they were still together, as if she'd been with her all along. But there was the death certificate: October 5, 1997.

Another file was marked *The girls*. Inside, Grace's birth certificate—December 1, 1992—and an imprint of her little baby foot from the hospital. She found Mary's too, born two minutes later; her little footprint mirrored her own. Several ultrasound photographs of the two babies—a notation below one read, *They're holding hands!* There was no birth certificate in the file for Lisa, but a couple of photos were clipped to some papers. The first was of Lisa, maybe three, staring into the camera, no smile, no light in her eyes. The second was a picture taken of her back, bare for the camera, bruised and cut. Grace looked at the paperwork attached to it. Adoption papers. So that was why she didn't see a resemblance. Was this the answer? Why Lisa had been so cruel, so unhappy about having sisters? She examined the papers: born June 3, 1985; adopted on July 6, 1988. She'd been abused, mistreated, born to a drug-addicted mother, one prior foster-home placement that lasted six months. Grace couldn't imagine the pain, the damage such neglect had caused.

Suddenly, light beamed through the windows in front of her like a strobe, as if she'd been caught stealing. Headlights. Someone was here.

She put everything down and moved to the side of the window. The porch light illuminated falling snowflakes. Lisa got out of the car, opened the back door, grabbed a couple of grocery bags, and walked toward the porch.

She was suddenly terrified of confronting Lisa about their history. She waited in the library, listening as Lisa came into the house, removed her boots and hat by the door, and dumped the bags on the kitchen counter. She looked down at her arm, at all those scars, the pain she'd been pushing down for years. She needed to face her now.

Grace took a step forward. The floor creaked beneath her and Lisa turned, startled. She looked at Grace as if she were a ghost.

Neither spoke. For a moment, they stared at each other. Lisa recovered quicker and plastered a smile on her face. "Hey! How are you feeling?" She didn't wait for a response but began unloading the groceries.

Grace walked through the living room and into the kitchen, taking a seat at the table. Lisa's back was to her. "I got a lot of my memories back today," she said.

Lisa paused in the midst of placing a cereal box in the upper cabinet. "What do you mean?" she asked, sliding the box onto the shelf.

"I mean our childhood. I remembered you and the things you did to me."

Lisa turned to her, arrogance distorting her expression. "Is this about the laundry chute?" She laughed. "It was just for fun!"

Grace hesitated. She'd felt so confident of the truth in Dr. Newell's office, but the reality was, she had no way of knowing what was real and what wasn't. She only knew she didn't want to be frightened any longer. "I've been having all these feelings, these hints of memories, terrifying anxiety. And then today I found out they were all buried memories of you. You did terrible things to me. You—"

"Oh, please." Lisa turned back to the counter. "You're being dramatic."

"You locked me in a trunk. You almost drowned Mary. You blindfolded us in the woods."

Lisa didn't respond except to pull a corkscrew from the drawer. Grace watched as she opened a bottle of wine, then walked to the cupboard for glasses. She stood there for a moment, her back to Grace. Was she angry? Was she dangerous? A shiver traveled up Grace's spine. She scanned the room. She might need to make a quick exit.

But Lisa turned toward her, a smile on her face, and carried two full glasses of wine over to the table and sat beside her. "Grace, I'm really sorry about all that." She handed her the glass and took a sip.

"We were kids. I didn't mean to hurt you. You forgave me for that stuff a long time ago! Come on, let's toast to having your memories back."

Grace stared at her, still angry, even more confused.

"Seriously? Are you going to be mad at me for things that happened when we were kids? It's ancient history!" Lisa's arm was outstretched, waiting for Grace to clink glasses. Her smile was disappearing, a storm cloud emerging.

Grace slowly lifted her glass, suddenly afraid. They toasted, and Grace took a sip.

The storm passed. Lisa returned to the counter. "Look, I got your favorite." She pulled out chicken breasts, pasta, and a bag of greens. "Chicken piccata. You remember that dish? With angel hair? It was the only good thing Mom ever made us. You remember?"

She didn't. There were still gaps.

"I bought it to celebrate."

"Celebrate what?"

"Well, I guess we need to celebrate two things now. Getting some memories back, for one. Sorry they weren't the good ones, but it is progress, right?" She rushed on before Grace could respond. "And it's only a matter of time before this murder silliness is behind us. So come on, drink up. You hungry?"

Could it be that Lisa was right? That Grace had forgiven her? That she was afraid and angry now only because she'd just relived it all in terrifying detail? Lisa had obviously had a tough start. Grace took another sip of wine. But no, she reasoned. Lisa had been lying to her. "You said Mom and Dad were bad people, that they hurt us. It's not true. None of that's true."

Lisa dropped the knife on the counter and spun. "It is true. They fucking hurt me, Grace."

"No, they didn't. Those burns on your arm aren't from Dad. You did that. I remember. You showed me." That moment in the woods came back in full view: Lisa, maybe fourteen, Grace only seven.

She'd shown Grace how to smoke, acting like a big sister, sharing secrets of growing up, but then she'd taken the cigarette, burning her own flesh, wincing slightly but laughing, explaining that sometimes it felt good to hurt, that it helped focus pain.

Grace looked down at her own scarred arm. "No one else ever hurt you." She regretted saying it the moment it came out. Obviously this girl had been hurt since the beginning.

Lisa opened the cabinet above her and slammed it again and again, focusing her rage. "Not true!" she repeated.

Fearing her erratic mood, Grace softened her tone. "Lisa, you needed help."

"Bullshit."

Grace looked away and saw her, Lisa, maybe eleven years old, yelling at their mother, slamming a kitchen drawer shut, over and over. "Why can't I go?" she kept repeating. "Why? I hate you. I hate you all." She'd thrown her plate across the room. Her mother had done nothing, said nothing, just held her head in her hands, trying to block out the noise. The wall in Grace's mind began to crumble as the images rushed back: Lisa punching holes in the wall of that room upstairs; throwing a chair across the kitchen; crying inconsolably, her head buried in her mother's lap on the couch; stomping up the stairs, kicking out the spindles. The rage, the repentance, the neediness. Lisa could never handle being anything but the sun.

"You need medication, Lisa. You've always needed medication."

"Bullshit. This is the only medication I need," Lisa said, raising the wineglass. "I need a little wine, and I need some freedom, and I need people to leave me the fuck alone."

And Grace had done that—she suddenly remembered. She'd stayed away since their parents' deaths, leaving Lisa to have the house, fearing the rage that would only grow worse if she staked any claim. Unfortunately, Dad's lawyer had never known their history and had assumed that Lisa would willingly share the money with her. It meant Grace had to come to the house for her checks each month. It was the only way she could afford school.

"You take your meds today, Gracie?" Lisa said.

"No. They make me feel worse."

She nodded. "That's how I always felt too." She turned back to the counter for a moment. Grace couldn't see what she was doing. And then Lisa was walking toward her, one hand fisted, the other holding a knife. "That's what I used to say," Lisa said. "They gave me sweats, insomnia, horrible dreams, awful side effects, but everyone said, 'Take the meds.' So now I'll say it to you too." She stood there, the closed hand now outstretched, offering two capsules and a tablet. The knife pointed directly at Grace.

Grace looked at the blade, then at her sister. Would she really do this? Lisa didn't move, didn't blink, her eyes getting darker. Grace raised her hand and accepted the pills. She slowly put them in her mouth. Lisa waved the blade at her, the silent instruction clear. Grace took a few sips to wash down the pills.

Lisa relaxed the knife then, grinning. "Good girl. Now!" She turned and went back to the counter full of groceries. "I brought home your favorite dinner. We should celebrate."

Grace didn't know what to do. Her rage was palpable.

"Come on and help me."

The raw chicken was splayed on the counter and Lisa began pounding it with a mallet, breaking down the muscle, spraying juice onto the counter. "We gotta get this nice and thin, you remember?"

There was anger and speed in her movements, power in her destruction, as the meat weakened under her will. Grace watched, mesmerized. Tomorrow. She would go to Officer Hackett. He would believe her. She would tell him what she'd remembered. Lisa was dangerous. They needed to investigate her.

Her head wobbled, too heavy for her neck. Her gaze fell to the linoleum tile. The pattern began to oscillate, and soon the whole room was spinning. She squeezed her eyes shut. Cinder blocks came crashing down and suddenly she was there: standing in her own house, Michael's house, in the yellow living room. Acid rose up in her chest, bile burning her stomach. She saw the bedroom, the blood, Michael lying on the bed, the gaping hole in his chest. And Lisa. Standing in the doorway, a man behind her. Tucker. Everything came back.

Her chest started heaving. She put down the wineglass and clasped her hands over her mouth to stop from screaming. But the tears couldn't be contained.

Lisa stopped working on the food and looked over. She must have seen it on Grace's face. "What are you thinking?"

She couldn't speak. She couldn't look at her sister's face. The reality of what had happened was now painfully clear.

Lisa grinned, a carnival grin. "You remember, don't you?"

She didn't answer.

"Well, I knew you'd remember at some point. Luckily, it doesn't matter anymore." She walked toward the table. "Boy, Grace, it's kind of nice to finally be able to talk about it."

Grace was shaking her head; she didn't want it to be true. The horror. She'd never broken up with Michael. She'd never been afraid of him. She hadn't gone to Lisa crying about leaving him on Friday night. That wasn't it at all. Everything Lisa told her was a lie. "Why . . . ?" she whispered.

"The 'whys' don't really matter anymore, do they? We're here now and this needs to end, because there's no fucking way I'm going down for Michael's murder."

Her legs felt heavy. Move, she told herself. Why couldn't she move?

Lisa took another swig of wine. "We saw you hit that tree. I thought maybe you were dead. I wanted to see if the car would burst into flames. I just wanted to see you die. Finally. I'd be rid of you and

I could tell the police you killed Michael, but we heard a siren and Tucker said we needed to get out of there." She sat at the table, like they could finally share how it all went down. "I tried to make him understand that if you lived, we couldn't keep the money, but that asshole was too stupid, too stoned to listen. He called me a psycho," she said, her voice laced with anger. "So that was the end of that."

Grace felt her body shutting down. This might be the end. She focused on slowing her breathing. Breathe, she'd thought, just before the deer crashed through her windshield.

"Frankly, I thought I was fucked. I was in such a panic. But when the hospital called and said you didn't remember anything, I almost laughed right into the phone." Lisa was still holding the mallet, smeared with raw chicken, waving it with excitement. "You didn't actually think I would go down for this, did you? I'm a lot smarter than you are, Gracie. Always have been."

Breathe.

"I knew I could play the doting sister and take care of my brain-damaged little Gracie, just long enough to be sure the evidence pointed nowhere near me. I just needed to keep you medicated and isolated. Not exactly hard out here. I had to make sure they saw that it was you."

"You're a monster."

"Me?" Lisa said incredulously. "You turned our parents against me."

"I didn't."

"You ruined everything. Everything was fine until you—"

"They loved all of us. Even you, despite everything."

"Bullshit."

Grace swallowed hard. It was difficult to speak now, every movement, even her lips and tongue, weighted and weak. "Is that why you killed them?" she slurred. She'd never been so bold as to accuse Lisa before, but she was never going to get away now. There was no more need to keep secrets.

"You poisoned them against me, Grace. It was your fault they died."

Grace's eyes closed; her head rested on her chest. "I told them the truth."

"You told them I tortured you and Mary."

"You did."

Lisa shook her head. "They were just games, Grace. But—"

"You killed them."

"I had to."

The words wrapped around Grace like a blanket, the admission she'd only dreamed of. Finally, it was over. She willed her head to rise so she could look at her sister.

"Woulda killed you too if you'd been home. None of this would have happened, Grace. Don't you see that? Michael would still be alive if you'd just died like you were supposed to right here with Mom and Dad. I wouldn't have had to spend the last two weeks as your fucking nursemaid—"

Grace cut her off. "What are you going to do now?"

"Well, I thought the police would have seen by now that it had to be you, but it's obvious they're getting off track, focusing on the money, so we need to end this. There's enough pointing your way that no one will be surprised when you off yourself."

Grace shook her head. "I'm not going to kill myself," she whispered, her body draining of all energy.

"You've been killing yourself all week. Taking dangerous combinations of drugs. Drinking that coffee. And then you couldn't take it anymore, so you took too many prescriptions. Fuck, these drugs can even cause suicidal thoughts. I should know. But then, so can being charged with murder and being tortured by the knowledge that you've killed someone. It's perfect."

Grace pushed away the wineglass.

"Shouldn't have had that wine, Gracie. Certainly not with those pills." Lisa laughed. "Hell, I thought you were already dead. You

275

shouldn't have made it through last night. I was ready to come home and find you dead in bed. That's why I got my celebratory meal here. I was sure that soup would have finished you off." She waved her finger, scolding. "Someone obviously didn't take all her meds yesterday. But no matter. This should do it."

Grace tried to stand, pushing her palms firmly against the table, trying to raise her body, but it had suddenly tripled in weight. When she finally stood, her legs gave out and she slid to the floor, knocking the wineglass onto the tile.

Lisa bent over her, almost whispering into her ear. "Can't move, can you? That's the plan. You're so stupid, Grace. You're all stupid people."

She tried to move but her muscles betrayed her. She tried to talk, but she couldn't. She was paralyzed. She screamed as loud as she could, but nothing came out. It was simply a memory of that sound, of terror.

"Say good night, Gracie."

She lay helpless as Lisa dragged her to the door.

TWENTY-NINE

BISHOP WAS ON HIS CELL AS THEY SPED along the road toward the Abbott house. Hackett could barely breathe. He could think of nothing but Grace's face, her beautiful eyes, the way she turned away when he made her smile, embarrassed by his attention and flattery. And that kiss. She'd chosen someone else, but it didn't make him want her less. And now, he just wanted to see her again, get her out of that house, away from Lisa, and find Tucker.

Bishop ended his call. "Kewanee found the footage of Cahill at the blackjack table when he won the ten K. A man of Tucker's description was sitting at a nearby table. There was an uproar of applause when it happened. The waitress came by and took that photo we saw on Facebook. Everyone around them knew exactly what had happened."

"So the waitress is in the clear. Is that enough to get Tucker?"

"Probably not. But he found parking lot footage of Cahill leaving the casino around noon, Friday. And behind him, getting on a Honda 2002 motorcycle, was our skinny, bleach-blond, tattooed Tucker."

"And there's no chance Tucker won some money too?"

Bishop shook his head. "From the time of Cahill's win to their departure in the lot, there's no footage of Tucker going to cash in. He didn't win anything."

"So Tucker planned to rob Cahill. He knew who Cahill was . . . and Lisa is playing a twisted game."

"Yeah," Bishop added. "We've got an APB out on the motorcycle and her car."

It was now after five and the landscape began to disappear into the void of darkness. The falling snow, thick and heavy, began to blow in the wind, decreasing visibility. As they turned onto the gravel road, Bishop slowed. He peered down the driveway before turning in. "She's here. Okay, we have no idea if there are any guns in that house. Don't let her out of your sight for a second. Let's ring the doorbell, hope she assumes nothing out of the ordinary, and cuff her. Once we've got her cuffed, we'll look around for Tucker."

"You think he's been hiding out here all week?"

"It's possible. Just tread lightly."

"Got it."

They rolled up the driveway toward the house and parked behind Lisa's car.

Lisa came flying out the front door, waving frantically, tears streaming down her face.

Bishop turned off the engine and gave Hackett a furrowed-brow look. There was no time to confer. They got out of the car.

"Detective! Thank God you're here!"

"What's going on, Miss Abbott?" Bishop said.

"It's Grace." She was sobbing hysterically. "She's gone! I don't know what to do!" She ran back toward the house. Bishop jogged after her and Hackett followed, scanning the landscape for a motorcycle. He kept his hand on his holster as he followed them inside, checking the living room as they passed.

When Lisa reached the kitchen, she took a giant swig of wine and then refilled the glass.

Bishop didn't reach for the cuffs. "What do you mean, she's gone?" he said.

Lisa wiped her tears, smearing the mess of thick black eyeliner across her face. Mascara streamed down both cheeks. "She said she remembered. She freaked out. I think she may have taken something." Lisa sniffled and grabbed a cigarette from the drawer, lit it with trembling hands, and inhaled deeply.

It was a lie. It had to be. Hackett looked at Bishop, who glanced his way before responding. Their strategy was obviously changing. "What did she take?"

"I don't know. She's on a lot of meds. She didn't seem like herself." She looked at Hackett then. "I knew something was off. She threw the wineglass on the floor."

Everyone's attention moved to the shattered glass. Grace was in trouble. But if they cuffed Lisa now, what would happen to her? Could Tucker have her somewhere? If they took Lisa in, would he panic and kill her?

Bishop must have wondered the same thing. He played along. "Tell us exactly what happened."

"I took her to see a lawyer yesterday. She insisted."

Hackett held his stance, fighting the urge to shake the truth out of her. "Did she say why?" he asked.

"I think she must have remembered something." She lowered her eyes. "She'd gone back to their house that Saturday morning; she'd said she was going to get her clothes." Lisa shook her head. "I should have told you before. I was trying to protect her. I didn't want to believe she could have killed Michael. So I took her to a lawyer. But I wasn't allowed in the meeting. Afterward, she was really upset. She cried the whole way home. Last night she wouldn't talk to me. She wouldn't tell me what was going on. I told her to rest. But tonight I got home from work and she was pacing all over the house. She said she remembered killing Michael. She said she couldn't go to prison, and then she ran out of here."

Bishop shot a wary glance toward the dining room, then stepped toward her. "Your car is here. The truck is here. Did she go on foot?"

"I guess. Yes. She ran toward the road."

"How long ago?" Hackett barked.

"Twenty minutes, maybe. Did you see anyone walking on the road? Oh, it's dark, who knows. You need to go look for her! Go find her before something happens."

Hackett went to the back door, where coats hung on several hooks. The one Grace had worn to the station was hanging by the others. "She didn't wear her coat?"

"No," Lisa said. "She didn't take the purse either. She was upset. She wasn't thinking. She wasn't going shopping!" Her anger began to trump the tears. She stomped into the living room. "Why are you still here? Go find her!"

"We want to find her," Bishop said, following. "We just want to look around, okay?" He nodded at Hackett.

"I told you, she's run off. You need to go." She tossed her cigarette into the fireplace.

Hackett drew his gun and threw open the pocket doors off the hall. The boxes prevented a full view, so he stepped carefully to check behind them. He then took the stairs, two at a time, to the second floor and pushed each door open with one hand, gun ready in the other. He moved through each bedroom, checking under the beds, in the closets, throwing back the shower curtain in the bathroom, each time fearing that he'd find Grace, bloodied and dead—the same fear he'd felt walking into Cahill's house that Monday.

He ran back down the stairs and shook his head.

"Check the basement," Bishop ordered.

"Why are you looking in here?" Lisa's voice rose. "I told you what happened!"

Bishop held an arm out toward her. "Let's sit down, Lisa. I think we should talk."

"If something happens to Grace, I'm going to blame you. You need to go!"

She was stalling, dissembling. Hackett raced down the stairs. The basement was filled with stuff, but there was no sign of anyone. He rushed back to the living room and trained his gun on her. "What did you do to Grace?"

"What are you talking about? I didn't do anything!"

"It was you," Hackett said, stepping closer to the couch. "In those photos with Cahill. You drugged him. We know it happened upstairs. Same room where your parents were killed."

She jumped up and paced to the mantel. "You're crazy!"

"Relax, Lisa," Bishop said, slowly pulling out his cuffs. "We don't want to hurt you. I want this to be easy and peaceful."

"Are you kidding me? What the fuck is going on?" She backed toward the front door. "I just told you, Grace killed Michael! She confessed! I didn't do anything!"

Bishop seemed to change strategy. He replaced the cuffs and raised his hands. "Calm down. Just help us find Grace and this will go much better."

They didn't have time for this. Grace was in danger. "Stop lying," Hackett growled. "The wallpaper in the naked pictures with Cahill was the same as your parents' murder scene."

Her indignation shifted into derision. "That doesn't mean anything. We fucked. Grace was jealous. Maybe that's why she killed him."

Bishop's stance was deceptively relaxed, his tone casual. "What about Tucker? We know he's your boyfriend. Where is he, Lisa? Does he have Grace? This will go much better for you if you help us."

"Tucker?" She looked at Bishop, then Hackett. "We broke up. I haven't seen him. He's not here. Look for yourself. I haven't seen him since Dave's party."

Bishop took a step forward. "If Grace turns up dead, it's not gonna look good for you and Tucker. You can make this better or worse."

"You're fucking crazy. I told you. Grace did it. Grace did it. Not me!"

The back screen door slammed against the side of the house, startling all three of them. Tucker? Heart pounding in his chest, Hackett went to the door. There was no one there; the wind must have blown it open. But when he stepped outside, he saw a wheelbarrow and shovel propped up against the side of the house. Small tire tracks extended into the yard, disappearing in the darkness. His stomach flipped at the thought of what Lisa and Tucker might have done, if Grace were already dead.

He raced back inside. "There's a wheelbarrow. And fresh tracks," he said to Bishop. "Goddammit, where is Grace?" he said to Lisa as he came at her.

Lisa stepped toward the stack of wood by the fireplace, her lying eyes wide. "I just carried in some firewood." Before either cop had a chance to react, she grabbed the poker from the hearth.

Bishop pulled his gun. Hackett held the barrel of his pistol pointed at her chest. "Don't do this," Bishop said. "I don't want anyone getting hurt."

She looked from one to the other. "Then stop accusing me of something I didn't do. You're killing Grace. Not me."

Bishop nodded at him. "Follow the tracks."

Lisa dropped the poker and ran for the front door. Bishop took a shot but hit the door frame. Hackett ran after her.

She sprinted through the front yard toward the road. He yelled for her to stop, but the darkness swallowed her up. Snowflakes had become a horizontal blur in the wind. He fired his weapon once. Twice. Four times. And then he heard a moan, a body collapsing in the snow.

Bishop came up behind him, his flashlight and weapon drawn, panting. "I'll call for backup and an ambulance and look for Grace. If Lisa's okay, cuff her."

Hackett couldn't seem to catch his breath as he approached her. What if he'd killed her? What if he'd killed the only person who could tell him where Grace was? He crouched beside her. The snow was starting to turn black around her body. His hands shook as he examined the damage. One shot had hit her leg. A second, her abdomen. She was conscious.

He jogged to the car and grabbed the first-aid supplies and a blanket from the trunk, jogged back, and wrapped the wounds as best as he could. He covered her in the blanket. "Don't do this, Lisa," he begged. "Help me save her."

Lisa's eyes, black as the night, stared, unfocused. "She deserves to die."

"Hackett!" It was Bishop yelling from somewhere behind the house. "Hurry!"

THIRTY

HACKETT RAN TOWARD THE WOOD LINE with his flashlight. "Get a shovel!" Bishop yelled.

He veered toward the shed along the wood's edge, broke the glass, and opened the door into the dark space. Nausea upended his stomach. He didn't know if he could stand to see it. Grace, buried in the frozen ground. Cold. He'd failed her.

He flashed the beam at the walls. There in the back—a shovel. He pushed aside the bags of fertilizer and stepped toward a tarp draped over a large pile of something in the corner. He stomach dipped again, fearing the worst. He couldn't breathe as he grabbed at the material and threw it back.

But it was just machine parts. He shined the light on them: two tires, a massive handlebar, a license plate. And then he saw the emblem. Honda. Tucker was here. He'd probably killed Grace. Rage filled him. He grabbed the shovel and ran out of the shed. "Where are you?" he shouted. "Flash your light for me!"

"I'm about ten feet deep in the woods, north side. Hurry . . ."

Hackett ran toward the voice. He found Bishop on his knees, using his hands to shovel snow and dirt.

"Oh shit." Even in the dim light, he could see the dirt mixed in with the snow in one large area. It stood out against the fresh snowfall surrounding them.

The ground was frozen, but this patch was freshly moved. He began digging with the shovel, lifting mounds at a time. A siren wailed in the distance, and a moment later, a red strobe swirled in the night sky on the other side of the house. The paramedics would see Lisa right away.

After about six digs, the shovel hit something. He gently pushed the blade down again. It was wood. "Here!" he said, shoveling the area around the sound more rapidly. Bishop knelt beside him. He unearthed what looked like a wooden box about six inches beneath the surface. But the box was small. Too small. Bishop continued to clear away the dirt and pull the box from the ground while Hackett jumped up, grabbed his shovel, and continued digging where Bishop had left off.

Sweat dripped from his forehead, clouding his vision, but he thought he saw something, maybe string, against the black dirt. He dropped the shovel, fell to his knees, and leaned in to see what was in front of him, nearly invisible in the dark. It was a few strands of hair. "Here!"

And that was when he knew—they were too late. Bishop joined him and they both grabbed at the dirt with their bare hands. "No, no," he said, over and over.

Bishop's radio crackled. He sat back on his haunches and answered. "We're in the back. Suspect out front, she's been shot. We've found something. Bring whatever lights you have."

Hackett heard footsteps running toward the woods; flashlight beams bounced in the trees. "Over here!" yelled Bishop.

Hackett ignored them. His hands had slowed, and he carefully, reverently brushed the dirt away from the body. His Grace. She'd been through so much; she didn't deserve to be bruised anymore.

Bishop flashed his light on the area, and as he skimmed the dirt off the exposed hair, he realized that it wasn't brown. It was bright blond. Faster now, he swiped the icy dirt from the face, exposing a nose, lips, and eyes. It wasn't Grace. It wasn't Grace. Tears flooded his eyes.

He looked up at Bishop, who'd resumed digging around the torso. He lifted an arm from the makeshift grave. It was covered in tattoos.

"I guess this is Tucker," Bishop said.

"Over here!" yelled one of the men from about thirty feet away.

Hackett leaped to his feet and ran toward their voices.

Several officers were huddled around the firewood stacked at the wood's edge. One of them left the group and ran back toward the house. Hackett brushed past them, rushing around to the back of the stack.

It was Grace, slumped over, facedown on the ground, like she'd been propped up against the wood but had collapsed. Her eyes were closed, her body covered in an inch of fresh powder. He pulled her against him, willing her to feel his warmth. Then he leaned into her chest, praying for sound.

THIRTY-ONE

GRACE OPENED HER EYES AND STARED up at the white ceiling tiles, those tiny holes that had held no answers a week earlier. In seven days, it had all come back: memories, images, and a reality she wanted desperately to forget. The sun was rising, the blinds casting a shadow across her hospital bed like the bars of a cage. She was trapped by images she could no longer block out. She closed and reopened her eyes, clutching to the fantasy that this might all be a terrible nightmare. But everything remained—the sterile walls, the snow-covered roof outside her window, the truth.

A soft knock at the door distracted her. Detective Bishop and Officer Hackett—*Justin*—entered, smiling tentatively, and approached the foot of her bed.

Bishop spoke up first. "It's good to see you, Grace."

Justin stepped closer. "You doin' okay?"

She remembered the gunshots echoing through the trees last night. "Is she . . . ?"

He glanced at Bishop before responding. "She's alive. Barely. I had to shoot, Grace. I'm sorry; she was trying to escape."

"I . . ." She struggled to find the right words. Justin stepped closer, but she couldn't look at him. "She tried to kill me," she whispered.

"We know, Grace. We know everything."

She closed her eyes as tears coursed down her cheeks. Did he?

"Lisa and Tucker killed Michael," Bishop said. "We can place her at his house."

"Cahill won ten grand at the casino on Friday," Justin said, as if he hadn't already shared that information days before. "Tucker was after the money. We found it last night, buried in a box in the woods behind Lisa's house."

"We found Tucker buried too," Bishop said. "He'd been stabbed."

Oh God. She turned to the window, not wanting to hear any more. She squeezed her eyes shut but couldn't close her ears.

Justin walked around the bed, pulled a chair in front of the window, and sat by her side. "They must have fought after it happened. Maybe she panicked. It's hard to know what she was thinking."

"Like I've told Hackett, sometimes we don't get every answer, but we get the ones that matter," Bishop said. "Do you remember anything, Grace?"

She looked into his eyes, unable to get out the words. She nodded slowly.

"Were you there?"

She nodded.

"What happened?" Bishop asked.

"I came in and found them. She saw me and I ran out of the house."

Justin leaned forward. "Were you out running?"

She nodded, allowing his words to guide her.

He smiled. "I knew it. I knew you didn't do it, Grace."

That smile. She'd been unable to forget it for days after they'd kissed. His face now was just as she remembered, intense and earnest. A wave of relief washed over her.

She looked at Bishop. "She killed our parents. She admitted it to me last night. I guess she figured I wouldn't live to tell."

"Did you always suspect her?" he asked.

The idea of this conversation made her want to summon a deep breath, as if going there required more strength, but when she tried, she felt a sharp pain in her chest and struggled to prop herself up. Justin jumped up and helped arrange another pillow behind her back.

"Thanks," she said. He'd shored up her strength so many times already. She kept her gaze on the bed. "When they caught someone and said Lisa had an alibi, I figured even she couldn't do that. But then about a year ago, I was at the house to pick up a check, and I overheard her and Tucker laughing about the man who was in prison. I don't even remember exactly what was said, but it seemed like Tucker knew who he was."

"Why didn't you go to the police?" Bishop asked.

"Michael thought it was a bad idea. Lisa was always one step ahead of me. I had no proof and I didn't need to give her another reason to go after me. We both knew she was dangerous. She's been torturing me for as long as I can remember."

"Like with those naked photos," Justin said.

She turned to him, relieved. He had figured out a lot. "Right."

"Well, we know he'd been drugged. If that makes any of this better. He didn't really sleep with Lisa. Or at least he didn't know he did."

"She's a monster," Grace whispered.

"She's not going to get away with it this time," Justin said.

"If she makes it," Bishop added.

Lisa dead. It would really be the end. The end of her twisted, psychotic games. She looked up at Bishop. He'd finally softened. His stance was relaxed, or maybe it was exhausted, those dark circles less menacing now that his silent suspicions were gone. She took in Justin's day-old stubble, the fatigue in his eyes, and became overwhelmed by guilt.

"I gotta say," Bishop said, as if reading her thoughts, "things weren't looking too good for you for a while there. But my partner here knew to keep pushing. He didn't believe that it could have been you."

Justin sat back in his chair, smiling. She reached out toward him, and he leaned forward and took her hand in his. She looked at their hands together. He was the reason she was alive, and free. "I remember you," she said.

He let out a sigh and chuckled. "I'm so glad, Grace. I don't think I've ever forgotten that kiss, and I didn't know what I'd do if you never remembered it—or me."

"I'm sorry I didn't show up that night."

"It's okay. I guess it really wasn't over between you two."

Her eyes watered and she shook her head. That wasn't it at all. "I wanted to come," she began, her voice wobbling. The details were now vivid in her mind. "It was just so complicated," she murmured, while inside, she relived that evening in full detail.

She'd come home prepared for a confrontation, her speech about growing apart rehearsed on a loop in her head. But when she'd walked in, Michael was there, ring in hand, tearful, down on one knee, talking about how long he'd loved her, how being with her had saved him. He must have seen the doubt on her face, because he'd collapsed onto the floor, practically begging her not to leave him. Making promises about cleaning up his act. "I'm not going to be like my father," he said again and again. "I'll be better."

Grace had joined him on the carpet. "Why are you talking about your father?" They'd agreed years ago never to mention his name. It was too painful for both of them.

"He's dead," Michael said, tears streaming down his face. "I got a call a few hours ago. He hung himself."

"Oh my God," Grace said, instinctively wrapping her arms around him. "I'm so sorry."

He grabbed her by the arms then, forcing her to look at his face. "That's not why I'm proposing, Grace. I swear. I bought the ring on Saturday. Please marry me."

Every excuse, every justification for leaving, melted away. She couldn't hurt him. He'd taken care of her for as long as she could remember, even as a child. So she'd said yes, despite her doubts. That kiss with Justin, that dream of starting something new, of moving on, was no more than a fantasy. Michael was hers and she couldn't walk away.

Justin put his other hand over hers, pulling her out of the trance. "It's okay," he said. "I understand, and I'm really sorry for your loss."

"Thanks." She smiled.

"Okay, then," Bishop said with a grin, "I'll be outside."

"Wait," Grace said. "What happens now?"

Bishop's expression turned solemn. "If Lisa survives, she'll go away for a long time."

She wanted to believe it, but she didn't. When she tried to sit up, her breath caught in her chest, and she winced.

Justin dropped her hand and gently braced her shoulder to stop her from the effort. "Your lung collapsed again last night. We almost lost you. You're very weak."

As she looked down at the tube still attached to her chest, her face grew hot. The tears came again. She wondered if they'd ever stop.

"What is it?"

She could barely get out the words. "I wish I didn't remember. I don't want to remember."

Justin took her hand again and held it with both of his. "It'll get easier. You rest. I'm just going to be outside. I've got some calls to make, but I'm not going anywhere."

THIRTY-TWO

HACKETT SAT IN ONE OF THE chairs lined up across from Grace's room, listening to a voice-mail message from his mother reminding him that Christmas was now four days away and he still hadn't let her know if he was coming home. She pleaded again for his return, even joked that his brother Joe was willing to take another punch if that's what was needed. Hackett smiled. Finally, he felt ready to see them. He looked at the hospital room door, sure that Grace had something to do with it. Olivia hadn't been right for him. He had always known that, or at least he should have known. Maybe everything did happen for a reason.

Bishop came out of the elevator, coffee in hand, just as he was deleting the voice mail. Bishop took the seat next to him and slapped his leg. "Glad it worked out for you, rookie."

"I'm sorry about all the lies. I really fucked up."

"I'm not arguing with you there."

"I might be in love with her. I don't know what I would have done if this had gone the other way."

"Well, luckily, we got our killer, and just in time for Christmas. So I guess I'll let this one slide. We'll call it a rookie mistake. I'm not about to ruin your career for it." Bishop held out his hand and

Hackett shook it before Bishop stood to go. "I'm gonna call the prosecutor and head home. But I'll leave you the paperwork."

Hackett smiled. "Of course. I'll get over there later. I just want to be sure she's okay. She seems pretty shaken." The truth was that Grace finally remembered him, and he wasn't ready to let her go again so soon. "Hey, boss, you mind if I ask you something?"

"Shoot."

"When we were arguing about the case and you asked me if I was referring to that Detroit case, what were you talking about?"

"Ah." Bishop sat back down. "Remember I told you about that case where we thought we had the killer but we kept looking for more, and in the meantime the perp killed again?"

"Yeah."

"It was my fault. The killer was a young girl, and I just didn't think she could do it. I ignored what was right in front of me. I've never forgotten that, obviously. I learned a lot from that case."

"Sure. And I guess you thought I might be doing the same thing with Grace?"

"And I thought if you'd heard about that case, you might think I was going after Grace just because of it." Bishop stood. "Well, I've gotta go. My family needs me at home, and this case certainly makes me appreciate family right now."

Hackett nodded. "Me too. And I'm sorry about your mother-in-law. Will you text me when the service is? I'd like to come."

"Sure thing, kid. Now get some rest, and get that paperwork done."

"Got it." Hackett grinned, watching him walk away, grateful to have been on this case, grateful to have Bishop for his partner.

He dialed his mother's house. Her tone reminded him that it had been entirely too long since they'd spoken. She avoided going right into the Christmas question and instead inquired about his new job.

"I'll be there, Mom," he said when she finally asked, for the hundredth time, whether he was coming home for Christmas. He pulled the phone away from her responding shriek and laughed.

She told him when they were planning the meal on Christmas Eve and who was coming. Dinner would include all the siblings, his brother Joe, Olivia, Joe's ex-wife, the ex's new guy, and about twenty kids. It was utterly dysfunctional, but he'd missed them—all of them. She asked if he'd stay for the night. They would all be heading to his older brother Tommy's house in the late morning for a brunch, and all the kids would bring their new toys. He thought of Donny, of not being with him on Christmas morning, and it still stung, but he figured this was the next best thing. Alice had been right—at least Donny was still family. They'd always be connected.

"And if you want to bring anyone, sweetie, of course that would be great," she added, ever hopeful that he'd move on and be happy.

He looked at Grace's door. The thought of her on his arm put butterflies in his stomach. She didn't have a family. Maybe she'd want a place to go for Christmas. "We'll see," he said.

After they hung up, he let his head fall back against the wall and closed his eyes, thinking of that kiss, her hand in his, her smile. The circumstances were terrible, but at least she was now free. He pictured sitting across from Olivia and Joe at the dinner table, and all the secrets they'd kept and the pain they'd caused. But with Grace by his side, he knew he would be okay. She was different. Secrets would never tear them apart.

THIRTY-THREE

GRACE'S GAZE REMAINED FIXED ON the closed door after Justin and Bishop left. She still couldn't contain her tears as the full implication of everything that had happened sank in. She couldn't believe it was over, that Lisa would go to prison, finally paying for everything she'd done.

The sun was rising, those shadows from the window blinds had moved, and she could feel that freedom was coming, like the toxic cloud hanging over her might soon be gone. She looked back out the window at the smoke rising from a chimney into the blue sky, scattering into the abyss. She willed her memories to do the same and closed her eyes. But she couldn't forget; every detail of her life, of that night and that morning, was forever burned into her brain.

There was a faint knock, and the door opened. A doctor came in and sat on the arm of a nearby chair. She was obviously not here for an examination.

"Hi, Grace. How are you feeling?"

The doctor's face had bad news written all over it. Grace answered quietly, "Okay," waiting for the other shoe to drop.

"I've been treating your sister." And there it was. "I understand from the police officer outside that she's the reason you're in here right now. And I'm sure your feelings toward her are pretty complicated. But she's lost a lot of blood. We operated, but there's extensive damage, and the next few hours are critical."

Grace turned toward the window. She felt like a monster, wishing her dead, but she couldn't hope for anything else.

"She's asking for you," the doctor said. "I certainly understand if you don't want to see her, but you might not get another chance, so I felt compelled to tell you."

Grace didn't respond, instead reliving the moment when Lisa saw her that dreadful morning, and the fear that had gripped her as she ran out of the house. The doctor stood up to go. "Well, think about it. I'll be glad to take you to see her if you decide—"

"Okay," Grace said. There was no one else left. She had to do it. It would be the last time she'd ever see her, no matter what happened next.

When the doctor wheeled Grace into the hall, Hackett rose from his chair. "Would you like me to come with you?"

She shook her head and he sat back down. "I'll be right here."

They rolled down the hall in silence and took an elevator to the floor above. When they entered Lisa's room, the doctor pushed the wheelchair close to the bed. Lisa was hooked up to various machines, and a plastic oxygen mask covered her face. Her eyes were closed. One of the machines beeped softly, consistently, confirming that, for now, she was alive.

"Can she hear me?" Grace asked the doctor.

She nodded. "Lisa," she said, leaning down toward her. "Your sister is here. Just as you asked."

Lisa opened her eyes and, with effort, turned her head toward Grace.

"I'll leave you two for a few minutes. Just push this button," the doctor said, indicating a red button near the bed, "and a nurse will help you back to your room."

Grace nodded, trying to maintain eye contact with Lisa, to stare down this monster, this woman who'd pretended all week to love her, to care about her, but she couldn't do it. She didn't feel triumphant. There were no winners.

Lisa slowly raised her arm toward her face and pulled at the elastic band holding the oxygen mask over her mouth and nose. Grace watched her struggle, unable, maybe unwilling, to help.

"We didn't think anyone would be home," Lisa whispered, barely audible. "His car wasn't there. You always run in the morning. We just wanted the money. We didn't—"

Grace cut her off. "I told the police you killed our parents," she said bitterly. "They found Tucker and the money you buried. It's over."

Lisa's words came out haltingly, as if each inhale caused more distress. "Tucker wasn't supposed to die." Her eyes began to water, as if she actually regretted her violence for once in her life. "It was an accident."

"Right. An accidental stabbing."

"He didn't understand. The second I saw your face, I knew you were going to tell the police that I did it. You'd tell them everything. They'd believe you."

Grace suddenly didn't know why she'd come. "You'll finally pay for what you've done," she whispered.

Lisa's eyes darkened. "You know I didn't kill Michael."

Grace shook her head. "I don't feel sorry for you."

"Why?" Lisa said, the utterance a monumental effort.

Grace looked away. She wanted to be tough, to act unfazed, to be satisfied by this outcome, the one she had wished for in those last moments as she raced away from the house. But she couldn't. The rage and shock and heartbreak suddenly came rushing back, drowning her in memories. So many memories. Too many.

She'd returned home from work around nine o'clock, exhausted despite the early hour, mostly because she'd spent the evening playing the blushing bride-to-be, trying to feed off the excitement of her coworkers and overcome the looming weight of a decision she might always regret. She'd hoped to spend the evening with Michael, certain that his excitement about their engagement would spark some in her as well.

But when she got home, she found a wad of cash on the kitchen table, bound by a rubber band, with a note: *Let's take a trip!* She fanned through the money. He was still gambling. Their house was a dump, they couldn't afford more, school was expensive, and yet here he was, risking paychecks and talking about a trip. She threw the winnings on the counter where empty beer bottles filled the space, and stared out the window into the dark woods, wondering if she could really marry this man. Wondering what that life looked like.

She needed to see Vicki—Vicki, who'd known them both forever, would tell her that it would be okay. She walked to the bedroom while typing a quick text to say she'd pop over in the morning after her run.

The lights and television were on, but Michael was sound asleep. She tried to wake him but he was like a dead man. On the night table next to him, her Xanax bottle sat opened. Only two pills left. He'd gotten into them. Yet again. She stripped out of her clothes and threw on an old T-shirt, heading back into the living room with the remaining Xanax so she could hide them again. And that's when the horror began.

The mail was on the coffee table, unopened, of course. Michael never paid any bills. She leafed through the stack before coming to the big envelope, addressed to her. Written on the back: *H B G.* She knew immediately that it was from Lisa. Lisa had signed every birthday card the same way—*HBG*, as if the initials of well wishes would do and the act of merely giving a birthday card, a duty forced upon her by their parents when they were young, was enough.

She'd braced herself as she tore open the envelope. Every year since her parents had died, Lisa had done something on Grace's birthday just to remind her that she was still playing her cruel games. The presents were always criminal, accompanied by just enough clues to make her suspect Lisa but never enough evidence to do anything about it—the keyed car on her seventeenth, the brick through the window on her eighteenth, the slashed tires last year. And now, some torment for her twentieth.

When she pulled out the photos of Michael and another woman naked, the shock of it, the reality, was unbelievable. She looked closer. She recognized the bedroom. Lisa.

Michael had always told Grace to stay away from her—she'd confided in him about everything Lisa had done to her, even her suspicions regarding their parents' death. It didn't seem possible he'd sleep with her. But then she saw the date written on the back: *12/1/13.* Her birthday. The night Michael didn't come home after work like he'd said he would. Instead, he'd been unable to remember anything, so messed up the next morning that she'd taken him to urgent care. There was no proving it, yet again, but Lisa was behind it. She and Tucker were always doing drugs. The evidence was right there—Michael didn't even look conscious in the photos. And Lisa was capable of doing anything that entered her twisted mind.

Grace had walked into the bedroom with the photos and stashed them in her bedside table. There'd be no waking Michael now. They could talk about it in the morning.

That's when she noticed the ripped envelope on the floor. It was addressed to Michael, the return address Oaks Correctional. His dad. He must have sent it before he killed himself.

The envelope was empty. She pulled back the sheets. There. In his hand. Maybe that's why he'd taken the Xanax. Maybe hearing from his father had been too much to bear. He'd refused to speak to him in all those years he'd been in prison, had said it would be too painful.

She slid the letter from his hand, hoping he wouldn't wake now, sure that this was an invasion of privacy, but she couldn't stop herself. She'd never faced Michael's father—she'd been too young when it happened—but he'd been part of why she'd felt so bonded to Michael, both of them irreparably damaged by the same man. She wandered back to the living room, reading.

Michael's father apologized for his drinking, for all the abuse. He said Michael was a good kid and hadn't deserved a dad like him.

But he didn't apologize for killing Mary. Grace's heart wrenched. The words—or maybe it was just her vision—turned bloodred on the page. *I'm sure I drove you to it and I just want you to know that I forgive you.* She read that line again. *I forgive you.* What? She kept reading and rereading, closing and reopening her eyes, certain she was confused.

But there was no other possible meaning. Michael—her Michael—had killed Mary? Her knees buckled and she fell onto the sofa, the paper shaking in her hands. His father recalled seeing Michael dump Mary's body, too drunk to react at the time and uncertain of what he remembered after blacking out. But ten months after his arrest, finally sober, he'd sat in that courtroom listening to the evidence, listening to his son and his wife recount the years of abuse. He wasn't sure what had happened that day, but he was sure that this was to be his punishment. He'd spent fifteen years in a cell, piecing together his sorry excuse for a life, the choices he'd made, and the fact that he couldn't even defend himself because of his addictions. *State-imposed therapy*, he called it. When he finally remembered the truth of that day, he vowed to take it to his grave, the least he could do to protect his son.

The words pierced like a knife, twisting through her gut. She'd even looked down at her stomach to see if it was bleeding, if her insides had spilled out. "Why?" she uttered, barely audible. "Why?" she screamed. She ran to the bedroom and shoved Michael, pummeled him, yelling, "Wake up! Wake up!" He didn't move.

She ran back to the living room, saw the picture of them on the mantel, and threw it across the room, watching the glass shatter as it hit the wall and fell to the floor. "We were five years old," she screamed into the empty room. "You loved us!"

It was just a whisper then, this voice that interrupted her confusion and shared a thought she'd never imagined. Michael, then fifteen, doing something unspeakable to Mary. She pictured her twin's face, twisted in fear, crying out for help. What did he do to her? The sobs came harder and she threw her hand over her mouth. She couldn't even say it.

Their history came at her like a speeding freight train. Michael, always by her side, taking care of her, loving her. He'd played with her for as long as she could remember. She thought of that first time he'd kissed her. She'd been only twelve. He was twenty-two! No wonder her mother was against the relationship. What kind of twenty-five-year-old man sleeps with a fifteen-year-old girl? All her life, he'd played the friend, the protector, the lover, when he'd been the reason she lost Mary. She stopped to wipe her face, grabbed a nearby tissue for her nose, now running and so clogged it had grown difficult to breathe, and stood motionless for a moment. Nothing was real. Their entire history an illusion.

"You sick, twisted fuck!" she shouted, her voice unable to contain her rage. He'd killed Mary; he'd let his father go to prison for her murder. She paced the room until she couldn't bear to think about it anymore. She stood at the sink, a full beer in one hand, the two remaining Xanax in the other, and forced herself to swallow the pills and drink the bottle in three gulps, wiping frantically as it spilled down her chin.

She walked into the bedroom again, sat on the edge of their bed, and stared at him, repulsed by that face she knew so well—every line, every look, every smile. She didn't know him at all.

The pills began to kick in, and she collapsed on her side of the bed, her insides still screaming, while her body began to shut down. Her only plan, in those last conscious moments, was to wake up

Saturday, break off their engagement, and finally get out from under the web of lies and deceit. She'd get away from Lisa while she was at it. She couldn't take this life anymore.

But she dreamed about it: Michael touching Mary, scaring her. In the dream, they were up on the hunting platform, and Grace was there, trying to save her, to pull him off of her, to stop it, but Mary fell, her body soaring through the air, the distance to the ground growing, as if she were falling from a cliff, while Grace reached down, screaming her name.

She sat up, shouting. She had to save her sister. And through the tears and the fury, she reached down and pulled Michael's shotgun from under the bed.

Her hands shook as she stood at the end of the bed and squeezed the trigger. And then the explosion came, like an alarm, blasting into the nightmare. She shrieked at the sight of the spray on the wall behind the bed, the sheer amount of blood that poured out of his body like an open faucet. She dropped the gun and ran to the bathroom, vomiting violently into the tub until her stomach had shriveled into a tiny ball of nerves.

The hospital door opened, pulling Grace back from the memory. A nurse popped her head inside, smiled at Grace, and left, like she hadn't realized there was a visitor, and Grace looked at Lisa, struggling to breathe, and finally whispered the horrifying truth of why she'd done it. "He killed Mary."

Lisa took a few breaths in the mask before moving it from her mouth again. "You're no different than I am."

Grace shook her head and wiped at her face. It wasn't true. Grace hadn't planned any of it. And sitting on the tile floor, covered in Michael's blood, she'd begun to shake, almost convulsively, processing what she'd done, but then what he'd done, that someone had already gone to prison for his crimes, and now she would too. Her mind began to speed up, like something outside of herself was taking charge. She needed to shower and get rid of the evidence; she needed to go for a run; she needed to go see Vicki, to be surprised when she came home to find him dead.

She took off the nightshirt she'd slept in, now covered in blood. After dressing in running gear, she took the letter from Michael's father out back and dropped it into the well, watching the paper slowly cascade into the black hole. She drove down Red Arrow in a daze, woozy from pills, beer, and blood, her only thought being to get rid of the evidence, to put many miles between it and her crime.

The roads were empty. Darkness surrounded her. Tossing the items into the woods seemed like a mistake, too easily found. But as she neared New Buffalo, she saw those apartments off to the left—Bellaire—and those four big dumpsters at the edge of the lot, sitting in the darkness, just beyond the spotlights of the parking lot. She envisioned trash trucks picking up those giant bins, crushing their contents before dumping them in a landfill, never to be found. She switched off her headlights and turned into the lot. It was full of cars, but there was no one in sight when she threw the items into a bin and ran back to the car.

But just as she put her hand on the ignition, she heard voices, laughter, beer cans being kicked across the parking lot. She slid down on the seat. Several people began walking out of the building, a party breaking up. She watched them stumble to their cars, and then she slowly turned back onto Red Arrow, hit the gas, and took off.

The sky began to lighten as she returned to the house, like time was moving faster. Soon everything would come to light. She grabbed the stack of mail, along with the empty envelopes, threw them into the trash, and headed for the front door to take her run.

But the back door creaked open. Grace froze. She heard a footstep on the squeaky wood floor and ducked behind the island in the kitchen. And then more footsteps. Someone was inside.

"Check in the bedroom." She knew that voice. Lisa.

And then Tucker's: "Where do you think he'd put it?" His footsteps moved down the hall.

"There!" Lisa said, her steps coming closer. She grabbed the wad of money from the counter. She was only a few feet away. If she turned toward the front door, she'd see Grace. Grace held her breath and squeezed her eyes shut, silently begging them to get out, praying for the chance to get away.

"What the fuck!" Tucker shouted from the bedroom. Lisa jogged back toward his voice. Grace's heart pounded against her chest, and she jumped up and grabbed the handle on the front door. The bolt was latched and just as she unlocked it—

"Grace!"

She slowly turned back.

"What the fuck did you do?" Lisa was slurring, drunk, stumbling toward her from the other side of the room.

She scanned the space frantically, terrified of Lisa's rage, of what could happen now. It wasn't me, Grace thought. *It wasn't me.* She backed up against the doorknob, twisted the handle as Lisa came at her, and ran out the front door.

Her hands shook as she tried to put the key in the ignition. She looked back at the house, threw the gear in reverse, and backed out of the drive, the tires spitting up gravel. Shifting into drive, she slammed her foot on the accelerator and flew down the road.

Lisa stole his money. "Lisa was there. She did it. Lisa did it," she began repeating under her breath. Lisa killed him. That's what she'd tell the police. She'd come in from her run and found her there. Lisa had sent those pictures. She was a killer. "I could never do that," she pleaded, crying, "I loved him," the desperation, the heartbreak driving her on. Lisa had killed their parents and allowed someone else to pay for their deaths; Michael had killed Mary, allowing his father to pay for her death; so now she would make Lisa pay for

Michael's death. It was the only thing she could think of, until the universe stepped in and threw her into a tree.

"I'm not like you," Grace said, her voice raised now as she wiped the last of the tears from her cheeks. "I didn't plan it. But Michael killed Mary. He stole my sister, my childhood." She could barely breathe; the air seemed filled with poison. But it didn't matter. There was nothing more to say. She would never speak of this again. Ever.

She leaned forward and pressed the call button. Suddenly, Lisa started wheezing.

No, not wheezing. It was like a chuckle.

Lisa lifted the oxygen mask to her mouth and took a painfully slow gasp that seemed to rattle in her chest. She looked at Grace, those dark eyes bigger now, their deep pools sparkling in the way that had terrified Grace when she was a child. "You're wrong," she whispered.

A nurse appeared before Grace could ask her what she meant. "Ready to leave?" she asked cheerfully, then frowned. She stepped to the bedside and replaced the oxygen mask on Lisa's face. "You should rest," she said.

"Wrong about what?" Grace blurted. She didn't care if the nurse overheard. What did Lisa mean? Wrong about Michael? But Lisa had closed her eyes, and her only response was the rattle-gasp, rattle-gasp of her breathing.

The nurse wheeled Grace into the hallway. *You're wrong.* The accusation bounced around her brain, looking for meaning. She wiped compulsively at her face with the fronts and backs of her palms, unable to soak up the damage. She couldn't be wrong. Michael's father had seen him. He'd seen him with the body. Even near death, Lisa was just playing her twisted games, trying to torment her one last time.

But what if there had been more to it? If Lisa had been involved, or if there had been an accident? What if Michael hadn't killed Mary? What would that make Grace?

Behind the closed door, the beeping of Lisa's heart-rate monitor continued faintly, regularly, then became one long, continuous note. Everyone knew what it meant. The nurse raced back, abandoning Grace in the hall. Other staff rushed in behind her. She listened to the frantic energy of the medical team until the sound stopped, the energy of the room drained, and several nurses and a doctor slowly exited, defeated. One of them put a hand on Grace's shoulder, as if there could be some consolation in having had the chance to say good-bye.

A different nurse wheeled her back to her room. She was speaking, but Grace only heard muffled sounds. The only clear noise that continued to ring out in her head was the blast of the gun and her own scream. She stared at the sterile white floor, but her mind was focused on Michael, surrounded by blood. When the elevator doors opened, Justin rose from his chair and smiled.

He followed them into the room and waited while the nurse helped Grace into the bed and left. He sat on the edge of the mattress. "You okay?"

She didn't know what to say. Everyone was gone. Lisa. Michael. His father. Tucker. She was free from her old life, but she'd never be free from the memory of that day, of what she'd done, or the torment of Lisa's last words. "She's dead," Grace whispered.

He let out a deep breath. "I'm here for you. Whatever you need."

She needed the truth. But she would never get it. And here was the one man who had utter faith in her, in her innocence. She could never tell him. How could he forgive her if he knew what she'd done? How could anyone? She'd have to live with it. Lock it away in some part of her mind. Her memories bound forever by secrets, lies, and uncertainty.

He reached out for her and she put her hands in his.

She didn't deserve to hold on, but she didn't want to let go. She couldn't let go.

ACKNOWLEDGMENTS

For fueling my drive and commitment to write this book, I thank the readers of *The Green Line*, who reached out to me through social media or wrote online reviews, expressing support, interest, and kind words.

In addition, I am indebted to numerous people whose support, love, or assistance made it possible to write this story . . .

First, to Jim, thanks for enduring, with good humor, a wife who occasionally forgot about dinner during the last year and sometimes zoned out during conversations, living instead in her make-believe world. I'm the luckiest woman, with the best husband, whose love and humor make my dreams come true. To Caroline and Jimmy, thanks for your excitement and interest in my stories—even when you aren't allowed to read them—and to my dear friends, near and far, your enthusiasm and kindness lift me up. Endless thanks also go to my mother, sister, husband, and father for their willingness to be confidantes, cheerleaders, critics, readers, and therapists all at once.

To Cynthia Quam, Julia Buckley, Martha Whitehead, Peter and Carolyn Ferry, thank you for your time, energy, and feedback on the manuscript in its various stages. You made such a difference.

Sincere thanks go to Michigan prosecutor Mona Armstrong for answering my incessant inquiries regarding crime-scene investigations, procedures, and practices; William Marx, police chief of the Buchanan Police Department, for answering all my jurisdictional issues and inquiries; and my dear friend Dr. Doris Nussenbaum for answering my inquiries regarding medications, treatments, and general medical mayhem. (Of course, all of these experts answered queries without the benefit of reading the full story, and if any errors have been made regarding these areas, they are solely mine.)

To Anh Schluep for her interest in this manuscript and to the whole team at Thomas & Mercer for shepherding the manuscript through the production process—thank you all. And to my editor Caitlin Alexander, who believed in the story and helped make it better, I am very grateful.

Finally, thanks to the Oak Park Public Library for providing a beautiful and warm refuge where I spent countless hours drinking Diet Coke and working on this book.

BOOK CLUB DISCUSSION QUESTIONS

1. Retribution is defined as punishment that is considered to be morally right and fully deserved. Do any of the crimes in this story meet that definition?

2. Vengeance is the act of doing something to hurt someone because that person did something that hurt you or someone else. Which crimes in this story would be considered acts of vengeance? Do you find any of the crimes justified?

3. Is it ever acceptable to commit a crime? For example, a woman who kills her husband after enduring years of abuse? Is it only acceptable if you fear for your own safety? What if the danger has passed?

4. At one point in the story, Vicki Flynn says, "We could all kill someone, couldn't we?" Do you agree with that? Is everyone capable of murder under the right circumstances?

5. If someone who commits criminal acts is mentally unstable (i.e., bipolar or schizophrenic), does that make him or her more sympathetic? Do we care if a murderer is mentally incapacitated? Should we? Are all murderers and violent assaulters in some way mentally incapacitated?

6. Generally speaking, in order to be convicted of first-degree murder, a defendant must have intended harm with premeditation. If the crime is intentional but essentially spontaneous, the crime is second-degree murder. If there is no intent, i.e., the defendant was incapacitated in some way or the crime is accidental, the crime is voluntary or involuntary manslaughter. Do you think the charge against the actual

perpetrator for Michael Cahill's death would be first-degree murder, second-degree murder, or something else? Why? Do you think the perpetrator in this story deserves legal punishment?

7. For someone with a sense of right and wrong, guilt, remorse, etc., can his or her conscience ever be punishment enough? Do you think that the concept of self-preservation is strong enough to prevent a generally righteous person from ever admitting guilt of a heinous act?

8. Should we feel sympathy for someone convicted of a crime he or she didn't commit? Is there sometimes poetic justice in locking away a bad person away, even if the reasoning is flawed?

9. At what age should children be held solely accountable for their actions? To what extent does a child's history (e.g., abuse) mitigate his or her responsibility?

10. There are a few examples in this novel of parents enduring extreme sacrifices for their children. How far would you go to protect your children? Would you go to prison?

11. Discuss the book's title, *Broken Grace*. Do you think Grace is broken from the accident or something else? Did your interpretation of the title evolve from beginning to end? Do you think she's "fixed" after regaining her memories?

12. The novel leaves something unanswered, something Grace will never know, regarding the death of her sister. What do you think happened? Does your answer affect your feelings about Grace?

13. How much of our memory can be trusted? Can we ever remember what happened in childhood with certainty, or does the filter of a single perspective inherently prejudice our memories? How reliable are your own memories of what happened two weeks ago, two years ago, two decades ago? Have you ever been certain that a childhood memory was absolutely true, only to have someone else who was present insist things happened differently? Have you ever had a memory that you grew less certain—or more certain—about over time? What changed?

ABOUT THE AUTHOR

 E.C. Diskin grew up in the suburbs of Washington, DC, and Chicago. Though she spent several years as an attorney in Chicago, she's now a full-time writer and mother of two. Diskin and her family live in Illinois with a cool old boxer and a sweet baby cavapoo.

www.facebook.com/ECDiskin
@ecdiskin
www.ecdiskin.com

Made in the USA
Lexington, KY
05 March 2017